YOUNG RENNY

YOUNG RENNY

MAZO DE LA ROCHE

DUNDURN PRESS
TORONTO

Project Editor: Michael Carroll
Copy Editors: Kelvin Kong and Jason Karp
Design: Jennifer Scott
Printer: Webcom

Library and Archives Canada Cataloguing in Publication

De la Roche, Mazo, 1879-1961.
    Young Renny / by Mazo de la Roche.

ISBN 978-1-55488-410-0

    I. Title.

PS8507.E43Y65 2009   C813'.52   C2009-901989-2

1   2   3   4   5   13   12   11   10   09

 Conseil des Arts
du Canada   Canada Council
for the Arts   ONTARIO ARTS COUNCIL
CONSEIL DES ARTS DE L'ONTARIO

Canada

We acknowledge the support of **The Canada Council for the Arts** and the **Ontario Arts Council** for our publishing program. We also acknowledge the financial support of the **Government of Canada** through the **Book Publishing Industry Development Program** and **The Association for the Export of Canadian Books,** and the **Government of Ontario** through the **Ontario Book Publishers Tax Credit** program, and the **Ontario Media Development Corporation.**

Care has been taken to trace the ownership of copyright material used in this book. The author and the publisher welcome any information enabling them to rectify any references or credits in subsequent editions.

J. Kirk Howard, President

Printed and bound in Canada.
Printed on recycled paper.
www.dundurn.com

Dundurn Press
3 Church Street, Suite 500
Toronto, Ontario, Canada
M5E 1M2

Gazelle Book Services Limited
White Cross Mills
High Town, Lancaster, England
LA1 4XS

Dundurn Press
2250 Military Road
Tonawanda, NY
U.S.A. 14150

ANCIENT FOREST™
FRIENDLY

For Edward and Anne Dimock.
Remembering the summer of 1934
and much before and after.

CONTENTS

I

The Rehearsal

Everything about the house had been put in perfect order. Workmen had been there to mend the roof, tighten the supports of the shutters, and give the woodwork a glossy coat of new paint. They had cut back the Virginia creeper which, in its exuberant growth, would have completely covered the windows and so excluded even the peering sun from the doings of the Whiteoaks in this early summer of nineteen hundred and six.

The gravel sweep had been raked into a pattern by the gardener and Philip Whiteoak hesitated for a moment before crossing it. It seemed a pity to disarrange it, though he considered the making of the pattern rather a waste of time. Still, he could not deny that the house looked very spruce, somewhat like a man with a close haircut and shave, and a new cravat about his neck.

Philip himself looked the very reverse of spruce. A stained corduroy coat covered his broad shoulders and muddy top boots his powerful legs. He carried a fishing rod and a basket in which glistened a dozen speckled trout. One of these had life in it still and now and again drew itself into a sharp contortion above the bodies of its fellows.

As Philip lounged across the gravel and up the shining steps into the porch, he wondered lazily which of his family he would see first when he entered the house. He rather hoped it would not be his mother, with whom he had had words this morning, or his wife, who would make him feel that he should have come in by the side entrance with his mud and his fish.

As a matter of fact it was his wife whom he now saw descending the stairs in a white embroidered dress with a wide flounced skirt. He went toward her, smiling a little sheepishly, yet really unashamed.

"Hello, Molly," he said. "You look as pretty as a picture."

She stood, just out of his reach, critically looking at his fair, flushed face and disreputable clothes.

"Oh, Philip," she exclaimed, "your boots *are* muddy! You might have gone —"

"No, I mightn't," he interrupted. "I wanted to bring my catch straight in to show it you. Aren't they beauties?"

She ran down the steps that separated them.

"Pretty things!" She clasped her hands on his shoulder and peered into the basket.

"We'll have them for breakfast. One is still living! I hate to see it gasp like that."

"He feels the heat, just as I do. I always suffer in the first warm days." He set down the basket and put his arms about her. "Give me a kiss, Molly!"

She drew down his head and pressed her cheek to his.

"I say, Molly, your cheek is just like a flower."

"And yours is like a grater! You have not shaved today."

"If you scold me I'll grow a beard and do the heavy patriarch. It might be a good idea. I don't get the respect I should."

"No wonder, with your mother so arrogant!"

"Never mind, never mind! She knows she can't bully me — and never could!" He smiled magnanimously and his eyes, of a particularly fine blue, flashed amiably.

When he was with Mary she felt that nothing else mattered. Her tall delicate figure swayed beside his. The light from the stained glass windows on either side of the front door threw amber and green splashes over her, hardening her fair hair into a metallic brightness.

"What has been going on this afternoon?" he asked.

"Nothing in particular, except that Meg is in town shopping and Peep has got his new tooth through."

He had a grunt of satisfaction for the last statement and for the first the exclamation: —

"I'll be glad when this trousseau is completed! Meggie can't get enough to satisfy her." But, though his tone was complaining, he smiled complacently.

"I suppose she thinks it's the last she'll get from you." Then she added quickly — "Of course, an occasion like this comes only once in a girl's life. She's bound to want to make the most of it." In truth Mary Whiteoak was so glad that her stepdaughter was to be eliminated from the family circle that she was willing to condone all Meg did. The thought of being free of that stubborn girl, always making things difficult for her, always clinging about her father's neck, filled her with bliss.

"Who took her in?" asked Philip.

"Renny drove them to the train. Vera Lacey went with her. She should be back at any moment."

"H'm. I hope Vera comes with her. Charming girl."

A severe-looking parlormaid appeared from the dining room and announced that tea was ready. At the same moment a door at the end of the hall opened and old Mrs. Whiteoak entered. She had passed her eightieth birthday, but she moved strongly and her broad shoulders were just beginning to stoop. Although the May day was summerlike, she wore a heavy black cashmere dress with a much shirred and pleated bodice and a wide band of black velvet on the bottom of the long skirt. A lace cap trimmed with rosettes of mauve baby ribbon added to her already commanding height. Her eyes, which had once been large, were still of an intense and brilliant brown. Temper and race were implied in the lines of her mouth, and her strongly arched nose defied her fourscore years.

"Late for tea, as usual, Philip," she exclaimed, in a strong voice, with more than a hint of Irish accent.

"No, I'm not late, Mamma," he returned, "I've been in for some time."

"You are late," she persisted. "You're not ready. Look at your boots and your coat and your hands. Look at him, Molly! He's a sight, isn't he?"

"I like the way he looks," said Mary contradictorily.

"Of course you do! You're that sort of a woman."

Philip handed the basket of fish to the maid.

"Here, Eliza," he said, "take these to the cook."

"Wait a minute, till I have a look at them," put in his mother. She bent eagerly over the basket. "Fine catch, eh? I'll have one for my supper, with lemon and parsley. Don't forget about the lemon and parsley, Eliza."

"No, ma'am." The maid was about to descend the stairs to the basement kitchen when a side door giving on to the lawn opened and Philip's two elder brothers came in and demanded to inspect the fish. Their mother took an arm of each and looked approvingly into their faces, flushed by exercise.

"Had a good game, eh? I could see you from my window. That's the way to keep supple —" she pronounced it *soople* — "a good game of lawn tennis before tea."

"I think," said Nicholas, brushing back his thick greying hair, "that I'm getting a bit heavy for tennis. I get very hot. And I'm fifty-three, you know. I think I ought to go in for croquet or golf."

His mother gave him a thump on the shoulder. "Get along with you! When you're my age, you may talk of taking care of yourself."

"I'll never be what you are, Mamma. You'll live to be a hundred."

"We'll see, we'll see." And, still clinging to her elder sons, she led the way to the dining room.

A substantial tea was laid on the mahogany table. A plate of scones had been split, buttered, and spread with grape jelly. There was a silver dish of toasted crumpets, and a glistening section of honey in the comb. There were mounds of fresh white bread thickly buttered. The old lady's eyes lighted and her strong lips parted in a smile that showed teeth that had once been fine, but were now loose and discoloured.

"Tea, Mary," she demanded, "and let it be strong. Three lumps of sugar."

Molly Whiteoak raised the heavy silver teapot, and her white forearm curving below the elbow sleeve of her dress held the eyes of her husband. He did not at once see the cup of tea that Ernest handed to him.

"Wake up, Philip," said Nicholas. "What are you dreaming about?"

"What should he be dreaming of, but his daughter's wedding?" said their mother. "It's going to be a great occasion, I can tell you. Nothing so fine has happened to this family for many a day. Very different from your marriage, Nick, that cost you a pot of money and landed you in the divorce court."

"All that was fifteen years ago, Mamma," observed Nicholas tranquilly.

"H'm — well —" she returned, with a snort, "there have been marriages since" — and she mumbled under her breath — "no better."

Philip's bright blue eyes were staring at her challengingly. He said: —

"There's been our marriage, Mamma. Molly's and mine. If Meggie and Maurice are half as happy, they'll be lucky."

"I'm not talking about any flibbertigibbet happiness," retorted old Adeline, hotly. "I'm talking about a marriage that is uniting two good families and two large estates. Meggie is doing well. I'm glad she is staying in the neighbourhood, too."

"Yes," said Ernest, dubiously helping himself to a crumpet, for he had inherited his mother's love of food without her digestion, "it would have been sad to lose our only girl. How our family runs to males! Mamma was an only daughter in a family of boys. She had three sons and only one daughter. She had three grandsons and only one granddaughter."

A shadow fell across Mary's face, for she had buried a five-month-old daughter. She cast a reproachful look at Ernest, which he interpreted as a warning against eating the crumpet.

"H'm, well," he muttered. "After a strenuous game of tennis, I don't believe one crumpet will hurt me."

"Don't come to me for sympathy," said his brother, "if you have wind on the stomach."

Ernest returned crisply — "I should never expect sympathy from you."

"Listen to the hardy athletes!" said Philip, spreading clotted cream on his scone and introducing it in one bite into his mouth.

Nicholas and Ernest smiled good-humouredly. Philip, at forty-four, was very much the younger brother to them, and they could afford to be tolerant toward him, for his generosity never questioned the length of their visits in his home. They had had their share of their father's fortune. His house and land, with a fair income, had been left to Philip, his youngest and favourite son. As long as their money had lasted, Canada had seen little of Ernest and Nicholas. London was their natural home, and they had only returned to Jalna when there was nothing else to do. Ernest still hoped, if some of his investments recovered, to spend at least a part of each year in England.

As for their mother, old Adeline, her feelings toward Philip baffled even herself. She loved him and sometimes almost hated him. She resented his being the master of Jalna, which, she felt, should have been left to her absolutely. How she would have brandished that ownership as a bludgeon and as a bait over the heads of her three sons! Unlike Nicholas and Ernest, she felt no tolerance toward Philip because of his hospitality. She was saving of her own fortune and established an air of mystery about it.

She resented Philip's physical resemblance to her own Philip, the husband she had loved with all the force of her fiery nature. But perhaps it was less his resemblance than his differences to his father that irritated her. Captain Whiteoak had been a soldier, with a body as straight as a sword. Philip was an easygoing gentleman farmer with an incurably indolent slouch. Captain Whiteoak had rapped out his words with military explosiveness. Philip spoke indolently. Captain Whiteoak had been a martinet to his children. Philip indulged his children to the point of spoiling. Captain Whiteoak had thought a good deal of the importance of his position in the Province, for, though he had never gone into politics, his opinion had carried weight in public questions and it had been usually voiced with vigorous conviction. Philip did not care how unimportant he was.

Yet father and youngest son had one trait in common. That was their imperviousness to criticism. It was this trait that baffled Adeline. She stared fiercely at Philip in his ruffianly-looking fishing jacket, his dishevelled hair, and realized it was beyond her power to change him. He refused to tidy himself before coming to the tea table to please his old mother. Her cup trembled with anger as she raised it brimming to her lips, and some of the tea was slopped.

"Mamma," Ernest said, nervously, "must you" — he hesitated.

"Must I what?" Her eyes moved from Philip's face to his.

"Slop your tea?" He finished the question with an apologetic air.

"Yes, I must," she retorted fiercely. "I must — I must — I must — and no wonder! If my son comes to table looking like a pig, is it any wonder

I eat like one? I must get a trough. Philip and I will muzzle our food in a trough and grunt together, eh, Philip?"

"Yes, old lady," agreed Philip. Not to be outdone in coarseness by his mother, he added — "Have some of the clotted cream. It takes a grand hold o' the gob."

Ernest and Nicholas chuckled, but Molly exclaimed: —

"Philip, you're disgusting!"

There was a sound of horses' hoofs on the drive and then a burst of young girls' laughter in the hall. The door was thrown open and Philip's daughter and her friend Vera Lacey came into the room. Vera, the young London relative of neighbours, was spending the year with her aunts. Her parents had sent her on this visit because of an undesirable love affair, and she had made up her mind to turn the punishment into a thoroughly good time. Her piquant face was powdered, in contrast to Meggie's, which shone from heat and excitement. Meg cast herself on her father's knee and threw her arms about his neck.

"M'm" ... they cooed together, gazing into each other's eyes.

"Isn't Meggie a spoiled creature!" exclaimed Vera. "She should have my father for a while. She'd get no hugs from him."

Mary Whiteoak threw an irritated glance at father and daughter. She had been Meg's governess before she had married Philip, and the girl had the same power of tantalizing that had made the child a pupil to be dreaded. Mary said: —

"Your father's tea will be getting cold, Meg. Aren't you going to tell us what you bought? Did you have your fitting at the dressmaker's?"

Meg ignored her and pressed little nibbling kisses against her father's cheek.

Before the coming of the two girls Mary Whiteoak had appeared, in the company of the three middle-aged men and the old woman, as nothing more than a girl herself. Now, before the exuberance of their authentic girlhood, she paled into a fragile woman, worn by childbearing.

"Yes, yes," urged old Mrs. Whiteoak, agreeing for once with her daughter-in-law, "leave off your snuggling, Meggie, and tell us about the town."

Philip put his daughter from him and turned to his tea. "This wedding," he said, "is going to put me on the rocks."

"It was such fun!" cried Meg. "And what do you suppose Vera did? She went up to a customer in Murdocks' and began to examine her dress, thinking she was a dummy! You should have seen the customer's face!"

"The shops are amusing after London," said Vera. "But let me tell you what Meggie did."

Meg interrupted her, and the two went into peals of laughter. Exhilarated by their bursting health, Adeline helped herself to more jam and demanded another cup of tea.

"You should have seen my trousseau," said old Mrs. Whiteoak. "There was elegance for you. I took it all the way from Ireland to India in eleven large trunks. My father hadn't got it all paid for, they said, at the day of his death."

Agreeable talk was at its height when the chenille curtains that hung at the folding doors which led into the library were pushed aside and Philip's eldest son, Renny, surveyed the group about the table. He was two years Meg's junior and was just entering manhood.

"Come in, come in," said Ernest testily. "You are letting an abominable draught on the back of my neck. I have been overheated playing tennis."

"Why is he always late for tea?" growled Nicholas.

"Please don't bring that muddy dog with you!" cried his sister, and the two girls shrieked as the cocker spaniel padded about the table, his fringed tail waving.

With a grimace, half-deprecating, half-impudent, Renny disappeared behind the curtains, put his dog outside, and reappeared at the door leading from the hall.

He was a tall thin youth with a look of wiry strength, whose arrogant features already bore a striking resemblance to his grandmother's. His skin, which in young boyhood had been creamy, was now becoming weather-beaten by exposure to sun and wind in all seasons. His vivid brown eyes flashed beneath brows so expressive that already a horizontal line across his forehead marked their animation. His hair, brown in shadow, flashed into burnished red when the light touched it. This rather extraordinary hair covered a head of definite, statuesque modeling of which Meg had once observed that if it came to beating it against a stone wall, the wall might get the worst of it. As growing boy and heir to Jalna he had been the object of so much criticism from his grandmother, parents, aunts, and uncles; his doings had been the focus of such constant speculation, encouragement, and reproof, that he carried himself with an air of wariness as though always prepared to face attack.

With his entrance the attention of the two girls was fixed on him, and Nicholas was forced to raise his voice and repeat to Meggie that he had had a letter from his sister and that she and her husband were sailing the following week for Canada.

"That will be nice," said Meg, vaguely, then added, with more warmth, "I do wonder what they will bring me for a wedding present!"

"Some cast-off bit of jet or pinchbeck of your aunt's," said old Mrs. Whiteoak, scraping the jam pot.

Meg pushed out her pretty lips. "They ought to bring me something really handsome."

"I am sure Augusta and Edwin will bring you a charming present," said Ernest.

"I don't see what makes you think so," said his mother. "Their presents are always tarnished or stink of moth balls.... More tea, Molly! Have you gone to sleep behind the teapot? Ha — that's right — plenty of sugar."

Nicholas put in — "They are bringing something more interesting than a present for you, Meggie. They are bringing a wedding guest, your cousin, twice or thrice removed — Mr. Malahide Court."

Meg stared. "I've never heard of him. What a name!"

Her grandmother glared across the table at her. "Don't you dare to poke fun at that name, miss!"

"I wasn't! I only said what a name!"

"You jeered! You know you did! I won't have it! I was a Court and there's no finer family living. And Malahide is a good old Court name. The Malahides married the Courts and lived in their castles when the Whiteoaks were yeomen, let me tell you! Perhaps you've forgotten that I am the granddaughter of an earl, hey? Have you forgotten that?"

Grandmother was working herself into a temper. She rapped the table with her spoon to punctuate her sentences.

"Keep your hair on, Mamma," soothed Philip. "We all know about our noble ancestors and realize that we're only poor Colonials ourselves. There's no need of getting upset about it."

"Malahide Court," said Ernest sententiously, "must be well past forty. I remember that he came to my school in England just as I was leaving."

"What was he like?" asked Nicholas.

"A miserable little shaver."

"Had he the Court nose?" demanded old Mrs. Whiteoak.

"H'm, well, I don't remember that, but I know he was no beauty."

"I am anxious to see him. I hope he will stop the summer."

Philip raised his eyebrows. "Let us see him before we hope that, Mamma."

Small feet were heard running in the hall and Mary's face turned, all alight, toward the door. It opened and her elder son, Eden, pranced in.

"I'm a pony," he declared, and galloped round the table. Mary stretched out her hand to catch him as he passed. She had lost three infants before his advent and felt no security in her passionate possession of him. He eluded her hand, but was seized by Meg and rapturously kissed. Both she and Renny evinced a demonstrative affection for their little half-brothers, taking, as Mary saw it, a perverse pleasure in coming between her and them.

Now Meg asked of him — "What do you suppose I have brought from town?"

"I don't know. A little engine for me?"

"You silly, no! But I have bought your page's suit. White satin with a lace collar."

"Oh." He was impressed. "May I try it on, now?"

His mother spoke sharply. "No, Eden, you must wait till tomorrow. Your hands are probably dirty and it will soon be your bedtime."

"See, my hands are clean!" He spread them out for inspection.

Meg took him on her knee. She put her lips close to his ear and whispered something which apparently satisfied him. He took the piece of cake Renny offered and, with a daring glance at his mother, began to eat it. The older people were still talking about Malahide Court and speculating on the reasons for his visit.

After tea the two girls took Eden to Meg's room and locked the door.

"The idea of Mother saying he must not try on his page's suit!" exclaimed Meg. "That is always her way — to spoil our pleasure if she can."

"It must be horrid," said Vera, "having a stepmother."

"It's abominable! Especially when she was once one's governess. She attacks one from both angles. But Renny and I don't knuckle under." She dipped the corner of a towel in her ewer and wiped Eden's face and hands. He looked very earnestly into her face.

Vera unfolded the suit from its wrappings. "It's nice," she said, "that you are so fond of her children."

"Please don't ever call them hers! She had them, — the best thing she's ever done, — but they are perfect Whiteoaks."

"This one looks like her, doesn't he?"

"H'm, he has her colouring, but he's just himself."

She had taken off his sailor suit and he stood in his vest before them, white, fragile, yet proudly built. Meg began to dress him in the white satin garments.

When they went down they found that the family had moved out to the lawn to enjoy the late sunlight. Philip, Nicholas, and Ernest stood together admiring the house. It faced the sun serenely, as though conscious that everything about it was in exemplary order. No crumbled brick or rotted shingle or sagging shutter was there to take from its air of solid well-being. The bulk of the stables was concealed by a group of stalwart evergreens, and stretching far behind it were spread the six hundred acres of farm and woodland, pasture, ravine, and winding stream that had been, half a century before, reclaimed by Captain Whiteoak from the wild.

Renny had picked up a tennis racket and was sending balls into the net. Old Mrs. Whiteoak possessed herself of the other racket and faced him.

"Now then! Now then!" she challenged. "A ball to your grandmother, young cock!"

Renny, laughing, sent one softly bouncing toward her. She ignored it and stood with the racket foursquare to her shoulder, formidable-looking in her large ribboned cap.

"You call that a ball! D'ye think I'm so weak as that? Come now — a good one!"

Renny eyed her menacingly.

"Renny!" cautioned Ernest, "be careful."

"Mind your own business, Ernest!" she ordered. "Am I playing this game, or are you?"

A ball shot straight at her cap.

She caught it on her racket and returned it over the net with no mean blow, but she could not risk another. She grinned triumphantly.

"Well, now, do you say I can play tennis?"

"You're a marvel, Gran!"

He laughed across the net and came to her. She took his arm and squeezed it.

"The girls are coming. See what they've done?"

Meg and Vera descended the steps to the lawn with Eden between them.

"Look, Daddy!" cried Meg. "A rehearsal!" She put the hem of her dress in Eden's hands and moved sedately across the lawn, followed by Vera.

"Splendid!" exclaimed Nicholas.

"By Jove, the child looks beautiful!" said Ernest.

Philip met his daughter and she laid her hand on his arm. "Now then, Mamma, you'll have to be the parson. Renny, can't you produce the groom?"

"I don't like rehearsals of solemn things," said his mother. "They bring bad luck. Come to Granny, darling, and show her your fine new suit."

But Eden kept fast hold of Meg's skirt, bearing himself with dignity.

Renny gave a shout. "Hello, there's Maurice! Come along, Maurice! What price the laggard groom!"

Maurice Vaughan advanced through a small wicket gate set in a hedge of cedar. He had crossed the ravine which divided his father's property from Jalna and had picked on the way a bunch of white trilliums.

"Good man!" exclaimed Philip, delighted. "He's here — nosegay and all!"

Nicholas began to boom the "Wedding March."

"What's it all about?" asked Maurice.

"A rehearsal," said Mrs. Whiteoak, "and I don't like it. I don't like it at all. I've a superstition about it."

Maurice came to his fiancée and put the lilies into her hands. He made a little old-fashioned bow, but there was a gravity in his face, a heaviness in his eyes, that took the light from Meggie's. She held the flowers to her, and asked: —

"Is anything wrong?"

He shook his head. "No. Well, my father is not very well. Mother and I are worried about him."

"I've known your dad all my life," said Philip, "and I've never known him well. Don't you worry about him. He'll outlive us all." He tossed up Eden. "Now what do you think of this for a page?"

Maurice smiled and Meg's face cleared.

Mary now came out of the house carrying her younger child, a boy of twenty months whom they called Peep. He sat very straight on her arm, determined not to be sleepy, though he knew he was being brought out to say goodnight. He had a skin of exquisite pink and whiteness, thin fair hair, and intensely blue, rather prominent eyes.

"Oh, I call it a shame to have put that suit on Eden!" she said angrily. "He will be getting a spot on it." But she smiled in delight at his beauty when he darted to her side.

"See me! See me!" he cried.

Renny followed him. "Give Peep to me," he said. "Then you can look after Eden."

Half reluctantly she surrendered the baby. He leaped, crowing, into Renny's arms. Renny carried him to where Maurice had moved apart.

He thrust the child's downy head against Maurice's face. "Take him," he laughed. "You'll be dandling a kid of your own one day. Let me see how it becomes you."

Maurice drew back as though struck.

"For Christ's sake, keep it away from me!" he said, thickly. "Renny, I must see you alone! You must get rid of those girls and come with me into the ravine. I've something terrible to tell you."

II

IN THE RAVINE

THE TWO BOYS passed through the wicket gate and descended the path into the ravine, just as the sun was sending its last rays there. The young grass and unfolding bracken fronds had taken on an unearthly green, while the trees, still caught in the sunlight, glistened and quivered in the light breeze. The trunks of the pines showed a distinct purple tone, while those of the silver birches diffused through their whiteness a pale inner glow.

The contrast between the movements of Maurice and Renny was indicative not only of the moods that possessed them, but of their very natures. Maurice plunged down the path, sending small stones rolling before him, scarcely seeming to see where he was going. Renny moved freely as a wild creature and nothing escaped his brilliant gaze. He stopped once or twice and appeared to be on the point of turning aside into the wood, when Maurice called back to him: "Are you coming?" and he returned to the path.

The river which flowed through the ravine, and which, in later years, became only a small stream through the building of a dam in an enterprise by which the family endeavoured to counteract the extravagances and bad investments of Nicholas and Ernest, was now in the fullness of its strength. It made a distinct murmuring sound as it moved through

its thickly wooded curves, breaking into clear gurglings when it encountered the dark opposition of a boulder or urge of smooth ledges of rock.

Renny made toward a bridge which spanned the river at its narrowest
point, but Maurice drew him to the shelter of some wild cherry trees.

"Come in here," he said, "where we can't be seen. You never know
when someone may cross the bridge. Why, look now! There comes my
father! When I think what I may be bringing on to his head, I could
drown myself in that river."

Renny fixed his eyes on the figure of the man crossing the bridge. He
wished he could escape from Maurice. He said: —

"Your father won't be hard on you for anything you've done."

The thin, upright figure crossed the bridge and began to make the
ascent with an alert step. Maurice followed his movements with misery
in his eyes. Mr. Vaughan passed so near them that they could hear his
heavy breathing.

Maurice groaned — "I'm in the devil of a mess! I don't know how
to tell you."

"Perhaps you had better not tell me," said Renny, with a gleam of
hope in his eyes. "I always find it better to keep my troubles to myself."

"But I *must* tell you! You've got to help me! You're the only one
who can."

"Out with it, then!"

Maurice threw himself on the grass.

"Sit down! Sit down beside me!"

Renny dropped to his side and offered him a cigarette, but Maurice
shook his head.

"No, no, I can't smoke! Renny, I'm in the most terrible mess. I don't
know what I'm to do." He rolled on to his side and clutched a handful
of grass. Then, as though the words too were pulled up by the roots,
he said: —

"It's a girl I've got into trouble. She's going to have a baby! If your
family find out — if my mother and father find out — I'm done for! And
it isn't as though I care about the girl. I hate her now that I know what
she's going to do. I've never loved anyone but Meggie."

"Who is she?" Renny asked in a cold voice.

The name came so muffled he could scarcely hear the name: "Elvira Gray."

"Elvira!" Renny repeated it on a note of wonder, and he looked at his friend, seeing him in a new, strange, sensual light.

A flicker of bravado passed over Maurice's face. He gave a short laugh.

"You've never thought of Elvira in that way, eh?"

"I've never thought of her in any way." He spoke gruffly and avoided Maurice's eyes.

"But I don't see how you could help noticing her. She's not like any of the other village girls."

"Well, she's pretty, I know. But I've never given her a thought." His mind turned to his sister and he broke out: "It's a damned shame! It's horrible! Meg can never marry you after this!"

Maurice sat up and said desperately: "Meggie must never know. She never will know. You must help me!"

"How the devil can I help you?"

"Elvira will go away. She has relations who will take her in, if she has money to provide for her and the child till she can get work…. Renny, you must see Elvira for me…. I can't see her again…. She makes terrible scenes…. It isn't safe…. We'll be caught…. Everything will come out."

"Do you think —" Renny spoke passionately — "that I can bear the thought of you marrying my sister — after this?"

"What difference will it make if she never knows? I'll be faithful to her. I swear I will! I'll never look at another woman! Surely you have heard enough talk in your family to know that this sort of thing sometimes happens. Men forget themselves." He spoke as an experienced man to a boy.

Renny muttered — "You should not have forgotten yourself."

"I don't need you to tell me that! I've been driven almost mad by remorse. I haven't had a decent night's sleep since she told me about the baby."

"Did she threaten to tell your people?"

"No, but everyone in the village will talk. You know what they are for gossip. Our families will be bound to hear of it. Elvira's aunt will be after me for help. In fact, she has been. I've given her money — all I could lay my hands on — to shut her up."

"How did this affair begin?"

"Elvira used to come into our woods to pick blackberries. I used to be about with my gun. I spoke to her and once I helped her to fill her pail. There was something mysterious about her. But I never loved her for a minute, mind you. I've never stopped loving Meg. Meg *would* have a year's engagement. She would scarcely let me kiss her. But every time I looked at Elvira I could see she wanted me to kiss her. Then one day last August I forgot myself. I took her in my arms.... I was lost then. It was just like a wild dream."

Renny said — "Yes? What was she like?"

"She was passionate and strange. She almost frightened me. I made up my mind I'd never see her again.... But — the very next time I went into the wood — she was there."

Renny's face hardened. "Why didn't you keep out of the wood?"

"I was a fool. But I wanted to be alone to think things over."

"Are you sure you didn't want to meet her again?"

Maurice flushed under Renny's eyes.

"I don't know. Perhaps I did. I was a fool. But I can tell you, I've paid for it!"

"I think you're just beginning to pay for it."

"By God! You're hard! I thought you were my friend. I thought you'd help me."

"I'm wondering if I want my sister to marry you now."

"I swear I'll be faithful to her for the rest of my life! Any man is likely to make one slip. It will disappoint your people terribly. It will break my parents' hearts — if this comes between Meg and me. Lord, what I've been through! Meg buying her trousseau, and Elvira clasping me about the knees and begging me to marry her! It's too much! I can't bear it!"

He threw himself on the grass and groaned.

Renny was moved to compassion.

"Look here," he said, putting his hand on Maurice's shoulder, "buck up! We'll do something about it. I'll see Elvira and we'll get her out of here at once. Have you the money for her?"

"Yes. My father has given me a cheque for my wedding expenses. I'll have to take some out of that."

"Does that mean you will cut down on Meggie's pleasures on your wedding trip?" Renny regarded him suspiciously.

"Lord, no. I can always get money."

"H'm — you're a lucky devil."

"Will you see Elvira tomorrow?"

"Yes."

"She must leave soon — before it's too late."

"When is the arrival expected?"

"I don't quite know. In about a month, I think."

"Well, aren't people talking?"

"She doesn't show her condition."

"She may be bluffing you."

"No. I'm sure of it."

"Are you sure the child will be yours?"

"I think it is."

"Well, as Gran says, this is a pretty to-do. I wonder how the old lady would take it."

Maurice replied eagerly. "She would be on my side. You can depend on that, Renny! She is a woman of the world. My parents have lived narrow lives. They're puritanical. Your people are different. They see things comparatively."

Renny made a guarded, nervous movement. "They wouldn't see this comparatively," he said. "They'd see it as an insult to Meg. I don't believe they'd want her to marry you."

"I think you're quite wrong. But no one need ever know, if you'll help me."

"Oh, I'll help you, as far as that goes! When I can I see Elvira?"

"I will arrange that. God, what a load you've taken off my mind!"

He stretched out his hand and clasped Renny's.

A chill rose from the river and a tenuous wreath of mist indicated its meanderings. The crinkled surface of the water took on an olive tinge, while the tops of the willows were still gilded by the sun. A kingfisher swooped and rose with a small fish in its beak.

Then, from beyond a willowed curve of the river, two swans appeared, sailing in midstream, with closely folded wings and arched necks. They were a pair that Renny's father had brought from England. The experiment had been tried several times, but these were the first that had thriven and made the river their own. Now, in an attitude of innocent scorn, they sailed past the two youths, their snowy whiteness reflected in the darkening water, a long silver ripple springing from either side of their calm breasts.

III

ELVIRA

THAT EVENING RENNY could not get the thought of Elvira out of his head. After he had taken Vera Lacey home and had left her puzzled by his abstractedness, he followed the road to the village and turned into the poor street where the girl and her aunt lived. He knew that the aunt was a dressmaker who had appeared, from nowhere it seemed, about five years ago. Elvira had been a thin-legged little girl then, with hair that stuck out in a dark halo about her pale face. She had liked horses, he knew, for he remembered her hanging about the gates of the paddocks at Jalna, watching the activities there. He faintly remembered showing off in front of her on the back of a wayward colt because he liked the way Elvira stood, with her head thrown back and her hands clasped against her breast, as though her excitement were more than she could bear. He did not think he had had more than a glimpse of her in the past two years. It was strange, he reflected, that Maurice should have had this intercourse with her — Maurice, who had never looked at any girl but Meggie; Maurice, who had always been detached.

He looked speculatively at the one lighted window of the cottage. He could see into a kitchen where the two women were sitting by the table drinking tea. The oil lamp set between them revealed their features with dramatic intensity, hardening what was already hard, as the line of the older woman's lips, making still brighter her coarse, yellow hair and restless eyes. At the same time it added a bloom to the smoothness of the younger's cheeks, a more vivid redness to her lips. She sat with elbows on table, staring across the saucer of tea she was cooling at her aunt, who peered into her cup, evidently reading a fortune from the tea leaves. A dressmaker's dummy, wearing a red blouse, stood in a corner.

Renny gazed fascinated. He had never before witnessed a scene like this: the poverty of the little room, its warm seclusion, — for a stove was glowing hotly, — the two engrossed in feminine intimacy. He had expected a look of gloom about the place, depression, apprehension in the women's faces. He had expected to see a heavy elderly woman in the aunt — not this haggard one with gypsy eyes and a small, red-lipped mouth. The two had the same sharp, delicately cut features, but Elvira's hair was brown. She rose and went to the stove, and Renny saw the fullness of her young body. It was true what Maurice had said, she was going to have a child.

He had a sudden feeling of shame at having spied upon her. He turned away and would have left as silently as he had come, but a cock in the outhouse heard his movements and gave a loud crow; the hens were disturbed and filled the air with alarmed cacklings. The older woman was on her feet in a swift, catlike movement. Before Renny could retreat she had glided through the door and had seen his figure against the hedge. He came toward her then, stepping into the shaft of lamplight. He spoke nervously.

"I hope I haven't frightened you."

"Oh, no," she answered coolly. "That is — I was a bit scared when I thought someone was after my hens — but, as soon as I saw you just standing there —" She gave a little laugh. "You're young Mr. Whiteoak, aren't you?"

"Yes," he agreed, trying to see her face, trying to make her out.

"I don't suppose you know who I am," she went on, with a peculiar, teasing note in her voice. "Folks who live in big houses with a lot of land about them never even hear the names of poor people."

"I know the names of everyone in the village," he returned. "How could I help? I've lived here all my life."

A frank warm tone came into her voice when she next spoke. "You're a great friend of young Mr. Vaughan's, aren't you?"

He answered abruptly — "He and I have been talking over this affair today. This is why I have come to see you."

A flicker passed over her face. She looked disappointed, he thought.

He asked tentatively — "Will you tell me when I can meet Elvira to give her the money?"

She answered rather sharply: "Elvira isn't meeting folks now. You had better bring it here to me."

"All right."

"Come tomorrow night. About this time? You and I could have a little talk. I'll make you a nice cup of tea and read your fortune from the leaves. I'm good at that. I was just reading Elvira's when you came."

"Oh." He wondered why Elvira had shown no interest in what had brought her aunt hurrying to the door. "What is Elvira's fortune?"

"She's going to have a daughter. A beautiful daughter who is to move in high society. But I'd like to tell your fortune. You've a face for a fortune out of the ordinary. I'll bet I could tell you things that would surprise you."

"Could you?"

"I can tell you one thing without ever looking in a teacup. You're going to be fascinating to women. You can have love for the asking. I guess you've had some already, eh?"

He gave her a dark, wary glance.

"Me! Why, I'm not twenty yet."

"Years don't matter. You came of age in love many a month ago."

Without answering he moved a little nearer to her and looked into her eyes. They were narrow, startling eyes that looked like jewels in this light.

"Strange where you got them," he said. "They're not quite human."

"What?"

"Your eyes."

"I'll tell you all about myself tomorrow night. I'm young, you know. I'm only ten years older than Elvira. We'll be alone. I'll read your fortune and tell you how I got my eyes." She gave a daring laugh and suddenly put her hand on his head. "My goodness, but you are fascinating!"

At this instant the lamp in the kitchen was lowered. Now it sent out only a pale bluish gleam. The cock, still restless, uttered a plaintive, protesting crow. He fell from his perch and could be heard scrambling back to it with troubled flapping of wings, and complaining from his hens.

There was something almost Biblical in the interruption — the dimmed light, the crowing cock. Renny cast an apprehensive glance at the woman, and, muttering that he would bring the money the next night, he leaped across the bit of garden where the spears of young green onions were pushing up and went out through the hedge.

On the walk home beside the dark stream that alternately revealed and hid itself like a woman longing for love, his mind was full of thoughts of Elvira and her aunt.

But the next night he did not go into the cottage. He knocked at the door, and when the girl opened it he thrust the envelope Maurice had given him into her hand, with a swift glance into her startled face, and disappeared.

IV

SIR EDWIN AND LADY BUCKLEY
AND MALAHIDE COURT

A RENEWED FURBISHING of the house took place on the eve of the coming of the relations from England. Eliza, in starched print dress and flawless white apron, went about with brush and duster seeking imaginary dust in the corners of the drawing room. Philip's entrance into the house filled her with conflicting emotions — horror of the mud he would almost certainly bring with him, pleasure at the sight of his stalwart figure and good-humoured face. Eliza was a fussy, irritable, energetic woman, yet, with all her being, she admired these opposite qualities of the master of the house. Indeed she gloried in his untidiness and would stalk down the stairs to the basement kitchen with the ashes he had knocked from his pipe to the floor, or the burrs he had pulled from his dog's tail and hidden under his chair, proudly displayed on her dustpan for the shocking of the cook and the kitchenmaid.

Beatrice, the kitchenmaid, usually called "Beet" by Renny, most appropriately because of her purplish complexion, was now polishing the walnut newel post which was carved in a design of grapes and their leaves and never passed without a caress from Adeline Whiteoak.

Adeline was immensely interested in the preparations, for she was full of pent up vitality which her aging body could not relieve. She had that year begun to carry a stick for the first time, and its aggressive thud could be heard through the house at all hours when she was neither eating, playing backgammon, nor taking a nap.

She pooh-poohed all the fuss that was being made, yet she wanted the house to look its best, not so much for her daughter and her son-in-law as for Malahide Court, whom she had never seen. He was a cousin, several times removed, of a branch of her family which she had always hated because of a feud long before her day. She had a prideful desire to impress him with the elegance of her surroundings, for she knew that her family had looked on her as buried in this colony. She was also greatly curious about the man himself. All the Courts were interesting. Devils they might be, but never dull or without distinction.

She stroked the polished grapes of the newel post and looked up at her husband's sword, hung in its scabbard on the wall.

"Ha," she said, panting a little, for she had just ascended the basement stairs after an inspection of the preparations down there. "You've a good polish on the old newel, Beattie, a very good polish. Nothing like elbow grease. Beats all the stuff advertised in the papers."

"Yes'm," returned Beattie, polishing harder than ever.

Old Adeline stood staring at the newel post, fresh and upright as the day it was planted there at the foot of the stairs. She could see her husband, straight and strong, descending them.

But it was another Philip who came into the hall, put his arm round her, and said — "How's the old girl? Pretty fit, eh?" he kissed her cheek, on which a few strong hairs grew.

She returned the kiss with a loud smack. "Yes, yes, nothing to complain of. Appetite good. But fussed up a little with all this to-do over the Buckleys and that Court fellow. Why must Molly always want things so spotless?"

"Now, Mamma, you enjoy seeing the old place look trig just as much as anyone."

She faced him with her underlip protruding. "Of course I do! But I can't agree that the Buckleys are important. What is he? A third baronet! How did his grandfather get the title? For discovering something about mosquitoes in Brazil. Mosquitoes! Bugs! I call it a lousy title, I do!" She grinned at him triumphantly, feeling that she had obliterated

Sir Edwin's claims to nobility. She had liked him well enough when he had married Augusta. A nice little man with ash-blond side whiskers and an upper lip that nibbled like a rabbit's at his words. He had taken her daughter out of her way and he had always been deferential to her, laughed moderately at her ribald jokes, even when they were directed at himself. But he showed himself snappy when she jeered at Augusta. He and Augusta had taken their unexpected inheritance of the title and a manor house in Devon modestly, but Adeline could not forgive her daughter for becoming her social superior. She resented the title, never acknowledging that she remembered it, invariably speaking of Augusta as "my daughter, Lady Bilgeley, Lady Bunkum," or some such name.

Her interest in Malahide Court became even more fervent as the hour for the arrival drew near. She racked her brain to recall the history of his branch of the family, alternately stressing its disgracefulness and the impregnable grandeur of the main stock. Long before the guests were due to arrive she was dressed for their reception in a mulberry-coloured cashmere, trimmed with innumerable puffings and bands of velvet. She wore an enormous brooch, and rubies and diamonds glittered on her handsome old hands. Her cap was a creation of lace and mulberry-coloured ribbons. She presented an impressive picture of a bygone day — formidable, rich-hued, full of a vitality that had something fine in its unquestioning assurance.

The pair of bays flashed along the drive, their hoofs scattering the patterned gravel. Now, through a space in the freshly unfolded leaves, a muscular shoulder was visible for a brief moment or a flank groomed to satin brightness. Hodge, the ruddy coachman, brought up the pair before the door with a flourish. It was high noon. A cool fresh wind blew the branches about, so that the intense shadows on the lawn changed their shape without ceasing.

Nicholas, Ernest, and Philip stood together on the steps of the porch. Hodge jumped down from his seat and went to the horses' heads. Nicholas opened the carriage door. Augusta, holding up her skirt, descended the steps and was thrice clasped in brotherly arms. Sir Edwin followed and genially shook hands. Then Cousin Malahide gathered up an incredibly long, thin body from a corner of the carriage, and advanced with a sombre smile to meet his hosts. Nicholas's strong eyebrows rose toward his crest of greying hair. He tugged at his moustache. Ernest answered the smile with a wry movement of his sensitive lips. Philip grasped the hand extended languidly to him.

"Welcome to Jalna," he said.

"I am sorry to hear," added Ernest, also shaking hands, "that you have had a rough voyage."

"A filthy voyage," replied Malahide Court. His voice was unexpectedly full and deep. His disparaging gaze took in the house, the flower beds with their geraniums just set out, the faces of the three brothers.

"How charming!" he said, addressing Sir Edwin.

"Yes, yes," Sir Edwin said nervously. "I've always loved this place. Shall we go in, Philip? Augusta and I are anxious to see her mother."

"And Mamma will be eager to see us," answered Augusta, in her contralto tones.

They mounted the steps, Philip and Sir Edwin coming last.

"Well," asked Sir Edwin, "what do you think of him?"

Philip answered deliberately — "I can't make him out. I'm wondering what we should do with such an exotic at Jalna."

Sir Edwin looked worried. "Well, well, do you really think him so odd? But he has a very good mind. He knows a great deal about ancient Greek sculpture. He and I have had some interesting talks."

"How did you happen to bring him with you?"

"Really, I don't quite know. He was paying us a visit and the time went on and — he just came with us."

"You mean you couldn't shake him?"

"Just that!"

"But why should he have wanted to come here?"

"I can't quite make out. I think that things were rather uncomfortable for him in Ireland. An allowance he had from his mother is temporarily cut off, so he cannot live in Paris, where he usually goes when out of Ireland."

"Well, well, we must make the best of him," said Philip, philosophically. "Perhaps he will amuse Mamma."

Mamma was receiving him as they entered, a puzzled grin fixed on her face as she peered searchingly into his.

He was all in black. If her ebony stick with its ivory handle had suddenly betaken itself from her hand and bowed over her rings, it might have made some such figure as Malahide Court. His face had the sallowness of old ivory. His eyes were heavy-lidded and glistening, his chin pointed. His nose, strongly arched, jutted from his narrow face, with a flourish of long, widely flanged nostrils.

"Now, and this is a surprise," said Adeline. "I'm glad to see you and I'll be glad to hear news of the family at first hand." She looked him over and added — "Are you in mourning?"

"Yes." He laid a hand, from which he had removed the black glove, on his cravat, and passed it down over his waistcoat. "For my lost youth." The hand might have been used as a model for the hands in portraits by the old masters.

Adeline chose to consider this a joke. She gave a sudden bark of laughter. The noise roused her parrot, Boney, half asleep on his perch behind a fire screen. He rose on his toes, peered over the screen, and broke into a torrent of Hindoo curses.

"*Shaitan! Shaitan ka bata! Shaitan ka butcka! Piakur! Piakur! Jab kutr!*"

He followed this tirade with loud cackling laughter.

"That's my parrot," said Adeline, proudly. "I taught him myself. I'll wager you didn't understand a word he said."

Malahide Court not only understood, but threw back at the bird other Hindoo curses that made Adeline stare admiringly.

The parrot was in a paroxysm of rage. Screaming furiously, he flapped his wings and would have flown into the newcomer's face but that he was restrained by the slender chain on his leg.

Lady Buckley thought the scene was disgraceful and told her favourite brother, Ernest, so. They stood together, arm in arm, happy in their reunion. At that moment Meg appeared in the doorway, eager to greet the arrivals.

Ernest asked of his sister — "How do you think Mamma looks? You have not seen her for two years."

"Splendid," returned Augusta. "I only hope I shall be as exuberant at her age."

"Then you must soon begin," returned Ernest, "for you certainly are not now and I don't know that I should like it. It would not at all suit your style." He looked at her admiringly.

In truth Augusta had never been so attractive in her life as she now was. Middle age became her. Her Queen Alexandra fringe, of a rich, possibly questionable brown, accentuated the tranquil dignity of her features. She wore too many chains, bracelets, and brooches, but always appeared aloof from fashion rather than overdressed.

Meg could scarcely restrain her mirth at the sight of Malahide Court, bending with arched back over her hand. This fascinating Irish cousin who, in moments of dreaming, she had pictured as capable of making Maurice a little jealous!

"Meggie's not used to hand kissing," said her grandmother. "She's a simple country girl."

"Then this will seem more natural." And he kissed Meg's round cheek.

Meg drew back, repelled by the touch of his face against hers, and to cover this Augusta exclaimed: —

"We must see the others! Mary and her children. And where is Renny?"

"He's never about when he's wanted," said Philip. "I don't know what he does with himself. Ah, here come Mary and the babe!"

She hesitated, tall and fair in the doorway, her child in her arms. He clutched her neck in his small embrace, his pink cheek pressed against hers.

Augusta kissed Mary all the more warmly because she knew that Adeline disliked her. She cooed to the infant on a deep, enticing note. He grasped a handful of the jet that trimmed the front of her dress.

"He is the image of Philip!" she declared.

"He is far more like his grandfather," said Adeline. "He's got my husband's very look and his flat back. Did you ever see such a back on a twenty-months child? Turn him around, Molly, so they can see his back."

Mary turned him around and all eyes were fixed on the plump back and downy head. Malahide Court was forgotten.

Augusta asked — "Where is Eden?" The little boy was a favourite with her.

A shadow of annoyance crossed Mary's face. "I can't imagine. He was dressed and had promised to wait for me on the landing, but he disappeared. I dare say he is off somewhere with Renny."

"Drat the boy!" said his grandmother. "Why doesn't he come? Wait till you see him, Malahide! You'll say you've never seen such a Court. Red hair and all."

Malahide Court poked at the baby with a long forefinger. "The perfect age!" he said. "The perambulator age; the carried-in-arms age; the nipple, diaper, and talcum age! Why did I ever live to outgrow it!"

They were staring at him, trying to picture him as a baby, when Renny, with Eden clinging to his hand, came into the room. The two were greeted by reprimands from the family, with the exception of their grandmother, who raised her voice above the others. "Come now, Renny, and show yourself to my Cousin Malahide. There's a fine lad, Malahide. You must see him on a horse. He'll make you think of my father, old Renny Court."

The two shook hands, eying each other, the one without enthusiasm, the other with astonishment, dislike, and a touch of hilarity.

Eden looked into the strange face bent above him with an intent, rather unchildlike stare, then he raised his eyes to his mother's and smiled.

"A very unusual smile," said Cousin Malahide, still holding the little hand. "There's a shadow of pain in it which shows that he already is conscious that true mirth does not exist."

"No wonder he looks pained," muttered Renny to Meg. "This fellow is making me sick. Do you mean to say we've got to have him about for weeks?"

"Even months," answered Meg. "Isn't he awful? His clothes — his waist! I believe he wears corsets! Look at Father's face!"

Philip's face was indeed a study as his eyes followed the figure of Cousin Malahide, who had left the group and was moving about the room examining the Chippendale pieces with the intentness of a connoisseur.

Later, when the one o'clock lunch was announced, and Adeline led the way leaning on Malahide's arm, followed by Aunt Augusta with Eden by the hand, and Mary with Sir Edwin, Renny elongated his body, drew back his diaphragm to nothingness, assumed a sneering simper, and offered his arm to Meg. She, producing as well as she could on her round girlish face the arch grin of the old lady, clung to it and urged him toward the laden table. The three brothers, bringing up the rear, observed the caricature with tolerance, even with malicious amusement. Philip said: —

"I pity that gentleman if those two young rascals choose to make his life miserable. Lord, what a waist he has! Do you suppose he can put a solid meal out of sight?"

But Cousin Malahide, though his eyebrows all but disappeared when he saw the meal before him, displayed an unexpectedly good appetite. He vied with Adeline in second helpings, praised the sherry, and after a few glasses became so amusing that they wondered if, after all, they might not find him good company.

V

THE VISITOR

IN THE DAYS that followed, the newcomer made himself thoroughly at home. He explored the house, from the basement kitchen, and what was rather pretentiously called "the wine cellar," to the attic. He was never embarrassed, no matter where he was discovered, always proffering some glib explanation of his curiosity and drifting unabashed into further investigations.

He devoted at least two hours each day to gossip with his old kinswoman, raking up for her pleasure one scandalous happening after another, recalling almost forgotten members of her family to her mind with whatever was most disgraceful in their lives. He went to see her before she was up in the morning, when she still wore her befrilled nightdress, and sat by her bed, and flattered her and fed her parrot with toast.

He showed too that he could ride a horse, his incredibly long thin figure seeming to become a part of the spirited mare Renny had hoped would throw him.

To Adeline this unexpected visit, this revival of interest in her past, gave a renewed strength and vivacity. She had been feeling the weight of her eighty-odd years, moving slower, talking less, eating more often and less at a time, becoming slovenly at table. The fact that she could not properly chew her food was depressing to her. She would cast a gloomy look about the table at her descendants crunching the crisp rind of the roast pork and mutter: "All very well for you! But am I to live on potatoes and gravy?"

"The apple sauce is very nice, Mamma," Philip would say, pressing his sister's foot under the table and, as he had expected, sending his mother into a rage.

"Apple sauce! Apple sauce! D'ye think I can live on such slop? D'ye think I can keep my strength on pap? D'ye think I want to sit by and watch my children and my grandchildren gorge themselves while I starve! I that have carried great lumps of children in my body and eaten plenty for the two of us!"

"Perhaps you ate more than you needed, Granny," suggested Meg.

"Ate — ate — ate —" mimicked old Adeline. "What a way to pronounce a decent word! I say *et* and my family says *et!*"

"I was taught to pronounce it *ate* at school, Granny."

"Then unlearn it! I won't have any silly finicking ways of speech in this house! *Et* it was and *et* it is, and I wish to God I could do it!"

She stared mournfully at the pork.

"Well," said Philip, "as I have been saying for some time, what you need is two good sets of artificial teeth. Then you could chew in comfort."

"Quite true," agreed Sir Edwin. "Very true indeed."

The old lady eyed her son-in-law disparagingly. "Yours don't seem to do you much good. You mumble your food like a rabbit."

"They have a way now," said Malahide, "of sticking some sort of needle in the gum which deadens the pain. I had four out that way and it didn't hurt at all."

His kinswoman peered into his face.

"I don't see any lacking," she observed.

"They were my wisdom teeth," he grinned. "That is why I came out here."

Adeline struck the table with the handle of her fork.

"I'll not bear it any longer," she said. "I'll have them out!"

Although, as Philip had said, he had been urging her to this step, he felt something like consternation at the sudden decision. He abhorred any distasteful activity, and his first thought was that his mother might demand his support in the operation. He defended himself at once. He leaned forward to pat her shoulder.

"Splendid!" he exclaimed. "It will be a great improvement. I know of an excellent dental surgeon. Edwin and Augusta shall take you to him."

Augusta drew back her chin.

"Impossible!" she declared. "It would be too harrowing to me to see my mother suffer."

"But I shan't suffer! Malahide says I'll not suffer."

"Mamma, I beg you not to ask this of me!" said Augusta. "Philip is the one to take you. It is his suggestion."

Philip looked suddenly sulky. "Let Nicholas do it. He is her eldest son."

Nicholas leaned back in his chair. "I feel as Gussie does," he said. "I could not do it under any circumstances. Ernest is the one to accompany Mamma. He has tact. He has a woman's gentleness and a man's fortitude."

Ernest's expression was bitter as he listened to this eulogy of himself.

"I suppose," he said, "that you quite forget that I was sick when I saw the vet extract only six teeth from a mare."

"I have sixteen," said his mother. "You will never do." She looked almost pathetically into the faces about her. "Am I to go to the dentist alone?" she asked.

"If you will have me," said Malahide, "I'll be charmed to accompany you."

The family turned to him with their first and last expressions of gratitude. Grandmother stretched out her hand and took his. She said: —

"Well, that's handsome of you, Malahide. It's a good thing I have you to lean on. It is indeed."

"Mamma, you know how it is," said Ernest. "We cannot bear to see you suffer."

"Suffer!" she retorted. "I will not suffer! And, if I must, it won't be the first time. I suffered enough when I brought your miserable little carcass into the world."

Ernest gave a chagrined smile, while his brothers burst into laughter and Augusta frowned in sympathy with him. Sir Edwin remained, as he always did, unruffled in their midst.

"Shall you have them all out at once?" he asked.

"We'll see, we'll see," she returned easily. "Malahide and I will use our own discretion."

Malahide smiled under his long nose, and Renny pinched Meg's thigh beneath the table.

In the two days that followed, Adeline showed no depression in the ordeal awaiting her. Rather she seemed exhilarated, and her preference for the company of her kinsman tended to exclude all others.

On the third day she ordered Hodge to bring round the carriage at ten o'clock. At a quarter past nine, she was dressed in her velvet dolman and heavy widow's veil, thrown back from her strong old face. She sat waiting in the drawing room by a window that overlooked the drive, her parrot on his perch at her side. She stroked him with a hand that trembled a little.

"Poor old Boney," she murmured. "Soon I'll be like you. Not a tooth in me head!"

He undulated his neck to rub his beak against her palm. "*Dilkhoosa … Mera lal,*" he muttered softly.

Five minutes before the hour of departure Cousin Malahide appeared.

"Ready and waiting, eh?" he said.

"I'm always prompt," she returned tartly. "I've been sitting alone for nearly an hour.... Look at that son of mine! Does he care how I sit alone?" She nodded toward the window past which Philip was strolling, rod in hand, an old coat sagging on him, his hair dishevelled.

"Where are your other sons?" asked Malahide, in a tone that emphasized their neglect.

"Nicholas is still in bed. Ernest is buried in a book. I should go to my trial alone but for you, Malahide. Ha — here come the horses!"

Hodge brought them up before the door with a flourish. Adeline entered the carriage rather heavily, her veil falling forward about her face. Hodge tucked the rug solicitously about her knees. Malahide patted her hand.

"It will be over soon," he said, soothingly.

The first brilliance of summer was undimmed. Noonday had not yet violated the freshness of the morning. The young leaves unfolded to their utmost and the fields generously spread themselves on either hand.

Where there had been one blade a week ago, there were now a hundred. Adeline thought: —

"The land is at the time of increase, but I am at the time of decrease. H'm — well, I'm not done yet. I'll get new teeth and I'll hold my own at the board. I wish I had one of my own children with me instead of Cousin Malahide."

She straightened her shoulders and looked past Hodge's back at the fine flanks of the chestnuts. Malahide took her hand in his.

He was still holding it when they returned to Jalna. Ernest hastened to the carriage door to open it for his mother. He looked anxiously into her face. Its colour was heightened, but, when she smiled at him, he saw, with a mixture of relief and dismay, that she still had her teeth.

"Why — why," he stammered, "Mamma, you have not had them out!"

She returned haughtily: "Did I say that I was going to have them all out at once? I did nothing of the sort. I said I was going them out. And I am. One a day, till they are gone! I had my first one out this morning. Look!" She opened her mouth wide and displayed the gory cavity left by a large double tooth.

Ernest peered at it squeamishly. "It looks very sore. Did you have the injections, Mamma?"

Still with her finger at the corner of her mouth, she answered: —

"Not I! The surgeon showed me the instrument, but I didn't like the looks of it at all. 'I'll not have it.' I said. 'Pull my teeth in the old-fashioned way,' I said. 'One a day till they're all out,' I said."

"She was positively Boadicean," said Malahide.

She was in great good humour. She talked throughout the one o'clock dinner of the skill, the kindness, the efficiency of the dentist. She had a word of praise for Malahide and his timely support.

"How many teeth has she?" Philip said gloomily of his elder brother.

"Sixteen," growled Nicholas. "She'll go on like this for sixteen days."

Philip hunched a broad shoulder. "Well, we must just put up with it."

"We should be thankful," observed Augusta, "that she can extract pleasure from the extractions."

But it was pleasure mixed with apprehension. Adeline was in a state of exhilaration from the time of her return home till she went to bed, but the next morning there was a different tale to tell. She woke with a cloud hanging over her. By the time she had taken her porridge and mumbled her toast, she was in a state bordering on panic. By the time she was dressed she was in a villainous temper. Fully an hour before the moment when Hodge was due to appear with the bays, she was established in her chair in the drawing room, staring gloomily between the folds of her widow's weeds. Alternately she compressed her mouth in iron determination or with caressing tongue dolefully sought the familiar surfaces of those well-worn grinders.

Her parrot, always sensitive to her mood, would ruffle himself on his perch, peck at the grey scales on his legs, and now and again, in a metallic whisper, give vent to Hindoo curses.

At this hour Philip was never to be seen. Nicholas had developed a timely attack of lumbago and spent his mornings in bed. So it was Augusta and Ernest who did what they could to help their mother through this trying period. They got small thanks for their sympathy. The hour never passed without some shrewd dig from her that made them wince. It was with deep relief that they saw Cousin Malahide enter and offer her his arm.

But the return! The fine hilarity of the return! The bays, eager for their noontime feed, would have broken into a gallop if it had not been Hodge's tempering rein. Their hoofs scattered the clean gravel of the sweep on to the freshly shorn grass. Hodge beamed as he sprang down to open the door. All the family were gathered to see her then. She opened her arms wide to the one who was nearest, and clasped him to her breast. "I've done it again!" she would exclaim. "And a rare old monster it was, with roots like serpents! I tell you the surgeon had nigh to lift me out of the chair to draw it! Malahide will tell you. He had it wrapped up in a bit of paper to show."

And Malahide, with a smirk of satisfaction, would produce the sanguine relic.

On and on for sixteen days, sparing the intervening Sundays, till she owned no tooth in her head! She and Boney sat together, he on her shoulder, rubbing his arched beak against hers.

"*Dilkhoosa … Dilkhoosa …*" he murmured caressingly; then, "*Nur mahal … Mera lal.*"

"Love names!" she would exclaim. "Beautiful Eastern love names! Ah, they know how to make love to a woman in the East!"

She was toothless and triumphant. She looked forward to having the dental plates installed in time for the wedding. They loomed before the family equally with Meggie's trousseau. She revelled in the thought of the good food she would eat then. Now she was reduced to little more than pap. But she did not starve. She unearthed from the depths of a chest of old-fashioned silver a marrowbone holder. A marrowbone was ordered and simmered for hours. Three times she descended the stairs to the kitchen to test its progress. She could scarcely endure the waiting till it was served at table. Then, with it thrust firmly into the holder, she dug out spoonfuls of the smooth dark meat.

"It's good," she declared. "It's very good. It will help to sustain me till I have my plates."

She called Eden from his place and thrust a spoonful into his mouth. "This will be good for him," she said. "It will give him bone and muscle."

But the little boy made a grimace of distaste and spat out the morsel to the floor, whence it was snapped up by Philip's spaniel, which sat up in front of Adeline and barked for more.

"No more, you disgraceful fellow!" she said, delving deep with her spoon, "but when I have finished, you may have the bone."

The new teeth were a miracle of efficiency. It was a brilliant day when Malahide and she drove home with them. If ever they caused her discomfort, she denied it. The teeth were strong, well shaped, and of a colour neither too light nor too dark. She spent well-nigh an hour grinning before her glass. But this display of them came near being disastrous, for Boney, seeing the unaccustomed glitter in her mouth, flew suddenly to her shoulder to investigate, and gave one of the front incisors such a peck that he almost dislodged it. For a moment she was afraid to look, afraid to probe the spot with her tongue, but when she discovered the tooth safe and sound she was overjoyed and said: "Thank God for that!"

She felt that she should make a present to Malahide in recognition of his support through the long ordeal. She went over the contents of her jewel box and selected an earring from an ornate pair long unworn. She gave him this, and he had the diamond taken out and set into a cravat pin for himself.

He would have liked to keep the gift a secret, but Adeline was not one to hide her light under a bushel. At his first appearance wearing the pin she drew the attention of the family to it with: "Well, now, and what do you think of that? That is what I gave Mally for standing by me when I needed it. And, let me tell you, he has no cause to be ashamed of that diamond!"

The family swallowed the new abbreviation of his name, but they could not swallow the pin.

Sir Edwin nibbled at his lower lip and then said: —

"It is very handsome of you, dear Mrs. Whiteoak, but surely, — really, you know —"

"Did the pin belong to my papa?" boomed Augusta.

"No, no," put in Ernest. "It is obviously a new one."

"The stone," said their mother, "came from one of my old earrings — the ones shaped like banners. The diamond hung from the tip of the banner."

"Upon my word," growled Nicholas, "I think it is a great shame to have broken them up. Surely you might have found something for Cousin Malahide without doing that."

"Beautiful, beautiful earrings," said Ernest. "I always admired them. Only the other day I wondered why you no longer wore them."

"Such workmanship," continued Augusta, "is not found nowadays."

"The day will come," said Sir Edwin pompously, "when it will again be appreciated. People will seek for just such ornaments."

Philip murmured: "If I had known that it was a case for diamond tie pins, I'd have toed the scratch myself."

Adeline turned to him. "Speak up! I can't hear a word you say. Am I getting deaf, d'ye think?"

Philip raised his voice. "I said I would have taken you myself if —"

"Of course you would! So would you all! You'd have gone with me in a body — carried me there and back — if you'd thought there was anything in it for you! But I didn't let you know. It was a test, if you like. Malahide had no notion I would make him a present, had you, Mally?"

"I hadn't a thought in my head," said Malahide, fingering the pin.

"Sixteen times he went with me to the dental surgeon's, with no thought of gain in his head." Adeline vigorously nodded her own in emphasis.

"But I really think, Granny," put in Meg, "that, as I'm going to be married, I might have been given any jewels you didn't want."

"Didn't want? Didn't want? Who said I didn't want? I wanted it very much indeed. That's why I gave it to Malahide."

"Just the same," persisted Philip, "it wasn't fair to the rest of us." He began to pull burrs from the tail of his spaniel and conceal them beneath the chair he sat on.

"Look what you're doing!" fumed Adeline. "It's disgraceful! If your father were here, he'd give you a piece of his mind."

"No, he wouldn't!" returned Philip tranquilly. "Dear old Dad thought everything I did was perfect."

Renny had come in, just in time to hear this much. He went behind his father's chair and put a hand on his shoulder. Philip turned up his face to his son's and they exchanged a look of affectionate intimacy.

VI

THE CHILD

ROBERT VAUGHAN, THOUGH he was seventy-three, woke with a sense of youthful pleasure in the summer morning. He was an early riser, but he lay still a little while in order to savour his contentment with life. Things were going as he had so long hoped they would, and feared they might not. Maurice, his only child, was an earnest youth, moderately studious, deeply interested in the affairs of the Province. It was certain that he would become a great man in his country, a leader in patriotic Liberalism. He was a trifle arrogant, but that was a natural attribute of his youth and his position. In a few weeks he was to marry Meg Whiteoak, the only young girl of the few neighbouring families which Robert Vaughan considered the social equals of his own.

From the time Maurice and Meg had been children, their parents had hoped for this; the Whiteoaks, on their side, with an acquisitive eye on the thousand acres, bought from the government by the first Vaughan, and the income of ten thousand dollars a year, mostly from good mining stocks, that went with it.

It was the first Vaughan, Robert's father, a retired Anglo-Indian colonel, who had persuaded Captain Whiteoak to settle on this fertile southern shore of Ontario more than fifty years ago. "Here," he wrote, "the winters are mild. We have little snow, and in the long fruitful summer the land yields grain and fruit in abundance. An agreeable little settlement of *respect-able* families is being formed. You and your talented lady, my dear Whiteoak, would receive the welcome here that people of your consequence *merit*."

Colonel Vaughan had not only persuaded the Whiteoaks to settle beside him as neighbours, but had taken them into his own house for nearly a year while their own was in process of building.

How well Robert Vaughan remembered that coming! He had only been a youth then, and the impression made on him by Adeline Whiteoak, in her brocaded silks, her bright patterned shawls from India, her feather-trimmed bonnets and beautiful beringed hands, was never to leave him. She was a being from another world. He had made much of little Augusta and Nicholas.

But the Whiteoaks never became absolutely of the country as the Vaughans had. The Vaughans had no further interest in the Old Land and never revisited it. But Nicholas, Ernest, and Philip had been sent to school in England, and many Atlantic crossings were made by the Whiteoaks.

Robert Vaughan thought tenderly of the young Meg who was soon to be married to his son. Before the summer was over she would be established in the large room across the hall which already had been freshly decorated to receive her. She was charming, she was pliable, in her Maurice's mother would have the daughter she had always longed for. Maurice's mother was sleeping quietly at this moment and Robert turned, putting his arm gently about her so as not to disturb her. Maurice had come to them late in their married life and, while all their hopes were centred on him, their attitude toward each other remained that of lovers.

The tone of the sunlight, where it touched the walnut bedpost, was deepening, yet he could not bring himself to leave the comfort of his bed and break the happy sequence of this thoughts. A small mother bird was beginning to feed her young in a nest above the open window, and he smiled to himself at their eager twitterings. He pictured her, balanced on the edge of the nest, selecting which open beak should be the receptacle for the fat worm she carried.

The sound grew more persistent — or was it another sound? Yes — it was distinctly another sound coming from below. Possibly a cat with its eye on the nestlings under the eaves.

But no cat had given that weak and tremulous cry! Surely it was the cry of a very young child! Yet — that was impossible — unless some countrywoman were below with her child. But he had heard no steps on the drive and his hearing was keen. The cry became louder — it was a wail. He got out of bed and put on his slippers and went softly down the stairs to the front door. No one but himself was astir. He stood in his nightclothes on the threshold bathed in the brightness of the sunrise.

There he saw, almost at his feet, a bundle wrapped in a plaid shawl. A note was pinned to the shawl and, as though he were watching someone else, he saw himself take the note, unfold it, and read the words written in a scrawling hand. "Maurice Vaughan is the father of this baby. Please be kind to it. It hasn't harmed no one."

The little face, barely showing above the shawl, was no more than the sheathed bud of a flower. The words he had read were horrible to him. He sank on the floor in a faint.

Noah Binns, a farm labourer, discovered him. He saw the crumpled piece of paper on the floor beside him. He picked it up, smoothed it, and read the content. No wonder the old gentleman was upset! Noah felt no surprise. He could have told a thing or two, if he had been asked. It was a piece of good fortune that he should be the bearer of this news.

He knocked loudly on the brass knocker. Simultaneously a maid came hurrying to the front door and Mrs. Vaughan put her head out of her bedroom window.

"Noah!" she called. "What has happened?"

"It's Mr. Vaughan, ma'am. He's swooned. I rang the bell as I thought you'd like to know."

The maid exclaimed to Noah: "You fool! Why didn't you raise up his head?" Then she saw the baby.

"What does this mean?" she gasped.

"It's the young feller's," said Noah. "His and Elvira Gray's. I've seen them in the woods together."

Mrs. Vaughan came running down the stairs, gathering her dressing gown about her.

"Robert!" she cried. "My dear!"

At the sound of her voice he opened his eyes.

"I'll get brandy," said the maid.

Mrs. Vaughan knelt down beside her husband and took his head on her knees. He hid his eyes against her dressing gown and groaned. She saw the note and took it up with foreboding.

"No, no," he said, loud and clear, "you mustn't read it!" But he had not the strength to prevent her.

She crushed it in her hand and turned white.

The maid came running with the brandy. "I've telephoned for the doctor," she said, trembling so that she slopped the spirits. Mrs. Vaughan picked up the child and felt the strange penetrating power of its fragile body.

Noah Binns stared at all three, missing no detail of the portentous picture they made. Mr. Vaughan was looking less pallid.

"Give me a hand, Noah," he said. "I'm feeling better. I can't think what made me faint. I never did such a thing before. Just the shock of finding this poor little child on the doorstep, I guess. An unfortunate village girl left it here hoping we would take it in. That's what the note said. She hoped we would pity it and take it in. Poor girl — poor girl — If anyone asks you what happened, Noah, just tell them that, will you?"

With Noah Binns's help he got to his feet.

"I'll tell 'em just what you say, sir," agreed Noah. "It's a good thing to have a proper story. They're a pesky lot to gossip here."

"Did you say you telephoned for the doctor?" Robert Vaughan asked the maid when they were inside the hall with the door shut behind them and Noah Binns's heavy boots stumping in the direction of Jalna.

"Yes, sir."

"Well —" he spoke testily — "telephone again and stop him, if possible. I am quite recovered. I cannot imagine why I fainted. Just the shock — well, a man doesn't expect to find a young baby on his doorstep."

"No, indeed, sir." The maid looked at him pityingly. "Shall I take the baby to the kitchen, ma'am?"

"No. I'll keep it with me till we decide what is to be done with it." Mrs. Vaughan felt weak with the weight of the child, as though it had a mysterious power to crush her down. She swayed as she and her husband reached the top of the stairs. He put his arm about her.

"You're not going to faint too, are you?" He gave her a ghastly smile.

"No wonder if I would!" She dropped into a chair, holding the infant on her lap. She looked at the familiar room, as though it were some sinister habitation into which she had suddenly been thrust. Even the face of her husband looked strange and unnatural to her. The only object in the room that did look natural to her was the face of the child, for it was the face of Maurice as he had looked when an infant. She gazed at it as though she would never look away. She undid the shawl and examined the little hands and feet.

"No one will believe that the child has no connection with us," groaned Robert Vaughan. "I might as well have given Binns the note to read and told him to blazen it forth to the countryside."

"No one can prove that it is Maurice's child. But it is — I'm sure of that! Why, Robert, can't you see it? Look at it from where I am. Can't you see his face when he was a baby?"

"The young wastrel! The young villain. The sly rake!"

Never in his life had he said a word against his son. Now they were torn from him painfully in a voice neither he nor his wife had heard before. She said: —

"If the Whiteoaks suspect Maurice of being the father, they will never, never let Meggie marry him!"

"They must not suspect him! We must prevent that, at any cost. I had rather take the fatherhood of it on my own shoulders, so help me God, I would!"

Mrs. Vaughan smiled at him wanly and pityingly. He looked older than she had ever seen him.

"Let us be thankful," she said, "that you secured the note. It would have been terrible if Noah Binns had read it."

He spread out the sheet of paper and read the words once more. "Who is she? Who is this girl?"

"I can't imagine ... Why, Robert, it's impossible! We're wronging Maurice in suspecting him for a moment. As though he *could* do such a thing! He's to be married in a few weeks, and to that sweet girl!"

"What did you say a moment ago about the resemblance?"

"I must imagine it."

He came and they bent over the child. It made a little hiccupping sound and a trickle of whitish liquid ran from the corner of its mouth.

"Oh, poor little thing!" Mrs. Vaughan wiped its chin with her handkerchief.

"What colour are its eyes?"

"Very dark blue — no, brown."

"H'm, Maurice's are grey."

"Robert, there's no resemblance. I was just hysterical."

"Well, we'll soon find out. I'll have an interview with that young man." He spoke grimly.

"But it can't be true! Oh, if only you had not fainted! We might have got the child away without anyone's knowing about it."

"Did what I said to Binns sound convincing?"

"Oh, yes." And again she looked at him pityingly.

He pressed his hands to his head. "My God, wife, what are we to do with the child — if the boy acknowledges it?"

"Robert, you do believe it is his?"

"Well, if the girl made up such a story she'd be a fiend. Everyone knows he is just about to be married."

"Girls have lied before."

The child made a sucking movement with its lips and began to cry. Its cry was unexpectedly loud and piercing. The two elderly people trembled like two conspirators. She hushed it with consoling pats.

"Maurice will hear it!"

"I have a mind to carry it to his room and face him with it."

"No, no, I think I had better go to him."

"I must see my son myself." He spoke with authority. He hurriedly drew on his clothes.

"Do be kind to him!"

"If he denies this, I'll go down on my knees and beg his pardon!"

He repeated these words to himself as he went down the passage to Maurice's room. He had never had a scene with him in his life. Between himself and his boy there had existed perfect understanding. And now —

He remembered seeing Nicholas Whiteoak, when he was almost the age of Maurice, knocked down by a blow from his father. Captain

Whiteoak had thrashed all his boys. His wife had even taken a hand in it. He had heard of the scene of which young Renny had been the centre when he had been suspended from college a month ago.

He opened Maurice's door softly.

Maurice was lying, his hand under his cheek, his forehead smooth. The blanket was pushed off and beneath the sheet of his body, with the strong legs bent, was the body of a man. Robert Vaughan looked down at him almost fearfully. Out of his slender, delicate body he had begotten this heavily built muscular one. Maurice was like his mother's people. Yet he had always felt in such close communion with his son. He could not believe, looking at him quietly sleeping, that he had had this shameful secret life. He touched him on the shoulder.

"Maurice!"

His son opened his eyes, blinked, half smiled.

"Yes, Father." He was not startled. It was not unusual for him to be wakened, to be persuaded to go out to enjoy the beauty of the morning or reminded that his mother liked him to breakfast with her.

"Maurice, sit up and read this."

Robert Vaughan put the crushed sheet of paper into Maurice's hand. At the same moment, the baby, as though in anguish of spirit, gave a loud cry in Mrs. Vaughan's room.

Maurice turned white. His hand that held the note shook. He stared at it fixedly, not able to read.

"Read it," repeated his father. "Read it aloud."

Maurice read, in a shaking voice: —

"'Maurice Vaughan is the father — '" he stared horrified at his own father.

"Go on," said Robert Vaughan gently.

"'The father of this baby.'"

Again the cry of the child penetrated from the other room.

"She lies!" Maurice burst out.

"Who lies?"

"Elvira Gray."

"Oh, my God!" Robert Vaughan sank to the side of the bed and covered his face with his hands.

"Father, don't! I tell you it isn't true!"

Robert Vaughan began to cry, his whole body shaking convulsively.

"Father! I can't bear it! What do you want me to say?"

His father uncovered a ravaged face.

"When did you meet this — this Elvira Gray? Where did it happen? Don't be afraid. Tell me everything."

Maurice's misery was complete. The sound of his father's sobbing, the sight of his face, were terrible to him.

"When did she bring it here?" he asked.

"This morning — before anyone was about. She left it on the step. Its crying woke me."

"She promised — she promised — !"

"What?"

"To go away. I gave her money."

"You gave her money…. Yes…. What money, Maurice?"

"Oh, Father, don't ask me that!"

"No. I don't need to ask you…. I can guess…. My God, when I think how your mother and I have trusted you — how proud we've been of you!"

"Dad, I wish I'd died before I brought such trouble on you!"

"Don't say that! We must face it together."

Maurice wrung his hands. His face was distorted by remorse and shame.

"Go on," said his father sternly.

"Mother and you will never be able to forgive me."

"Maurice, I beg of you, tell me everything. I must know what to say to the Whiteoaks."

Maurice groaned.

"If they know the truth of it they will never let Meg marry me." He felt that he had reached the depths of despair. With his face hidden in his hands he poured out the story of his meetings with Elvira.

VII

MESSENGER OF FATE

MEG WHITEOAK WAS awake early that morning. She was stirred from her dreams by something new and exciting in the sweet summer air. Or was it some delicate current stirring in her own nerves? She made no attempt to discover which, but lay looking out of half open eyes through the white frilled muslin curtains of her window at the gently moving treetops. She liked to see the trees move gently so, like stately ladies fanning themselves. She liked the indolent morning conversation between two pigeons just above the eaves. She stretched out her bare white arm and let her glance slide along its glistening surface. She noted the pinkness of her palm and her pretty oval nails.

This room and all that was in it were so much a part of her that it was beyond her imagination to picture herself as removed from it. Yet she knew that very soon she would be sharing Maurice's room at Vaughanlands. She would take some things from this room to make it seem more homelike. The two little Dresden-china girls on the mantelshelf. The water colour by Uncle Ernest of the rose-covered Devon cottage, the sepia print of Queen Louise, and the oval gilt-framed Sistine Madonna that stood on her writing table. She would also like her comfortable stuffed chintz chair and the chenille curtains that hung at her door. Mrs. Vaughan had bought a new bedroom set for the young pair, the bed elaborately brass, the dressing table and washing stand of white enamel. Meg had suggested this herself, for she was tired of heavy walnut and mahogany furniture.

It was surprisingly warm this morning. Summer was really here. A puff of scented air that was almost hot pressed between the curtains and caressed her face and arms. With a strong movement she kicked the bedclothes from her and lay smiling in her long white nightdress. She spread her pink toes to the warm air. She felt deliciously conscious of her body this morning, as though it were a strong young plant rejoicing in its coming fruition.

A thick light brown plait lay over each shoulder and ended in a close glossy curl. She took these curling ends in her hands and dangled them.

She heard a quick snuffling sound beneath her window, then an excited bark. It was her father's spaniel, Keno, who was never let out in the morning except by Philip. Her father must be up then, off to catch a fish or two before breakfast!

Meg jumped out of bed and ran to the window. She put her head between the curtains and looked down. Her eyes were dancing. Her lips parted in a mischievous smile.

She saw her father in his corduroy Norfolk jacket, wading boots, and a disreputable Panama hat. He had laid his rod on the grass and was taking something from his pocket. It was a pocket comb, and he began at once to comb the wavy black hair of Keno's ears. The spaniel looked up and saw Meg leaning across the sill. He whimpered with pleasure and tried to prance about, but Philip held him firmly by the ear.

"Quiet, now, Keno! Behave yourself! We must have this loose hair combed out, you know." He gave the dog a gentle cuff.

Meg's cheeks dimpled. The stone sill felt cold and hard against her breast, but she did not mind. She pressed closer to it as she leaned out and made encouraging signs to Keno. His eyes were starting with excitement. He licked Philip's hands and drew away from the comb.

Meg was just going to clap her hands to startle her father when she saw the figure of a man hurrying up the steep path from the ravine. As she turned her face in that direction a rich opulent smell came to her nostrils from the depths of moist earth and sun-warmed foliage there.

Always afterward, when she thought of that morning, she was conscious of that smell.

Noah Binns came through the wicket gate and crossed the lawn in a jog trot. Meg drew behind the shelter of a curtain. Philip straightened himself at the sight of Noah's face, and the released spaniel reared himself toward Meg and rolled his eyes joyously. For the space of a moment the crystal of the summer morning was suspended.

"Hullo, Noah," said Philip. "What's up? It's the first time in my life I've seen you move out of a snail's gallop."

Noah gasped — "I've a turrible piece of news fur you!"

Philip stared at him, his eyes prominent.

"Mr. Vaughan found a baby on his doorstep a bit ago and he fell in a swoon, and I came along and there was a piece of paper lying on the ground, and I looked at it and it said the baby was fathered by young Mr. Vaughan, and it wasn't no great shock to me, fur I've saw the two of 'em whisperin' together in the woods more than once."

"Which two?"

"The young feller and Elvira — the dressmaker's niece. They were a pair up to no good, that was plain."

Philip spoke slowly. "A young baby, you said. Did you see it?"

"Ay, I seen it. Wrapped in a shawl and its face not as big as my fist. The girl couldn't have wasted much time fetchin' it, fur it looked young if ever a critter did."

"What was done with the child?"

Noah's eyes twinkled. "Mrs. Vaughan, she come down when she heard it cryin' and took it up. She was in a turrible state, too. I guess there won't be no weddin' now, sir, eh?"

"To hell with you and your impudence!" said Philip. He looked regretfully at his fishing rod and basket lying innocently on the green grass, at Keno grinning up at him. Then he picked up his things, chirped to his dog, and went back into the house.

Noah Binns looked after him resentfully.

"Dang him!" he said. "Dang 'em all!"

VIII

The Whiteoaks Ride Out

Philip slowly mounted the stairs, a troubled frown on his forehead. None of his family was yet up and his feet made no sound on the thick carpet. Outside Meg's door he hesitated. Poor little girl, let her sleep happily while she could! The spaniel knew her room and well remembered having seen her at the window. He made as if to scratch at the door, but Philip caught him by the collar and gently dragged him along the passage. He opened the door of his own bedroom and closed it behind them.

His wife was fast asleep, the frill on the high collar of her nightdress giving her a quaint medieval appearance. She had thrown herself diagonally across the bed now that his big body was out of the way. Keno planted his paws on the side of the bed and licked her full on the mouth.

She started and pushed him away. "Oh, Philip, how could you let him do that?" She rubbed her lips on a corner of the sheet.

"I call that a gentle awakening," said Philip, sitting down beside her. "Very different from the rude one I have in store for you."

He was always teasing her. Now she was on her guard against him.

"I call that rude enough," she answered, playing with Keno's ears, for the dog had also established himself on the bed.

"I'm in earnest, Molly," Philip said. "Something awful has happened. An infant was left on the Vaughan's doorstep this morning, and it's said young Maurice is the sire of it. I'm afraid poor little Meggie's marriage is off. I thought I'd let you know first. Then I must tell Nick and Ernest. We'll go over to Vaughanlands and raise hell. We'll see what Robert Vaughan and that young whelp have to say for themselves."

Mary stared up at him, dazed by the suddenness of the blow. Meg's marriage off! It couldn't be! It would be too dreadful! That marriage toward which she had strained for a year! That freedom from Meg's presence which seemed like paradise! Why, in the last few months they had become quite friendly over the preparations for the wedding!

"But — Philip — it may not be true! Who told you?"

"Noah Binns. He saw the baby. He saw Robert Vaughan in a faint and read the note accusing Maurice. Unless he's quite cracked it must be true."

"What Noah saw — yes. But probably just a pack of lies as far as Maurice is concerned."

"Let's hope you're right, Molly! We'll soon find out! I'm going now to rouse Nick and Ernest."

"I'll behave as though nothing had happened, at breakfast. Where shall I say you three are?"

"In the stable. Spitfire dropped a foal last night."

He went softly to Ernest's room and entered without rapping.

Mary rolled over and hid her face in the crook of her arm. Black depression swept over her. It was true! The engagement would be broken off and Meg would remain at home for years to come, possibly as long as she lived. There were few eligible young men about. Meg was the only cause of discord between Philip and herself. He had always shamelessly spoilt the girl. Mary remembered her as she had first seen her, when she had come to Jalna to act as governess to the two motherless children. They had been running wild for a year. Philip had gone upstairs to fetch them and she had sat waiting in the drawing room, impressed by the stately proportions of the room, still more impressed by the fine proportions of Philip himself, his handsome blue eyes, his indolent smile. She had sat, holding herself together, determined, if possible, to get the post, to make friends with these children.

From the moment when Philip had brought them, one by either hand, into the room, she had found them a formidable pair. Meg, with her round, inscrutable face, her critical stare. Renny, with his look of a small wild thing captured. Meg had been ten then, with a mop of unkempt golden brown hair, the frill of a drawer leg showing beneath her frock; he eight, positively unwashed, his red hair growing to his collar, his brilliant brown eyes and extreme thinness giving him a fierce, half-starved air. "What they need," Mary had thought, "is a woman's tenderness." But they had not responded to hers. They had been intractable, mischievous, difficult, from the first. She could not make them into the semblance of the well-behaved children she had last taught in a Warwickshire rectory.

She had read poetry to them, she had played the piano and sung to them, hoping to soften them, but they would escape to the orchards, the ravine, the woods, and peer out at her suspiciously, as though she were a being from another world.

But before long she had been too much in love with Philip to worry over the delinquencies of his children. For six months she had had him to herself before his mother and older brothers, made suspicious by a remark in a letter from him, had hastened from England to put a spoke in her wheel. But they had not been able to do it. Philip had been as stubborn in his love for her as he was in all else. They had married within the year.

Now he and his brothers were on their way to Vaughanlands. It was not yet half-past eight. It was characteristic of them that, though they were accustomed to a solid breakfast, they gave no thought to food when business such as this was on hand. They rode abreast, Nicholas and Ernest on dark bay geldings, Philip on a bright chestnut mare with a white blaze on her face. The two elder were dressed with care in London-made riding clothes. Ernest had placed a flower in his buttonhole, but had later taken it out as unsuitable to the occasion. Philip rode bareheaded, in his disreputable fishing suit. Keno trotted close to the heels of the mare.

Robert Vaughan saw the three horsemen approach along his drive. They rode abreast and the sleek flanks of their horses now and again touched, giving the animals that sense of companionship they loved. Robert Vaughan looked out on them as one of his ancestors may have looked from his bleak house on the Welsh borders at a band of galloping marauders. But he came to meet them with a firm step.

In the dining room, where an untouched breakfast was laid, Philip broke out: —

"Well, this is a hell of a mess your son has got into! By God, I'd like to have brought a horsewhip with me!"

"I don't wonder you are upset," said Robert Vaughan. "It has been a terrible blow to me."

"Upset!" exclaimed Nicholas. "Upset! That's putting it mildly."

"How did you find it out?"

"That worm Binns told me," answered Philip. "You didn't expect him to hold his tongue, did you?"

"Where escapades materialize into squalling infants, they can't be concealed," said Ernest. "The whole affair is a dreadful insult to my niece."

Philip added loudly — "Yes — an insult to Meggie! Where is he? I must see him!"

"He has gone off to the wood," said Robert Vaughan. "He is completely crushed, poor boy!"

"Poor boy!" shouted Philip. "What about my poor girl?"

"Yes," growled Nicholas. "what about her? She's shamed before the countryside. An innocent young girl — and a Whiteoak."

He had added fuel to the flame.

Ernest's voice was thick with rage when he said: —

"Not a woman of our family was ever treated like this before. Maurice has behaved like a scoundrel."

"I know it. I know it," Robert Vaughan agreed distractedly. "But you know what a loose girl can do with a young man."

"If he is weak enough," said Nicholas.

"Where were your eyes?" demanded Philip. "The trouble is that you have utterly spoiled Maurice."

"Do you know everything your son does?" asked Robert Vaughan, goaded to anger.

"I'd like to see him make a mother of a village girl and get away with it! If he did what Maurice has done I'd break every bone in his body!"

"Oh, no, you wouldn't! You'd —"

"You say I lie?"

"No, no, but —"

"If my son, I repeat —"

"But listen, Philip —"

Ernest put in — "Mr. Vaughan expects us to be calm."

"Picture yourself in our place," said Nicholas.

"How can he?" exclaimed Philip. "He has no daughter!"

"No niece," added Ernest.

"He has a son," said Nicholas, "who has ruined Meggie's life. Humiliated us all."

Robert Vaughan looked about to faint again.

"Is there no possibility," he asked, "of hiding this from Meg? A home can be found for the child at a safe distance from here. Maurice tells me Elvira and her aunt have given up their cottage and are going to relations somewhere."

"I'll wager," said Nicholas, "that the woman is the girl's mother and no aunt. I've heard things about her."

Philip moved to Robert Vaughan's side. "Do you imagine," he said, "that I will let my young daughter marry a man who has made a mother of a village slut?"

"If my father were living," declared Ernest, "nothing short of a horse-whipping for Maurice would have satisfied him."

Philip turned a dark red. "Fetch the boy in here! I have something to say to him!"

They raged about Robert Vaughan, they in their prime, he beginning to feel the weight of his years, till he staggered and took hold of the back of a chair to steady himself. He managed to say: —

"I'm afraid I can't talk any longer about it. It's been a terrible morning. If it's all over — if nothing can be done — but — I can't stand any more." He looked ghastly.

"If only Noah Binns did not know of it!" said Ernest.

"We could never hush it up," said Nicholas, "Not with the servants here in the secret."

"The whole affair," Philip added, "makes me sick."

"It makes me sick too," Nicholas growled. "And what I don't understand is how things could have reached such a point and neither Robert nor Mrs. Vaughan suspected anything."

"Were you never able to conceal your doings from your parents?" retorted Robert Vaughan.

"Not to that extent."

"No," agreed Ernest, "and we never took up with village girls ... excepting Philip once — and he was stopped in time."

Philip looked resentfully at Ernest. He went to the sideboard and poured a drink for Robert Vaughan. He saw the table laid for three.

"I apologize," he said, "for keeping you and Mrs. Vaughan so long from your breakfast."

Robert Vaughan gulped down the brandy. "Help yourselves," he said, "I'm sure you need something."

The three brothers moved in unison to the sideboard. A more temperate atmosphere prevailed. Talking the affair over more quietly, they agreed that such things had happened before; that marriages with inauspicious beginnings had been known to turn out very well. It seemed to Robert Vaughan's ears too good to be true when Philip Whiteoak said, with an almost friendly ring in his voice: —

"Well, the marriage is too important to our two families to be shelved. We must try to put this unfortunate happening behind us and go on with the preparations."

"Thank you," said Robert Vaughan, "I can promise that Maurice will never again — why, he did not care two straws for the girl — she tricked him into it."

"H'm — what is she like? Pretty?"

"Why — I'm sure — I don't know. I dare say."

"I've seen her," said Nicholas, "Rather an elfin creature."

"The aunt is attractive too," said Ernest, "in a sharp gypsy way. Yellow hair."

Philip laughed — "Old Ernie knows all about them!"

He took his brother by the shoulder. "Are you sure you are not the guilty father of the infant?"

Nicholas chuckled. Mr. Vaughan gave a wry smile. Upstairs the child cried.

"What is it?" asked Philip. "Not a boy, I hope."

"No. A girl."

"Good. Call her Pheasant."

Robert Vaughan thought — "Shall I ever understand these people

— know how they will take things?" He repeated, rather petulantly: "Pheasant! Why Pheasant? It's a very strange name for a little girl."

"I'll tell you why I chose it. As I was riding here a pheasant rose out of a clump of bushes and showed herself in the sun. She was lovely and bright and it occurred to me what a pretty name for a girl."

Nicholas poured himself another drink. "You're a most extraordinary fellow, Philip. Fancy choosing a name for your prospective son-in-law's bastard at a time like this!"

"But I do choose it," returned Philip stubbornly.

"It shall be as you say," said Vaughan, who cared little what the child should be called.

Philip drank his second whiskey and water at a gulp. "Let's see her," he said, almost genially. "I like babies."

"My God!" exclaimed Ernest. "Not newborn babies! Above all, not this one!"

"I like them all. Can't you fetch her down, Robert?"

"Won't it look very suspicious to the servants?" said Ernest. "We're going to face the thing out, aren't we?"

Robert Vaughan answered — "I will simply say that a poor woman left the child on my doorstep with a note asking me to succour it. We have been charitable people, I think, so the plea will not seem unnatural. I will say that we have agreed to provide for the child. Our housekeeper is leaving to live with her invalid mother. She would be glad, I am sure, to take it into her care. She will be going quite a long way off."

"That sounds possible," said Ernest. "The principal thing is to deny any intimacy between Maurice and Elvira."

"The same story will do for Meggie. She must never hear the truth," said Nicholas.

"Poor girl," groaned Robert Vaughan.

"I'd like to see the child," said Philip again.

Nicholas gave Robert Vaughan a look that said: —

"We may as well humour this strange brother of mine."

Robert Vaughan objected — "I agree with Ernest that it will look very suspicious to the servants — my bringing the child to you."

"Rot!" said Philip. "It will put them off the scent."

Robert Vaughan acquiesced. He went slowly out of the room, a thin drooping figure, his sparse hair brushed smoothly across his increasing baldness.

"Looks old, doesn't he?" observed Nicholas.

"He is old," said Philip laconically. His eye was on his spaniel, who now raised himself against the breakfast table and drew a slice of meat from the platter.

"Keno — you brute — drop it!" ordered Nicholas.

"Too late to stop him," said Philip. "He's hungry. So am I."

Ernest moved nearer the table and looked down at the neglected viands spread there. "Cold ham — looks very nice too. Egg cups — they'll be having boiled eggs as well. No porridge spoons — sometimes I think I'd be as well without it. It's really too filling."

Nicholas was pouring himself another drink.

"Well," he said, "this has been a ghastly business. But, thank God, we've been able to patch it up! It's a lesson for young Maurice. He'll likely run straight for the rest of his days. There's the comport Mamma and Papa gave Robert's parents on their silver anniversary."

Ernest came to examine it. Philip had seated himself on the broad window sill. He was watching his spaniel meticulously cleaning with his tongue the spot on the floor where the ham had lain. His face looked downcast, yet not unhappy. He accepted life as it came, with only an occasional outburst of protest.

Mr. Vaughan returned to the room with the child on his arm. He had felt confused coming down the stairs, had even thought for a moment that this was the infant Maurice he held. Mrs. Vaughan had taken off the plaid shawl and the baby appeared in a clean white dress. Its tiny head was misted with dark hair. Nicholas, with a sardonic smile, Ernest, with a deprecating grimace, came at once to inspect it. Philip made no haste to move from where he sat. He had lighted his pipe and was enjoying the first fragrant puff. He held one of Keno's ears between his fingers, handling it gently as he smoked.

"How old would you say it is?" asked Nicholas.

"Between two and three weeks — my wife thinks."

"It's much better looking than they usually are at that age," observed Ernest. "Tell me, did Maurice know of its birth before this morning?"

"No. He had had word from the girl that she and her aunt were leaving. He had been certain that the child would be born in the place where they are going."

"Disconcerting for him — this!" said Nicholas grimly.

Robert Vaughan turned toward Philip.

"You asked," he said sternly, "to see the child."

Philip rose and came almost nonchalantly and bent over it. "Nice little thing! A pretty little girl. I hope that housekeeper will be kind to her. How does it feel to be a grandfather, Vaughan?"

Robert Vaughan shrank from the words as from a menacing hand. "I can scarcely be called a grandfather — in the ordinary way," he said in a shaking voice.

"Damned ordinary, I should say," observed Philip. Through pouted lips he gently blew a cloud of smoke into the infant's face. It drew its features together in a comical way and sneezed.

Philip smiled amiably.

"I always do it to my own," he said. "It's amusing to watch them."

His elder brothers were anxious to return to Jalna. They wanted their breakfast, and there was the business of breaking the news to their mother. It had been agreed that it would not be safe to keep it from her, for she would have been suspicious at once and never ceased with questioning and probing till the truth would out. She and Mary and Augusta, combined with their men, must shield Meggie.

They rode away, as they had come, in the warm sunshine, their horses' flanks sometimes touching, Keno trotting close to the mare's heels. Mr. and Mrs. Vaughan watched them from their bedroom window. "Thank God," he said, "that's over! Now you must come and try to take a little breakfast, my dear."

But she was not interested in her own breakfast. A feeding bottle that had once been used for her son had been filled with warm milk, and she held the rubber nipple encouragingly to the child's mouth. But it turned away its face, whimpering, and sought, with nuzzling head, for the young breast to which it was accustomed.

IX

MEG

Now she minded the sharpness of the stone sill against her breast. She minded it very much. It seemed to cut into the tender flesh, to cut into it cruelly, right to her very heart. She was sure that the sharpness and chill of the stone had penetrated to the core of her heart. She pressed her hands there and crept back into the bed. She crept into it and drew the covers, first up to her chin, then quite over her head. All she thought at first was — "How cold I am! How cold and sharp the sill was!" Then she saw, before her tightly shut eyes, Keno's face turned up toward her window with his fixed spaniel's grin. As she pictured it, the grin became more and more terrible to her, till she shook like a leaf with fear of it.

She opened her eyes wide. She saw nothing but the dim paleness beneath the bedclothes. She smelt the delicate fragrance of her own body. She remembered the warm bath she had had the night before, how she had sat in the old bath from which the enamel was peeling, and scrubbed the firm whiteness of her flesh with a flannel well lathered with Windsor soap. She had been so happy she had scarcely known what to do with herself, but had lathered and splashed and only half dried herself, and left the huge bath sheet in a heap in the middle of the floor.

Now a voice came to her penetrating the bedclothes drawn over her head. It was the voice of Noah Binns and it said: —

"I've turrible news fur you. I guess there won't be no wedding now."

The words came first in a kind of sickly whisper that seemed to enter into her consciousness through her very pores. Then they were repeated louder and louder till at last they were shouted at her so that the very sheet vibrated with the thunder of them. She had a strange sensation of being under water and discovered that she was dripping with sweat. She sat up and pushed the bedclothes from her. One of her plaits had wound itself tightly about her neck. She felt as though it were deliberately trying to choke her. With a gasp she unwound it and held it in her hands, looking blankly down at the glossy curl on the end. Then she twisted the plait in her hands, wringing it and dragging at it as though she would pull it off. She threw herself back on her pillow and suddenly began to make whimpering noises. The next moment she thought she would break into loud screams and disturb the house from its sleep. But she caught the plait in her teeth and, biting on it with all her force, was able to restrain herself. At last she lay quite still.

She had a fresh and happy adolescence free from dark thoughts and morbid speculations concerning sex. Maurice had been the man she was going to marry; after the wedding he would take her to Vaughanlands to live. She had put all troubling thoughts away from her. Her mind had been filled by the preparations for the wedding. But now all the hints of lust that she had ever heard, all the phrases that puzzled her when she had read her Bible, were made clear, clarified beyond all other earthly things, made into the very sinister soul of the world. She lay motionless for a long while, deliberately recalling all she could of these things. One or two obscene words she had heard came into her mind. The gong sounded for rising and, after a little, she heard Eden's voice laughing and chattering and the baby Peep crowing with joy. The pigeons above her eaves, which had flown away in search of breakfast, now returned and again took up the tale of their billing and cooing. Little they know, she thought to herself, little they know!

Now the household was astir, and the familiar sounds calmed her. She began to consider how she should face her family. She knew that what had happed was a terrible and humiliating thing for a girl about to become a bride. She wondered how her father, her uncles, and her grandmother would take it. She wondered if Renny would ever speak to Maurice again.

She thought of one or two similar episodes in old-fashioned novels she had read. In one instance the heroine had shrieked and repeatedly fainted. The other had met the disaster with tragic aloofness. She felt that she must prepare herself. It was better, she thought, to have heard the news as she had so that she might prepare herself in secret.

It was odd that the sounds in the house should be so normal. She heard Aunt Augusta talking to Molly in the passage about Peep's new tooth. She heard Renny whistling gayly in his room. Perhaps her father had told no one, but had hurried to see Mr. Vaughan and tell him what he thought of Maurice's perfidy.

It was awful to think of Maurice as perfidious. She had always looked on him as little short of perfect. She had been so glad that he was tall and fine-looking like her father. She had thought that naturally she and Maurice would have a lot of children.

Meg tried to remember what Elvira looked like, but could only recall a pair of dark slanting eyes and hair that looked as though it seldom felt the brush. Yet this strange girl had come into her life and ruined it. Meg remembered her wedding dress, shimmering and white, inside its snowy wrappings in her cupboard. For the first time tears ran from her eyes. She buried her face in the pillow and cried convulsively.

She lay crying a long while. The house was still. Once she heard the hoofs of horses cantering in the direction of the stables. Once she heard the sharp tap of a woodpecker on the maple tree beneath her window. Both sounds seemed full of melancholy to her, like sounds heard in the depth of the night.

After a long while a tap came low down on her door.

"Who is there?" she asked.

"Eden. Mamma says would you like your breakfast in bed for a treat? She'll bring it to you herself."

"No. I don't want breakfast. Go away!"

"Oh." His tone was disappointed. He still hesitated at the door. She remembered how he had looked in his page's suit and had to smother her sobs.

"Meggie! Were you saying anything?"

"No, darling. Meggie has a headache, tell Mamma. Tell Mamma Meggie doesn't want any breakfast."

"All right." But he did not go away.

After a little his voice came again. She could hear him breathing into the keyhole.

"Meg, are you crying?"

"Goodness, no! Do go and tell Mamma!"

He trotted off.

Again she relaxed into a flood of tears. She did not try to control them, for the unhappiness of weeping was bearable. She remembered how, when she was a child, she could cry and cry. She remembered the sound of Renny's yells of rage and despair when he was little. Would Renny offer to fight Maurice, challenge him to a duel? She pictured them facing each other with revolvers in the ravine at dawn. She heard the sad murmuring of the river.

Another step sounded outside her door. There was no tap, but it opened softly and Mary put in her head.

"Meg, dear, aren't you quite well? Don't you think that a cup of tea would be nice? We had the first strawberries on the table this morning. Eden said he thought you were feeling ill." There was an excited quiver in her voice. She was keeping a hold on herself. Meg was conscious of a faint sense of satisfaction in the thought that Mary was trying to pretend that everything was as usual while she had known the worst from the very beginning.

"I don't want anything," she answered.

Mary came quickly to the bedside and looked down at her tear stained face.

"Why, Meggie —"

Meg sat bolt upright, her blurred eyes staring into Mary's.

"I know all," she said. "I heard Noah Binns tell Daddy everything."

Consternation drew the colour from Mary's lips. For a moment she did not know what to say, but just stood staring back at Meg, stammering — "Why — why — oh —"

Then she pulled herself together and sat down beside Meg and put both arms around her. "Poor little girl! It's awful for you, I know. I mean, to have heard such a thing. But you mustn't believe it! I don't believe a single word of it. You must try to put it out of your head and go on as though nothing had happened. It's nothing but cruel, spiteful gossip."

Meg drew herself away. "Is Daddy downstairs?"

"Yes."

"Did he go over to the Vaughans?"

"Yes. He and your uncles went."

"What did Maurice say?"

"They did not see him. They saw Mr. Vaughan."

"Did they see the baby?"

Again Mary put her arms about her.

"If I were you, Meg," she said, "I would not let myself believe this hateful gossip."

"But — supposing it isn't gossip? Supposing it's true?"

"You must not think it is true. You love Maurice. Maurice loves you. I have seen his eyes follow you with a most loving look in them."

Meg pushed her away. "Send Daddy to me, please! I want him to tell me what he thinks."

"Can't I say anything to help you? If only I could be your friend in this time —"

Meg turned her back and buried her face in the pillows.

She lay listening to the sound of Mary's steps retreating down the stairway. She wished she could hear what they were saying below. Suddenly she sprang out of bed and ran across the room into the passage. She leant far over the banister and strained her ears. All the family seemed to be talking at once. She could just distinguish Aunt Augusta's contralto voice through the sonorous tones of the men, and her grandmother's, old and harsh, raised suddenly for a moment.

She would stay listening, she thought, till she heard her father coming into the hall, then she would run back to her bed and lie rigid on it with her eyes tightly closed. He would have to speak to her several times before she would answer.

She started as she heard Renny's steps coming along the passage. She tried to dart into her room, but she could not escape him. She turned and faced him, pathetic in her white nightdress, her brown plaits with the curls on the ends.

"Renny," she said, "I'll *never, never* marry Maurice! It's all over, I tell you! You wouldn't have me marry him, would you?"

Renny gave her a sideways look. He would have liked to escape her. He did not answer, but gave an embarrassed smile. His face looked inscrutable to her, masculine and knowing and old. She thought — "He has known all about this sort of thing for ages, while I am only beginning to find out!"

She asked sharply — "Did you know about it before this morning?"

"A little," he answered.

"A little! What do you mean by that?"

"Well, Maurice had spoken of Elvira to me."

"Oh, and to think that Mother would ask me to behave as though nothing had happened! To go on with everything! To believe that it was all gossip!"

"I supposed a good deal of it is gossip." He moved down the stairway below her so that their faces were now on a level.

She looked into his face furiously. "Is the *baby* just *gossip?*"

He drew back from her, standing flat against the wall. Philip came into the hall below. He saw them as he reached the foot of the stairs. He had a sudden recollection of them watching from above when there was a party going on. But they were no longer children. He had his hands full. Renny watched his approach with relief. Meg put her arm across her eyes and began to cry.

"What are you crying for?" asked Philip. "There's nothing to cry about."

"Oh, Daddy, how can you say that?" She fell sobbing into his arms. "My heart is broken!"

Philip stroked her hair. "Meggie, Meggie, don't cry so! You'll be ill. Come, we'll go into your room and talk it over. Renny doesn't believe in this story, do you, Renny?"

"That's just what I was telling her."

"He does! He does! He knows every word of it is true!"

Philip drew her into her own room and closed the door behind them. He sat down on the side of the bed and took Meg on his knees. Her plump young body was an armful. She looked searchingly into his face.

"Daddy, I want you to answer me just in one word. Do you or don't you believe that Maurice is the father of this baby?"

"Meggie, what I think has happened is —"

"One word! I said one word! Oh, Daddy, don't you lie to me too!"

Philip's forehead was puckered in distress. He answered sombrely — "Yes."

Her last hope, if she had any, was shattered. She threw herself out of his arms and lay in a dishevelled heap on the bed. She began to roll convulsively from side to side. She caught the hem of the sheet in her teeth and bit at it.

"Meggie, stop it!" said Philip sternly. He gave her a sharp slap on the cheek.

She lay still, looking up at him out of eyes so swollen by weeping that they were almost closed. He could scarcely recognize his child.

He rose heavily and went to the washing stand. He dipped her sponge in the ewer and came back to her and began gently to bathe her eyes. "Poor little girl," he comforted, "poor little daughter."

She caught his hand and kissed it.

"Oh, Daddy," she sobbed, "I'll stay with you forever!"

There seemed to be no limit to her tears. As fast as he wiped them away, others streamed in their place. He asked desperately: —

"Shall I send your mother to you?"

"No — no!"

"Granny, then?"

"No!"

"Your aunt or one of the uncles?"

"I don't want anyone!"

"Would you like to be alone for a bit?" He felt that he could not stand the strain of this much longer.

"Yes."

"If I leave you, will you promise me not to roll about or anything?"

"Yes."

"You'll be quite still and try not to worry?"

"Yes — I'll lie quite still."

He straightened her pillows and drew her nightdress neatly about her ankles. Then he covered her, touched her plaits, and said — "Nice hair."

When he reached the door he turned back and said seriously: —

"You must not imagine that this sort of thing has never happened to an engaged girl before. It's very rough on you, I'll admit. But young men are often wild, you know. This will be a good lesson for Maurice. Far better have it happen before marriage than after. He'll probably be a good husband to you all his days." He went out and closed the door.

Downstairs he lingered in the hall for a moment, looking through the open door at the lawn, where one of Eden's rabbits, escaped from its hutch, nibbled its sunny way. Philip sighed, thinking that there would be no fishing for him that day. He glanced at the grandfather clock and saw that it was not quite eleven. God — what a day! Already it seemed like a week.

He turned into the library where the family had gathered. Little breakfast had been eaten that morning and Eliza had just carried in a tray with a pot of tea and a plate of scones. His mother was sitting behind it, the shadow of disappointment on her face lightened a little at the sight of the food. Malahide Court lounged beside her on the couch. He wore a pensive expression. Sir Edwin sat upright near a window reading a fortnight-old copy of the *Times*, his eyeglasses pushed near the end of his nose so that he might look over them at his collected relatives-in-law when he chose. Ernest had an open copy of *Quo Vadis* on his knee, but his reading was only an effort to appear calmer than he was. He was deeply shaken by the events of the morning. He was longing for food, yet doubtful if he should eat when so agitated. Nicholas sat puffing stolidly at his pipe and motioned Philip to a chair at his side. Augusta, in a wine-coloured cashmere dress with a lace jabot, held Eden on her lap, and Molly sat close beside talking earnestly to her. The folding doors that gave into the dining room were open, and under their arch, his hands deep in his pockets, Renny moved nervously about. He gave his father an anxious look as he entered. The lace curtains at the windows moved gently in the light breeze.

"Well," Adeline demanded. "How is the girl taking it?"

"Very hard, indeed," answered Philip sadly. "She's never stopped crying. As a matter of fact, I thought once she was going to have a fit. She rolled over and over and bit the sheet!"

The breath of the family escaped in a universal "tck."

"She should have had a clout on the head," said Adeline.

"She did," said Philip.

"Ha! That was good! Bring her to her senses."

"I call it nothing short of brutal," observed Ernest.

"Oh, it was just a tap," said Philip, "but it quieted her, poor little thing!"

"The point is," put in Nicholas, "is she willing to go on with the marriage?"

"It's impossible to say at the moment. She doesn't want to see anyone. She just wants to be let alone."

"The very best thing for her," said Augusta. "The quieter she can be kept for the next few days the better. Speak soothingly to her, give her plenty of tempting food. Perhaps a wedding present might divert her mind. I think she can be brought to see reason!"

"She must," said Adeline. "Have some tea, Philip." She began to fill the cups with tea. Ernest rose and, with *Quo Vadis* in one hand and a plate of scones in the other, circled the room. Soon they were all eating, drinking the heartening beverage which they felt they badly needed, for they had had a severe shock to their pride and their long-cherished plan had been all but wrecked.

"What I can't tolerate," said Adeline, "is the thought that Robert Vaughan and his wife, with never any but this one chick to look after, should not have known what he was up to. I call them a weak-kneed, spineless, milk-and-water doddering old pair of half-wits!"

"They have spoilt the boy," said Ernest.

"They were always talking about how clever and how good he was," added Nicholas.

"I think," agreed Augusta, "that they were very boring on the subject of their son's perfections. I am convinced that they thought him superior to our young man."

Philip chuckled. "Yes. When ours was suspended last term Vaughan made no pretense of hiding his gratitude for the high-minded qualities of his son."

"Well, he'll do no crowing after this," said Nicholas. "Young Renny deserved to be suspended, it's true, but his scrape had nothing to do with girls."

Renny's grandmother looked at him fiercely from under her heavy brows. She began to speak, but found that she had taken such a mouthful of scone that it was impossible. Her family regarded her politely and with a little concern as she grew red and tried in vain to swallow.

"Take a mouthful of tea, Mamma," urged Ernest. "It's dangerous to fill your mouth so full of dry scone."

Her fierce glance became furious as she directed it from Renny's face to Ernest's, but she took his advice and swallowed half a cupful of tea. With it she got rid of the scone and turned to her grandson.

"If you," she said thickly, "ever dare to lay a bad hand on a village girl, I pity you!"

A rumble of agreement came from the lips of her sons.

The subject of Adeline's threat stood in the arch of the doorway, his mouth twisted in an embarrassed smile. His bright gaze travelled from one face to another.

Eden was sure that they were scolding Renny again. He slipped down from his aunt's lap and went to him and pulled at his sleeve.

"Let's go for a walk, Renny, shall we?" he whispered.

Renny laid his hand on Eden's round, soft neck.

"Take your hand off the child's neck," commanded their grandmother. "You'll make him humpbacked walking with him so. You're always at it."

Renny grinned, but did not remove his hand.

"You defy me!" cried Adeline!

"Now that you remark it, Mamma," said Ernest, "I am conscious that Renny never comes near the child without putting his hand on his nape. It is very bad for Eden, as you say. Have you noticed the habit, Philip?"

Philip stared at his sons.

"I've noticed," he said, "that Renny is very fond of the child. Stand out here, Eden, and let us see if your neck is straight."

Mary said, with a resentful tone in her voice: —

"I am often worried by the way Renny is always handling Eden. I think it's bad for him. And Eden expects it. He runs to Renny the instant he sees him."

"And why not?" exclaimed Adeline. "That's perfectly natural. What isn't natural is that Renny should put the weight of his hand on the child's neck."

"You won't want me to put my hand on anyone, eh, Gran?" He gave her one of his odd, slanting looks.

"No cheek, young man!"

Sir Edwin put in — "The spine of a young child is very tender. A curvature might easily result."

"Stand out here, Eden," said Philip sternly. "Let us have a look at you."

Renny gave his brother a gentle push and the little boy advanced into the middle of the room, his cheeks flushed, his head drooping.

"What did I tell you!" cried Adeline. "The child's neck is bent!"

"Hold up your head, sir," ordered Philip.

Eden raised his head a little. He was half-frightened, half-pleased at being the centre of this discussion.

"Higher!" There was anxiety in Philip's voice.

"He can't!" cried Molly.

Augusta said — "Eden is admirably, nay, perfectly proportioned. If Renny has induced a curvature —"

"Of course he has," interrupted her mother. "There's no if about it! I've seen it coming."

"Then it was cruel," cried Molly, "not to warn me!"

"You never give heed to what *I* say."

Ernest said — "I remember a dwarf I once saw in Algiers —"

"Oh, I remember him," said Nicholas. "They said he'd been brought up in a cage."

Sir Edwin observed — "No need to go to foreign countries to see strange examples of contorted humans."

"My God," interrupted Philip, "give the child a chance! He's frightened." He stretched out his arm and drew Eden between his knees.

By this time Eden was enjoying the situation. When his father put a hand on each side of his head and endeavoured to straighten his neck he held himself tense, with knit forehead and lips drawn back as though in pain. Philip looked about blankly.

"It's true!" he said. "The child can't straighten! How was it we didn't notice it before?"

"Oh, my little darling!" sobbed Molly.

Adeline set down her cup of tea and rose. She caught Eden by the head and raised him off his feet. The little boy screamed. When she freed him he stood glaring, straight as a rush.

"There now," she said triumphantly. "I have uncrooked it!"

"I don't believe there was anything wrong with him," said Philip. "Run off and play, Eden."

Molly drew him toward her and kissed him passionately, but he escaped and ran after Renny. When he overtook him in the porch Renny's hand mechanically moved to rest on the child's nape. With a snuggling movement Eden pressed close to it.

"Where shall we go?" he asked, with an adoring look upward.

"Where do you want to go?"

"To the river."

"All right."

"Am I humpbacked?"

"You're straight as an arrow!"

"Why do they say I am?"

"Just to be after me."

"Why? Don't they like you?"

"Of course they do. You can't understand."

"I love you, Renny. When I grow up I'm going to be just like you. We'll have fun together, shan't we?" He strode eagerly at Renny's side.

"Loads of fun. See that kingfisher!"

A flash of wings, of the same shade as the horizon beyond the wheat fields, moved from the broad branches of an oak on the riverbank and dropped to the sunlit water below. Ripples circled from the spot where beak and scale met, the bird rose leisurely, the young trout gleaming in his bill. The sun poured down its benign fire. It was the first really hot day.

Renny ran down the steep path to the water's edge, grasping Eden firmly by the hand. Sometimes the little boy lost his footing completely and dangled helpless, but he was not afraid with that strong hand holding him. He laughed as he knelt on a broad stone and saw his reflection peering up at him.

The stream still flowed in its springtime strength, urging its way with agreeable gurgling sounds into the most secret grassy nooks and slaty crevices. In midstream it was dazzling to the eyes, but in the shadow it held a cool olive tone. It seemed to delight in itself and all its movements, flowing either swift or slow with equal careless assurance.

Eden raised troubled eyes to Renny's.

"Where do you suppose the trout is now, Renny?"

"In the kingfisher's tummy."

Eden reflected. "I don't like to think of that."

"I do."

"Why?"

"Because the bird was hungry."

"Don't you mind the little fish being eaten?"

"Not a bit."

"Then neither do I."

Renny took his arm and pointed. "See the swans!"

The pair came sailing round a sedgy curve side by side, their breasts, full and white, seeming to caress the water. The movements of their feet could just be seen.

They approached the boys with an air of haughty indifference, but when they were opposite the male turned and, with an angry gleam in his eyes, raised both wings and spread them, opening his beak wide. For a moment he remained poised in this fine attitude of menace, then calmly he lowered his wings, arched his neck pridefully, and, with an air almost benign, sailed after his mate.

"Keep away from him," warned Renny; "they have a nest somewhere."

Eden watched the pair disappear behind an overhanging willow with a rapt look on his face. His ears were filled with the gentle murmurings of the river. The stone beneath him was warmed by the sun. Beside him knelt his fearless, his indomitable hero, his brother. His heart swelled with pride and a troubling joy he could not understand.

X

Retirement

Philip, as he was knocking out his pipe into a flowerpot in which a rakish cactus was producing its puny flower, found Eliza's eyes on him. She brought an ashtray and set it invitingly on the table beside the pot. But Philip doggedly continued in his own way, though he was somewhat embarrassed. To distract her attending from himself he asked: —

"Has Miss Meggie eaten her tea?"

Eliza, fully informed of the happenings of the day, answered: —

"No, sir. Not a bite. Nor dinner neither. I set nice tempting trays outside her door, as you ordered, but she made no answer when I rapped, and the trays had not a morsel taken off them."

Philip stared, disconcerted. "Why, this is awful, Eliza! The child hasn't had a bite all day! She'll be ill!"

"That's what I'm expecting, sir. I knew of a young lady once who went very queer after a disappointment in love. She wouldn't comb her hair and it grew in a great clump on the side of her head like a crow's nest."

"Tch! Well — we must make her eat. Is there anything special you can have made to tempt her? A nice omelette?"

Eliza considered a moment. "Miss Meggie likes dumplings with jam better than anything. Perhaps, if Cook made her some for her supper and you would carry them up to her yourself, she might give way."

"She must! See to it that there's plenty of jam on the dumplings."

Eliza did not at the moment answer. With a corner of her duster she was gathering up the ashes from the flowerpot. Then, with another corner, she wiped from the leaves of the cactus any possible contamination, while Philip looked on unabashed. Then she said: —

"Strawberry jam will be best."

But all their plans to tempt Meg were unsuccessful. Though Philip creaked up the stairs bearing the temping supper tray cautiously, and begged her to open her door, there was no answer. Really frightened, he exclaimed: —

"Meg! Are you all right?"

"Yes, Daddy." Her voice came muffled.

"Then do open the door and let me bring you this nice supper. It's a surprise. Something you like very much."

"I couldn't possibly eat."

"But, my dear, you must! You'll be ill. Come now, I command it."

There was no answer.

"Do you want me to break the lock?"

"Please, Daddy, let me be! That's all I ask!"

It seemed cruel to harass her. He said soothingly — "Look here, Meggie, I shall set the tray here and, when I have gone, just open your door and peep out at it. Will you promise me?"

"M'm — yes."

He creaked down again.

"She's as stubborn as a mule," he said to his mother.

"You have only yourself to blame," she returned.

"Do you mean I have spoilt her?"

"I mean you begot her."

When they went to bed there still sat the tray, the jam congealed on the dumpling, the tea and cream untouched. But Keno had eaten the chicken, the gnawed wing bone lying not far off.

Adeline waited at the foot of the stairs. Philip leant across the banister and whispered hoarsely: —

"She's not touched it!"

"God bless me, that's a long time to go empty!"

"Over twenty-four hours."

Adeline gave a little grunt. "Well, we must give her time, poor child. She'll get over it. By morning she'll be ready for breakfast. Get to your bed, Philip. You need your rest after such a day."

She turned into her own room on the ground floor behind the drawing room. It was her favourite room in the house. It was enriched by memories beautiful, voluptuous, painful, passionate, heart-rending. For over fifty years she had lain down to sleep in this room, on this very painted bedstead on which she had lain in far-off India. Its glowing birds and flowers looked as fresh today as then. But her body had changed from that of a young woman to an old. In this bed she had lain in the arms of Philip, her husband. In this bed she had borne his children. Here Philip had died — a man well past sixty but looking, in his fresh colouring and vigour, not more than fifty, she would swear. He had been carried into the hall from his stables, for he had been kicked by a horse. She had run frantically down the stairs to him. He had raised his head and exclaimed in his deep tones: —

"Just look, Adeline, what that brute has done to me!"

She had looked and had restrained her cry of horror. They had carried him into this room, laid him on this bed, and in less than an hour he was no longer her Philip, but a dead man whom she held close in her arms, passionately trying to force some spark of her agonized vitality into his breast.

For an instant the scene came back to her now. Her heart halted in its beat as she painfully bent her metal gaze on all its details. But she put it from her as she had for years forced herself to do. She would not waste her strength in mourning. She drew a deep breath and went to the window and opened it. "Must have more air in here," she said aloud. The night air entered neither warm nor cool, touching her flesh with a strange intimate caress.

Her new teeth hurt her gums. Not once since she had got them had her family seen her toothless. But now she was alone. She took them out and put them in a glass of water that awaited them. Her reflection in the glass drew her attention. That strong, sunk-lipped reflection bore a vivid likeness to her old father. "Old Renny Court," she murmured with a whimsical grimace.

Oh, the exquisite relief of having the plates out! It gave her a rested feeling. She no longer wanted to go to bed. She had a mind to call one of her sons to come and sit with her. Still, they had had a hard day, poor fellows. Nicholas would be glum if he were routed out. Ernest would be too talkative and Philip would probably fall asleep under her nose. On the whole she had better put up with her own company.

She went to her parrot which, with head tucked under wing, perched on the foot of her bed. She put out her shapely wrinkled hand and stroked his hunched green back. A quiver of recognition passed through him, but he did not unsheathe his head. He made a guttural protesting sound low in his throat.

"Poor old bird," she said. "Poor old Boney! He needs his rest too."

Reluctantly she unpinned her brooch and stuck it in the red satin beaded cushion on her dressing table. Her fingers began to fumble with the long, closely packed row of buttons down her front. Still the thought of going to bed was repugnant to her.

An old lilac tree grew outside her window. It pressed too close, cutting off the air, and she often threatened to have it removed, but she could not find it in her heart to give the order. She had watched it grow from a tiny slip, when it was only a wand-like thing, had often given it a drink from her ewer. Now its heavy white plumes claimed the air before it entered her room. Between its leaves she could see the glimmer of the waning moon as it drooped into the ravine.

Suddenly she had a desire to go out into the night alone. It had been a very long time since she had done this. Always there had been Nicholas or Ernest or Philip to give her his arm. Surely she must be getting very old when her family guarded her so. She did not want to be guarded. She wanted to come and go as she willed, under sun or stars. She raised her long, strong arms and stretched. She felt tired, worried, yet somehow exhilarated by the happenings of the day. She could not settle down into her bed. She must have air.

She must be very cautious in unlocking the heavy front door. How beautifully, how smoothly it opened! No tawdry building in Jalna such as was done nowadays! But she must be careful not to let it clang. She crossed the gravel sweep and stepped on to the cool freshness of the lawn.

She could see the glimmering of the moon low down behind the trees. A silver birch stood out in front of the evergreens as though advancing to meet her. All its little leaves had caught the moonlight. Far below she could hear the rustling of the stream.

She had on thin shoes and she could feel a delicious response to the life of the deep earth in the soles of her feet. They seemed to be full of eager nerves pressing toward the earth. She savoured each step. Her quick eye saw the shapes of rabbits moving about in the shadows.

She went to the silver birch and laid her hands on its silky bole. Her palms were conscious of the life of the tree pulsing beneath them. She thought of the layer upon layer of thin bark binding the birch. She remembered how her Philip, on their fifth wedding anniversary, had cut in this very tree two hearts pierced by an arrow from the bow of rather a gross-looking cupid. Her fingers sought the scar of this wound and tenderly pressed it. A constriction came in her throat. After all these years she could still feel sentimental about it!

Near by she saw the bulk of an old latticework shelter for a well that was seldom used now. But it was good cold water. She knew that. She would have a drink of it, out here in the night alone. She would feel the cold iron of the pump handle in her palm.

The shelter stood at the edge of a small shrubbery where the white buds of syringa were beginning to show. Inside it there was a damp smell and she saw the silver wheel of a cobweb. On the mossy wooden stand a glass jar held water for priming the pump. She grasped it in both hands and poured it into the opening at the top. She began to move the handle up and down. It made a harsh grating noise, but in a moment the bright water gushed from the spout. Before she had time to step back her feet were splashed.

She filled the rusty tin mug and drank deeply. The icy water invigorated her.

"Ha, that's good!" she said, setting down the mug, and she drew her hand across her chin, on which the short strong hairs were wet. Near the pump, almost hidden by a clump of ribbon grass, she spied a bee's nest as large as a man's hat, glimmering palely, a smooth sphere, a sleeping world of fierce activity. "If Eden got into that …" she murmured. "Must tell the gardener …" Yet the thought of having all the little bees smoked out troubled her. "Their world," she thought "as much to them as Jalna to us…. Storing up honey for their old age … their winter…. Let Eden take his chance…. I won't tell of them."

She looked up at the dark bulk of the house and saw Meg leaning on her window sill, white and fair in the moonlight. Stubborn little baggage…. Meg had been watching her and now drew back into the shadow.

Adeline crossed the lawn and stepped beneath the window.

"Come along down," she said, "and we'll have a stroll together."

"No, Granny. I couldn't."

"I'll tell you some things about young men I've known, if you'll just come down."

"I don't want to know anything more."

"Pouf! You don't know anything."

"I don't want to know anything."

"You can't spend the rest of your days in that room."

"I'll spend the rest of my nights here!"

Her grandmother gave a snort of laughter.

"I pity you then!"

Still half laughing and grumbling to herself she turned away, went round the house, and passed through the little wicket gate to the top of the steep bank of the ravine, from where she could look down on the river. Now it shimmered in the moonlight, now hid itself among rushes and circled a great boulder that had fallen from above, now moved impatiently, as though in haste to be done with all its winding, now gave itself up to the indolent pleasure if its reedy bed.

She wished she might go down to the water's edge, but she dared not risk the climb in return. It would be humiliating to have to spend the night down there. She grasped a low projecting bough and leant on it, gazing down at the stream. In her mind she followed it through valleys and fields, back to its source among the hills. Then, as a river, she traced the course of her own life. Eastward — eastward and southward, back to her marriage in India. Westward and northward, back to its source in the misty hills of County Meath. She was a tiny child, lifted to her father's shoulder to look out on the great world.

XI

SLIGHTED LOVE AND LIGHT O'LOVE

THREE NIGHTS LATER another midnight prowler was reviewing his past. This was young Maurice, who, unable to sleep, or even to endure solitary inaction, had taken his horse from the stable and galloped along the silent road, trying to quiet his brain, to exhaust his restless body. But swift as he galloped, his thoughts were equally swift. Neck and neck with him raced the dark steed of his shame, his disappointment. The past he reviewed was held in one short year, from the time Elvira and he had first met in the woods.

What had driven him from the house was the sound of his child's crying. He had seen the light in his mother's room and known she was up tending it. He hated the sight of the child, the sound of its voice, the very thought of its fragile body interposed between him and Meg. The thought that he had got that body from his own was horrible to him. He resented the protective love which he saw in his parents' eyes when they spoke of it.

The moon was high in the deep blueness of the summer sky when he passed Jalna. His mare was so accustomed to turning in at that gate that he had had to draw a restraining rein. Now the house loomed dark and forbidding to him. Should he ever enter it again? With a feeling of desperation he wheeled the mare, jumped down, and opened the gate. He led her across the lawn and under the window of Meg's room.

"Meg!" he cried softly. "Meg!"

There was no answer, and he picked up a handful of gravel and threw it against the pane.

"Meg! Meg!" he called desperately.

He heard a stir inside the room. She appeared, framed like a picture in the moonlight. He had always thought Meg pretty, but now she looked beautiful. It was horrible to think of losing her. She, looking down on Maurice's upturned face, as he stood with the bridle over his arm, felt the romantic tragedy of her situation as she had not before. She was faint from lack of food. A sudden exhilaration swept over her. She would not have had things different from what they were. From the safe refuge of her room, she could look down on Maurice's remorse, unmoved.

"Oh, Meggie!" he said. "If you only knew how I hate myself! — If you'll give me another chance — I'll do just what you want for the rest of my days! Oh, Meg, you're too sweet to be cruel! — You must forgive me!"

She looked down at him without speaking.

"My God!" he exclaimed. "Are you made of ice? Can't you speak to me?"

She sat silent, in that same strange exhilaration.

"If only you knew," he went on, "how I have suffered! It's a wonder I'm alive. When I think how I've made Mother and Dad suffer and what I've done to you — life looks as black as the grave to me. But if only you'll take me back, I'll be a different sort of fellow! Oh, Meg, take me back! Say you'll forgive me!"

She listened to all he had to say, listened till he stood gazing up at her, silent, afraid of her. Then she spoke in an even voice, though with a hint in it of the elocution lessons she had learned at school.

"It is all over. I cannot marry you, Maurice. I shall never marry anyone."

He could not and would not believe her. He gathered all his strength for a last struggle. He came close under the window and began again at the beginning with — "Oh, if only you knew how I hate myself and how I love you!" Incoherently he tried to explain all, and got completely tangled up in his explanations and threw himself on the ground and groaned. The mare stood quietly beside him, cropping the grass.

Renny had been wakened by the sound of Maurice's voice and could not help hearing what he said. He was sorry for Meg, but, as Maurice poured out his heart without drawing so much as a word from her, Renny became impatient and Maurice's groans brought him to his feet.

He stood a moment irresolute. Should he go to Meg's door and beg her to be more forgiving? No, that would rouse the family. The miracle was that they had not already been roused. But, of course, the uncles and aunt slept on the other side of the house. His father could only with difficulty be roused when once he had given his mind to sleep, and it was doubtful whether his stepmother would interfere in what she would certainly hope might be a reconciliation.

Barefooted, Renny ran down the stairs and joined his friend beneath Meg's window. Her profile was raised toward the moon and, if she were aware of his coming, she made no sign.

"You can't go on like this," he said, in a low tense voice. "Hiding in your room — letting your heart be broken — You must pull yourself together, Meggie! Maurice will help you! I'll help you! I'll stand by you both and we'll see this thing through. Why, Meggie dear, think of all your pretty clothes and the presents beginning to come in! You can't go on like this!"

He knew how to touch her. Tears began to run down her cheeks. But she would not give in. With a dramatic gesture she closed her window and drew the shade.

Each of the family in turn came to reason with her. She had begun to eat the tempting meals that were sent to her, and this gave them hope. Mary brought Eden, dressed in his page's suit, and the sight made her burst into tears, but nothing moved her from her decision. She would not see Maurice again.

Her interview with her grandmother was the most stormy. Adeline completely lost her temper and, for the first time but not the last, used her stick and gave her granddaughter a sharp rap with it. Meg's scream brought Philip to the scene, and he and his mother had a fierce altercation. He would not have his little girl, he said, forced into any distasteful marriage. And it was small wonder if Meggie couldn't stomach a bridegroom who had just made a mother of one of the village girls.

These happenings had a strong effect on Renny. His mind became occupied with thoughts of sex as it had not been before. Brought up in the knowledge of horse breeding and the getting of stock, and among men who were roughly outspoken, his adolescence had not been troubled by subtle or morbid imaginings. Sex was natural, it was right. There was in it the nature of a teasing, sometimes calculating, game. He and Maurice had talked little of it. Renny had felt a shyness with Maurice on the subject because Maurice was engaged to his sister.

But now all was changed. The engagement was off. Maurice and he were seldom long together before Renny would bring up the subject of Maurice's affair with Elvira. Maurice, bitterly introspective, poured out the details of their meetings. He took some comfort in remembering Elvira's clinging tenderness towards him. But he had nothing to tell of Elvira's aunt beyond the fact that he had visited her cottage a few times to see Elvira and that he had not liked her. She had made him feel uncomfortable. There was something strange and foreign about her. Sometimes he had wondered if she were not Elvira's mother.

"That's impossible," Renny had put in. "She's not more than ten years older than the girl."

"Wait till you see her in daylight," said Maurice.

"What did you think of her looks? Not so pretty as Elvira, eh?"

"She's not pretty at all! But she has attractive eyes — there's something about them that holds you. She may have been pretty once."

"Do you know where they have gone?" Renny asked in a low voice.

"Yes. To a village about twenty miles north of Brancepeth. Just a hamlet, I think. They have relatives there."

Casually Renny found out all he could from Maurice of the place where they had gone. More particularly he made inquiries from a village girl who had been a friend of Elvira's. He was honest with himself. He did not say to himself — "I have a fancy for knowing where those women are. Some day I might be going that way." Definitely he thought — "I must know where they are and I shall not rest till I have seen them again."

But the difficulty was to find an excuse for absence from home. He would not say that he was going to visit a friend. In truth he had no friends near with whom he was intimate enough to visit. The companionship of Maurice had always been enough for him in the holidays, and he would not lie to Philip.

He remembered that a colt had lately been sold to a man who lived not far from the hamlet where the women had gone. He would offer to deliver the colt himself.

His father looked at him dubiously.

"But the colt is only half broken," he objected, "and, between you and me, he's a cantankerous brute and I doubt if he'll ever be anything else."

"Is that why you offered to deliver him?"

"Yes. And that's why I sold him cheap. The man's got a bargain if only he can stick on him!"

"Well — I can."

Philip knit his fair brows. "I don't like it. It would be a pretty retribution for me if my eldest son had his neck broken in the shuffle."

Renny laughed nervously. "Will you let me do it?"

There was something in his laugh that made Philip look at him shrewdly.

"What are you up to?" he asked.

"Nothing dangerous," returned Renny.

"H'm — well, if you break your neck, don't come to me for sympathy," He turned away.

Renny started out early next day. It was going to be hot. Already the heat haze quivered above the treetops. The shadows beneath them had a luminous quality. Little red cones, nibbled from the evergreens by squirrels, lay scattered on the drive. The bed of geraniums beside the croquet lawn blazed brilliant.

He could see the fruit glistening on the mulberry tree near the gate. He turned the colt at a walk from the drive and crossed the lawn. It moved easily beneath him with a restrained energy. It turned its large liquid eyes suspiciously towards the painted post of the croquet set.

Renny drew rein beside the tree and picked a handful of the berries. He sat eating them and wondering what the journey would mean for him. Scotchmere, the chief of the stablemen, a thin weather-beaten man with sandy hair, appeared at the gate to open it for him.

"You've a nice day's work ahead of you, sir," he said, grimly, as Renny passed through.

"Rot!" said Renny cheerfully. "I like him and he likes me."

"Well, good luck to you! And, if he cuts up too bad, give him the whip."

"Not if I can help it!" He clapped his hand softly on the colt's flank and it broke into a smooth canter on the white dusty road.

Scotchmere looked after him. "By gum," he said aloud, "he's the ridin'est critter I ever set eyes on!" This was his favourite description of the eldest son of the house.

Anyone who saw him cantering down the road would have thought the description a good one. His body moved so rhythmically with the canter of the colt that it might well have been imagined that the same bloodstream vitalized both or that the youth's pelvic bones sprang from the spine of the colt.

They covered a mile or more of the quiet road without incident. A light playful breeze sprang from the lake. Renny was delighted with his mount.

"You're a darling!" he exclaimed, patting the muscular shoulder. "We'll be good friends all the way, eh?"

For a little longer all went well, then a crumpled piece of paper stirred in the ditch beside them. The colt stopped, then leaped forward as though electrified and shied almost into the ditch. Renny spoke soothingly.

"All right ... all right, old boy ... all right."

But the colt refused to be soothed. All through the great barrel of its body Renny felt the quivers of irritation, of smouldering rage. The rhythm of its hoofs on the road became broken. Its hard naked ears were pricked, one forward, one back.

They passed a farm wagon without mishap, the steady farm team plodding on through the yellow dust. A group of school children scampered shouting out of the way.

Then a motor car approached from a turn of the road. They were still rare in the country and it was the first Renny had met when on horseback.

"Oh, curse it!" he muttered. "Hold on, boy — hold on — you're all right! *Hell*."

The last exclamation was drawn from him by a hoot of the motor horn. The colt raised itself like a circus horse and stood poised on its hind legs as the car approached. Renny could see the faces of the two occupants turn pale and his own features relaxed into a grin.

The colt reared, as though made of grey stone, its hoofs, looking enormous, menacing the two in the car. It waved its iron hoofs like two missiles it was about to hurl in on them. The driver tried to turn aside, but the ditch and a heap of broken stones lay there. Renny tried to force the colt to its haunches, but it was careless of the pain of the bit. The faces of the motorists were contorted by fear as the car rattled past, the man ducking his head to escape the hoof that curved nearest. The stench of gasoline was ejected from behind the motor. The yellow teeth of the colt and the white teeth of the boy jeered.

The smell of gasoline was loathsome to the colt. All its being from nostrils to rump was insulted. It gathered itself together for a bound of escape, then was conscious of the wrench its jaw had received and, instead of bounding forward, it backed, with arching flanks, against the frail fence that separated the road from the steep bank overhanging the shore of the lake. The fence gave way, breaking like twigs, and Renny expected to find himself on the shore below with the weight of the colt on top of him. He struck his spurs into its flanks and flogged it with the crop. Violently the colt rushed from the bank, which was already crumbling.

They were on the road again and the colt was galloping as though to rid itself of the fears and hates that pursued it. Renny let it have its head and laughed in relief at his escape. They turned into a rough road diverging from the lake and rode for a long while under the heat of the mounting sun. They came to a steep hill and the colt, whose glossy sides were darkened by great patches of sweat, slackened its pace to a walk. But still it kept a wary outlook for offence. A barking dog set it once more rearing.

Among the shouldering hills, as though it had sought seclusion there, they came to a village with a small hotel where Renny remembered having gone with Philip at the time of the village fall fair. He had the colt put into a stall and himself rubbed it down. He ordered the hostler to give it a drink and a light feed. The colt looked almost subdued. Its eyes were pensively half closed. Renny's hair was dark with sweat. His clothes clung to him. After he had washed he devoured two chops, a mound of potatoes and peas, and a slice of apple pie and cream. The first early harvest apples were just in. Cooked, they had a golden transparency, the cream was yellow and thick. He ordered a glass of beer and lighted a cigarette.

He had never felt more self-reliant, more master of himself than now. The tempestuous journey of the morning made Jalna seem far away. He looked in retrospect at the events that had been taking place there. Meg's blighted love seemed suddenly affected. He felt a faint contempt for Maurice's despair. He would handle the affairs of his own life differently. He began to wonder just why he was seeking out the two women. He wished he knew the older one's name. It irritated him to have nothing to call her in his mind. It was she whom he wanted to see. A desire to be with her again, to talk to her, had been gathering within him like a storm. He felt that he would be desperate if he could not see her. Just what he wanted of her he would not let himself think. His mind shied from the thought as the colt from what was new and strange. In his thoughts of her he saw himself reflected in a distortion, as his image might be reflected in a dark woodland stream.

As he was paying his bill the hostler came in.

"That colt of yours," he said, "has busted the bucket and chewed a piece out of the manger and kicked the hoss in the next stall. I guess you'll owe the boss something for damages."

The proprietor and Renny returned with him to the stable.

The colt rolled his eyes at them over his shoulder. His long tongue was hanging out of the side of his mouth, as though in derision. In the stall next to him an elderly man was putting some ointment on the hind leg of a quiet aged mare.

"That's a vicious brute you've got," he said. "How he managed to kick my mare, I don't know. But you can see the gash he's given her."

Renny made sounds of sympathy. He gently touched the injured leg. The mare looked at him kindly.

"What are you putting on it?" he asked.

The man showed him the tin.

Renny's brows went up in amazement. "I should take it off if I were you," he said. "My people have bred horses all their lives and nothing would induce them to use it. Now I'll recommend something" — he turned and put a coin into the hand of the hostler, at the same time giving him the name of the preparation — "that will heal the cut in short order. We never use anything else in our stables."

"Thanks," said the owner of the mare glumly.

"You'll be glad," returned Renny, "that she had this little accident when you find what a wonderful remedy this is. I do hope you'll always keep it on hand in future." He went to the mare's head and stroked it. "Nice old girl! How old is she?"

"Twenty-nine."

"By George, I'd never have thought it! She looks about twelve, and what a set of teeth!"

He applied the ointment himself and helped the man to harness the mare to a buggy. His adroit hands tightened a strap here, eased one there. The mare turned her head and nuzzled him with her long soft lip. Her owner pocketed the tin of ointment, pleased in spite of himself.

Renny picked up the badly dented bucket, examined it, and turned with a grin to the hostler. "You wouldn't expect me," he said, "to blame my colt for refusing to drink out of a leaking bucket. He's not used to that sort of thing. I noticed that it was dribbling when you were carrying it to him."

The hostler, crestfallen, peered into the bucket.

"What about the manger?" demanded the proprietor. "It'll need a new side."

Renny turned over petulantly. "If you trouble me any more over this bit of mischief my colt has done, I'm dashed if I will come here again."

"Well, well," muttered the proprietor, "we'll say no more about it."

Renny paid his bill and was left alone with the colt.

"I hope," he said reproachfully, "that you will behave yourself on the rest of the journey."

The colt looked down its long grey nose and laid back its ears. As Renny was putting the bit in place, the colt caught him by the shoulder and ripped the sleeve of his coat halfway down his arm.

"You would, would you?" he exclaimed, and gave him a furious cuff.

It worked the bit forward in its teeth, flattened its stark ears, and lifted its leg to kick. Renny hugged its head to him. "No, no, no, you shan't!" He backed the colt out of the stall and mounted it in the yard. The hostler and a stableboy stood by as the colt disdainfully passed.

"Look at the gentleman's coat!" jeered the hostler.

"It's tore half off his back," said the boy. "He ain't got control of the beast. He can't ride for sour apples, can he?"

Renny turned the colt toward the boy, but it danced with him out of the yard.

It seemed that the rest of the way would be more peaceful. The heat of the sun might well have taken the spirit even from the colt. But it still showed its irritability by sidling along the road and constantly shaking his head.

It was late afternoon when they came to a railway crossing guarded by gates. Renny heard the whistle of a train in the distance. The gate attendant rang a bell and the gates began to drop. Renny drew in his rein, wondering how the colt would take this new experience. At the same moment the motor car which had met them in the morning came up behind, the driver nervously sounding his horn.

A snort of horror shook the colt to its bowels. It bounded forward under the first of the gates, but before it could cross the track the second gate fell and horse and rider were caught in front of the onrushing train, which loomed horribly large and threatening.

The gatekeeper, in a panic, tried to raise the gates, but the mechanism balked. They did not rise. The colt's hoofs clattered on the shining rails as he reared and wheeled.

The gatekeeper snatched up a green flag and ran toward the locomotive, waving it sharply. Renny faced the colt to the gate, struck him sharply with the crop and, with hands and knees giving their message of confidence, rode him straight for the jump.

With tail and mane streaming the colt rose and swam over the barrier. Had it ever jumped before? Renny did not know, but he grinned exultantly at the feel of the bounding body beneath him. He turned in the saddle and thumbed his nose at gatekeeper, locomotive, and motorist, his bare white shoulder showing through his torn coat.

He loved the colt. In a passion of loving he bent and kissed its neck. With its yellow teeth showing, its nostrils arched, it flew like an arrow along the road.

It flew into a thunder shower, but in its exultation never noticed the flash that whitened the road or the rolling of the clouds together.

It did notice the spatter of drops on its hide and imagined they were given by the rider who held it between his thighs. It flew faster and faster.

"Why, you're made for a race horse!" exclaimed Renny. "I wish to God Dad had never sold you!"

The dust lay dark, flattened on the road. The leaves, new washed, cherished the last drops of the pain. All bright colours blazed at each other as though in challenge. Little birds essayed their evening song or preened their wet plumage.

Just beyond a hamlet in a hollow, the farm where the two women had come lay on the side of a steep hill. A red sunset cloud hung above it like a banner.

Renny felt a strange new shyness. What should he say when he arrived? In what different ways should he approach Elvira or her aunt, according to which he first met? He realized that his coat was torn, that he was wet through. As he and the colt moved slowly along the farm lane their heads hung in weariness.

By the side of a barn a load of hay was drawn up. A man in a dripping shirt was forking hay to the loft above. Just inside Renny could see Elvira distributing the hay on the floor of the mow. Her long cloth skirt was pinned up so that it reached just below her knees, but, as though to counterbalance this immodesty, her hair had loosed itself and hung in a dark mass about her shoulders.

The childish poise of her head as she peered down at him was moving to Renny. She looked innocent, isolated in the twilight of the mow. He thought of her as the mother of Maurice's child. Yet Maurice hated the remembrance of her.

"Hullo, Elvira," he said, riding round the load of hay so that it stood between him and the man.

"Oh, how do you do, Mr. Whiteoak," she returned sedately, leaning on her fork.

"I had to come this way," he went on, "to deliver this colt. My father sold it to a Mr. Ferrier, not far from here, so I thought I'd drop in and ask how you are."

"Oh," was her only answer. She looked timidly down on him as though not knowing what to do, as though wondering whether she should put aside her fork and come down to him.

The man came round the load of hay and looked aggressively at Renny. "Is it John Ferrier you mean?"

"Yes."

"He don't live near here. He lives ten miles away, at Creditford."

"Ten miles is nothing to this colt," said Renny. "You're lucky to have saved this load of hay before the rain came. It looks nice and dry."

"It is," returned the man, gruffly. "What I've got to do now is to stow it in the mow before dark. There'll be more rain tonight." He looked at the red cloud that hung above the hilltop. "Come along, Elvira. We've wasted enough time." He set to work again.

"I've never seen a girl do farm work before," observed Renny. "It looks strange to me."

"You'd see lots of it where I came from," said the farmer. He threw a forkful of hay, as though with intentional carelessness so that some of it fell over Renny and the colt. The colt started and laid back his ears. Renny dismounted. "Look here, let me help you! You'll never get it in before dark at this rate."

"Thanks," muttered the farmer. "There's an empty stall in there." Fork in hand, he led the way to the stable. He gave Renny a small basin of oats for the colt.

Renny mounted the steps to the loft and Elvira obediently handed him her fork. He looked no better than a hired man, she thought, with the red sunburn on his face, his untidy hair and torn coat. Very different from Maurice. The sight of him brought back all her old life. Her heart ached with longing as she stood in the twilight watching his swift manipulation of the hay.

He and the man worked well together. The load diminished as the colour faded from the cloud. A thin piping of locusts began on all sides. A cow lowed in the stable below.

The man looked up at Elvira. "Why don't Lulu come and do the milking?" he demanded.

"Shall I go and tell her?" asked Elvira. She turned to Renny. "This is our cousin, Bob," she said. "We're staying here."

Renny and Bob assented to the introduction, as though they had just met. Bob said: —

"I'll go and tell Lulu. Then you can go to the house and get some supper for us." He felt that Renny and Elvira wished to be alone for a little.

When they were, she looked at him questioningly.

"Your child is well," he said reassuringly, then added — "but you couldn't have cared much for it or you'd not have done what you did."

"Lulu made me," said Elvira simply.

"The devil, she did! And you do just what she says?"

"Yes."

"Well — I guess it's better off as it is. The Vaughans are going to keep it. Maurice says his mother loves it like her own grandchild already."

"Have you seen it?" She twisted her thin, chaff-strung fingers together.

"Yes. It's a sweet little thing. I looked in the window of the sitting room and saw it."

"How was it dressed?"

Renny considered, leaning on the hay fork. "Well, it had on a long white dress and some sort of woolly pink jacket with a bow under the chin."

"That sounds nice," she said, and gave a little smile of pleasure at the picture.

He turned to her abruptly. "Do you think Bob will mind my coming here to see you and Lulu?"

"No. He'll be glad you helped him with the hay. He's glad to have us here. His wife's in bed with her fifth child. He'll not say anything."

"Gosh!" exclaimed Renny. "are there nine of you living in that cottage?"

She nodded and repeated — "Bob's glad to have help." She held out her palm, on which a blister showed. "Look!"

Renny took her hand in his and saw, at the same moment, the older woman called Lulu coming along the path carrying a milk pail.

The sight of her made him forget Elvira's existence. He looked down at Lulu and noticed her smooth supple walk, easy as an animal's. Her hair was drawn in a smooth knot at the back of her head. She had a spot of rouge on each cheek and she wore a clean white cotton dress with large red polka dots on it. A red ribbon was wound twice round her neck and the bow fastened in front by a brooch with a yellow stone set in it.

He stood, a tall thin stripling, watching her nonchalant approach. To hide the quick beating of his heart behind careless words, he said: —

"Do you always dress up like that for milking?"

She looked up at him boldly, swinging the pail.

"I always dress up when I know you're here," she returned.

Elvira asked — "Shall I go up and lay the supper?"

"Yes — that's a good idea." The woman smiled up at her. "Bob has gone in to see Lizzie. She's feeling a bit lonesome for the sight of him. I told him I'd give a hand with the hay. He's worn out."

"Dressed like that!" exclaimed Renny, astonished.

Lifting her skirt, she clambered onto the top of the load and picked up Bob's fork. There was not much hay left to unload. Elvira descended the ladder from the loft and went toward the house. She walked stiffly, as though she were very tired.

"Poor kid!" said Renny, looking after her.

"Don't pity her! She's had her happiness. We all pay for that."

"Have you had yours?"

"I've had my share."

"Have you paid for it?"

"Twice over."

"You don't look as though you'd minded."

"Oh, I'm a hard one!"

He gave an excited laugh. "So am I! I don't mind paying."

"*You!* You're only a baby!"

"If you talk to me like that — I'll go."

"Surely it don't matter to you — anything I say."

"I came all the way here to see you."

"Why?" She looked at him provocatively out of her yellowish slant-ing eyes.

"Don't you remember asking me — that night? You said you'd tell my fortune from tea leaves and tell me where you got those queer eyes."

"*Queer* eyes! I like that."

"Well — aren't they?"

"Don't you admire them?"

"I didn't say I didn't."

"Well, *do* you?"

"I repeat that they're queer."

"So are yours!"

"Mine! I don't see anything queer in them."

"I see the devil in them."

"It's your own reflection."

"Aren't you a clever boy! Now I say your eyes are as dark as a thunder-cloud with lightning behind it and your lashes are blacker than they've any right to be."

"Yes — and my hair is like the sunset and my teeth like tombstones and my nose like a battle-axe — Oh, I'm a most poetic-looking devil!"

"However did you tear your coat so?"

"The colt tore it off me. He was jealous of my affection for you."

"I'll kiss him for that!"

"Good! I want you and him to be friends."

For answer she took a forkful of the hay and threw it up at him. He caught it and spread it on the mound on which he stood. Another and another followed. A tall strong woman with a small breast and a head that moved swiftly on her supple neck, she worked with fierce energy, while he, with his trim loins and legs braced apart, received the hay on his fork in an almost angry eagerness. The hay was so dry that the loft was full of its dust. He coughed and rubbed his nose on his sleeve.

As the last brightness was received into the earth and the cloud on the hilltop gathered other smaller clouds to its bosom, the last of the hay was stored. Below in the stable the colt whickered and the fowls quarrelled over the best positions on the perches.

Renny put the farm horses in their stalls and watered them.

"I wonder," he said, "why your cousin didn't come back?"

"He was tired out. I told him we'd finish the hay. He's putting the kids to bed. He's a good fellow about the house. Elvira's laying the table." She began brushing bits of hay from her dress, and putting her hair in order. Renny regarded her dispassionately, but was conscious of the inference of all her gestures.

"Am I invited to supper?" he asked. "I'm starving."

"Of course. Let us go now." Her tone was matter-of-fact. As she walked ahead of him along the path, she did not once glance over her shoulder.

"We're going to have more rain," he said.

"Yes. Bob will be glad he's got his hay in."

They found Bob in the kitchen buttoning a sturdy girl of four into a flannel nightdress. A baby, half naked, was crawling about the floor. In spite of his squareness Bob looked gaunt. His face was heavy with weariness. His coarse fingers were deft about the child.

Elvira had had no time to ready herself. Her hair still hung about her shoulders and her cloth skirt was pinned up, but she had set out a substantial meal on a clean white cloth. There were fried potatoes, cold pork, pickles, fresh wild raspberries, Sultana buns, and yellow Canadian cheese.

Bob turned to Renny and said: —

"Elvira tells me you're a swell. Maybe you won't eat with the common folks like us. I guess I shouldn't have let you help with the hay."

"Rot! I'm starving and I liked helping with the hay."

"That's all right, then. I'll take these kids up to bed." Bob took a child under each arm and clumped up the narrow stairs to the room above. Through the thin partition came the faint cry of a young infant.

Elvira looked questioningly at Lulu. "Have I got plenty to eat, do you think?"

"Good Lord!" exclaimed Renny. "It's a spread!"

Lulu said, in a low voice — "What a pity there aren't just the three of us! We could have fun."

"Yes," said Elvira. "There's no fun in Bob."

Bob clumped down the stairs and passed his hand over his forehead. "It's as hot as hell up there," he said. He raised his face to the stairway and called — "Shut up, you kids, or I'll be after you!"

The scuffling and giggling of the children ceased.

"Will you like to wash?" Elvira asked of Renny.

She led him to a stand in the corner of the kitchen where she had placed a basin of water, a clean towel, and her own cake of pink, rose-scented soap.

He rolled up his sleeves and dashed the water over his face, neck, and arms. "Gosh!" he thought, under the delicious coolness, "if the family could see me!" He grinned into the basin.

Bob was glad to have another male to talk to, especially one who knew something of farming. What Renny did not know about he hid under an air of sagacity. But what Bob really wanted was a listener. He talked on and on, expounding his theories, telling of his trials and disappointments. Like many farmers he ate little, but urged Renny to repletion. The two women sat silent, their eyes fixed on Renny. There was dead silence in the next room and upstairs. An alarm clock on a bracket ticked in extravagant and watchful haste.

Lulu brought a round glossy teapot from the stove. "Now," she said, "what about that fortune?"

Bob's face relaxed into humorous condescension. "Don't you let her tell your fortune," he advised. "She'll give you a bad one."

"Why?" asked Renny, leaning back and lighting a cigarette. Bob was already puffing at his pipe.

"That sort of woman always brings bad luck."

"Now that's a hard thing to say," declared Lulu.

Bob reached out and caught her dress in his hand. "Well, Lulu, you know what I mean. What I mean is you're not steady and safe like my Lizzie in there. But you've been good to me, there's no denying that! You and Elvira too."

Lulu sat down and stared into the teapot. "I guess it's stewed long enough," she said. She stirred the leaves and poured a cup apiece.

They drank simultaneously, with almost the air of conspirators in a rite. Summer lightning woke the landscape beyond the door into swift brightness.

"Now," said Lulu, crossing her legs, "who shall I do first?"

"Not me," said Bob. "Last time, you told me the potatoes would be blighted, and they was…." He stared glumly into his cup. "And the time before, you told me that my missus was going to have another girl — and she did! No more fortunes for me!"

"How can you say that!" exclaimed Lulu. "Didn't I tell you you were going to have a handsome visitor within three days?"

"So you did," said Bob. "I remember. But I guess he came to see Elvira."

"He's not my visitor," said the girl sulkily.

Lulu turned to Renny. "Whose visitor are you?" she asked, looking at him out of half-closed eyes.

He was suddenly boyish, embarrassed. Bob rose and pushed in his chair. He said — "Well, you settle it among you. I'm going to do the chores."

"I'll milk the cows," said Lulu with a sharp, almost commanding tone in her voice.

"All right."

The two women drew their chairs close on either side of Renny and peered into his cup.

"Well," he asked, "what do you make of it?"

"I see," she said slowly, "love and fighting, but not much peace."

"Who wants peace?" He laughed. "If I'd wanted peace I should not have come here."

"I see women loving you — I can't make them out."

"I hope I shall be able to."

"One of their names begins with an A and one with C."

"What's the matter with B?"

"Everything. She's a bitch without a name."

He laughed softly. Thoughts were stirring wildly in his head. "Tell me more about this nameless one."

"She'll come and she'll go, but you won't forget her."

"Will she let me love her?"

"For a night."

Elvira rose and stood with her hands clasped to her breast. Tears were standing on her cheeks.

"What's the matter?" asked Renny.

"I feel lonesome all of a sudden."

"She's the funniest girl," said Lulu. "She's always been like that." After one glance at Elvira her slanting gaze returned to the cup. Renny put his arm about her waist.

"I see the colt," she went on.

"What is he doing? Kicking the other tea leaves about?"

"No — but he isn't getting where he's headed for."

Renny became instantly serious.

"That's bad. If I don't get him there I'll be in trouble with my father."

"I see your grandmother on her deathbed," she continued.

He looked aghast. "Good heavens! Not for a long time, I hope."

"Yes — a long time off."

"Would you mind telling me," he asked, "how she's leaving her money?"

Lulu gave a malicious smile. "She's leaving more of herself to you than any of the others."

"Good!" he laughed. "Her money is herself. She hangs on to it for dear life."

Lulu went on. "I see responsibility. Lots of it. People clinging on to you."

He raised his head pridefully. "I don't mind that."

"But you will love one place more than any one person." She set down the cup. "I don't see anything more. I must go and milk the cows. It's got dark."

Bob came in carrying a lighted lantern.

"I've done the chores," he said, not looking at Lulu or Renny. "You said you'd milk the cows, Lulu."

"Yes," she said, taking the lantern and lowering the flame, which smoked.

As they went down the path a cool breeze drew from the moist earth all the sweet scents sleeping there. There was no moon, but a host of far-off stars distilled a pale light. Under the low stable roof the two cows turned broad reproachful faces toward Lulu. The farm horses had been turned out, but the colt lay, an angular grey bulk, in the shadow of the stall, from which his eyes glanced softly in the lantern light.

Lulu sat down on a stool, curving her graceful legs beneath her, and laid her forehead against the red flank of a cow. From its hard udder she drove a stream of milk against the bottom of the pail.

Renny stood leaning against the end of the stall. "You're a wonderful woman," he said. "When I first saw you you were a dressmaker —"

"Not much of a one," she interrupted. "I often spoiled the materials they brought me."

He went on — "When I meet you again you are a harvester. Next thing you're a fortune teller. Now you're a milkmaid!"

"Well," she said lightly, "I've had time to learn a good many things. I'm no chicken."

"I don't suppose," he asked inquisitively "that you'd tell me how old you are?"

"No." She spoke curtly. "I wouldn't."

She milked the second cow, then turned them both out into the night, slapping their bony hips as they passed her and stumbled meekly over the uneven step into the yard.

The same fitful heat lightning softly illumined the fields. Lulu went to a well in the stable and plunged her arms to the elbow in the cool water.

"I hate the smell of milk," she said.

He stood looking at her gravely. He said: —

"I guess I had better be going. I must find some place for the night."

The lightning played across her features.

"We could go and sit in the mow for a bit if you like," she said, as though indifferently. "But if you think you'd better be going ..."

"If Bob wouldn't mind — I think I'll sleep here in the hay. The colt's played out."

"Are you?" she asked, and her teeth gleamed.

He put both arms round her and drew her to him, kissing her hotly on the mouth.

"Well, then," she whispered composedly, "we'll go up."

They mounted the ladder and she threw herself down, but at a little distance from him. He stood, so tall that he must bend his head under the sloping roof.

"Why don't you sit down?" she asked.

"I'm all right." His voice shook a little.

She undid her brooch and the red ribbon from her neck.

"I hate pressure on my throat," she said. "I wish the fashion was to go bare-necked. Here, put these in your pocket. If they get into the hay I'll never see them again."

He put the ribbon and brooch carefully into his pocket.

She stretched her arms and yawned.

"Well," she asked lazily, "what do you want to know?"

His voice came out of the dusk. "You were going to tell me how you came by those eyes."

"It was my mother's doing. Her husband was a good man. He was a respected man. But my mother got intimate with a Rumanian gypsy who came peddling things.... I was all she had of him."

He came and knelt at her side.

"Let me look into them," he said, his breath coming short.

She touched his white shoulder that showed through the tear in his coat. "It's too dark for seeing," she whispered.

The lightning flickered softly, seeking the cobwebs in the loft, touching the hay into a scented brightness.

He laid his hand on her lips and she kissed it. With a swift movement he drew it the length of her body, outlining its curves, to her feet. Then he held it above her as though in menace — as though he had drawn some weapon she had had concealed about her.

She sank before him, sighing as though wounded.

XII

THE RETURN

HE WAS WOKEN by a grinding, tearing sound. His face was against the hay and he felt half stifled. He kept his eyes shut and stretched out his hand to feel if Lulu were there. His hand slid across the depression where her body had lain. He opened his eyes and sat up, his fresh cheek seamed by his fragrant pillow.

Through the cracks of the loft the sunlight came slanting, bright-edged. He sat thinking of the night past, neither proud nor repentant, but pierced through by the new strange experience, as the virgin twilight of the loft by the dusky sun rays.

He would have remained there thinking for a while, but the sounds below disturbed him. Was the colt into some mischief?

With a supple movement he rose and descended the ladder. As the colt recognized his legs, it ceased to gnaw the boards of the stall and gave a welcoming whinny. When his head appeared it lifted its lip and showed its big teeth in a grimace of relief. Splinters of wood clung to the stiff hairs about its mouth. A great gouge was torn from the manger, the straw of its bed was kicked into the passage.

He went up to it warily, but it stretched its long head toward him and began talking in subdued rumbles of the long lonely night and its anxiety to be off.

Renny clasped its massive neck in his arms.

"Good boy," he murmured. "Nice old boy! Whose nice old boy is he? Whose pretty old boy?" He was filled with a sudden, deep sadness at the thought of parting with the colt.

As they stood so embraced, Elvira appeared in the doorway. She looked cool and fresh, but a little startled, like a doe surprised in the forest.

"Won't you come and have some breakfast?" she asked.

"Just look," he exclaimed, "what this young devil has done!"

"It doesn't matter. The stable is falling to pieces anyway."

"But it does matter! I must pay Bob for it."

"He wouldn't take anything."

From a shiny new purse Renny took our a five dollar note. "Here," he said, "you give it to him after I am gone."

She took it. Then she said hesitatingly: —

"I want to tell you how sorry I am about your sister ... the bad thing I did to her."

He drew a deep sigh. "Yes," he said heavily. "It has spoiled her life, she says."

Elvira looked up at him miserably. "I loved him, but I'm sure now that he never loved me. Does she know that? It might make it easier for her to forgive him."

Renny answered stiffly — "My sister must do what she thinks right."

He brought water to the colt, fed him, and followed Elvira to the cottage. His mind turned to Lulu. How would she meet him in front of the others? He wished he might have seen her alone first.

But here she was in the kitchen, which was made clean and tidy, giving the four little girls their breakfast. Bob was already in the fields.

Renny glanced inquiringly at Lulu from under his lashes. He moved shyly toward the breakfast table, then turned to the washing stand in the corner. The children followed his every move fascinated, their spoons suspended, the bluish milk on their porridge undisturbed.

Lulu laid a clean towel on Renny's shoulder and gave him a little push. She was complete in her self-assurance. When he slid to his chair opposite the children she leant over him and poured cream from a jug over his porridge. It dropped in thick yellow gouts. Her attitude implied that nothing was too good for him.

She sat at one end of the table and Elvira at the other. Renny tried to joke with the little girls, but they only stared at him in speechless trepidation. Elvira sat silent, still feeling rebuffed, and Lulu seemed bent only on serving Renny.

But when she stood beside him as he saddled the colt, and he turned and faced her expectantly, she said: —

"No. Don't come again. We've had our time together. It's over."

"Over!" he repeated incredulously.

"Yes — you can't keep coming back here. It'll be something for you to look back on, just as it is. But I'm not the sort of woman to want a boy hanging around."

"But you did want me, didn't you?"

She smiled enigmatically.

"You did!" he repeated angrily, and moved toward her.

She drew back and exclaimed almost savagely: —

"Don't dare touch me! I only want you to go!"

The look in her face satisfied him. He was no longer angry or hurt. He mounted the colt and, arranging its mane with his fingers, said: —

"I suppose if I ever do come this way you'll refuse to see me?"

"Yes — I'll refuse to see you."

"Do you never want to see me again?"

"Well — I'll not say that."

"Aren't you going to give me one kiss before I go?"

She came to his stirrup and held up her face, hard as a sculptured mask.

He bent down, then drew back. "Do you expect me to kiss that?"

"It's the best I can give you."

"Were you disappointed in me?"

"My God — no!"

She reached up, as though in a frenzy, and pulled his face down to hers and kissed him passionately. Then she turned away and walked swiftly along the path.

As he cantered down the road he had thought of all that had happened since he had left Jalna. It had been a strange time and he wished he might go straight home without delivering the colt to its new owner. The thought of parting with it now drove all other thoughts from his head. This morning he felt a new gracious understanding between them. His will was now the colt's will. When he turned into the road that led to Mr. Ferrier's, a black cloud hung over him.

It was nearly noon when the colt trotted docilely in at the gate. Mr. Ferrier, a bluff, purple-faced man, advanced to meet him.

"I expected you yesterday, young man," he said severely.

Renny looked at him out of a woebegone face. "I myself expected to be here, sir," he answered.

"Then why weren't you here?"

Renny stroked the colt's mane.

Mr. Ferrier looked the pair over. "You look as though you had been through a good deal."

Renny drew down the corners of his mouth and dismounted. He put the bridle into Mr. Ferrier's hand.

"Now see here," said Mr. Ferrier, "I want you to tell me why your coat is torn half off your back, why your clothes look as though you'd spent the night in a haystack, and why this animal's hide is stiff with sweat and dust. If you refuse to tell me, I'll inquire your father about it."

"The truth is," returned Renny, "I had an awful time getting here."

"I want no half-truths!" shouted Mr. Ferrier. "Is or is not this animal vicious?"

The colt answered for himself. He opened his mouth wide, then shut it with a grinding champ of his teeth full in the face of his new owner. Mr. Ferrier drew back in terror. He threw the bridle from him as though it were a poisonous reptile. Renny caught it and stood grinning sheepishly.

"Take him away!" ordered Mr. Ferrier. "I refuse to keep him! I'll let your father hear from me! Thank God I haven't given him my cheque! And just let me tell you, young fellow, those people you horrified in the motor car yesterday were my brother-in-law and his wife. They told me of the dastardly behaviour of this beast on the road and on the railway line. Your father will get a letter from me that will make his hair rise!"

Renny experienced an added sharpness in all his senses as he galloped along the homeward road. He felt that he could see the very veins on the smallest leaves of the new washed trees. The smell of the saddle, of the colt, of the warming earth, rose to him with piercing perfection. The feel of the horse beneath him, the measured thud of its hoofs, Lulu's remembered kiss warm on his lips, filled him with joyous vitality. Life burned in him like a torch.

XIII

Family Pleasures

Philip and Mary stood on either side of a swing that hung from a low branch of an oak tree beside the croquet lawn. In the swing Eden sat clutching the ropes tightly, ecstatic at the experience of being swung through the air from one parent to another. His mother would push him gently on the back and, at about every fifth swing, his father would catch his feet, hold them a second, and send him back to his mother with added momentum.

The baby, Piers, toddled about, drawing a small wooden horse on wheels. But he was becoming old enough to have feelings of jealousy when his brother was the centre of interest. He stalled his horse under the drooping branches of a syringa in flower and came toward the swing, frowning.

"Me! Me! Me!" he demanded.

"Look out!" cried Philip.

Mary snatched up the child in her arms. He pushed at her breast. "Me!" he repeated, pointing at the swing.

"Put him on my lap!" cried Eden. "I'll hold him."

Mary placed the little one carefully on Eden's knees and, supporting him there, swung them gently to and fro. But the baby would not have it so. With one chubby hand he grasped the rope himself and with the other tried to push Eden from the swing.

Philip threw Mary an amused glance. "He is going to be a rough one," he observed. "You sit in the swing, Molly. Perhaps he'll tolerate your holding him."

The change was made. Mary spread out her frilly skirt, settled the baby in front of her, and Philip, holding his pipe in his teeth, sent them flying toward the leafy greenness. Piers shouted with joy; Mary's skirts blew back, displaying her white embroidered petticoat and slim black silk ankles.

"Oh, how lovely!" she cried.

Eden, hearing the sound of horse's hooves at the gate, darted through the shrubbery and appeared directly in front of Renny and the colt as they entered the drive.

The colt reared and held itself rigid for a moment, then moved on its hind legs, as though preparing to dance.

Eden rushed toward it shouting "Whoa! Whoa!"

"Get back, Eden," ordered Renny, "you little fool!"

The last word was jolted from him in a grunt as he was hurled to the ground from the colt's back. Philip ran to the scene, his final push to the swing so uneven that Mary was left precariously zigzagging.

The colt now stood quite still and let Philip to take it by the bridle. He did so, and his full blue eyes swept over it and his son.

"Well," he said slowly, "you're a pretty pair!"

"It was Eden's fault," said Renny, "He must learn not to run out on the drive like that."

Philip asked — "And what about the pickle you're in? Is that Eden's fault?"

Mary came through the trees carrying the baby on her arm. At the sight of Renny's cheek, which had been scratched on the gravel, and his generally ruffianly appearance, she screamed. At the sight and sound of his mother's distress Eden too gave a shrill cry.

"Enough of that!" exclaimed Philip testily. "If anyone should scream I am the one. Now," he turned to his eldest son — "explain!"

Renny passed his hand over his head. "Mr. Ferrier refused to keep the colt."

"Refused to keep the colt? But why?"

"The colt bit at him, Father. It all but took the face off him. I couldn't ask him to keep it after that."

Philip groaned. "And to think I haven't his cheque!"

Renny proceeded. "And he tore my coat, as you see, and he nearly jumped into a motor car with two people who turned out to be relations of Mr. Ferrier, and he ate the manger at the hotel, and I nearly lost my life at a railway crossing because of him. I'm lucky enough to have got back at all after what I've been through!"

Philip laughed derisively.

"It's all very well for *you* to laugh," said Renny.

"What on earth shall we do with the brute?" asked Philip, looking ruefully over the colt.

Renny answered eagerly: —

"He's a splendid fellow, Dad! I've never known a colt I liked better. He will be a fine jumper. All he needs is the right handling. I'm the one to do it! Please let me school him! There's nothing I'd like so much."

Philip looked thoughtfully into his son's eyes, then he said — "Very well, I agree. But if he persists in this biting habit — Eden! Keep away from his head, will you!"

Renny jumped to the saddle and Eden cried — "May I ride with him to the stable?" Piers too held out his arms toward Renny.

"No! No!" said Mary. "You must keep away from that horse. Renny, I do beg that you will be careful of the children!"

Renny looked at her teasingly. "It will be quite safe to give them a ride that far," he said.

"Philip," she cried. "Do you hear him? You must tell him never, never to let the children near that horse!"

"Never, never let the children near that horse," repeated Philip tranquilly. "And, by the way, where did you spend last night?"

Renny looked at him blankly. "Why — I — why — I —"

"What the devil are you stuttering about?" asked Philip. "I asked where you spent last night?"

"At a little farm not far from Mr. Ferrier's."

"What was your reason? The hostler from the hotel met one of our men and told him you had an early lunch there. What were you doing between then and bedtime?"

"Well — you see —" He went into a detailed account of the incident on the railway line.

Philip looked thoughtful. "What I don't understand is why you should pass that crossing on the road to Mr. Ferrier's. It was quite five miles out of the way."

"I got lost."

"You couldn't possibly get lost on that road. It's as straight as a string."

Mary's eyes were alight with mischief as they looked into her stepson's troubled face.

"Now what I think is," went on Philip, "that you went out of your way to see some girl and stopped the night somewhere you had no business to be. I have an idea that you went to see that girl Elvira for Maurice. You took her money, perhaps — Am I right?"

"There's no use in my trying to hide anything from you," growled Renny, and he gave the colt a slap and galloped in the direction of the stables.

Before he was halfway there he wheeled and galloped back. Eden ran to meet him.

"What are you going to do, Renny?" he called out.

"Go back and tell Daddy that Maurice had nothing to do with it."

Eden, delighted to carry a message for his hero, dashed back.

"What is it, darling?" asked Mary.

He answered promptly. "Maurice had nothing to do with it, Renny says."

Mary stroked his hair. She pushed out her pretty underlip petulantly.

"What's the matter, Molly?" asked Philip.

"It seems to me we are never enjoying ourselves together but Renny appears on the scene and spoils things. Or, if he does not appear, you are wondering where he is and what he is up to."

"He's just at the troublesome age," returned Philip. "But I'm glad he is no liar. Shall I give you another swing?"

She shook her head. Then asked — "Why do you suppose he spent the night at that farm?"

What he supposed Philip did not intend to tell her. To change the subject he said — "Just look at Peep! He's stuffing himself with mulberries!"

The baby had been picking up the fallen berries and now, at the sound of his name, turned and faced them, his cherub's mouth purple. When his mother slapped his hands he burst into screams of rage, striking back at her with his round fists. She carried him to the house.

Philip laughed and the sound of the gong for the one o'clock dinner came from the house. Taking Eden by the hand, he moved slowly across the lawn, his mind troubled by the behaviour of his eldest son. Had this affair of Maurice's turned Renny's mind toward sex in its darker aspect? He had been interested in girls, his attentions to Vera Lacey had been the subject of amusement to the family, but there had been never anything serious, anything secret in his excursions, before this. Philip knew that Elvira and her relative, — sister or aunt — God knew what! — had moved in the direction of Mr. Ferrier's. But surely — not Elvira! That would be too shocking. And certainly not the older woman. Yet there was that message sent back by Eden — Maurice had nothing to do with it. Renny had been off on his own. He had certainly had a rough time with that colt. Well, let him keep it and see what he could make of it! As Scotchmere said — he was the "ridin'est critter!"

Eliza met him in the hall.

"Mr. Ferrier wishes to speak to you on the telephone, sir," she said severely. "I told him it was dinner time, but nothing would stop him. He has called up three times this morning."

"Run along with Eliza, Eden," said Philip, and humped his broad shoulders above the telephone in the library to listen to a vehement outpouring of accusations against his son, his colt, and himself.

When he entered the dining room his mother turned toward him with an accusing look and a piece of dumpling poised on her fork.

"Do you see that, Philip? That's my last mouthful of dumpling. My plate's cleared. We didn't wait for you. Molly and Edwin and Augusta said wait. But Nick and Ernest and Malahide and I said no, and we outweighed them." She thrust the piece of dumpling into her mouth.

Philip helped himself to the pot pie. "It was Ferrier," he said, "raising hell about the colt."

"I see that he is back," observed Nicholas. "I am not surprised at that. I always said he was vicious."

"I'm afraid you will have difficulty in getting rid of him now," added Ernest.

"Begin bad, end bad," put in Sir Edwin.

Augusta said, dictatorially — "Harness him to one of the farm wagons and let him work. That will prevent his becoming incorrigible."

Adeline peered across Malahide at her daughter. "What do you know about horses, Lady Bunkley? Put a thoroughbred between the shafts of a farm wagon! I say no! It would break his spirit."

Sir Edwin turned to her. "It seems strange," he said mildly, "that a woman of your great intelligence, Mrs. Whiteoak, should not be able to remember her daughter's name."

Adeline looked abashed, as only Sir Edwin could abash her. "Well, well," she muttered, "I'm losing my memory. I'm getting old."

"Renny says the colt is a good one," said Philip. "He wants to school him for high jumping. I think I'll let him have his way."

"Just for a change," said Ernest, and Mary threw him a glance of agreement.

The door opened and Meg, followed by Renny, came in. To cover the embarrassment of his own entrance he had persuaded her to this first venture into family life. At her appearance a warm emotion of tenderness and relief stirred those about the table, with the exception of Mary and Malahide, she regarding the young girl with irritable wonder and he with amused curiosity.

Her uncles drew out her chair, which was between theirs, and she sat down in it shading her face with her hand. Philip eagerly investigated the pot pie in search of a tempting morsel for his daughter.

"The wing," said Adeline, "give her the wing! That's the thing to tempt delicate girls. Make 'em feel like flying, eh, Meggie?"

"Yes, Granny," answered Meg, and tears began to roll down her cheeks.

"Meg, Meg, do try to control yourself!" exclaimed Mary.

Philip surveyed the plate he had arranged as though he would, out of his own heart, put virtue into it for her healing, then passed it to her. Nicholas patted her shoulder and Ernest picked up her table napkin which had fallen, and spread it carefully on her knees.

"What's the matter with her?" asked Eden.

All the family said *"Ssh"* at once, and he subsided into contemplation of his aunt's many ornaments.

Philip now heaped a plate of what remained of the pie for Renny, who attacked it hungrily. But if he hoped that his absence of the night before was to receive no further notice, he was mistaken.

"Where did you stop the night?" asked Nicholas.

"At a farm."

"But why was that necessary?"

"I had a dickens of a time with the colt. Didn't Father tell you?"

"What farm did you stop at?" inquired Ernest.

"A little farm — poor people — never saw it before."

"What was the farmer's name?" asked his aunt. "I used to know the names of the farmers for many miles about."

"Why, Auntie, you knew nothing about that part of the county," said Renny irritably.

"I might," persisted Augusta. "Just tell me the farmer's name."

"Bob. I didn't ask his surname." He wished they would let him enjoy his dinner in peace.

"What family had he?"

"A lot of little girls. Another one had just come."

Philip sat watching him with a whimsical smile, but said nothing.

Meg suddenly spoke. "Vera told me this morning that those terrible women have gone in that direction. Perhaps you spent the night with them."

If she had dropped a bomb in their midst the family would have scarcely felt more consternation. They looked from her to Renny, who laid down his knife and fork and stared at his sister aghast.

Philip spoke first. "She doesn't know what she is saying, poor child!"

Augusta said, in her ominous contralto: —

"Her mind is deranged. And no wonder, after all she has been through. It is not the first time I have known that to occur after a blow on the head."

Grandmother struck the table with her spoon. "D'ye mean to say, Lady B. —" She was afraid to mispronounce her daughter's name because of Sir Edwin, yet disdained to say it correctly. "D'ye mean to say that Meg is deranged because of the little tap on the pate I gave her?"

"I should not be surprised, Mamma."

Her mother grinned at her. "You've had harder ones."

"But *not* following on disappointed love, Mrs. Whiteoak," returned Sir Edwin blandly.

"Was there a bump on Meg's head?" asked Eden.

Meg burst into tears and rose from the table.

"There now, there now," said Ernest consolingly. He put his arm about her and led her weeping out of the room.

Philip looked ruefully at her untouched plate and heaved a sigh. "Look at that!" he said. "She hasn't eaten a bite!"

"She will come right," said Nicholas. "We must just be patient. In the meantime I may as well have this wing. I had nothing but dark meat." He helped himself to the wing.

To draw the attention of the family from Renny, Philip began to talk somewhat truculently of the good points of the colt and so raised an animated discussion. Ernest returned, with word that Meg had gone to her room, but had intimated that she might eat a little of the sweet, if it were carried to her.

So Philip creaked up the stairs carrying a large piece of gooseberry tart, smothered in cream, to his daughter. When he came back his hair was dishevelled, his face flushed.

"Philip, just look at your hair!" exclaimed Mary.

"The darling was hugging me," he said, in a voice not quite steady, and a cloud darkened Mary's face.

From the dinner table Philip went straight to a white garden seat that circled a fine oak on the lawn, and established himself there with his pipe. When Renny appeared on the porch Philip raised his hand and beckoned to him.

Renny came slowly across the warm grass and sat down beside him. Philip asked: —

"Have you anything you'd like to tell me?"

"Yes," muttered Renny.

"About last night?" encouraged Philip mildly.

"Yes. I did go there — where Meggie said."

"Ah.... Yes, but not for Maurice?"

"Maurice knew nothing about it. I just went ... on my own account."

Philip puffed hard at his pipe, which showed signs of going out. His eyes rested admiringly on the flaming bed of geraniums. "A fine colour, aren't they?"

"H'm-h'm," muttered Renny, glancing sideways into his father's face. He added quickly — "I didn't go to see that girl of Maurice's, but the older one. Elvira's aunt."

Philip watched the bees humming heavily about the geraniums. He asked, in a low voice: —

"You'd known her before? When she lived here?"

"I'd met her — just once. I had gone to take money to Elvira from Maurice. He didn't want to see her again. He was afraid of another scene with her. He was terribly upset."

"So — he pushed my son into a brothel, to save his own feelings — damn his eyes!" Philip spoke quietly against the mouthpiece of his pipe, the even puffs from which were not interrupted. He added, after a moment — "I'd like to go to his house this moment and thrash him under his father's nose."

The indolence of Philip's speech somehow softened all his threats. Renny moved closer to him along the bench. He said huskily: —

"There was nothing between us at that first meeting. Except a bit of chaffing. I'd seen her through the window reading a teacup, and she said she'd read my fortune if I would go to see her."

"And did she?"

"Yes."

"What did she tell you?"

"Oh, mostly rot!"

"And didn't she promise anything else — that first night?"

"She said she'd tell me how she came by such strange looking eyes."

"Had she come by them honestly?"

"Her mother had got intimate with a Rumanian gypsy."

"Is she pretty — this woman?"

"No — not pretty. But you can't keep your eyes off her." Remembrance of the night surged through him. He wrung his fingers together between his knees. "I don't want to talk about her, Father. But I had to tell you why I was there."

Philip asked quietly — "Did you sleep with her?"

Renny's voice was scarcely audible. "Yes."

"The bitch! And you not twenty yet! And your first experience!" He turned his full blue eyes on his son. "It was, wasn't it?"

"Yes. There was something about me — that first night we met — that made her think differently. So she didn't know — I don't believe she's the sort of woman you think she is, Father. She says I must never go back to see her again." He spoke with boyish simplicity.

"Well, that is handsome of her," returned Philip. "Renny, I want you to promise me something. If you feel tempted to go back to that woman, I want you to come to me and ask me for money. I'll send you off somewhere. Go with you myself, if you'd like to have me. In the meantime, there's the colt! You must try to see what you can do with him. And you'll soon be going back to college."

"I guess you'll be glad when I do go, Dad," said Renny contritely. "I'll do what you say and — it's awfully decent of you to let me have the colt. I'm afraid you spoil us — just as Mother says."

Philip took his son's hand and squeezed it.

"Well," he said, as cheerfully as he could, "you and Meggie must turn out well, else I'll be blamed for it. I'm sorry this happened. And right on top of the other affair, too. It seemed quite unnecessary. But — so much of life *is* unnecessary! You'll find that out as you grow older."

XIV

Peace in Thy Palaces

In the week that followed Cousin Malahide was not idle. It gratified something in his dark and circuitous nature to verify Meg's haphazard thrust at Renny. When he had his facts assembled he spread them out in front of Adeline, as a peddler might spread his wares. She pounced on them, and though furious with Renny, exulted in spite of her self in the assurance that her grandson was a Court, and that her father, old Renny Court, lived again in the youth.

But it was late Saturday night; she was too tired for any scene so vital as this disclosure must portend. On Sunday morning there was the church service to be gone through, then Sunday dinner, which must be enjoyed without interruption, and her forty winks afterward. She lay in bed, the gentle glimmer from the night light throwing an enormous shadow of her parrot across the ceiling, while she counted the number of hours which must pass before she could lay bare the truth.

There was no malice in her toward her grandson. But she had the desire to show Philip that he had brought up the boy badly, that he had never taken her advice or even asked for it, that he had failed both as father and as son. She counted the seventeen hours that must pass before she would take the wind out of Philip's sails.

It seemed to her that she had scarcely slept at all, that she had had nothing but little cat naps all through the long hours till the first beam of sunshine stole the parrot's shadow from the night light and spread it elongated against the yellow wall.

The next thing she knew there was Eliza, her print dress standing stiff about her, with the breakfast tray, the large brown egg in the silver egg cup, the pile of buttered toast, the pot of marmalade, the two golden popovers wrapped in a snow-white napkin. She took no porridge on Sunday mornings so that she might have room for, and the ability to digest, two of these, which were a special treat of the day.

She took the egg cup and held it to the light to see if it might be tarnished a little. If it were she would let the servants hear from her. But it was bright as a coin fresh from the mint and, with a little grunt half of disappointment, half of pleasure, she set about chipping the egg.

The parrot drew up his grey eyelids, fluttered his wings, and gaped, showing his dark tongue. He cocked an eye at the napkin containing the popovers, for which he had an inordinate liking.

"No, no," she said, shaking her egg spoon at him. "You're a greedy fellow! Go back to your sunflower seeds!"

But she relented and rather clumsily began to undo the napkin. As he saw that he was to be indulged he sidled up and down the footboard of the bed wriggling with pleasure, undulating his glossy neck, opening and closing his claws while he said in his nasal tones: —

"Chota Rami — Dilhi — Dil Pasand!"

He gave her no peace till she had tossed him the fragments of one of the popovers and had hurriedly demolished the other lest it too might be begged of her.

"You're a regular playboy, you are!" she exclaimed. "You and Cousin Malahide are a pair!"

Before any of the others she was ready for church, sitting by one of the windows in the drawing room in her velvet cloak and heavy widow's weeds.

The next to be ready was Eden, in a white sailor suit, a ten-cent piece clutched in his small hand. He dragged an ottoman beside his grandmother's chair and sat down on it, observing: —

"Mamma said I was to stop with you till she was ready so I'd keep clean. Look, I've got ten cents for church. It's the most I've ever had." He displayed it on his palm.

"Look out that you don't put it in your mouth."

"It wouldn't matter if I did," he answered with dignity. "Mamma washed it before she gave it to me. I wonder why?"

"Just one of her flibbertygibbety ways," answered Adeline brusquely.

Ernest came in immaculate in morning coat, his top hat on his arm. His mother looked him over approvingly. "You look nice," she said.

"And you look handsomer all the time," he returned gallantly, and kissed her.

She beamed for a moment and then said — "Mary has washed this child's offering. It will put these new germy ideas in his head. I don't like it."

"There's something exquisite about Mary," said Ernest. "A fastidiousness that I would not have changed. And, when one thinks of it, it is more seemly to offer a thoroughly cleansed coin at the altar rather than a dingy one which may, the day before, have been passed across a bar."

"You make me tired," retorted his mother. "Money is money wherever it comes from. D'ye mean to say," — she extracted a fifty-cent piece from her bag and slapped it down on the occasional table beside her — "D'ye mean to say that my money isn't as good as Mary's?"

"Of course it is," Ernest answered soothingly. "Nevertheless I do admire Mary's delicacy."

The Buckleys appeared just as Hodge drew up the bays in front of the door. In her Sunday attire Augusta looked rather an overpowering mate for Sir Edwin, but he carried their two prayer books and steered her protectingly down the steps to the carriage, where Ernest was already establishing his mother and Eden clambering to the box beside Hodge. They drove in the best carriage, which Captain Whiteoak had had made in London many years before. Philip himself drove a smart grey mare, with hogged mane and tail, dam of Renny's colt. Mary, Nicholas, and Meg were with him. Malahide was still abed and Renny was walking to church across the fields.

It was Meg's first appearance in public and the world to her had a strange new look. The season had indeed matured greatly while she had kept to the house, but to her it seemed that summer was over, that the grass looked dry, the flowers drooping, and that the great clouds coming up from the west were forerunners of autumn.

She was sure that everyone in the church would know that her engagement with Maurice was broken off, and why. She wondered how she would face them all. Even now, in the carriage, the only thing that kept her from breaking down was the sight of her father's broad shoulders in front of her.

When they reached the steps he offered her his arm instead of giving it to Mary as he usually did. So she entered the church as she had often pictured herself doing, but not to her marriage ceremony. She clutched his arm in her silk-gloved hand and wondered if she could walk down the aisle. Their pew seemed very far away and the throbbing of the organ rather frightened her.

"Oh, Daddy, I can't do it!" she said.

He could not hear her words, but saw the movement of her lips and smiled at her. Soon she found herself passing the pew where Admiral Lacey, his wife, two daughters, and granddaughter sat. Their faces turned toward her and she felt a sudden forlorn dignity in her position.

As she knelt she peeped through her fingers across the aisle at the Vaughans' pew. Mr. Vaughan was there looking very sad, Meg thought, and Mrs. Vaughan, broad and erect, facing the world across her son's shame. Maurice sat with folded arms and bent head. Meg could not see his face.

Renny was late as usual, and when he slid into the seat beside Meg she felt that some of the security of her everyday life had come to her with him. She glanced at his face and saw it proud and aloof, with an expression she could not fathom. They all knelt together and began the general confession.

Eden was between his mother and Nicholas, but desired very much to be with Renny and Meg. Mary wanted him to be good and sweet. When he fingered the whistle at the end of his lanyard or shook his money between his palms she took his hand gently in hers and held it. There was nothing gentle in the look Uncle Nick gave him when he wriggled. It made him hang his head and colour, yet he could not keep still.

"May I sit beside Renny?" he whispered.

Mary shook her head and gave him a little prayer book with coloured pictures to look at. He looked at the pictures disconsolately and tried to make out the words under them, but could not. He slid on to his backbone so far that he would have slipped from the seat had not Nicholas caught him and set him up with a jerk.

Now they stood up to sing a hymn, and Eden hung over the pew looking at the belongings of Ernest, Grandmother, and the Buckleys. He found that he could reach the handle of Aunt Augusta's umbrella. She looked round at him and shook her head. Philip reached across Mary and moved Eden beside him. He snuggled there a moment, then, as they resumed theirs seats, whispered: —

"Daddy, may I sit between Renny and Meg?"

Already they were making room for him. Philip let him pass and he pressed in between them. He smiled up happily into their faces. He pushed a hand into theirs. Meg's was plump, velvety. Renny's thin and muscular.

The family filled two pews with their bodies and the little church with their strong voices. They set themselves in good earnest at a hymn, as hunters at a jump. Now it was "The Church's One Foundation" which rose from their throats in a tempo always a little in advance of the organist. Meg tried to sing it too, but when they came to "From heaven He came and sought her — to be His holy bride," her voice failed her and she could only clutch Eden's hand and stare dumbly at the blurred page of her hymn book.

The young clergyman was not quite High enough to please old Mrs. Whiteoak and her two elder sons, not quite Low enough for Philip and the Buckleys. The Laceys were on the High side, the Vaughans on the Low, and, being an amiable young man, he varied the ritual as much as possible, so that while neither side was satisfied neither was absolutely affronted.

He chose as his text today: "Peace be within thy walls, and prosperity within thy palaces." It was a text well chosen to please the Whiteoaks, though not deliberately on Mr. Fennel's part. They leant back in their broadcloth and velvet to enjoy it to the full. Adeline took out a large black satin fan on which purple violets had been painted by the elder Miss Lacey, and waved it slowly to and fro. Peace, prosperity, and palaces — all good words, she thought. They all began with *p,* too, which was her favourite letter, since it began her dear husband's name. It stood for other vigorous words, such as pride, pomp, purple, prejudice, pageantry, pillory, pike, and, on its lighter side, pianoforte, piffle, and pooh-pooh. She fixed her still bright brown eyes on the rector and drank in all he had to say of peace within the home and the dangers of too much prosperity, till, to her mind, he became a little long-drawn-out, and her thoughts wandered to the shock she had up her sleeve for her family.

She became drowsy and would have dozed but for a fly that tormented her. He flew finally to the back of the pew in front and, folding her fan, she ended his activities with a sharp blow that made everyone look in her direction. She gave a pleased smile and settled her veil about her shoulders.

It was Communion Sunday, as Meg realized with dismay. She could not — nothing on earth could persuade her — face the possibility of kneeling at the altar in terrible proximity to Maurice. Yet if she left the church before the celebration, it was all too probable that he would leave too and they would walk down the aisle together — not united, but sundered forever!

As she hesitated Philip leaned toward her and said — "You and Renny go and take Eden along." He gave her a warm protective glance.

She woke the little boy, who stumbled between his elders along a side aisle and through a small door opposite the Lacey's pew. Vera joined them outside.

"I couldn't stay," she exclaimed, "when I saw you two leaving, so I whispered to Grandpa that I had a frightful headache, and the old dear nodded, but the aunts looked very disapproving!"

Meg put her arm through her friend's and felt a sudden lifting of the spirit, finding herself out under the sky with other young people. There was no sign of Maurice, for he had gone out by the front door and concealed himself among the gravestones till they were out of sight.

Renny, by the light of his late experience, saw Vera with new eyes. He perceived her delicate charm. But he presented a new air of taciturnity toward her, walking at the side of the road with his hand on Eden's neck and ignoring both the girls.

Vera said, in an audible whisper to Meg — "What is the matter with the son and heir? He looks very aloof this morning."

"I expect he is brooding on Cousin Malahide," returned Meg. "We both hate him, you know."

"I don't wonder! I think he's an *impossible* person."

"We hope and pray that he will go back to England with Aunt Augusta and Uncle Edwin."

"But surely he'd never let them go *without* him!"

"That's exactly what he would do! Poor Daddy suspects it, I know. I think the truth is that Cousin Malahide hasn't two coins to rub together at the moment, and his only hope is visiting round among his relatives."

"And *what* a visitor!" Vera began a ridiculous imitation of Malahide Court. Her aim was to divert Meg and she succeeded. The two girls walked along the dusty country road giving little shrieks of laughter.

Renny threw an antagonistic glance at them. At this moment he was disliking the presence of all womankind. The thought of the unwanted Malahide remaining in the house infuriated him.

"If he stays," he said, savagely kicking a stone out of his way, "I will make Jalna too hot to hold him!"

"What shall you do?" questioned both girls.

"I'll have to think about it," he answered glumly.

They left Vera at her grandfather's gate and returned across the fields to Jalna. Eden was very much awake now and darted about them, finding something at every turn. A snail shell or the nest of a bird filled him with delight.

In the hall Renny put his arm about his sister's waist. "I like having you about again, Meggie. You're coming down to dinner, aren't you?"

"I suppose." She stroked the polished grapes of the walnut newel post.

Cousin Malahide was coming down the stairs.

"What a charming picture!" he drawled.

"Are you being disagreeable?" asked Renny abruptly.

Malahide turned up the corners of his mouth beneath his long nose.

"Good heavens, no! I love you both too well for that!"

They were shamed at the thought of being loved by him, chagrined by his refusal to quarrel.

Eden held out his snail shell. "Look what I found!"

Malahide took it and laid it out on his palm. He said, with a wry smile: —

"How I envy the snail — carrying his house on his back!"

Meg, remembering Vera's imitation of him, began to shake with secret mirth. She was at the stage of recovery that lies between tears and laughter.

Renny turned and went out of doors again, followed by Eden. Malahide's arm slid round Meg's shoulders. "Won't you let me comfort you?" he asked.

Meggie still shook with laughter. They were standing so when the first carriage arrived at the door. Meg disengaged herself and ran quickly up the stairs. Malahide advanced to meet his old kinswoman.

"So you are back, my dear Adeline," he said, "refreshed in soul and ready for the good meal I can scent in preparation! How marvellously well you all look! As for me, I have dozed a little, after a stark night of anxiety over my affairs. I had a most unkind letter from my mother yesterday. I can only compare her to those fabled monsters who devour their young. Could anyone accuse me, Edwin, of not being an affectionate son to her? You have seen us together. And you, too, Augusta!" He took an arm of each of the Buckleys and escorted them into the drawing room.

Adeline threw back her veil.

"I am as hot as a toad in sand," she affirmed. "Somebody fetch me a drink."

"What would you like, Mamma?" asked Philip. "Water? Cider? Sherry?"

"Our own cider," returned his mother. "There is nothing better at this time o' day."

It was a good choice, for the cider at Jalna, made from Admiral Lacey's recipe, was excellent. They sat and stood about drinking it, while the four sleek carriage horses in the stable were being rubbed down and given their own refreshment.

"Peace within thy walls and prosperity within thy palaces," said Ernest. "A very good sermon, I thought. I like the young rector very much indeed."

"If only he had not that beard," said Mary. "It looks very unbecoming with a surplice, in my opinion."

"In mine," said Augusta, "the beard is very reassuring. It counteracts the popish tendencies which he undoubtedly has. I close my eyes at times rather than observe what he does in front of the altar."

"You show your poor judgment then, Lady B.," said her mother. "Ritual is the best part of any service."

Augusta looked down her nose. "I inherit my Papa's distaste for High Church practices.

Adeline's eyebrows shot up.

"It's a pity you have inherited nothing from him but a fault."

Sir Edwin put in mildly — "In Augusta faults are transformed into virtues." He wiped his side whiskers with a mauve silk handkerchief.

The dinner passed in peace, and it was not till the family was assembled for tea that Adeline made her disclosure.

In a pause she remarked, as though to her teacup: —

"Spoil a boy and what thanks does he give you? None. He does his best to disgrace you."

Her sons looked at each other. Had she one of them in her mind?

Malahide wrapped his long legs about each other and said: —

"I certainly was never spoilt. Whenever my parents could think of nothing else to do they beat me."

Nicholas, Ernest, and Philip again exchanged a look, this time of sympathy with Malahide's parents.

Sir Edwin said — "I was brought up firmly but kindly. My father would reason with me for hours and now I am thankful to him for it, since it developed me from a young barbarian to what I am today."

"Of course," Adeline agreed heartily, "any son would thank any father who made him toe the scratch. It's the spoilt boy that brings shame to his father's house."

Meg rose from her ottoman. "If you are going to talk about *that,* Granny, I cannot stay here."

Her grandmother looked at her kindly. "You have finished your tea. Very well, my dear, you had better go. I want to say just what I feel — for once."

Meg went quietly from the room and there was a perceptible moment of drawing closer to Adeline, who, with underlip thrust out, sat staring straight in front of her. Renny sat looking at his clasped hands with an air of wary attention.

His grandmother now turned to him abruptly. She asked — "Where did you spend the night of the day when you set out to deliver the colt?"

He raised his eyes to her face, but did not answer.

She turned to Philip. "Do you know where your son spent that night?"

"Yes," he returned, "I know. No need to talk about it, Mamma."

"You know —" she repeated violently, "you know nothing of the sort! You know just what the young rake has chosen to tell you."

"I know that he spent the night at a farm about ten miles from Mr. Ferrier's."

"Yes — and whom did he sleep with?"

"He slept with a woman — the older one of the two who got young Maurice into trouble."

His mother's fiery glance turned to Renny, who faced her with his lips drawn back from his teeth.

At Philip's words Sir Edwin uttered an exclamation of distaste and pulled nervously at his whiskers. Lady Buckley drew back her chin and with an air of speechless affront. Nicholas made a sound between a chuckle and a groan. Ernest turned red and exclaimed — "My God!" Mary drew in a quick breath and caught her underlip between her white teeth, and Malahide Court would his legs together where he sat on a sofa by himself and fingered his diamond tie pin.

"How rural!" he murmured.

Adeline's face quivered with humiliation. She had prepared a fine scene between herself and Philip. She had prepared a flamboyant part for herself to enact before her family. She felt, for the moment, defeated, cheated, deprived of her prestige. The sight of the boy grinning at her revived her. She leant towards him, supporting her hands on her stick.

"So," she said in a rasping voice, "you saved your face, you young whelp, by confessing to your easygoing, spineless father!"

He did not answer.

"Haven't you a tongue in your head?" she demanded violently. "Can you do nothing but sit there grinning at your Grandmother? Oh, I warrant you had plenty to say to that trollop! Lots of sweet words to lavish on her! Where did you have her, I'd like to know! Come now, out with it! Take that grin off your face and tell me where you had the troll!"

"In the mow," he answered in a level voice. "In the new hay."

"In the hay!" groaned Augusta. "A Whiteoak in the hay, like any common yokel!"

"He ought to be horsewhipped!" growled Nicholas.

"It is to be hoped it won't get out," said Ernest. "What a piece of gossip for the countryside!"

Philip said to his mother — "How did you find this out?"

"Oh, I have ways of finding out!" she retorted. "I haven't lived for eighty years on this earth for nothing!"

"I think you ought to tell me," he persisted.

Renny turned to him fiercely. "I'll tell you! No — let him tell you himself — ask Cousin Malahide!"

"You honour me," answered Malahide, "with a perspicacity I do not possess."

"If you want to know," said Adeline, "I will tell you. Malahide *did* find out. But only because I begged him to. He had no personal interest in it whatever, had you, Mally?"

To have his part in the disclosure made public was the last thing Malahide desired. He pulled at his lower lip and said deprecatingly: —

"Please leave me out of it, dear cousin. You have much more important things to discuss."

Augusta interrupted with — "These women should be forced to leave the Province. To think they would cause two young boys to lose their virtue!"

Philip said gravely — "I feel that Renny's excuse in this affair is the disturbance to his mind by all that has taken place. It's most unfortunate. But he has made a clean breast of it. No more should be said on the subject." He took out his pipe and began to fill it.

Nicholas said — "You're too much inclined to let things slide, Philip. When the boy was suspended last term, what did you do about it? Absolutely nothing."

"And the result is," said Ernest, "that things have slid, as Nicholas puts it, into this!"

"My sons," declared Adeline, "would have been flogged if they had been sent home from school. But your son is pampered and petted —"

"My son is as manly as yours," interrupted Philip angrily.

"But has he the self-control?" asked Augusta.

"Good Lord!" said Philip. "Has our family been famous for self-control? Had the Courts self-control? What are these stories of life in Ireland that Mamma and Malahide are so fond of raking up?"

Adeline proceeded — "My grandson went unscathed after his suspension. It made him feel master of himself! He'll do what he pleases and no deference to you or to anyone! Now I say something must be done about the affair of this woman. And you are the one to do it. You've shilly-shallied long enough!"

A murmur of assent came from the others. Their eyes looked accusingly at Philip. He began to wonder if perhaps he were to blame for Renny's behaviour. He puffed at his pipe in silence for a space, then turned to his son. "I wish," he said ruefully, "that we could have kept this matter between ourselves. As it is — I think you must not see Maurice again before you go back to college. I expect he's been a bad influence for you."

"Not see him!" Renny repeated. "What do you mean, not see him?"

"I mean keep away from him. Have nothing to do with him."

"That's right," agreed Nicholas.

"A pity you did not say that long ago, Philip," said Ernest.

"Maurice's influence has been bad from the first," declared Augusta.

Renny exclaimed hotly — "It's ridiculous! Maurice and I can't be kept apart. We're neighbours — we're friends — how can we keep apart?"

Adeline struck her stick on the floor. "By doing what you're told, for once in your life, you independent young vagabond! The first thing we know, we'll be having a brat left on the doorstep of Jalna!"

"Mamma!" cried Augusta. "How can you say such a thing!"

"I say it and mean it! A woman's a woman whether it's mattress or hay!"

Renny sprang to his feet. "I'm going!" He said bitterly. He turned to his father.

"Are you in earnest?"

"Yes. I want you to keep away from Maurice — absolutely."

"May I see him long enough to tell him?"

"Certainly — but no longer."

Renny turned to Malahide.

"I wish," he said savagely, "that you would come outside with me!"

"You're very much the schoolboy still, aren't you?" said Malahide, with a sneer.

Renny flung from the room. Eliza, who had been keeping the tea wagon outside till calm should reign within, wheeled it with dignity through the door. Sighs of pleasurable anticipation greeted it.

In the hall Renny stopped. He stretched up his arms and closed his hands. He stretched his body taut and blew out a great breath of resentment and hate for Malahide. From the drawing room came the sound of his grandmother's voice, harsh and dictatorial, laying down the law about him, he supposed. He raised his eyes to the carved fox's head on the top of the hatstand and made a grimace at it.

XV

MAURICE AND RENNY

"AND SO," CONCLUDED Renny, bitterly, "we're to be cut off from each other just when we might manage to get a little pleasure out of this beastly disappointing summer."

"We should have been parted in any case," returned Maurice. "Dad and I have decided that it is best for me to go away for a while. I have cousins in Nova Scotia, you know. I am going to visit them till this affair blows over."

"If you wait for that," said Renny pessimistically, "you'll be grey-headed when you come back. Nothing is ever forgotten here."

"Still, in a few months it won't be so difficult for us. In our own house, I mean. Now when we meet each other we feel embarrassed. We spend our mealtime in making polite conversation, trying to pretend that everything is all right. It's ghastly!"

"Why do you pretend?"

"Well, one has to. Mother can't tell me at breakfast that she spent a sleepless night because of my behaviour. Dad can't say why it is he has no appetite. And — if I told them what was in my mind … It just can't be done! We've got to keep up a pretense of ordinary life, but it's a terrible strain."

"Yes," agreed Renny, "it must be."

"I'm tired out with it. I must go away."

Renny sighed. "I suppose it is better for you. But I'm sorry you're going."

They were walking down the narrow sandy road to the lake. Maurice caught his friend's arm in his hand and held it close. "You've been a brick to me through all of this," he said. "I've spoilt everything for you just as I have for Meg and myself. It's too awful! Let's go to my boathouse and take out the canoe. Your father can't object to our having a paddle together when we'll be separated for so long."

"Good," agreed Renny, "I'd like that. As for Father, he'd never have said such a thing if he hadn't been driven to it by Gran."

"But," exclaimed Maurice, "why are they making all this fuss now? I don't understand."

"You don't understand because you don't know everything. You don't know that I went to see Elvira and Lulu. That was what got the wind up."

Maurice stopped in the road and faced him. His grey eyes were sombre in his dark pale face.

"You too," he said heavily. "You went there! Good Lord! What made you do it?"

Renny flashed him a challenging look.

"I wanted to see Lulu again."

"Lulu!" Maurice echoed the name in mingled relief and consternation. "Lulu!" Why — why on earth — well, I can't believe that you were attracted by her."

"Why not?"

"Well, she's years and years older than you are, for one thing. And she's rather an ugly looking woman."

Renny began to walk quickly along the road. He muttered — "To my mind she's a beautiful woman."

Maurice overtook him and gave a high, embarrassed laugh. "Well — if you think so — but I don't see what you could have found to say to her. She made me uncomfortable."

"You didn't understand her," said Renny gruffly.

"Upon my word, I'm surprised that you did. I shouldn't fancy her your style at all. But perhaps it just means that you have more discrimination than I have."

"She's wonderful."

A silence fell between them as they padded, in their light canvas shoes, over the warm earth. They turned into a narrow winding path and, in a moment, the lake lay before them and the deserted white sickle of the shore. The lake was rippled like blue silk and level cloud shapes barred the horizon. They were a nameless colour, neither blue nor rose, nor gold, but a mingling of all three.

The two boys slid the canoe across the sand and sprang into it, Maurice pushing off with his paddle. In three strokes they had entered into a new world, a liquid translucent world freed from the troubling bonds of the land. They had taken off their jerseys, and their smooth torsos, as they bent above their paddles, were bronzed by the afterglow. The rhythmic movement of their arms, the crystal drip of water from their paddles, gave them peace. They saw the events of the past weeks in a calmer light. As they moved farther and farther from shore they became detached from themselves, and each looked into his own mind as into a still well.

"You say," said Maurice, at last, "that she is wonderful. Does that mean that she has let you love her?"

"Yes."

"Were you long at the farm?"

"I stayed there one night."

Maurice looked at his friend's back, watched its muscles moving against the shapely bones, watched the proud way he held his head and how his ears lay against it.

"I don't believe I've ever understood you, Renny," he said.

"There's nothing in me to understand — except as you might understand the colt."

"Well — I guess he's not easy to understand." It was a relief to speak of the colt. "But I'm glad you're to have him. Shall you school him for the Show?"

"Yes. I don't know what I can make of him, any more than my father knows what he can make of me."

"I'm terribly sorry that I led you into this," said Maurice. "It was all my fault."

"I didn't need any leading. I should have found my way."

Maurice had a moment's chagrin. He had felt superior to Renny as an experienced man to a boy. Now Renny seemed to have advanced beyond him. His affair with Elvira seemed immature and trifling. He said: —

"Will you tell me something about Lulu? What is she like to talk to? She always seemed to be laughing at me."

"Oh, I can't remember anything she said!" He began to paddle strongly. The canoe moved swiftly forward. The clouds at the horizon had merged into a great conflagration of colour that engulfed sky and lake.

XVI

An Exchange of Presents

IT WAS LATE when Renny went to his room. He found on his dressing table a pair of ivory hair brushes and beside them a card bearing the words — "A token of affection from Cousin Malahide." He looked at the brushes and the card, not believing his eyes. He turned back to the door, then again came to the dressing table and reread the message.

"The dirty dog!" he ejaculated. "As though I'd have his brushes!"

He took one in either hand and examined them. Handsome ones, certainly. He had admired them in Malahide's room when first he came. But to have them given to him as a token of his affection, at a time like this! He began vigorously to brush his hair with them. Back from his forehead and temples, up from his ears, down to his nape. Good brushes — excellent brushes — he should like to take them to Cousin Malahide's room and give him a whacking with them.

Instead he took them to his sister's door.

"Meg," he whispered, tapping, "may I come in?"

Her light was still burning. Her voice came heavy with drowsiness. "Come in. I was just going to put out my light."

He closed the door behind him and came and sat on the side of her bed.

"Look," he said, holding out a brush in each hand, "what Malahide has given me! He left them on my dressing table — 'as a token of affection'! What do you think of that? What the devil shall I do to him?"

Meg examined the brushes. "I'd certainly keep them," she said.

She looked charming sitting up in her frilled nightdress with its long sleeves and high neck, above which her girl's face blossomed and her tendrils of bright brown hair shone in the lamplight.

"Keep them!" he repeated, fiercely. "Keep them! What I want to think up is the most insulting way of returning them."

"Well, after all," she said, "he ought to give you a present. He knows he has been horrid to you and he is trying to make up for it. Besides, Granny has been giving him presents, so it is only fair he should return the compliment."

"What a mind you have!" he exclaimed peevishly.

"I have a logical mind," she returned, "which you have not and never will have."

He gave her a long, searching look, trying to read her, trying to understand this being, so close to him, of the very flesh of which he was made, yet uncomprehendable as a book in a foreign tongue.

He gave up the effort and said — "What I am afraid of is that he will not leave when Auntie and Uncle Edwin do. If he doesn't, God knows when we shall be rid of him. He may stay till Christmas — all the winter!"

"Oh no," cried Meg, "that would be too horrible! We must make it so unpleasant for him here that he will be glad to go!"

"When are they leaving?"

"In a fortnight. They're seeing about tickets tomorrow."

"Meggie, can you think of anything we might do to get even with him for what he's done to me? Something so insulting that he'll be bound to go, after it?"

"Let me think," she said, and covered her face with her hands.

There was silence while she sat with bowed head and he gazed hopefully at her. The grandfather clock in the hall struck its twelve sonorous tones.

"You're not going to sleep, are you?" he asked.

She uncovered her face and turned it reproachfully on him.

"Do you imagine," she said, "that a plan to get rid of such a bundle of black iniquity can be thought of in a second?"

"I suppose not. But have you got an idea?"

"Yes…. But it will all depend on how well we can do it. Supposing we write an insulting verse to him and teach it to Eden and have Eden recite it in front of everyone."

He was disappointed at the suggestion. It lacked the violence he desired, but he said, encouragingly: —

"That's a good idea. But you'll have to write it. I'm no good at that sort of thing."

"We'll write it together!" Her face brightened with a mischievous light he had not seen there for a long while. He grinned in response.

"How shall we begin?" he asked.

"We'll begin with the vocative. I'll do the first line….

"O Malahide —"

Now you go on."

"I can't abide,"

he added at once.

"Good!" she exclaimed.

He knit his brows. "I can't think of anything else."

"Of course you can! You must."

He proceeded, with a scowl: —

"The way you've spied —
The way you've lied —"

Meg carried on triumphantly: —

"You are a snide!"

Renny uttered a snort of delight. "Go on, go on," he implored, "while you're in the vein!"

With an exalted expression she concluded: —

> "I wish you'd died
> In Ballyside —
> O Malahide!"

Renny's lips were stretched in a grin of approval.

"Now let me say it over from the beginning." But she could not repeat it for laughing. She buried her face in her bolster and he laid her pillow on her head to smother the sound of her mirth. "What a one you are for laughing!" he said, but he was pleased with her.

A bat flew in at the window and began its naked, black dance, soft and punctual, up and down the room.

Meg sat up and stared at it from the ambush of her sheet.

"Oh, put it out! Oh, kill it!" she said in an anguished whisper. "If it gets into my hair it must be cut off!"

Renny caught up a towel, folded it into a weapon, and tiptoed, lean and silent, after the bat. It flitted always where he was not, like the spirit of opportunity, the answer to desire.

"Ha, I've got you!" he said, again and again, but when he raised his weapon the bat was pirouetting with its shadow against the ceiling.

"Oh, mind the lamp!" she cried, as the flapping towel snatched the air from the glass and the flame sank and the smoke poured up through the lamp chimney. But the lamp did not go out. The flame rose again to show her Renny triumphant, holding the bat in a little nest in the towel.

"Want to see it?" he asked.

"No, no," she answered, shrinking, but in spite of herself had to peer fearfully at it nipped between his finger and thumb. From out of the towel its evil face peered back at her. Its body swelled with spite.

"It's a return gift," said Renny, "for Cousin Malahide."

With the hair brushes in one hand and the bat concealed in the towel, he stole from the room and rapped softly on Malahide's door.

It opened, and Malahide appeared clad in a black silk dressing gown, open to the waist. His neck, without the high collar, was smooth as ivory. On his breast was a patch of glossy black hair.

"Cousin Renny!" he exclaimed. "I'm so glad to see you! Come in! Did you like my present?"

"So well," said Renny, with a bitter grin, "that I've brought you one in return!"

He stepped into the room, laid the brushes on the dressing table, and, with a bold gesture, released the bat. It danced from its captivity, ugly as fate, and circled above their heads.

Renny slid swiftly out of the room and closed the door behind him.

XVII

Recitation

Eden was captured the next day by Renny and led to Meg's room. He had been told that he was to share a secret with them, and his back was stiff with pride. He stood looking expectantly from one face to the other, at Meg settled in her chintz-covered chair, and at Renny lighting a cigarette as he lounged on the wide window sill.

"Now," said Renny, "you know that Cousin Malahide is going away. Meggie and I have decided that it will be nice for you to recite something for him — a sort of goodbye verse in front of all the family. So we've brought you up here to teach it to you."

Eden looked blank. "Is that all? I thought there was a secret."

Meg took his hand in hers. "It is a secret. No one is to know anything about it but us three. Renny and I have made up the verse, but we're too old to recite it, and you recite so beautifully."

Eden was unimpressed. He said, "I don't want to."

Renny and Meg exchanged glances. This lack of enthusiasm on the part of their speaker would never do. Renny said: —

"Now, look here, if you recite this piece properly I'll tell you what I'll do. I will take you for a glorious ride on my colt. He's perfectly safe now, but you mustn't say anything about it. The whole thing is a profound secret."

"All right," said Eden at once. "How soon will you take me on Gallant?" The colt had been so named by a combination of his dam's name, Saucy Gal, and his sire's, Duke of Brabant.

"As soon as you have said the piece," returned Renny, "and we've escaped with our lives."

"Sh," warned Meg.

Eden had a good memory. In a quarter of an hour he could recite the doggerel accurately.

Two days passed before the propitious moment came. Remembering the promised ride, Eden kept the secret. The Laceys and Mr. Fennel had come to tea, and a game of backgammon and two tables of whist had been arranged.

Admiral Lacey and Adeline were seated at the backgammon board in the middle of the room. The Admiral, a man of just over seventy and of a build so solid and a countenance so red that he looked a formidable opponent, faced her with friendly truculence. His wife, short, stout, and pink-faced, sat at a table of whist with Sir Edwin as her partner, and Augusta and Philip as opponents. At another table the two Miss Laceys, who were in their late forties and had fluffy hair turning grey and complexions like young girls, were engaged at play with Nicholas and Ernest. There had been a time when they had hoped very much to be engaged with them in the business of life, but the brothers had spent much of their time in London and had there met women more congenial to them, as they had thought, and certainly less restricted in their outlook. Now Nicholas, looking into Violet Lacey's blue eyes, wondered if he would not have done well to marry her. On her part she still cared for him, but about his head glimmered a sinister halo of divorce. She doubted if she could face that. Still, the sight of his large handsome hands shuffling the cards moved her strangely. Her sister Ethel and Ernest kept up a flow of badinage of the sort fashionable in the nineties. At a third table Mary, Malahide, and Vera Lacey watched Mr. Fennel do a card trick prior to a game of bridge.

After a period of great heat there had been an electrical storm and the air was now unseasonably cool, so that the snapping of the wood fire was agreeable to the human occupants of the room, though not to Keno, the spaniel, who wished to lie on the rug in front of it, or to Boney, who eyed the blaze askance from his perch, at the same time keeping the eye next the company closed, as though in distaste for their frivolity.

Renny had not appeared for tea. Now he came in and went straight to Mary with an air of unusual deference.

"I'm sorry I'm late, Mother. I had to go to town and I got caught in the rain and was wet through. I've been changing."

Mary, always ready to be friendly with her stepchildren, smiled at him. Meg appeared in the doorway with Eden by the hand. She had not yet quite resumed her place in the family. Now her coming was greeted by sympathetic smiles. She said sedately, after speaking to the guests: —

"Eden has come to say goodnight. Hurry up, dear, and get it over with."

"But," said the little boy excitedly, "I want to say my piece first."

"What piece?" asked his father.

"My goodbye poem for Cousin Malahide."

"A goodbye poem," repeated Malahide. "That's rather premature, isn't it?"

"But I must say it!" insisted Eden. He placed himself in front of Malahide Court and recited in a clear treble: —

> "O Malahide!
> I can't abide
> They way you've spied,
> The way you've lied.
> You are a snide —
> I wish you'd died
> In Ballyside,
> O Malahide!"

No one had initiative to stop him, while the subject of the poem, turning a sickly yellow, cast a look of bitter chagrin at Adeline.

She was the first to speak.

"Come here," she said to the child.

Feeling important and pleased with himself, he marched to her side. She took his chin in her hand and started into his eyes.

"Who taught you that?" she demanded.

Well schooled, he returned — "I made it up."

"A likely story! Made it up! I say — who taught you that verse?" She emphasized the last five words with five successive raps on the table.

Eden's face quivered, but he persisted. "I made it up myself."

"Please don't mind," said Malahide.

"I *will* mind! I'll get to the bottom of this!"

"Plenty of time later," said Philip, very red in the face.

"Yes, yes," agreed Admiral Lacey, "let us go on with the game, Mrs. Whiteoak."

"I will not have my kinsman insulted and let it pass!"

"I'm sure," said Mrs. Lacey soothingly, "that none of us understood it, in the least."

Adeline turned her head from one to another of the assembly. "Is there anyone here," she demanded, "who is so *imbecile* so not to understand the meaning of that recitation?"

Both the Miss Laceys chimed in together — "I didn't understand a word of it! Really I didn't!"

"Childish nonsense," said the Admiral.

"Childish devilment," declared Adeline. "I'll get to the bottom of it. I won't have Malahide insulted." An ominous colour suffused her face.

Nicholas sat tugging at his grey moustache. Ernest and Ethel Lacey dared not look into each other's eyes. He pressed her foot under the table. Augusta boomed: —

"The child is the mouthpiece of others."

"Quite so," agreed Sir Edwin.

"Mouthpiece or not," said Adeline, "I'll have it out of him!"

Eden wriggled his chin out of her hand and fled to his mother.

"I did make it up," he insisted proudly. "Every word of it. Shall I say it again?"

"Yes," said his grandmother, "I want to hear it again."

Mr. Fennel had, with admirable coolness, worked at his card trick all this while. Malahide kept his eyes on the cards as though his life depended on the working out of the trick. Meg, seated on the piano stool, was as impassive as the Dresden-china shepherdess on the mantelpiece. Not so Renny. An uncontrollable grin stretched his features. He was standing beside the parrot's perch and, half in nervousness, half in malice, tweaked a feather from its tail.

With a torrent of curses in Hindoo it spread its wings and flew to the backgammon board, scattering the neatly placed men in all directions.

Adeline stretched out a long arm and pulled Eden from his mother's lap.

"Now," she commanded, "say your piece again, child!"

"Mamma —" began Augusta.

"Hold your tongue, Augusta," said her mother.

"Steady on, Mamma," growled Nicholas. "We can have that later."

"Yes," said Violet Lacey, "we'd love to hear it later on, dear Mrs. Whiteoak."

"No need to wait. I remember the first line myself: 'O Malahide —' Now go on, Eden." She had soothed the parrot and he sat preening himself on her shoulder.

Eden, with more than a hint of mischief on his face, declaimed: —

> "O Malahide!
> I can't abide
> They way you've spied,
> The way you've lied.
> You are a snide...."

Uncontrolled laughter broke from Nicholas and Ernest. Renny, with a sudden flourish of his hand toward Malahide, concluded, in a derisive tone: —

> "I wish you'd died
> In Ballyside,
> O Malahide!"

Philip said — "Renny, take Eden away. I'll see to him later."

Renny shouldered the small boy and glided out of the room.

"Somebody bring Malahide a drink," ordered Adeline. "He looks queasy."

Ernest got up with alacrity.

"Could I have a drop of something too?" asked the Admiral.

"We'll all have something," said Nicholas.

Malahide was restored somewhat by the sherry. The greenish shade left his skin and it resumed its normal ivory tint. He gathered his forces and smiled wanly at Adeline. Her choleric colour had faded and she was now enjoying herself. She leant forward and started sympathetically at Malahide.

"I was never so ashamed," she said. "As I've heard the peasants in Ireland say — 'You might light a candle from the same in me eye.' But, never fear, Malahide, our young man will smart for this. I know well that its root lay in him and I'll not bear that he should intimidate any guest of mine."

"Well, after all," said Mary, in impulsive defence of her stepson, "it's only natural that Renny should retaliate."

Philip beamed at her.

"I don't understand," said Mrs. Lacey inquisitively.

"It is better left unexplained," said Augusta.

"We'll have him flogged," said Adeline. "You must lay your stick about him, Philip."

"Impossible!" said Philip. "I must just ask Cousin Malahide to forgive him, if he can."

Malahide raised his head. "I have already done that, Philip. But what I shall never forget is the superb manner with which the little boy spoke his lines — unsettling as they were to me. His poise is perfect."

"Ay, he's a clever young rascal," said Adeline.

Mary was delighted by Malahide's praise of her child.

"He is really amazing," she said eagerly. "The things he says! You'd hardly believe."

"He's too precocious," said Philip, yet pleased, in spite of himself.

The Admiral said — "Now, when I was his age, I used to stand up in front of a roomful of people and recite, 'My Name is Norval,' at the top of my lungs."

The men were replaced on the backgammon board; the cards dealt. Boney uttered sounds of content and Keno scratched the hearth rug into a more agreeable disposition for his fire-baked body. Another rainstorm dashed against the pane, and the roof spread itself hospitably over all beneath it.

XVIII

GARDEN PARTY

THE RESULT OF this disturbance was to divide the family into two parties. One was for Malahide's remaining there, the other against it. On
the one side were the Buckleys, who very much preferred leaving him
at Jalna, for they feared that, if he returned with them to England, he
might settle down in their house for the winter. A business affair of
Ernest's was important enough, in his eyes at any rate, to recall him to
London, and he was leaving with his sister and brother-in-law. Nicholas,
who was remaining, looked on Malahide as rather an amusing addition
to the family party, and a unique companion for Adeline. He enjoyed
hearing them talk together. Adeline herself, having cast her protective
power over Malahide, would not lightly withdraw it, and the fact that
she wanted him to stay made opposition to this infuriating to her. On
the other side were ranged Philip, Mary, Meg, and Renny, a solid family
within the family, the two younger members of which were ruthless in
their determination to oust the intruder.

No coldness or indifference on their part had any effect on Malahide,
neither could Philip be brought to the point of telling him directly to get
out. Philip strolled about with his dogs at his heels or fished or oversaw
his stables or farm, tolerant and good-humoured toward both parties,
but not to be driven by either of them into a definite step.

It was decided that some sort of entertainment should be given as a send-off for the Buckleys, and also to show that the family was not subdued by the breaking of Meg's engagement to Maurice. Meg was to appear in public self-contained, and in appearance, heart-whole.

Augusta chose a garden party as the form of entertainment most pleasing to her. Heavy rains had made the lawns and borders green and luxuriant. The house, inside and out, was looking its best, the whole an ideal setting for a large gathering.

The family was heart and soul in preparation for the fête. Mary saw to the putting in perfect order of the house. The windows were polished, the mahogany and walnut of the furniture brought to a satin shine. She and Ernest conferred over the arrangement of flowers, choosing pink and crimson roses and pink carnations for the drawing room, yellow and cream dahlias for the dining room and library, while tall delphiniums and variegated phlox ornamented the striped marquee erected on the lawn. The rest of the family were more interested in the arrangements for refreshments, both solid and liquid, and the band which was to be stationed behind the shrubbery.

The state of the weather caused some anxiety, for it showed itself capricious during all the week preceding the party and, on the very morning, sparkled and showered alternately. But at noon the sun came out hotly, the lawn was dried, and the scene looked all the gayer for the washing.

It had been difficult for Meg to choose which dress of her trousseau she would wear. Each one had been so carefully considered as a part of her wedding trip. She would have preferred to buy a new dress for this occasion, but Philip would not hear of it. He had been put to too much unnecessary expense as it was.

She stood irresolute between a pink-flowered organdie and a pale green tulle when she heard Renny passing her door. She called him in.

"Which shall I wear?" she asked, her lips trembling as she put the question, for, at the moment, she felt that she could not bear to face all those people.

He looked dubiously at the dresses spread on the bed.

She said — "Mother says the pale green will look more elegant, but Vera is for the pink. She thinks I'll feel more confident in it."

"Put on the pink," he said, at once. "You'll feel more cheerful. It's just like Mother to choose green."

"All right. But really Mother is being quite agreeable, considering that she isn't getting me off her hands, as I suppose she's been hoping to all this while."

"H'm." He put his arm around her. "Well, never mind, Meggie. I wasn't wanting to get you off my hands, at any rate."

She pressed her face against his shoulder. How comforting to have such a brother, she thought.

He said suddenly — "Look here, Meggie, we haven't done a thing to Malahide this week!"

"Not since I put salt instead of sugar in his tea. And he drank it without a word."

He dismissed such schoolgirl tricks with a shrug.

"I wish," he said, "that we could think of something really devastating to do today."

"I wish we could," she said wistfully. "Perhaps Mother could think of something. She hates the thought of his staying on as much as we do. She's as sick as mud about it."

"We can manage without her. Still, if she is on our side, so much the better."

He stood, holding his chin in his hand, buried in thought, and showing as strong a likeness to his grandmother as is possible between a stripling and an old woman. Suddenly he raised his head abruptly and exclaimed: —

"I have it! What do you think of this?"

He poured out his plan, in which she acquiesced with the abandon of one seeking distraction from melancholy.

Their plan was just completed and Meg was breathless with her tremulous laughter when the door opened softly and Eden's golden head was intruded.

"Oh, hullo," he said ingratiatingly, "may I come in?"

"Yes," said Meg, "and shut the door after you."

He came to Renny and asked — "I want the ride on Gallant. You've never taken me and you promised if I said the piece!"

"Well, Mother said your nerves were upset. Why have you nerves like that?"

"They were upset because I wanted to go and you wouldn't take me." He looked up accusingly at Renny.

"I'll take you today. Before the garden party." He turned to Meg. "It will be well for me to be out of the way, in case questions are asked."

At three o'clock all was astir in the house for the final preparations. In their bedrooms Adeline, Augusta, Mary, and Meg dressed themselves with unusual care, Adeline trying on five different caps before she found one to suit her. Sir Edwin had reached the stage of knowing that he must have help from Augusta or he would never get his collar and cravat fastened properly, when an agitated rap sounded on the door. He opened it a little way and discovered Malahide, who said anxiously: —

"What do you suppose, Edwin! I can't get into my room! I've got Eliza to help me and she can't open the door either."

"Did you lock it when you left?"

"Now can you imagine my doing such a thing? No — this is a trick! I have been purposely locked out of my room."

Sir Edwin was worried and could not help feeling annoyed with Malahide. Augusta spoke from the corner, where she had taken refuge.

"You must get a ladder."

"Couldn't the lock be taken off?" asked Sir Edwin.

"The locks of Jalna," she returned, "are not made to be taken on and off. Malahide will have to enter his room by the window."

"Perhaps we had better see Philip about it."

"Philip has just this moment come up to dress. Mary had to go to the stables herself to fetch him. If he is disturbed now, he will never be ready to receive his guests." Augusta too felt an unreasonable annoyance with Malahide.

He wavered disconsolately in the passage, twice bending his eye to the keyhole of his room as though by sheer force of will he would project himself through it. From all the bedrooms about him came the sound of splashing water and eager steps.

A quarter of an hour later servants and the hired waiters from town stopped in their journeys between house and pavilion to watch Malahide

Court's long form ascending a ladder to his window while red-faced young Hodge steadied it below.

Almost immediately he descended the ladder and looked despairingly into the face of Hodge. "My clothes are not there," he said, "Nothing that I own is there. They have taken them away."

Hodge looked at him with mingled scorn and pity. Secure in his own Sunday garments, he could offer no suggestion.

Eliza was passing with a tray of wineglasses and Malahide appealed to her. "What had I better do, Eliza? They have taken my clothes away."

Eliza well knew whom he meant by *they*. She said: —

"Well, sir, you are about Mr. Ernest's height. Perhaps he might lend you some things."

Malahide jumped at this suggestion. He hastened into the house and to Ernest's room. Ernest appeared, in answer to the knock, fully dressed even to the carnation in his buttonhole. He listened sympathetically.

"I'm very sorry for this, Malahide. Mamma will be much upset, too. Come in and I will see what I can do for you."

Ernest had an excellent wardrobe. He soon provided Malahide with all that was necessary, though a perfect fit he could not provide, being himself less narrow in the shoulder and less long in leg and arm. Still Malahide was presentable and was ready to descend the stairs at the same time as Philip and Mary. He decided to say nothing to them of the incident, but to allow Ernest to inform them of it when he thought best.

Philip cast him a glance of amusement and whispered to Mary: —

"By the Lord Harry! What a fit! He looks more than ever like a tadpole!"

Mary scarcely heard what he said. She was worried by the disappearance of Eden just when he should have been dressed. "I *can't* think where he is," she said anxiously. "He was playing about after lunch, the servants say, and he was warned to not go away. But when Katie was ready to dress him he could not be found. It is very worrying. First you — and now Eden. I really have had enough to do without that."

Philip hunched his shoulders. "Don't worry, darling. The first guests are arriving. The Laceys, of course. And there are Mrs. Vaughan and Robert. Poor old boy, he looks very ill!"

In the brilliant sunshine the guests, in summer attire, poured on to
the lawn as from a cornucopia of gayety and colour. The band played
as husband and wife, with Adeline on one side and the Buckleys and
Malahide on the other, received their guests. Meg, looking charming in the pink organdie, assisted by Vera and Nicholas and Ernest,
helped to make things go smoothly and found it easier than she had
expected, though she dared not look in the direction of Malahide and
she concealed a real anxiety for Renny and Eden. What might not the
colt have done!

The baby, Piers, in a white dress and blue sash, toddled sturdily
among the guests, pressing his way between the legs of gentlemen who
held cups of hot coffee in their hands or reaching toward the trays of
pink ices which invited him. He ignored the pats and kisses that were
lavished on his downy head.

Eden had been told by Renny to watch for his going in the direction of the stables. He was then to run, not after him, but to the bridle
path which led through the wood, where they were to meet for the ride.
Eagerly Eden watched for the figure of his brother and, when he perceived him lounging across the croquet lawn, he set out as fast as he could.

His heart was still beating quickly when Renny, mounted on Gallant, rode up. The next moment he was perched on the colt's back with a
strong arm encircling him. It was glorious.

Along the velvet path they cantered, the dark green wood on either
side. They passed a field of yellow wheat set in the wood, then a rabbit fled out of their path and the colt danced in pretended fright. They
circled the field in pursuit of the rabbit.

Eden laughed delightedly. "I like it! I like it! Oh, I'm glad I said the
piece! Renny, will you take me for lots of rides on Gallant?"

"We'll see." He held the small body close. Nice little fellow.... He would
take care of him always ... him and Piers ... better to have small brothers
like this than chaps of one's own age one would be sure to quarrel with.

Eden wanted to ride out on the road, but Renny refused that. If there
were any mishap, he would never hear the end of it. Besides, it was time
they went back to dress. Three times they had cantered the length of the
bridle path. He wheeled the colt and turned his head in the direction of

the stables. He glanced at his watch and was alarmed to find that it had stopped. It was his first wrist watch, brought to him from London by his uncles, and it was not behaving well. Good Lord, he thought, we shall be late for the party and I shall catch it!

He gave the colt a slap and they sped toward the stables. Then he remembered that he must set Eden down before they were seen. He had just drawn the bridle when a motor car, driven by one of the guests, appeared, panting along the drive. A pair of carriage horses just come to a stand before the stable pranced and backed from the approaching car. Another latecomer drove up in a dogcart, and his horse, a rangy black mare, broke into a gallop and came toward the colt. The band struck up a lively march.

Renny could not put Eden down in such a position. The colt reared and stood on his hind legs. The motorist, new at driving, accelerated and crashed into the palings of the paddock. In a moment a mare and her twin foals had escaped from it and were careering, with squeals of delight, in the direction of the marquee. The carriage horses continued to prance and back till the rear of the carriage was locked in the motor car.

The colt, uttering a clarion whinny, galloped thunderously after the mare and foals. All four, like an advancing storm, bore down on the garden party.

"Look out, look out!" shouted Philip to his guests, and ran towards the colt's head.

Nicholas and Ernest hastened to protect their mother. Augusta snatched up the baby, who screamed and kicked her. Ladies, in wide flounced skirts and enormous Merry Widow hats, darted about the lawn like frightened tropic birds. One dropped a frilled pink sunshade, which rolled over and over toward the colt. He leaped aside, evading Philip's outstretched hand, and plunged in the direction of a table laden with cakes and ices. The mare and her foals, as though executing a spirited folk dance, pranced with loud whickerings among the guests. The bandsmen, unconscious, behind their screen of shrubbery, of the disturbance on the lawn, burst into still livelier music.

"Save Eden!" screamed Mary, wringing her hands. "Oh, Philip, save my child!"

Eden, excited to the point of exaltation, tried to find something on the colt's neck to grasp, but its mane had been lately hogged and his fingers encountered only the slippery hard hide. It reared again, stood upright like a grand grey statue, then bucked twice, the second time throwing both riders into the middle of the table. It wheeled then, galloped along the drive, knocking over a gentleman in immaculate pearl grey, and sped through the gate on to the road. The mare and her foals ceased executing their folk dance and followed him.

Renny picked himself up and looked to see whether Eden were hurt. Mary had him in her arms frantically examining a scratch on his cheek.

"I'm all right, Mamma," he cried. "It was a splendid ride!"

Mary turned her white face to Renny. "You might have been the cause of his death," she said.

"Where his headlong ways will lead him, God only knows," said Augusta.

Everyone crowded about them. The guests commiserating, the family blaming. Renny received both with a hangdog air, alternately wiping the blood from a cut on his forehead and the ice cream from the front of his jersey.

By degrees a certain feverish order was restored. Stablemen were dispatched by Philip to seek the horses. The wreckage of the refreshment table was gathered up. Malahide Court made himself useful in calming the ladies, and Adeline treated the whole matter with a fierce kind of humour. It was an escapade after her own heart.

"The whelp is always into mischief," she said, grinning amiably. "There is scarcely a day of our lives but what he puts us to shame." But she bridled with pride in him.

There had been so much excitement that no one had noticed the change in the weather. The sky, which had been all too brilliant, was now overcast. A few large drops struck the roof of the marquee. A wind whispered and moaned beneath the music of the band. Then rain began to fall in a sharp shower.

There was no time to get to the house. The guests crowded beneath the spreading branches of the trees. They looked curiously at a cart drawn by a sorry-looking nag, all bones and tangled mane, the like of which had never before been seen at Jalna. A shock-headed boy was perched on the seat. He drew up and sat in the rain in front of the guests.

Philip's blue eyes became prominent as he looked at this monstrosity. He waved a peremptory hand to the boy, who slouched on the seat gazing at the horse's ears, apparently in a trance.

The shower stopped and the gathering crowd moved with inquisitive accord in the direction of the cart.

They had already seen that it was heaped with luggage. Now they saw that the trunk, the suitcases and bags, each bore a bright steamship label on which was written in clear lettering: "Malahide Court — Ballyside Hall — County Meath — Ireland." All eyes turned inquiringly to Malahide. He stood in his short-sleeved, short-legged suit, in a collar somewhat too large, looking the picture of chagrin.

"Excess luggage!" he exclaimed, to Ethel Lacey.

"And so you are leaving too," she said. "I had not known it."

"Nor I. Indeed this apparition is all spite. Philip and Molly would be devastated if I were to go so soon."

Philip cast his eyes over the poor old mare which drew the cart. He said to Renny: —

"How did you come by this nag?"

"I bought her from a rag picker."

Philip made a wry face. "And now I have the pleasure of shooting and burying her." He turned sternly to his son. "Get up on the seat and drive to the stable and tell Hodge to have her put away. When you've done that, make yourself presentable and apologize to our guests for the disturbance you've created."

If he had thought to humiliate Renny he was disappointed. His son jumped to the seat of the cart and took the reins blithely. But the poor old horse from sheer weakness refused to move, and stood with gaunt legs straddled and bony head drooping. Its great nostrils were stretched in misery, and suffering had given it human eyes of despair.

Eden had been taken into the house. Champagne corks were being drawn, for a health was to be drunk to the voyagers. The sun burned brightly between rotund white clouds. The band played airs from *Floradora*. There was no sign left of the unhappy incident save the loaded cart before the house, and from it the guests determinedly kept their eyes averted.

Ernest came to Philip and said irritably: —

"You must get that dreadful sight removed. It's appalling. It makes the house look like an Irish peasant's shanty. Have you no authority over that boy?"

"Good God, I ordered him away long ago!"

"He is still here. It's disgraceful!"

Philip strode across the lawn to Renny, who still drooped on the seat of the cart, beside the feeble-minded stableboy, with an air of meek submission.

"You young ruffian!" exclaimed Philip. "Why the hell don't you do what I tell you to?"

"She won't budge," returned Renny.

"H'm." He gazed angrily at his son, then said — "Give her a touch of the whip."

Renny struck the protruding ribs a sharp blow. But the mare, instead of responding, made as if to lie down on the gravel. Philip rushed to her and held her up.

"Whatever shall we do?" he asked helplessly.

His mother, leaning strongly on her stick, hurried to his side.

"Have ye no gumption at all?" she demanded. "Unload the cart and give it a push from behind."

"Good!" said Philip. "That's the idea!"

Eliza came to his side and they began to lift off the smaller pieces. Two young men heaved off the trunk.

While this was being accomplished Adeline had a sugar basin brought to her and, laying several lumps on her palm, held it out to the mare.

It pointed its loose lips suspiciously, blew, and then, as in a dream, took the sugar from her hand.

"Now," said Philip, slapping his hands together. "Away with you!"

But the mare would not willingly lose sight of her benefactress. When Renny chirruped and touched her with the whip, instead of moving along the drive she placed her uncared-for hoofs on the soft turf and followed Adeline on to the lawn.

"Back, back," shouted Philip. "Back the brute, Renny!"

But Renny seemed incapable of controlling the mare, and Adeline, not ill-pleased, marched toward her guests thus attended.

It was with difficulty that the mare's course was diverted, and during the rest of the garden party, which everyone conceded had been delightful, Malahide Court's luggage remained in a melancholy mound at the front of the house.

XIX

A Variety of Scenes

That night, heavy with midsummer and lighted by a sultry moon, found Meg and Renny walking along a half-hidden way that led from the bridle path through the wood to a rough open space at the back of the estate. Trees had been felled here and their trunks, not yet removed, were being covered by brambles and wild grapevines. A few wild apple trees showed their imperfect yellow fruit, and dark groups of sumac thrust up their tawny red spikes. Goldenrod was coming into flower, and the first pale stars of the wild aster, while the bergamot scented the air with its pungent sweetness.

Renny put his arm about his sister's waist and said: —

"She ought to be about here somewhere. I gave her a grand feed of oats and turned her loose." He peered anxiously about.

"All the family think she is underground by now," said Meg.

"And so she should be," he returned, "but I hadn't the heart."

"But she's such a terrible looking creature, Renny."

"I know — but I hadn't the heart. Ah, there she is!"

From behind a group of sumac a mare ambled toward them, a long wisp of grass hanging from her mouth. Her belly, depending from her sunken back, bulged with her good feed. She stood in front of them meekly, her suffering eyes looking resignedly into theirs.

Renny grasped her head and opened her mouth. "Look there, Meggie, she has her teeth! She can eat. It would be cruel to take her life." He released her and she continued humbly to munch the wisp of grass.

"I know. But you can't keep her hidden here for long, and when she is discovered, I don't know what the family will say. I should think you would feel yourself in trouble enough with the colt lost and all. Where did they find the mare and her foals?"

"In a wheat field. They'd trampled it a good deal. I expect Father will have to pay for it."

Meg made a little sound of concern, then said — "But you did look nice, in spite of your cut face, when you had got into your white flannels. Everyone said so. Everyone thought the affair of Malahide's luggage was a huge joke. But nothing can drive him away. I'm quite hopeless. We shall have to endure him. Relatives seem to think they can stay forever at Jalna."

"Well, he can't! Mark my words, we'll be rid of him before I go back to college!"

Meg looked at him admiringly, but her eyes were troubled. "I don't know what Father will say if anything more happens. He was really angry this afternoon, for him. As for Granny, she has taken Malahide completely under her wing."

"Don't worry, Meggie. Everything will be all right. Scotchmere and I are setting out tomorrow to search for the colt."

But it wasn't necessary to search for Gallant. The next morning, just as Philip appeared with his fishing rod and basket, and Keno at his heels, a shabby buggy turned into the drive. It was driven by Elvira's cousin Bob, and seated beside him was Lulu leading the colt by a rope halter.

As they advanced Philip surveyed them with a doubtful welcome in his eyes.

"So," he said, "you've found my colt."

"Yes," answered Bob, getting out of the buggy. "I saw him wandering about and I asked the neighbours if they knew where he belonged, and they said here. I can tell you, mister, he's a tough one to handle. He all but chawed the head off me when I took him in."

The colt rolled back his eyes and yawned in unconcern.

Philip's eyes were on Lulu. An extraordinary looking woman, he thought, to be in company with this fellow. She returned his look with interest.

Philip turned to Bob. "Did you say you found him on the road?"

"Well — he was sort of hanging around. He'd come in my lane."

Philip laid down his rod and basket and, taking out a leather pocket-book, extracted from it a five dollar note and handed it to Bob.

He mumbled his thanks, and as the spaniel approached the colt it lifted a hoof to strike.

"Whoa, now, whoa," said Lulu soothingly. She shortened the halter and put her hand on the colt's head.

"You're evidently not afraid of him," observed Philip.

"I understand animals," she answered, and her eyes met his. He remembered what Renny had said about Lulu's strange eyes and he thought — "So ... this is she! And she's taken the opportunity to come and see her young man."

At this moment Renny came out of the house to go in search of the colt. He looked tall and rather sombre. He had never known what it was to be awkward or hobbledehoy. Now his face closed on the secret he and Lulu had between them. His brown eyes turned warily toward his father. He waited for him to speak.

"I think," said Philip, "that these two are friends of yours. I expect you'll like to thank them for bringing back your colt. He had returned to the farm." He looked squarely at Lulu.

The colour rushed into her face, but she gave a loud reckless laugh. She got down from the buggy and came toward him with the halter on her arm.

"No, no," he said, "give it to my son. He's responsible for it." He threw Renny a shrewd glance.

Renny ran down the steps and took the halter. The colt drew a great breath and blew it out in exaggerated relief to be home again. It moved its chiselled head up and down between the woman and boy as though conjuring them to some fresh adventure.

Young Hodge, driving a dogcart in which he was to take Philip and Nicholas some distance for fishing, now swung round the curve of the drive. Nicholas came out of the house, bearing his rod and limping.

"On time, for once, eh?" said Philip, smiling.

Nicholas grunted. "I was slow in dressing. I've had rather a nasty pain in my knee at times lately. It caught me this morning in a devilish fashion."

"Gout," declared Philip, clambering into the dogcart and taking the reins from Hodge.

"Gad, I hope not! Give me a hand, Hodge."

Hodge alighted and assisted Nicholas to the seat.

"Don't you see that the colt is back?" asked Philip.

"That's good." Nicholas suddenly saw Lulu and stared at her with curiosity.

"Yes. It was kind of those people to bring him home." Philip sat solidly on the seat with a tight rein, waiting for Lulu to be gone.

Bob said sheepishly — "Well, I guess we'd better go, Lulu."

She stood, smiling, brazen, waiting for Philip to drive out. Hodge ran to the gate to be ready to shut it after them.

Bob said — "I guess you'd better go first, mister. Your horse is a good lot faster than mine."

"No — you go first," returned Philip genially.

Bob looked at Lulu, but she seemed to have lost the use of her legs. Behind the colt's head she whispered: —

"Come again. Tomorrow — if you can."

Her smile had stiffened as she got into the buggy and was driven off.

"Odd-looking woman," said Nicholas. "Who was she?"

"Never saw her before. She looks as hard as nails."

Renny was tightening the colt's girth. Now he sprang on its back and the colt danced about the dogcart as though in fear.

Nicholas said — "I should think you'd be ashamed of yourself. My mother will not soon forget how you horrified her guests. As for Cousin Malahide, he has treated the incident with the contempt it deserves."

"I have not finished with him," said Renny, "and you may tell him so!"

Before Nicholas could answer, Philip had flicked his horse with the whip and it was trotting briskly between the evergreens along the drive.

Adeline had not forgotten how Malahide had been treated, nor did she let anyone else forget it. At short intervals during the day she gave way to sharp outbursts of indignation.

Pleased to find herself at one with her daughter on the subject, she made frequent excursions into Augusta's room, so hindering Augusta in her packing that never before were her belongings in such confusion. Yet Augusta was pleased to part from her mother on such happy terms and even more pleased to be going without Malahide. But she gave a sigh when she heard the sound of Adeline's stick once more returning along the passage. Now she had brought a present to Augusta. It was a length of purple velvet she had had put away for years.

"Have a dress made of it," she said, "or an evening cloak or *peignoir*, if you prefer that. I'll not need it." She draped it across her daughter, who craned her neck to see her reflection in the glass and could not help noticing how sallow it made her.

"I think you had better keep it, Mamma," she said.

"No, no, it is for you. I've been intending all along to make you a present. And there's Edwin, too. I'd like him to have something. I'll go back to my room and see what I can unearth."

"But all this going up and down stairs is very bad for you, Mamma," said Ernest, who had just come to the door.

"Stuff and nonsense!" she returned. "You're only jealous because I've nothing for you!" She gave him a playful tap on the arm.

Augusta and Ernest, left alone, shook their heads over her untimely activity. "If only," said Augusta, "her presents weren't so bulky! And if only they were things one could use!"

"Leave the velvet with Mary," advised Ernest. "She will take care of it for you."

Augusta declared proudly. "I should not want Mary to know that any present of my mother's was not acceptable to me. Besides, I should not dare. She would be sure to find out."

Sir Edwin entered, his keys in his hand. "I have locked my trunk and my bags. Everything is admirably stored away."

Augusta said grimly — "You will just have to unlock again. Mamma has gone down to get you a present."

"But I can't — I really can't, Augusta!"

"Not a word, Edwin — you must. It would upset her dreadfully if you were to refuse."

"If only," said Ernest, "she would give a chap a present of money!"

Adeline's return, somewhat laboured after repeated ascents of the stairs, was now heard. She carried in her arms a French china clock which had stood on the mantelpiece of her room, but had not gone for years. She smiled archly at Sir Edwin.

"Something for you, Edwin," she panted. "You must keep it in your own room and, when it strikes, you will know it is time to come back to Jalna." Her smile wavered as she said these words, for she was not quite sure that their sentiment conveyed just what she had intended.

"Delighted!" said Sir Edwin gallantly. "Charmed, I'm sure!" He stood looking about him helplessly, the clock in his arms.

"Now, I suppose, this lad will be jealous," said Adeline, taking Ernest's arm. "Come along with me and I'll find you something, never fear!"

He went, but at the bottom of the stairs, he stopped. "My luggage is strapped, Mamma, but if you really want to give me a present, I should be most grateful for even a small cheque."

Her face fell. "I'm that unnerved," she said, "by all the to-do yesterday that I couldn't hold a pen to make out a cheque. Look at my hand, how it shakes." She held up her shapely old hand, now trembling as though from ague.

Ernest regarded it glumly. "I could guide it, Mamma," he suggested.

"'T wouldn't be legal. They'd be saying in the bank that you forged my name. No — not now. Maybe I shall send you a cheque on your birthday." She marched on toward her room, feeling distinctly huffy.

Her door closed behind her, she drew her brows together and pouted her lips in displeasure. Ernest had no right to be asking her for money. He'd had enough from his father, and from her more than he should have had. She said to Boney: —

"I'll give presents *when* I like and to *whom* I like, and of the *sort* I like. Nobody's business."

Boney sidled along his perch, ruffling himself so that the scarlet feathers in his green wings and tail were displayed. A quiver passed over his pale blue crest.

"*Kutni — Kutni*," he said in a jeering tone. "*Shaitan ka katla — kambakht!*"

If anyone needed money, she thought, it was Malahide. Yet he was pleased — touched to the heart — by any present she gave him. She had a mind to give him a present of money now, while she was in a giving mood. And if Ernest found out, well — it would serve him right!

She smiled maliciously and went to the writing bureau, on top of which stood a framed photograph of her husband, and fumbled in the top drawer for her book of blank cheques. She found it and her pen, a slender ivory handled one she had brought from India, too delicate now for her old fingers. But she gripped it and, peering and blowing at the cheque, she filled it in for a hundred dollars and signed her name — Adeline Whiteoak — with a flourish.

She examined it critically. The ink was rather thick; still, it was quite legible — a good signature, a good name. She put her second finger to her mouth and cleansed it of the ink stain.

She went to the red woollen bell cord and gave it a tug. She said, when Eliza appeared: —

"Find Mr. Court for me. Tell him I'd like to see him here."

"Thank you, 'm," said Eliza stiffly. She did not approve of Mr. Court.

Malahide came, a lift in his spirits at the summons. He found life at Jalna intolerably boring at times.

"Here," said Adeline, thrusting her cheque into his hand, "a little present for you." She regarded his sallow face affectionately.

His fingers closed on the cheque. "Ah, my dear!" he exclaimed. "You are too generous!"

"Wait till you've examined it before you say that," she returned brusquely.

"As though the amount signified!" he exclaimed. "It is your spirit that is generous. What can I say? Nothing that will express what I feel! Here I am — stranded without means — depending on your hospitality — and you are not only the spirit of hospitality, but of liberality as well!"

He took her hand and pressed his lips to it. She smiled down on his head. "Look at the cheque," she repeated shortly. "It is not for a large sum, but I thought it would come in handy."

He straightened his back and took in the figures.

The door opened and Ernest's long delicate nose was introduced. He fixed his eyes on Malahide and the cheque with an expression of dismay.

He did not know whether to advance or retreat, but his mother saw him and commanded: —

"Come in, come in, you're making a draught."

Ernest entered and said, in a tone which he tried to make casual: —

"I came to tell you that the luggage is being carried down. Our time is getting short and we thought you would like to be with us. We are having tea on the lawn."

Malahide had somewhat hastily thrust the cheque into his pocket. He smiled from Ernest's gloomy face to Adeline's bold one, and said: —

"Yes, yes, we must spend our last moments together! How sad it makes us to think you are going, doesn't it, Cousin Adeline?"

"Oh, we'll get along," she said cheerfully. "I'll look after Malahide and Malahide will look after me!" She tucked her arm into his.

Ernest said — "Don't you think you had better come with us after all, Malahide? I am afraid I shall be very *de trop* with Augusta and Edwin. They are so devoted to each other."

"Too late, too late!" said his mother, giving him a waggish look.

"I think it could be managed. Really, I am afraid you will find it very quiet here as the nights draw in."

"I was never better entertained in my life," returned Malahide. "No, as long as Cousin Adeline wants me to stay, I'll remain."

Ernest stood aside to let them pass. Then he went into the dining room, where Nicholas was mixing himself a drink of whiskey and water.

"Nick," he said gloomily, "we've made a horrible mistake. Philip and Renny are quite right. Malahide is a menace. We should have seen how he was getting round Mamma. Think of the diamond cravat pin! He should be leaving today."

"I hate these partings," said Nicholas, sipping his whiskey, "and for my part I am glad that Malahide is staying. I find him very entertaining. So does Mamma."

"Entertaining! I should think so. And she is paying for the entertainment. And so, indirectly, are you! Just as I went into her room now I found him pocketing a cheque."

Nicholas looked much disturbed. "Well — h'm — that's serious. I had no notion she would give him money. Why, it's awful! Have you any idea what the cheque was for?"

"No. He tried to conceal it. Mama had that teasing look she assumes when she thinks she will annoy us — and me, in particular. We have been fools, Nick. I see it now!"

"Well —" Nicholas set down his glass and wiped his moustache — "it's too late to chuck him out now, but I certainly shan't encourage him to prolong his visit."

They joined the others at tea, which was more lavish than usual, but less enjoyed. Ernest took the opportunity of telling the Buckleys, in a whisper, the disturbing news of the cheque. Renny was troubled by Lulu's appearance of the morning, and Philip, conscious of his son's mood, was troubled too. Mary and Meg felt chagrin at not having been able to get rid of their uninvited guest. And Adeline had less appetite than usual because of the unease of the preparation for departure and a twinge of remorse for her treatment of Ernest.

Over them all was the feeling that the object of the visit had not been fulfilled. It had been made to celebrate a wedding and no wedding had taken place. Meg sat in their midst trying hard to be brave, to live down the disappointment, but still abstracted and often melancholy.

The little boys were taking tea with the family as a special treat, dressed in white as they had been at the garden party. Augusta took Eden on her knees and whispered to him: —

"You won't forget Aunt Augusta, dear, will you?"

"No," he answered firmly, "I won't forget you and I'll say 'God bless you' in my prayers and I'll go to visit you when I'm big and you'll take me to the zoo."

Augusta held him close. "I wish I could take him back with me," she said. "I shall miss him so much — and Peep too."

Philip said — "Molly and I will take all the children to visit you one day, Gussie."

Augusta looked as though she thought that would be too much of a good thing. She said: —

"That would be delightful. But, speaking of visiting, I do think that Edwin and I have made a very long visit at Jalna. I think long visits are a great mistake."

Sir Edwin added — "Yes, yes, we have stayed a very long time."

"You've been very welcome," said Mary. "It makes all the difference in the world who visitors are."

"Yes, indeed," said Meg. "Some people could never stay too long, while others …"

"I agree," said Ernest, "that visits should not be prolonged and, even while Jalna is my home, the time comes when I know I should return to London."

"Don't be sanctimonious about it," growled Nicholas. "You know you're glad to get back."

"One thing that *I'm* glad of," put in their mother, "is that Malahide Court is staying on. He'll be a great comfort to me." She laid her hand protectingly on Malahide's knee.

Hoofs now sounded on the gravel and the carriage appeared. Hodge drew up in front of the door.

"He's too early," said Ernest, looking at his watch.

Eliza came out of the house and spoke to Hodge. She then crossed the lawn and approached Philip. She told him something in a low tone. He turned a startled face to the others.

"What do you suppose has happened? Robert Vaughan has had a stroke! Poor man, this affair has been too much for him."

"Just when we are about to leave!" said Augusta.

"A great blow for Mrs. Vaughan," said Sir Edwin.

"I wonder what young Maurice will think of himself now," growled Nicholas.

Mary exclaimed — "I have felt something — a shadow — all day!"

"I remember," said Ernest, "how shaken he seemed that morning when we three went to see him. He could not at all keep himself in hand as we did."

All discussed the calamity in sorrowful excitement, with the exception of Adeline, who sat, a hand on each knee, staring straight in front of her. At last she said: —

"A stroke, eh? Robert Vaughan a stroke. D'ye think he'll be about again, Philip?"

"There is hope, Mamma."

"Ha, that's good! Must go to see him. Cheer him up. Where did you say he's affected?"

"Down one side — the left."

She shook her head in commiseration and rubbed her hand up and down her left thigh.

Sir Edwin looked at his watch. "By Jove!" he exclaimed, "we have no time to spare!"

"To think," said Augusta, "that I must go without seeing poor Mrs. Vaughan! Mamma, you must give her our deepest sympathy."

"They'll get along. They'll get along. Don't you worry," said her mother tersely.

But now the family goodbyes must be said. Sir Edwin, Augusta, and Ernest were in turn enfolded in Adeline's strong embrace. To the last she whispered: —

"Ye mustn't mind me giving a little present to Malahide. 'Twas nothing of any account."

Ernest looked relieved but still a little dubious. He whispered back — "Don't imagine that I grudge anything that gives you pleasure, Mamma. But, if I were you, I should not urge him to stay on. After all, it is Philip's and Molly's house and it is obvious that they dislike his presence."

He had said the wrong thing when he referred to Mary as having a share in the ownership of Jalna. His mother pushed him from her.

"Jalna belong to that one! Jalna belong to that flibbertigibbety wife of Philip's. You talk like a fool!"

"Sh, Mamma, she'll hear you! All I meant was …"

But he was given no time for explanation. Nicholas pushed him toward the carriage. The bays were sweeping the gravel with their polished hoofs. Peep was being held up by Renny to throw kisses. Mary was snatching Eden from under the horses' heads. Meg, all her trouble brought back by the news of Mr. Vaughan's illness, was weeping on Philip's shoulder. Malahide tucked Adeline's hand in the crook of his arm and beamed, protectingly. He waved a glad farewell to the occupants of the carriage, as the dark branches of the hemlocks stretched out to hide them from view.

XX

An Old Coat
and an Old Mare

THE EARTH SEEMED to have wearied of heat and now, though it was still August, groped toward the chill walls of autumn. With the departure of three guests, Mary's burden of housekeeping was lightened. She began to recover from her disappointment over Meg's broken engagement. The relations between her and her stepchildren were happier than ever before. Eden, whose health had given her much anxiety, was now sparkling with vitality and Peep was as sturdy as a child could well be. There was this to be said for the company of Malahide: it gave her more of Philip, the intimate companionship she craved.

She loved his horses and dogs almost as well as he did. They would stand in the orchard watching a sow suckling her litter, with quiet pleasure. Happiest to them both were the hours they spent by the river, hidden by thick growing shrubs, while she read poetry to him and he lay watching the pale sunshine dapple the fine skin of her face and throat. What Mary could not and would not do was to go fishing with him. There he had the solitude which his nature demanded.

Adeline was less content in these days. The departure of her children left a blank not easy to fill. She leant on Ernest more than she realized, and she felt a keen sense of irritation when he was not at hand to wait on her, to supply that particular something which his personality offered. She missed the Buckleys, too, even Sir Edwin's crisp protection of Augusta from her sometimes barbed remarks.

Her head grew weary from late sittings at the card table or backgammon board. Malahide was a better player than she, and she was shrewd enough to reject his suggestion that they play for money. Yet he did win money from both Philip and Nicholas at bridge.

One morning a stirring wind blew across the countryside, driving the clouds before it. They melted into the horizon beyond the lake, and the sky arched itself in summer blueness. The sun caressed the late flower buds into bloom.

Adeline longed for something active to do. Through all her body she had a sense of the futile inaction of the past weeks. She made up her mind that she would go about more. She would take some long drives. She would go to see Robert Vaughan, who was now able to sit up, the stroke having been a slight one. But on this fine blowy morning the first thing she should do would be to put her Philip's clothes out in the sun and brush and shake them thoroughly, against the ravages of moths. This she did once every year at about this time. Her son Philip always helped her because Ernest shrank too much from what, to him, was a depressing ordeal, and Nicholas invariably drew her attention to new moth holes and advised her to give the clothes away or to burn them.

Now she went out at the side door to where she had heard Philip's voice, in conversation with the prospective buyer of a horse, and called to him: —

"Philip, my dear, come here! I have something I want you to help me with."

Philip's back was toward her, and before turning round he hesitated. There was that in her tone which told him what his task was to be and his heart rebelled, on such a morning as this. He stood sulkily, as he had often stood when a small boy, reluctant to answer the summons.

"Philip," she called sharply, "are you woolgathering that you pay no heed to me?"

He turned slowly and came toward her, taking off his dilapidated Panama hat and passing his hand across his fair hair.

"I was just thinking," he said deliberately, "that I have about a thousand things to do this morning."

"You're taking your time about them," she returned sarcastically. "But there's one thing, Philip, that you must do. You must help me give your father's clothes an airing. The time is past due for it and there's a fine cleansing wind."

He came and put his arm about her waist. "Wouldn't you like a nice drive in the phaëton, old girl?" he asked coaxingly.

"No," she answered with resolve. "We'll air your father's clothes."

Philip made a resigned movement of his shoulders and said — "Very well, I'll have the boxes brought down."

The limpid notes of an oriole came to them in late summer sweetness, from where he swayed near by his empty nest. Philip said: —

"He doesn't trouble his head about the past. He enjoys his present — before the winter comes."

His mother turned her head sharply to him. "Am I a bird?" she asked. Then she added, in a gentler tone — "No, Philip, we must not shirk it. We'll do the clothes."

Philip had the three trunks brought down from the attic and ranged on the grass plot at the back of the house where lines for drying clothes were stretched. He took the keys which his mother handed to him and unlocked them one after the other. As the lids were raised the smell of camphor came from them, and the smell of cloth long shut away from human flesh and air and sun. Philip began to take out the garments and lay them on the grass.

Adeline had brought from her room two old ivory backed brushes with the initials "P.W." on them in silver. She handed one of these to Philip.

"His own brushes," she observed. "Proper to brush his clothes with them."

Philip took up a coat of a warm brown-heather mixture tweed and looked it over.

"You are to have those brushes," she said.

"I'll like that. My initials."

"Little Piers can have 'em after you."

"Yes. I'll see to it. This coat looks in pretty good condition."

She came, brush in hand, and examined it. The coat, still bearing the print of the vigorous body that had rounded it, seemed almost to expand, as though drawing a deep breath of the outdoor air.

Adeline touched it gently.

"Men's clothes," she murmured. "Touching things they are — when the man's gone…. A woman's clothes — so much silk or velvet or cotton or lace — flattened out — no more than dead leaves dropped from a tree…. But — look at that coat now! No, — give it me — let me brush it…." Her voice broke. She took the coat and began energetically to wield the brush.

One trunk contained the dead man's evening clothes, his finest linen, silk scarves, and velvet smoking jacket. Another his tweeds and riding clothes. The third the uniform he had brought from India. One by one they shook the garments, brushed them, and hung them on the line. The scarlet and gold of the uniform caught and held close the sunlight.

Philip took up a tasseled velvet smoking cap and put it on his head. "Look, Mamma," he said.

She gave him a searching look.

He asked — "Do I look like my father in it?"

"Yes…. But your face is in a different mould…. It hurts me to see you in the cap. Take it off."

She turned again to her brushing of the tunic.

"If you could have seen him in this! Ah, but he was a figure! You don't see his like nowadays."

"But I did see him in it!" he said. "Don't you remember? He wore it at some fancy-dress affair when I was a small boy. I thought I had never seen anyone look so grand."

"No — and never will again."

He opened the long narrow compartment in one of the trays. "Here are his pipes," he said.

She came and looked. On every amber mouthpiece the lips of her beloved had pouted; through every stem drawn in the sweet smoke for his pleasure.

"No harm can come to them," she said. "Shut the lid."

In concern she saw that the garment she was holding had a large place eaten by moths on the breast. She drew her son's attention to it.

"It's the one he wore — that last day," she said "D'ye think we shall have to burn it?"

"Yes," he answered. "I told you that a year ago. Look!" He took it from her and held it to the sun. "It is falling to pieces. If you keep it they will all have to be burned."

She gazed at the garment, her strong old features carved in the image of compassion.

"I'm sorry for the coat," she said. "'T was the last one he wore."

"I will look after it." He took it gently from her. "I'll burn it back in the woods where he used to shoot."

"Thank you, my dear." She took the sleeve of the coat and held it to her lips. Her hands shook as she proceeded with the brushing of the garments.

When all were hung up on the line, swaying and swept by the clean wind, Adeline felt very tired. She would go to her room and rest, she said. She looked the other way when Philip picked up the coat and walked off with it hanging limply from his hand. She found Eliza and told her to keep an eye on the clothes that they were not touched.

Philip walked slowly along the bridle path, then turned from it to the little winding path that led through the wood and on to the waste land where Renny had left the worn out horse. His spaniel, Keno, trotted soberly after him.

He felt the land that he owned beneath his feet. He saw the same sky arching above. And here was his father's coat in his hand and he himself walking in strength and security. What was death? Was it his father's hand reaching out through the sleeve of the coat to grasp his and draw him into that blackness where he would be effaced? Or was it his father living on in him, striding as he strode, over the land they loved? He remembered his mother's shaking hands and her dry eyes that burned with compassion. I am made in a softer mould, he thought, and his own eyes filled with tears.

He gathered twigs and broke the dead branch of a pine into short pieces. He folded the coat and laid it on top of these, then struck a match and set fire to them.

The hesitant little flames were slow to attack the cloth. They snapped and crackled among the twigs, then hid themselves in the shadow of the coat. But presently through its folds tendrils of smoke came creeping and then the flames were coaxed into life. It was in a blaze, all but one sleeve which flung itself out as though there were an arm about it that sought to be free.

As Philip stood staring at the small burning mound he heard a slow dragging step behind him. He turned sharply and saw the old mare, her bony knees bent, her inflated belly sagging, stumbling past. Again he saw the human eyes that suffering had given her, but she did not see him nor did she see the blazing of the fire. Her eyes were fixed on something beyond and she stumbled heavily toward it, her rasping breath coming with difficulty. She uttered a whinny in which there was a note of gladness.

Philip had thought she was underground weeks ago. A tremor passed through him as though he had seen an apparition. Could it really be she, he wondered. This mare's mane and tail were brushed and her harsh hide curried to a semblance of decency.

He was about to step from behind the bushes which concealed him when he heard the sharp report of a gun. He hastened after the mare, saw her stagger, drop to her knees, and fall in a strange angular heap. He saw Renny running towards him, his gun in his hand. His face was white.

"Father! I might have killed you!"

"You might," returned Philip quietly. "Will you please explain what this means? And why are you shooting this poor old mare which should have been dead long ago?" The spaniel ran to the mare, sniffed it, and made a sound between a howl and a bark.

Renny's features broke into a line of dejection. "I thought I could save her," he said mournfully. "I've fed her and watered her and curried her — and she could eat. But, try as she would, she could not get well. She was dying. So — I had to do it at last." He swallowed with difficulty. "I'm sorry. I should have had her shot when you told me, at the first."

"Look at her!" exclaimed Philip sternly. "You ought to be ashamed to have let her live so long!"

"I thought she would get better. She was always so glad to see me. Why — she came to meet me just now — when I was going to do that to her!" His face was contorted as though he were about to cry.

Philip looked at his son, at the dead mare, at his father's coat lying in shining layer upon layer as though it were made of cloth of gold. He sighed.

"This is a strange way," he observed, "to spend a fine morning." He patted Renny on the shoulder. "Come, come," he said soothingly. "I can't have you going on like this. Just be glad that you didn't put a bullet into your dad!"

But Renny did not soon gain self-control. Philip suspected that his nerves were overwrought. He led him away from the sight of the dead mare and they stood leaning over a gate together, looking on a field of ripe grain. Renny lighted a cigarette and Philip, with a sigh of relief, filled his pipe. Keno entered the field and began to run here and there, snuffing the ground. Only the movement of the grain showed where he was.

Renny laid his arms along the top bar of the gate. He felt the smooth wood in his hands and saw that his father's hands too were touching it. Between them they possessed the gate and the yellow field and the land, and life itself. He moved his hand toward Philip and gave him a furtive caress.

"I'm sorry," he repeated, "I should have done what you told me to. But she was so hungry — I hadn't the heart to kill her." And he added, wonderingly — "But she couldn't get well — eat as she would."

"I have been going over my dad's belongings," said Philip, "and I had to burn one of his coats — the last one he wore. Your Granny felt badly about it. It's surprising how things hurt."

Renny watched the ripple of grain that marked Keno's movements in silence for a space. Then he said: —

"What I want more than anything is to ride Gallant at the Show."

"It would mean missing some time at college."

Renny clasped his head in his hands, and muttered — "Think how I left it! If only I could get a first at the Show — I'd go back with a better face."

Philip looked at the stripling's wiry form hanging over the gate. He thought of the dead mare and of his own dead father's coat. He did not know why thinking of these things should weaken the firmness he felt he should show towards Renny, but weaken him it did. He said doubtfully: —

"I don't know if it will be good for you. I'm afraid your grandmother and your mother and uncles won't think so."

"There's nothing Gran likes so much as to see us get a first at the Show. As for the others — they've too much to say about me. I'm always being discussed. When I come into a room where they are collected I can tell by their faces they've been talking me over. Sometimes they don't even stop when I go in. And, of course, Gran is into it, too," he added bitterly.

"Well, well," said Philip, "it shows how important your behaviour is to them. But do you really believe you could win on Gallant?"

Renny turned his intense gaze on him.

"I'm sure I could! There's nothing on earth I want so much!"

"Have your own way, then," said Philip half testily. "But see that you keep your mind on the colt. Keep that yellow-haired woman out of it."

"I'll never give her a thought," said Renny.

XXI

A Horse to Ride

ADELINE MADE UP her mind that Malahide Court should accompany her on her call at Vaughanlands. At first she had thought to go by herself to see her old friend, congratulate him on his recovery, which was more rapid than they could have hoped for. But she was really afraid to leave Malahide at Jalna without her protecting presence. She did not know what Renny or Meg might do. Philip and Mary, she was afraid, would be only too pleased to see things made uncomfortable for him. Even Nicholas had of late assumed a surly attitude toward her kinsman. She was certain that Ernest had disclosed the fact that she had been giving Malahide money. Well, they were all tarred of the same brush, wanted everything for themselves, but she was equal to them.

She looked about her critically as the carriage rolled along the Vaughans' drive. It was a poor place, she thought, compared to Jalna, lacking Jalna's dignity and fine arrogant chimneys, but it was a pleasant place, and the sight of Robert Vaughan, wrapped in a travelling rug, on his chair on the verandah, warmed her heart.

As soon as Malahide had assisted her from the carriage she began to mount the steps impatiently while she held out in her right hand a basket in which she had brought him a jar of port wine jelly, some Malaga grapes, and a pound cake.

"Now," she said, a little breathlessly, "just see what I've brought you! Nothing that will do you harm. Everything that will do you good. No — don't try to get up! It's enough for me to grasp your hand and find you a live man instead of a dead. You did give us a scare. And here's my cousin Malahide come to inquire after ye."

Robert Vaughan shook hands with them both rather tremulously. He gave them a bright fixed smile, trying hard to feel strong. Mrs. Vaughan came out of the house and saw that Mrs. Whiteoak was established in the most comfortable chair with a cushion at her back.

"Ha, that's good!" said Adeline. "And it's splendid to see you making such a good recovery, Robert Vaughan. It's small wonder you were ill after all you were through. If I hadn't been made of extraordinary tough stuff I'd have been on my own back. It's a terrible thing to see your only grand-daughter disappointed in love and a little baby left on your neighbour's doorstep where one should not have been due for ten months, at the least."

Mrs. Vaughan looked uneasily at her husband, but the case, thus strongly stated, seemed to have done him no harm. He sat staring into old Adeline's face with an eager look, as though he were drawing new vitality from her abundance. Mrs. Vaughan said: —

"We are thankful that Robert has got along so well. And you have all been so kind in sending him things. Shall I take the basket from you, dear?"

But Adeline interposed — "No, let the man hold it on his knee. It will cheer him up to look at those nice titbits waiting to be eaten. Eat a few of the grapes now, Robert. They'll do you good."

Obediently he took a grape in his pale fingers while she looked on benignly. She said: —

"You must be well in time for the Horse Show. You must not miss that, you know."

His face lighted. "No, I must not miss the Horse Show. Of course, I have never been so keen as you are, but I generally have a good horse to show. This year I have a very promising mare which I thought would do well in the high jumping. But" — a slow colour crept into his face — "I'm afraid I shan't be able to show her now. Maurice was to have ridden her and — he's still away, you know."

"You should have sent for him! You should have brought him to your bedside and said — 'Now, young man, see what you've done to me!' That's what I'd have done!"

Robert Vaughan gave a wan smile. His wife exclaimed: —

"Oh, but that would have been cruel! It would have broken Maurice's heart."

"And serve him right! But that's neither here nor there. What I'm going to say is — why not let my cousin here ride your horse? He'd do it gladly. And rides like a centenarian — or whatever they call those beasts. Don't you, Malahide?"

Malahide had been sitting limply, with legs outstretched, in a low wicker chair. A kitten had appeared and walked the length of his wand-like body from ankle to neck. It stood now on his chest, rubbing first one cheek, then the other, against his chin. Malahide seemed hypnotized by its attentions.

"Do you hear what I'm saying, Mally?" demanded Adeline.

He opened a slit of one languid eye. "I'd be delighted, I'm sure," he said. "I can ride any sort of nag."

Robert Vaughan looked ruffled, and Adeline hastened to explain: —

"Malahide thinks that all horses that are not Irish are nags."

"This horse had an Irish sire. She's from your own stables, Mrs. Whiteoak."

"Of course, I know her well. I will take Malahide to see her before we go, if you'd like him to ride for you."

Robert Vaughan could not believe in Malahide's horsemanship, but the thought of having someone to talk to about his mare, of watching its schooling for the Show, revived his spirits. His interest in horses had been cultivated chiefly by his proximity to the horse-loving tribe at Jalna. Perhaps because of that his chief pleasure in showing his beasts lay in outstripping the Whiteoaks. He had heard rumours of Renny's colt.

After further conversation, in which Malahide only faintly joined, Adeline said to Mrs. Vaughan: —

"Let us leave the men to talk things over. I'd like a word alone with you, my dear."

As she passed Robert Vaughan's chair she gave him a comforting pat on the shoulder. "It will put new life in you to see Malahide mounted. He's bound to win for you."

Robert Vaughan looked up at her admiringly.

"It shows how much you have my recovery at heart," he said, "when you are willing to help me win from Jalna."

"Your mare," she returned, brusquely, "was bred in our stables and will be ridden by my kinsman. It would be all to our credit."

Inside the sitting room she said to Mrs. Vaughan: —

"Now, then, let me have a look at the child."

Mrs. Vaughan had been expecting this and she shrank from it, but she could not refuse.

"I will bring her down here," she said, "so you need not climb the stairs."

"I'm better able to climb them than you are," said Adeline, "I'll go up."

They found the infant asleep in a bassinet in Mrs. Vaughan's dressing room. In one hand it grasped the rubber tube of a feeding bottle, the nipple of which was still wet. Downy dark hair clung in moist rungs on its head, which, like the bud of a flower, pushed, tender and relentless, from its sheath. As they looked down on it, its lips widened in a secret smile that flickered a moment across its face and was gone.

"It hears the angels," whispered Mrs. Vaughan.

"More likely it's just wet itself," said Adeline.

As though in reproach the baby opened its eyes. They looked up, in deep, dark brightness. Mrs. Vaughan took it up and laid it against her broad breast. She crooned to it.

"You love it, eh?" said her visitor.

"Ah, I can't help loving it!"

"H'm, well, you've a stronger stomach than I have! Now I think I'll take Malahide to see the horse."

Mrs. Vaughan was deeply hurt. She did not offer to accompany them to the stable. Her excuse was that she must not leave her husband.

Adeline clung fast to Malahide's arm as she trudged toward the stable. With the other hand she clutched the voluminous folds of her dress, showing her broad-toed shoes that were planted arrogantly, as though the path questioned her right to tread on it.

"A poor, paltry little stable," she said. "Yet it and that house were the finest about here, till we came and built Jalna. That was a bitter pill for Robert Vaughan's father, I can tell ye. I and my husband and my two children — little toddlers, then, — stopped with the Vaughans while our house was being built. It was all we could to do keep the peace. And every time he had the chance, young Robert was for making love to me. I don't suppose he has ever told his own boy that…. Not that I took any interest in him. He was too callow for my taste."

"If only I had been there when you were young!" exclaimed Malahide. "I would have made you love me."

She gave him a roguish look. "Well, well, it would have kept you busy — with my Philip about!"

"I'd have done it!" he declared, a smile lighting his swarthy face.

In the stable they found the tall three-year-old being groomed by a stableboy. Adeline compressed her lips and looked her over appraisingly. She said: —

"She can jump. I've seen her. And she has a good disposition — with just a spark of the devil in her — a promising combination for man or beast. I'm just the reverse — a devilish disposition with just a spark of good!"

"And I am here to fan that spark!" he said.

"Get along with you! Now, how do you like the looks of her? Her sire cost my son four hundred guineas. This mare takes after him. Renny's grey colt is the mare's half-brother and is the image of his dam, who is a disappointment."

Malahide stroked the mare's flank.

"I'll win with her," he said languidly, "if I have to jump her out of her hide to do it."

"And I'll go to see you, I will! I enjoy a good contest. But, mind you, that grandson of mine can ride. 'The ridin'est critter that ever lived,' Scotchmere says. But we'll beat him, Malahide! We'll punish him for putting that flittermouse into your room and the doggerel he taught Eden, and all his other bad behaviour. And I'll show my son Philip that my kinsman can beat his son and that all this humouring of him leads to nothing."

"I am of a forgiving disposition," said Malahide, "but I don't mind telling you that — to borrow one of the young man's elegant expressions — I'd like to lick the daylights out of him."

XXII

RIVALS

IT WAS NOT long before it was known that Malahide Court was to ride Robert Vaughan's bay mare Harpie at the Show. It was recognized that the event was in the nature of a duel between Malahide and Renny. There was also a subtle feeling (first insinuated by Meg) that, if Gallant were the victor, the slight to her by Maurice's delinquency would receive a blow in her honour.

The fact that Malahide was to ride a horse belonging to an outsider did not increase his prestige in the house. Nicholas regarded him with more suspicion than ever. Philip turned a broad shoulder toward him when possible, while Molly and Meg were never alone for five minutes that their conversation did not turn to his hateful presence in their midst, his affectations, his clothes, the chances of getting rid of him. In Renny the feeling of animosity had so risen that he could no longer trust himself to speak with civility to him, but kept an aloof, yet vindictive silence when they were in the same room.

Malahide and Adeline were now ranged on one side with the rest of the family on the other, with the exception of the two little boys, who were unconscious of the situation, though Eden knew that Meg and Renny were not pleased with him when he was friendly to Malahide. Yet Malahide fascinated him and he would sit on his knee absorbing the strange Irish folklore which Malahide had had from his nurse. Many a night the little boy lay in his crib, his head under the clothes, shivering with fear, but unwilling to tell the cause of his agitation lest he might be allowed to listen no more.

The heat of the summer had given way to the bracing brightness of early autumn. Adeline was feeling extraordinarily well. The new teeth had made it possible for her to masticate her food thoroughly, and the benefit she so derived showed in her good spirits and general alertness. She frequently laid aside her stick, on which she had began to lean rather heavily, and walked with a firm tread, even as far as Vaughanlands.

She was enjoying the situation to the full. She magnified it to the status of fine intrigue and bold cast for power. As she and Malahide ascended the deeply shaded path beyond the ravine, on their way to Vaughanlands, she entertained feelings such as an empress might have had, with her favourite at her side and the rest of the court scheming against her.

Nothing could have been better for Robert Vaughan's recovery than this gay, caressing autumn weather and the exhilaration of watching Malahide school Harpie for the contest. He was able to walk as far as the paddock where this took place, and there he and Adeline sat, just outside the palings, while Malahide, with skill and grace and iron determination, put Harpie through her jumps. When Robert Vaughan thought the horse was being treated a little harshly he would put up one thin hand and call out — "Careful, careful, Mr. Court. Kindness is everything."

Adeline would grin and wish that she and Malahide might have the mare to themselves. It was soon perceived, by those who looked on, that the bay had never jumped so well as she was now doing, that she was likely to be one of the best horses in the Show.

At the same time Renny was schooling Gallant, advised, derided, criticized, and cheered by his father, uncle, stepmother, and sister. Vera Lacey, too, was often there, adding her high-pitched adjurations to him flying past. Every groom, stableboy, and farm labourer who dared leave his work was on hand to watch, jealous for Jalna; and they dared much when Philip was absorbed in the activity of his boy.

It could not be said of Gallant that he had a good disposition. Irritable, sensitive, spiteful to a degree, he capered over the course, sidling from the hurdles as though in terror, backing against them instead of going over them, kicking and biting at all who approached him save Renny, yet soaring like an eagle when he did consent to jump, skimming the highest bar with the assurance of a seasoned jumper.

Those leaning against the palings of the paddock were moved to great excitement. Sometimes they feared that the boy's neck would be broken. Sometimes Philip would utter a proud sire's shout of approbation or Nicholas would clap his hands and send the colt spinning down the course in a frenzy of fright.

"Look out — look out!" Philip once warned him. "Don't frighten the colt!"

Nicholas retorted — "If he can't endure the sound of a single hand clap what will he do in a thunder of applause — and a band thrown in?"

"True, true," sighed Philip. "He must get used to it."

After that the onlookers let themselves go, making all the din they could. Time and again the wiry rider was thrown to the ground. When he laid himself down at night he groaned with the pain of his bruises.

Of all those who watched the schooling of the colt not one was more absorbed by it than Eden. He stood close by Philip's side, watching the feats and failures of his hero. This year, for the first time, he was to be taken to the Show. Even the baby, Peep, was sometimes a spectator, and learned to add his lusty shout to Philip's.

The presence of Adeline at the schooling was a source of irritation to the family. For come she did, day after day, and stood, a majestic figure, at the palings, her hands firmly grasping them, her widow's weeds in classic folds about her shoulders. They felt that, as she had cast in her lot with Malahide, she was taking a mean advantage in so closely observing all that was going on at home.

All knew that, on an occasion when Scotchmere had been sent to Vaughanlands to see how Harpie was coming on, he had been arbitrarily ordered off by Adeline, who expressed herself as scornful of such prying. Never had it been the custom, she said, in Captain Whiteoak's time to send spies into a neighbour's stables.

Yet when Philip, more than a little chagrined by her watchful presence and sardonic comments, said to her — "I suppose you are keeping

Cousin Malahide and Robert Vaughan well posted about what goes on here," she returned amiably — "I like to see what my grandson is doing. And if I seem to be on Robert Vaughan's side, it is because I'm sorry for him. He was a sick man and this interest in the Show is lifting him out of himself. To be sure, he brought on his own little trouble, for he spoiled his son, and the ingratitude of a spoilt child is sharper than the stallion's tooth." And she marched to her room and shut the door.

Philip stared after her, scratching his chin, on which there was a two days' growth of yellow beard, and said: —

"Very well, very well, old lady! But you can't make me believe that you are not for Malahide and all against us."

Adeline was, for the only time in her life, heart and soul against a Jalna horse. Many a time she had been against her family. But, even while she felt the qualms of a traitor, she experienced no weakening in her desire to see her kinsman victorious, her championship of him justified. Then, too, Harpie's winning would be the most potent tonic possible for Robert Vaughan, a salutary dose for her own family, and an exquisite triumph for herself.

The renewed intimacy with the doings of the stable exhilarated her. For so long she had been an onlooker. The very putting on of heavy shoes, so that she might make an excursion into the barnyard, after the schooling of the Show horses was over; the very smell of the harness room and the acrid scents of the barnyard, filled her with an urgent vitality.

While Philip and Nicholas were able to regard their mother's behaviour with a certain degree of tolerance, Molly and Meg could find no excuse for it. To Molly it was a direct reflection on Philip; to Meg, on herself. Neither dared openly to reproach mother-in-law and grandmother, but in private they poured out their anger against her and their contempt for Malahide.

Renny was of a nature too ardent for self-control in such a situation. He and Adeline were at daggers drawn. He would stalk past her without so much as a nod in her direction, and when she, affronted, exclaimed — "Can't you speak to your grandmother, unmannerly cub?" his fiery eyes met hers with a hostile stare and he retorted — "What have you to say to me but to find fault and jeer?"

One afternoon he came in tired and aching. He had not only been helping Scotchmere with the schooling of several horses, but he had been crowded against the side of the stall by Gallant, and was consequently in a bad temper. He saw that his grandmother was the only other occupant of the sitting room. She too looked flushed and tired, and she was searching through a velvet bag which she always carried for her spectacles, which she was always losing. She rose stiffly from her chair and went to the writing desk and fumbled among the papers there.

"H'm, must have left them in my room," she muttered, and drew a sigh.

Renny sat stolidly, pretending to read a sporting paper, while she hobbled out of the room and down the passage. But he gave a quick glance into her face when she returned, and had a feeling of shame. He wished he had got the glasses for her, even though she was such an old Tartar. There was something in the sight of her, as she settled her spectacles on her nose and took up the latest copy of the *Churchman*, that touched him. If they had remained long alone in the room together there might have been a reconciliation, but Meg came in and began whispering to him of some detestable act of Malahide's. Their grandmother heard the name and sharply rebuked them. Malahide himself entered and, sitting down by Adeline's side, talked to her in a low tone, occasionally even whispering behind a sallow hand.

The brother and sister went out and stood together at the foot of the stairs, lounging against the newel post. Patches of light from the coloured-glass window above the door fell on them, the violet one throwing a strange shadow on Meg's fair forehead and a crimson splash turning Renny's hair to flame.

"You look funny," she said. "The stained glass has given you a kind of halo. But what a saint! Patron of the stables!"

"I'd not wish for any better job, if I were a saint," he returned. "As for you, you look as though someone had given you a bash on the head."

He felt happier now that he was out here with Meggie. He lighted a cigarette and offered a puff to her.

She closed her full lips on it, murmuring — "M'm — I could soon get to like them! I wonder if I shall ever smoke."

"I don't think I want you to."

"Do you know what Vera does?"

He pretended a lack of interest. "No idea — something idiotic?"

"No — not idiotic — but you'd never guess."

"Smoke in her bedroom?"

Meg nodded. "Yes, she does that too. But you know how you've admired the colour of her lips? You said you wondered why they were so much redder than mine. Well, I can tell you. She paints them! I saw her do it. She made no bones about it."

"Do her aunts know?"

"Heavens, no! But she says London girls think nothing of it. She's frightfully advanced."

"She'd be in a pretty fix if someone kissed her. The paint would come off, wouldn't it?"

"She says it's proof against that. She's tried it."

He stared. "Since she came out here?"

"I shouldn't be surprised. Vera's not made for seclusion."

His mind flew over the likely young men of the neighbourhood, who were few.

"Who with, I wonder?"

She dimpled, and whispered — "Perhaps Cousin Malahide!"

The mention of his name between them recalled all their machinations against him.

"Look here," said Renny, and led the way into the drawing room. He went to where Boney sat craning on his perch. The parrot was in an alert mood and liked the sound of their laughter.

Renny sat down in front of him and said: —

"To hell with Malahide!"

Boney listened, interested. He sidled along the perch, giving Renny a waggish look.

"To hell with Malahide!" repeated Renny in an imperative tone.

"Whatever are you doing?" said Meg.

"Shut up! Now listen, Boney! To hell with Malahide! Do you hear that? Say it!"

"Don't imagine you can teach him as quickly as that. Besides, he talks almost nothing but Hindoo. You'll have to go about it slowly, in a darkened room, if you want to succeed. Oh, may I be there to hear if he springs that on Gran and her satellite!"

"He will!" Renny took a bar of chocolate from his pocket, broke off a morsel and put it into the parrot's claw. There was nothing Boney liked better. As his dark tongue drew it in his eyes rolled beseechingly at Renny and he said in Hindoo — *"Peariee — Peariee — Peariee lal!"*

"No you don't!" said Renny. "You must say — 'To hell with Cousin Malahide!' before you get any more."

"You are wasting your chocolate," said Meg. "You had much better give it to me. You'll never teach him without being discovered."

"Peariee — Peariee lal," repeated Boney, in a wheedling tone.

Renny flicked him with his finger. "To hell with Malahide!"

With a covetous look at the chocolate Boney swooped and took it from Renny's hand and returned with it to his perch. Adeline and Malahide entered the room followed by Nicholas.

"Well now, well now," said Adeline, "what's my Boney got?"

"We thought chocolate would be good for him, Granny," said Meg innocently.

Adeline was mollified. "But not too much, children, not too much."

"Chota Rani," crooned Boney, his beak full of chocolate.

Nicholas gave a suspicious look at the brother and sister from under his shaggy brows. He wondered what they had been up to. Unaccountable, idiotic young things. He would not be that age again, if he had the chance, and yet — there had been a mad sort of pleasure in life then, which there certainly was not now. But he had paid for his experience and he would not lightly give it up.

The pair drifted out of the room and up the stairs. Meg, who had been fond of visiting the neighbouring houses, no longer cared to go out. She took little exercise and was growing plump. The skin of her face and hands had a clear pallor. She yearned toward Renny's coming and, when he was in the house, seldom was away from his side. Sometimes she felt longings for Maurice, but she put him resolutely out of her mind.

She had divined Vera's secret reaching out toward Renny. Vera was always bringing their talk to him and his doings. She pretended to laugh at him as an unformed youth, and when she was with him she liked to air her knowledge of London ways, to present a hard, bright surface to him, but Meg had seen her change colour when he came into the room. She had seen her wear the same dress, over and over again, because he had said he liked her in it. And there was no use in Vera's saying he was a boy. He was a man — with that set to his head and that look in his eye.

But she was his sister. She was secure in her possession. She would always have him to play with, to quarrel with, to show off in front of other girls. She put her arm round him as they went up the stairs.

"That was a close shave," he said. "I must have Boney where we'll not be disturbed."

"*Do* you think he can learn to say it?"

"In no time! We must do what we can to upset Malahide's nerve."

"Nothing short of a bomb would do that."

"I believe you're right," he answered gloomily. "But anyhow it gives me satisfaction to bait him."

Her mind was on Vera. She said, when they had sat down on the window seat of the landing: —

"Vera is awfully anxious for you to win at the Show."

"She wouldn't be a friend of ours if she weren't."

"She talks of nothing else."

He looked gratified.

"I don't see how I can fail," he said, "if Gallant doesn't absolutely refuse to jump, as he did this morning."

"You should have laid your crop about him."

"No, that won't do." He rubbed a bruise on his shin and then said thoughtfully: —

"*So*, she paints her lips?"

"Yes. You ought to see her do it. She paints carefully enough to make them a pretty shape."

"It's a wonder she would let you see her do it. She might know you'd tell me."

"She's the soul of frankness."

"That's a deception."

"Not if you make no pretense of hiding it."

"She hides it from her family."

Meg lifted a plump shoulder. "They don't count. It is only you who count with Vera."

He turned down the corners of his mouth severely. "I should not care to kiss a girl with painted lips."

"Well, I don't suppose you will kiss her."

"I don't suppose so."

"Renny — have you ever kissed anyone? I mean outside your family?"

"*Wouldn't* you like to know?"

"Tell me!" She clasped his arm and spoke in a wheedling tone.

"Of course I have."

"Many?"

"Several."

"Lately?"

"Well — not long ago."

"Since you were sent home?"

This reminder of his suspension irritated him. He withdrew his arm from hers and rose.

He said — "I'm going to have a bath. I feel filthy."

"You do smell rather horsy."

"It's a good thing Vera isn't here."

"She wouldn't mind! She'd admire you if you smelled of fire and brimstone."

He asked — "Does she know I am suspended?"

"Yes. I told her you had quarrelled with the riding master and had knocked him down."

He laughed. "What did she say to that?"

"She thought it was thrilling."

He went to his room thinking of Vera, but when the door had closed behind him his thoughts turned to Lulu, her strange eyes, her lithe body and strong arms. He stood in the middle of his room frowning, the remembrance of his night with her rising like a rock round which his thoughts circled and eddied in unsatisfied insistence.

But from this time he was conscious of Vera in a new way. A new element entered into their relations. He was watchful of her, and she realized that she was no longer just Meg's friend, but a girl to whose presence he was sensitive.

Malahide spent more and more time at Vaughanlands. It was a relief to have this new door open to him. But, though he might spend the middle of the day in the company of the Vaughans (Robert Vaughan found him a delightful companion), he was always back at Jalna in time for tea, in time to take his place at the backgammon board or bridge table, to appear to toy superciliously with his food at supper and yet, in some mysterious way, to sweep his plate clean. He and Adeline held long conversations in which the others had no part. At first these had been entertaining, with their allusions to the Court family and their life in Ireland, but as time went on and the same scandals and episodes were reiterated and the same people mimicked in Malahide's simpering tones, the irritation of the family became almost unendurable. His presence became like a hair shirt to their proud body. His attitude toward Adeline was slavish. When she made one of her shrewd and sometimes witty remarks he would shake with silent laughter. When she launched a stinging comment at one of the family he twisted his long legs together and writhed in appreciation. At whatever game he played with her she was invariably the winner, so that she was always pleased with him.

He was so languid that it was difficult to believe the tales Scotchmere told of his prowess in jumping. An air of mystery was thrown over the schooling of Harpie, so that little was heard of her progress. Adeline and Malahide were constantly making veiled allusions to her. They had an irritating way of speaking of her as "H," as though her very name were a mystery, and Malahide began to speak of Mr. Vaughan as "my dear friend, Robert."

Ten days before the Show, Renny and Scotchmere could no longer bear the strain of schooling Gallant under observation from the opposing camp, for Malahide was occasionally appearing beside the paddock with Adeline on his arm. A smooth piece of pasture beyond the orchards and woods was now chosen for the schooling and the hurdles were placed there. Renny and Scotchmere rose early and led the colt to his training unseen, leaving a dark trail across the dew-grey grass.

Here they worked, the youth and the colt, with Scotchmere perched on a rail fence, a straw between his yellow teeth, settled pessimism on his weazened, sandy face. But as this was his habitual expression at the time of schooling, Renny was not cast down by it. The colt and Renny understood each other better every day. Not so, it appeared, Harpie and Malahide. Word leaked through from Vaughanlands that she had come to hate her rider, that she sidled away when he touched her, that, good-tempered though she was, she quivered with irritation when he settled himself in the saddle. "And no wonder," observed Scotchmere, "for, if ever I seen a snake on horseback, it's him. No wonder he was drove out of Ireland."

But no one questioned his ability to ride or the fact that, under his tuition, the mare was developing into a beautiful jumper. Disquieting rumours came every now and again.

XXIII

WOODLAND QUARTETTE

IN THESE AUTUMN days a softness came into the air, from the moment when the sun had swept away the sharpness of night. It was not like the bright warmth of summer, but crept out from under the trees and spread itself over the land like a palpable veil. All the striving of the season was over. All the struggle against fiery heat and withering wind and arrogant storm. There was nothing left to do but dream. The heavy clumps of goldenrod were dreaming. The mauve clouds of wild asters were dreaming beneath the weight of pollen-drenched bees. One by one the wine-coloured plumes of the sumac fell to the grass, as in a dream. The wild strawberry plants, dreaming that it was spring, sent out frail white flowers. Rabbits in the swarthy stubble moved silently, like creatures in a dream. The body of the old mare, which Scotchmere neglected to have buried, now lay, divested of flesh, a prehistoric mound of strange bones, an aerial fortification for the seething ant hills below. Ten thousand locusts sang their song of the futility of effort, but all the birds were silent.

Even Scotchmere, usually ruthless in his energy when the training of horses was concerned, had pushed his battered hat to the back of his tow head and was prowling over the shaggy grass in a fence corner where once, thirty years ago, he had lost a fifty-cent piece. In all these years he had never given up the hope of finding it, and whenever he had a slack time he fumbled and scratched, like a terrier after a lost bone, now on this side of the fence, now on that.

By degrees Renny and the colt too cared less and less for their strenuous activity. The colt stood in his stern perfection as though carved from grey granite. Oh his back Renny drooped, as though all his will had left him and he waited to be swayed by the breath of mere instinct.

He was unconscious that anyone had approached him till he felt a quiver run through the flesh of the colt. Then he moved his gaze from between its alert ears and saw a slender hand, a forefinger marked by needle pricks into which the stains of farm work had penetrated, slide along Gallant's side. It touched him on the knee.

He looked down then into Lulu's suntanned aquiline face.

She returned the look boldly, armed by what they had in their past meeting. She smiled and said — "I was about this way and I thought I'd drop in to see you."

Seeing her face thus slanting up at him from below, he felt a sudden quiver in his flesh, comparable to what the colt had felt at her touch, but with the added agitation of their remembered embraces.

There was more severity than sensuality, however, in his look as he replied — "You came at a bad time. I'm schooling the colt for the Show."

She ignored his first remark and exclaimed — "My, but he'll be a fine jumper! I wish I might see him. Do you think you could send me a ticket?"

"I don't want you to be looking on," he said sullenly. "You might put me off my form."

She laughed daringly. "Me put you off! Never! I'd put you on! Just when the other fellas might be winning you'd suddenly see me staring at you with all my eyes and you'd clear every barrier like a bird. Come on, say you'll send me a ticket!"

"All right," he answered, still sullenly. "I'll send you a ticket. What's your surname? I have never heard it."

"Address it to Mrs. Lulu Lepard…. How do you like the name? Does it suit me?"

"It's the Missus I'm thinking of," he replied "I didn't know you'd been married."

"Oh, I've been married! More than once, too, though not at that little church on the knoll, where your folks go."

"Is your husband living?"

"Don't ask me about any man but yourself! You are the only one I care about. I thought I was dead to men — dead and buried to them — till you came along." She began to stroke the glossy leather of his riding boot.

He looked down at her, frowning. He put down his hand and touched the back of her tanned neck, then drew it away.

"What's the matter?" she said. "Don't you like me any more? Look how I like you! I'd let you rip my breast open with this spur, if you wanted." She lifted his foot and pressed the spurred heel to her breast. It tore the thin cotton of her dress and made a deep scratch on the white flesh beneath.

"Don't!" he cried fiercely, and drew his foot away. Then the hardness went out of his face and it was tormented into lines of desire that took all its boyishness from it. "Lulu," he murmured, "my girl — my Lulu — what shall we do?" His hand sought her breast and he touched the mark made by the spur.

He saw her face darken with anger as she stared at someone approaching. It was Scotchmere, disconsolate after his fruitless search.

"Send him away!" she whispered. "Send him off to his stable! Think of the quietness here! Send him away!"

Scotchmere plodded on toward them, filled with resentment as he discovered her there, for, as he loved horses, so, in proportion, he hated women, with the one exception of old Mrs. Whiteoak.

Renny's vision blurred. Before his eyes he saw dark, unknown groves and the dim figures of Lulu and himself.

"Ye're gettin' on fine with the jumpin' aren't ye?" sneered Scotchmere. "Has the colt gone slack, or is it you?" He came and jerked the colt's bridle and it flung up its head and showed its teeth at him. "Come now — come now — would you bite at me? But perhaps you're just sick and tired of standin' slack."

"Do you let this stableman order you about?" asked Lulu.

Scotchmere retorted — "We've got our work cut out for us, Mrs. Whoever-you-are." But, though he would not say her name, he showed plainly that he recognized her. He began to tighten a strap of the stirrup, muttering to himself.

Renny sat between the two, motionless, but when Scotchmere's light eyes gave him a piercing look his lips framed the words, "Don't go."

Scotchmere straightened himself and said — "Well, now, shall we get to work? If you want to see some fine high jumpin', missus, you'll see it here. This young gentleman is the ridin'est critter I ever set eyes on — whatever else *you* may find in him."

Lulu showed her teeth in a straight white line — a forced, bitterly disappointed grin.

Renny resolutely kept his eyes averted from her, as he wheeled the colt and trotted down the track. As he headed Gallant for the first hurdle, he saw, out of the sides of his eyes, Lulu and Scotchmere in angry altercation. There was no mistaking the vindictive thrust of the man's head, the woman's jeering laugh.

Everything was wrong with the colt. It sidled from the hurdles as though it had never seen them before. It tossed its head in fury at the flies. It behaved as though it had gone lame. It laid its ears flat and lolled out its tongue.

Renny had wanted to show Lulu of what mettle Gallant was made. In some subtle way he had transferred his amorous proclivities to his desire to display the colt, as though in its leaping his manhood might have leapt. Again and again he wheeled and rushed Gallant at the hurdles. The colt either balked or jumped sideways, scattered the rails or attempted to climb them. All its great naked flashing body was pregnant with perversity. The broken rhythm of its hoofs was a low thunder of hate.

In anger Renny lashed it with the crop and the colt snorted and bucked, throwing up torn pieces of turf. It made itself into a ball and hurled him over his head. Then, with a clarion neigh, it battered along the track and in a wild leap cleared the gate. The pine wood appeared to open to receive it, and into this natural stable it galloped, neighing as some prehistoric ancestor may well have done.

Renny lay on his back looking up into the faces of Lulu and Scotchmere with equal hate.

Lulu bent over him. "He's hurt! Oh, my poor, beautiful boy!"

Scotchmere gave a loud guffaw. "Hurt! Not him. I guess he's had two hundred falls in his life so far. He's just mad — boiling mad at you. Haven't you spoiled his morning's work? Haven't you turned the colt wicked, so we shall never win anything by him now? You ought to kneel down in this here field and pray to God to forgive you. Why He made horseflies and women like you to be pests — He only knows! This here's a school for horses, not rips. So you can take yourself off or I'll let the boss hear a thing or two."

Lulu snatched up Renny's crop and stared fixedly at Scotchmere.

"If you hit me," he said, "I'll hit you back and the young gentleman can bear witness why."

She looked down at Renny. "Are you hurt?" she asked in a small voice unlike her own.

He answered — "No, but you'd better go."

She exclaimed recklessly — "Oh, I'm going — never fear! You'll never see me again — be sure of that! Do you think I'm a loose one that doesn't mind being insulted? Look here, this Scotchmere is a cheat! He cheats your father! Haven't I heard tales of him in the village? My God, how crooked he is!"

"You say that!" said Scotchmere, turning green.

"Yes! And more! I say that you was always prowling round my house of night — tapping at the window — whining to be let in!" She planted herself, laughing in his face.

"Blast your soul!" said Scotchmere. "Every word you let through your teeth is a lie. I'll call on the law! I'll have you up for libel! I'll have you up for seduction! This young lad hadn't a bad thought till you put them in his head."

"You've blasted me, and I'll blast you, in real earnest," said Lulu. "And the horse, too, if it wasn't that I love this boy."

Renny sat up. "Don't say you'd blast the colt, Lulu! That's a terrible thing to say."

His face changed, as he spoke, for he saw his father approaching in company with an apple buyer who had come to inspect the orchard. In the distance Philip took the figure of Lulu to be that of Mary. He removed his hat and waved it.

Lulu smiled at Scotchmere. "Mr. Whiteoak has nothing against me," she said. She stood for a moment irresolute, then turned with a swaying step and moved toward the wood, the trees seeming to open to receive her as they had received the colt.

XXIV

THE SAME DAY

AT NOON OF the same day Renny followed the meanderings of the river, from where it skirted the wood, after having flung a protective arm about the churchyard, down into the ravine where it spread itself into a shallow basin. A smooth slab of stone formed the bottom of this, and cattails, wild honeysuckle, and elderberries drooped about it. Here he would bathe, for it was too far to go to the lake, dog-tired as he was. He and Scotchmere had had a morning's work to recover the colt, which had crashed through undergrowth, galloped across fields, and at last had been captured on the public road trotting in the direction of the farm where he had spent one sultry night. The three had returned to the stables in common resentment.

Renny threw himself on the grass and took from his pocket three peaches he had picked on the way, for he had had little breakfast and it was an hour till the one o'clock dinner.

He laid the three in a row, in order of their mellowness, the first showing a ruddy gold cheek, the second blushing less warmly, and the third with only a faint pinkness beneath its velvety skin. The most mature he held to his nostrils, sniffing it with an air of distaste rather than relish. His unseeing eyes held in them the reflection of Lulu's supple form as she moved toward the darkness of the wood. She had come all that way to tempt and for nothing less. And how had she come? Was Bob in their secret? He experienced both relief and chagrin at her discomfiture.

He bit deep into the peach and, as its nectar lay on his tongue, he made a wry face, for he was suddenly aware that he was not alone, but that Malahide Court was seated in the shallow basin below reading a book while he soaked himself in the tepid water.

If a serpent had raised his head in his retreat, he could scarcely have felt more aversion than he felt at the sight of Malahide's small glossy head arching out of the stream. He looked and looked, as though the singular contours were new to him, and for some bizarre reason must be impressed upon his mind.

He felt surprised at the strength of the shoulders which he saw exposed and a grim amusement at the choice of such a spot for reading. He recognized the cover of the book as belonging to a novel by Rider Haggard. He finished his peach without tasting it, his eyes fixed on Malahide, who sat motionless as one of the tree roots which projected from the riverbank, save when he raised a dripping hand to turn the page.

Seeing a loose boulder near him, it entered Renny's head to precipitate it down the bank into the basin and give Malahide a fright, but at that moment the two swans, followed by their troop of cygnets, the first they had successfully reared, swam round a curve. As they emerged from the greenish shadow into the sunlight the male swan became aware of the alien presence and halted abruptly in his gliding progress, curving his neck strongly and opening his beak. His mate and his cygnets also became statuesque, gleaming in their whiteness on the face of the stream.

As the swans paused, transfixed, Malahide became wearied of his book or had perhaps reached its last page. With a wide gesture he flung it on the bank and settled himself into a position of still greater repose, unaware that his movement had further angered the male swan, who swam quickly in his direction, only stopping when close behind him. If he would attack Malahide, thought Renny! Oh, to be the witness of a combat between the two! If only he could have broken the barrier of language and cried out something in the tongue of swans to incite them to anger!

But their leader now turned with careless grace, as though anger were unworthy of him, and moved in stately fashion, followed by his train, round the curve from where they had come.

Malahide, unaware that he had been observed by bird or man, now rose from the water and walked gingerly across the burning hot stones at the water's edge and disappeared among some bushes.

Renny had no longer any desire to enter the pool. He sat staring gloomily down at it, his thoughts now turned from Lulu to what the outcome of the struggle between him and Malahide might be. Would the colt be upset by this morning's happenings and perhaps lose his nerve or become irrevocably willful? Feelings of melancholy, to which he was seldom a victim, settled on his spirit like birds of prey.

He must do something active to be rid of them. He rose and climbed the path as it mounted the side of the ravine toward the lawn. On the smooth stretch of grass he saw Meg and Vera gathering grapes from the luxuriant vines that draped themselves along a trellis. They were filling a large woven basket that stood on legs, talking and laughing softly together as they worked. Nothing did Meg so much good as Vera's presence. Vera lifted her out of herself, filled Meg with interest in the affairs of another.

When Meg saw Renny appear she made an excuse to go into the house, so that, as he reached Vera's side, he found her alone. It seemed to him that he saw her now for the first time. He looked at her with a curiosity so evident that she coloured as she said: —

"Are you coming to help us? My aunts are determined to make grape wine. They are to have all I can gather for them."

He did not answer, but still continued to look at her.

"There are two varieties here," she said, trying to speak naturally, "the deep purple and this lovely greenish gold. Of course, I'm telling you something you know already, but which do you like best?"

"Those greenish-yellow ones are rather the colour of your eyes," he answered, "so I like them best."

She did not know whether to accept this seriously or to make light of it. Though Meg talked so much of her brother, Vera felt that she knew nothing of him. She said: —

"It doesn't sound very attractive."

"But it is. And, while we're on the subject of you, I wish you would tell me why your hair is short and curly when the other girls wear pompadours."

"I had scarlet fever before I left England and it had to be cut. It came in curly like this. I suppose you think it hideous!"

He looked at her sombrely. "I had heard that it was a different sort of fever you had."

She knew how to take this. She laughed — "Oh, that! An affair, you mean. It wasn't very serious on my part. But my parents thought a year out here would be good for me. They think travel is broadening for a girl's mind — just as well for a young man's. What do you think?"

"I think it should do anyone good to see Jalna," he answered.

"And what about the son and heir to Jalna?" she said mockingly, but moving closer to him.

He could find no answer. He took the scissors which Meg had laid in the basket. He drew a heavy golden-green cluster from its hiding place under the leaves and snipped it off. It lay shimmering like the Pleiades in the arc of his palm. Vera bent to cut a bunch from the base of the vine and he saw the close chestnut tendrils of hair on her nape. Here was his answer, he thought. He laid the grapes in the basket and snipped off a lock of hair.

"Look," he said, "what I've done!"

She turned her face up to him, keeping it expressionless as a mask. She breathed — "Why did you do it?"

"Do you mind?"

"No — but I want to know why. Just to tease me?"

"No."

"Why, then?"

"I don't know."

"Yes — you do. You've a deliberate look in your eyes."

"Well, because I wanted something of you that I could keep." He took out a shabby leather notebook and laid the lock in it. Then he knelt beside her in the shadow of the grapevine and his arm slid about her. He saw the whiteness of her skin, exquisite as though the sun had never touched it, the glistening fineness of the skin about her eyes, the golden freckles on her nose like the pollen of a flower. She realized that he was going to kiss her.

Meg, coming softly across the grass, saw them holding each other close. She saw the abandon of Vera's attitude and drew a deep breath of envy and disapproval. How *could* Vera! Never, never could *she* have kissed Maurice like that. Why, Vera was behaving like a village girl! She would let her know what she thought about it. And Renny, her *own* brother … no wonder young men were — what they were!

How angry he would be if she went close to them, stared down at them hiding there! Then she saw their faces as they drew apart, looking in each other's eyes, and she glided away. She could not interrupt them — not with that look in their faces! They were like people in a dream. And he had said that he would not kiss a girl who painted her lips! This showed what a man's word was worth! She despised them all.

Vera had come to spend the day with her. Meg looked with curiosity at Renny and her when they came into the dining room, but their faces showed no trace of emotion. Deceivers — clever deceivers — Renny looking innocently into his father's eyes, Vera being sweet to Grandmother, who gave her a hearty kiss.

"Come and sit by me, my dear, and tell me what is the latest news from London."

Adeline saw between Vera and Malahide, well pleased with herself and them. She said to the girl: —

"You must come to Vaughanlands and see Malahide on Harpie. You'll see riding such as you've never seen and jumping such as you've never seen. You'll get a great dindle out of it, I promise you. They're a fine combination. Now, that grandson of mine is always being thrown. Those that have seen him stripped say that he is covered by bruises. His mount rages over the country side with a hue and cry of grooms after him. All these things come to my ear." She smacked her lips with satisfaction and added — "More of the veal, Philip. Cook has just the right flavour in the dressing. Give Malahide more of the veal."

She was in such spirits that she could not settle down to her afternoon nap and cast about in her mind for something they might do. A remark from Nicholas gave her the idea. He said: —

"I drove along the shore road this morning. The lake is like glass."

"Good!" she exclaimed. "We'll have a picnic. You girls shall go in bathing. Would you like that, Vera?"

"Oh, I'd love it!" Vera's eyes sought Renny's across the table.

"I like to watch young people bathing. Used to do it myself when it was considered rather improper. Why, I've heard that in Elizabeth's reign the students up at Cambridge were whipped or put in the stocks if they took a bathe in the sea. Well, for my part, I have my good soapy tub once a week — winter or summer — and it's done me no harm."

"I don't think I'll go in," observed Malahide. "I had a bathe in the river this morning and it was quite enough." A black lock clung limply against his forehead. He was feeling the unseasonable heat.

"Now," continued Adeline briskly, "the question is, what shall we eat?"

Before this could be answered the resources of the larder had to be ascertained. Fortunately it was well stocked, and Adeline, Mary, and Eliza conferred amicably on the packing of the hampers. Philip went to the cellar and brought up several bottles of wine and raspberry vinegar. The cook was set to work on the making of a large coconut cake. Eden collected his bucket and spade and the sailing boat he had got on his birthday. The baby was roused early from his nap and screamed lustily throughout the final preparations.

Hodge grumbled a good deal at taking out the bays in the midafternoon heat, but promptly at half-past three he had them drawn up before the door. The party divided themselves between the phaëton and the surrey driven by Philip.

Once they had left the spreading oaks of their own road, the sun beat hotly down on them. Grandmother's face was a dark red under her heavy widow's bonnet, but Malahide turned more pale and it was difficult for him to conceal his dissatisfaction with the outing. Many of the party would have been glad to have left him at home, but Adeline desired his presence, and that was enough for him. Nothing could appease the infant, Piers, until Philip took him on his knee and let him clutch the ends of the reins in his tiny hands. Eden's straw hat blew off into the ditch and the horses must be stopped and Renny go back to fetch it. He did so with bad grace and, returning, jammed it so far over the little boy's eyes that now he began to kick and cry. Vera and Meg sat in a seat together, their arms about each other, whispering and laughing. Meg could not remain disapproving. Vera fascinated her, now more than ever.

They turned into the narrow road that led to the lake, where the trees were not tall enough for shade, but standing close enough to keep out what breeze there was. The road was little more than a sandy path, and at its end the horses must be left and the hampers carried to the shore.

The walk over the soft sandy path was an effort to Adeline. She leant heavily on Nicholas's arm, but pressed forward eagerly to the sight of the lake, which so far this summer she had seen only from her carriage.

Rugs were spread on the coarse grass that grew beneath a group of windswept willows that sent their roots deep into the sand and were tenacious in their growth in spite of drought and storm and winter gale.

What a relief to be settled in their shade! To uncover heads and fan flushed faces with straw hats! There was no one else on the beach. They had the wide sandy stretch and the glittering blue expanse of the lake to themselves.

The bottles of raspberry vinegar that stood icebound in a bucket were opened and glasses were filled. Almost solemnly, their pleasure was so great, the family looked at each other as the sharp, sweet, ice-cold liquid, with its flavour of fresh raspberries, cooled their throats. Even Peep was given a taste, but made a wry face and hiccupped it up again. Eden drank his without taking breath and begged for more. Adeline spilt a little on the deck of his sailing boat, and exclaimed — "Now, I christen this vessel for you — 'Shamrock!' And good luck to her!"

Nicholas and Philip smoked their pipes, lounging comfortably on the sand. Renny, with a look over his shoulder at Vera, took the children to the water's edge. Vera followed and Meg sat disconsolate, feeling that she was not wanted by them, yet longing for their company. Mary took out her work bag and began to darn one of Eden's socks. Malahide lay passive, sifting the fine sand through his fingers and now and again giving Adeline a smile of secret understanding. Hodge had loosed the horses and led them across the sand to the water's edge. They bent their heads and drew in deep draughts. A pair of sandpipers walked briskly about, with sidelong glances at the party. A small steamer laden with school picnickers moved slowly past, just near enough for a faint cheer to be audible from her decks.

Adeline gave a grunt of satisfaction. "Nothing like a picnic," she said. "I like 'em and always shall. Another drop of this raspberry vinegar. Meg, don't look mopey, child. If you won't marry, you won't marry, and that's all there is to it. Thanks." She took the proffered glass and put her lips to the cold ruby fluid. Then she took out her heavily chased gold watch.

"There's just time for a nice bathe before tea," she said. "You ought to go in, Philip. It might take some of that fat off you."

"Philip fat!" cried Mary. "He's nothing of the sort! He's just nicely covered. He's a perfect figure."

"Well, you ought to know," returned Adeline, staring at her.

Philip answered complacently: —

"I've brought along my bathing suit. Have you, Nick?"

"Not I. I can't endure bathing in fresh water."

"What about you, Malahide?"

"I bathed in the stream this morning. I found it very depressing. I don't think I shall go in again. Your mother and Nicholas and I shall judge your performance."

"Come along, Molly," said Philip. "Let's have a dip."

Molly, all eagerness, put away her darning and produced their bathing suits and towels. Dimples showed in her slender cheeks. She called: —

"Eden, Eden! Do you want to bathe? Bring Peep along and come to Mamma!"

Philip shouted to his eldest son and flung him a faded bathing suit. Vera and Meg scampered to the shelter of a cluster of cedars where Mary was already undressing. Adeline, her massive veil falling about her shoulders, had taken the little boys in charge. As she pulled off their few garments she remarked to Nicholas: —

"Here, on this very spot, I used to undress you and Ernest when you were just so high. You were a little rip, but Ernest was always squealing and timid. I don't know how your father and I got him. Really, I don't…. Stand still, Peep, and let Granny put on your vest." For the baby, who owned no bathing suit, there was a shrunken wool vest which inadequately covered his sturdy infant body. Having them ready she administered a hearty smack on their buttocks which, knowing it was playfully done, they received with shouts of laughter. Eden, grasping Peep's hand, led him across the sand to where the sparkling blueness invited them.

But before they reached it they were caught up by their father and carried shrieking on his shoulders into the lake. Mary and Meg appeared in blue kilted bathing suits trimmed with white braid, but Vera's was white with a sky-blue sash and she had wound a scarf of the same colour about her curls. The shortness of her skirt brought an element of Continental daring to the scene.

The three young women and Philip were soon splashing in the water, passing the children from hand to hand. Philip swam outward with both on his back till Molly's shrieks recalled him. Vera filled Meg with envy by swimming two dozen strokes. Her pretty scarf was soaked and her hair curled more closely than ever.

"Renny! Renny!" cried Eden. "Teach me to swim! Take me out with you!"

Renny came slowly across the sand toward the bathers. He had been watching them from the shelter where he had changed. He looked at Vera, wondering how he could manage to be alone with her. Yet, when they were alone again, what should he say? Make love to her or pretend that all was as it had been before? What would a girl like Vera expect? Let her make the first move, he thought, let her lead the way into whatever bypath of love she chose. He was ready to follow.

"Renny! Renny!" shouted Eden, clinging to Renny's hand and lifting his own feet from the ground, as though by sheer weight he might command attention.

Ignoring him, Renny went toward Vera, his eyes saying — "Now, what do you want of me?"

"Renny! Renny! *Will* you teach me to swim?" Eden beat him with small angry fists.

"Yes," answered his brother. "This is the way."

He picked him up and strode into the water with him across his arms. When he was waist-high he threw Eden from him with a splash. "There, now, swim! That's the way I learned."

Eden struggled, sank, rose floundering and choking, all legs and arms, churning the water in his anguish. Mary came to his rescue, her eyes blazing.

"What a way to treat him! My poor little boy!" She gathered him to her, comforting him.

Adeline called from the shore — "Molly, put him back! Don't coddle him! Upon my soul, the word 'mollycoddle' was invented for you!"

"See me float!" cried Meg. "I'm a marvel at floating."

"You could not sink if you tried," laughed Philip, and she began to splash him.

Vera dropped lazily to the water and struck out in a graceful breast stroke. Renny swam on his side, his cheek on the water. With compassion he saw how she struggled to keep up with him, not to give in.

Suddenly she cried, in fright — "Am I out of my depth?"

He laughed and stood up beside her and supported her in his arms. He saw the flash of her white legs in the greenness. She clung to him, laughing into his face.

"It's so different," she said, "from the sea. It feels so thin. There's nothing there. Have you been in the sea?"

"Yes. I went once to Nova Scotia with Maurice."

"Oh, I wish you could swim in the Mediterranean! It's so lovely!" She spoke breathlessly.

"I wish I could." So, she wanted to behave as though nothing had happened. And with all this wide blueness about them! Was she afraid? He added, in a low voice — "With you."

She gave a nervous little laugh. "You could teach me. I don't swim very well."

"But how few girls do! I'll give you some lessons. I'll teach you to dive, if you like — when the Show is over. But I must go back to college — I forgot that."

"Give me a lesson now."

She surrendered herself to him, his hand under her chest. He felt the throbbing of her heart. "Like this," he said, "and so — don't be afraid — let yourself go — you're too tense." The living water curled about them. He felt the firm ripples of sand beneath his feet. The sun blazed. "If we were here," he thought, "at night ..." His hands tightened on her. He restrained her movements and, with a slanting look at the shore, where the others were playing with the children, he bent and pressed his lips to hers. She put her wet arms about his neck and held him.

When they returned the preparations for the meal were already on the way. A fine white cloth had been stretched on the sand, across which the trees now cast an agreeable shadow. Philip had laid two fires inside two circles of flat stones piled on top of one another. And on one of these the teakettle already sang. He told Renny to bring more driftwood, at the same time giving him a suspicious look. What had the boy been up to out there? He had seen him bending above Vera in an attitude too motionless for a lesson in swimming. Eden came running with his arms full of dry twigs and, when Renny added smooth driftwood to the flames, they raged vehemently about the kettle and under the large frying pan which Meg now placed on the second fire.

"What are you going to cook in that, Meggie?" asked Renny.

"Ham and eggs. My face is almost blistered. You do it for me?"

"A boy cook ham and eggs!" cried Vera. "He'll be sure to ruin them."

"Not he! He'll fry them better than I could."

Vera lingered fascinated by his side while he laid slices of ham in the pan, but seeing Philip's contemplative eyes on her, she turned away and began to talk eagerly to Nicholas.

One by one the golden yokes were discovered in the transparent whites. Renny squatted by the fire, his face intent, his cheeks burning red from the heat. His wet bathing suit clung to his curved lean body.

The waiting for the meal was becoming intolerable to Adeline. Leaning on her stick, she plodded up and down through the sand, now peering into the bucket where the wine lay cooling, now surveying the cloth on which Mary was arranging plates of bread and butter, thick ginger cookies, the coconut cake in a shroud of white shreds, and a bowl of halved peaches. Beside this stood a large glass jug containing thick cream. At the other end of the cloth she had placed a dish of potato salad on crisp lettuce leaves and a golden wedge of Cheddar cheese.

Adeline's mouth watered. She set her teeth together and trudged back to the fire.

"Keep dipping the fat over the tops of the eggs," she instructed Renny. "Mind what you're doing — you'll have the pan upset!"

He had turned his head aside to avoid a puff of smoke in his eyes. He had just picked up the last egg.

"Careful!" warned Meg. "That egg is to be boiled for Peep. He wouldn't eat his dinner because of the new tooth that he is cutting. Mother thought he should have an egg for his tea."

"Look out!" cried Adeline, "you're spilling the fat!" She poked him in the ribs with her stick while the fat, taking fire, flamed menacingly. Renny dropped the egg from his hand. It broke on the stones and slid, sleek as a lizard, into a crevice.

"Good heavens!" cried Meg. "See what you've done! Whatever will Mother say!"

"I'll have to tell her," said Renny. "These are done." He handed the pan to Meg and went to Mary, who was tying the baby's bib. If she had been angry about his treatment of Eden, what would she be now?

"Look here, Mother," he said. "I've broken Peep's egg. What shall we do about it?"

"Egg — gegg — gegg —" crowed Peep.

"Oh, how could you be so stupid?"

"Gran poked me with her stick and the smoke went in my eyes at the same moment. I'm awfully sorry." He looked miserably down on the baby.

"Well," said Mary, "he'll just have to have bread and milk, poor lamb!"

But someone had left Peep's bottle of milk in the sun. It was quite sour. It was too much for Mary. She raged to Philip.

"I've never seen such behaviour with food in my life," she exclaimed. "Your mother simply ravens about the frying pan and makes Renny lose his head so that the baby's egg is broken. Now Meg has left the jar with his milk in the sun. She's so careless. What am I to do? I shall simply have to take him and go home."

Philip knocked out his pipe on the sand. He said, calmly — "There's a farm near by. Let Renny go and get some milk there for the kid."

"Mik — mik — mik —" cried Peep, holding out his hands for the milk jar.

"I'll go with Renny for the milk," said Vera. "He might spill it. I shan't mind at all."

"Nonsense!" said Adeline, who had just come up. "Thin some of the cream with warm water. I've given that to my children hundreds of times."

"No," refused Mary. "He must have the milk."

Renny and Vera set out. Again their chance to be alone! They hurried along the smooth path in their bare feet. While they waited at the door of the farmhouse they looked at each other and smiled. They could not draw away from that gaze, nor yet could they look steadily. Their glances wavered, dipped, and rose again like gulls on the wing. She longed to touch his glistening brown shoulder. They laughed and made foolish remarks about the chickens that gathered round them. They carried the little pail of milk between them along the path.

In a quiet spot they set down the pail, and now they were in each other's arms.

"Vera," he breathed, "I do like you!"

"Oh, Renny, we should not be doing this!"

"I thought you were hard, but you're a sweet thing."

"You're adorable!"

"How much do you like me?"

"More than you me."

"You couldn't. I like you this much." He told her by kisses.

She whispered — "I'm mad for you, Renny!"

"God — if we didn't have to go back!"

"We must. They're waiting." She drew away from him and hurried along the path.

Once in sight they were greeted by orders to hasten. Ham and eggs had been kept hot for them. The party was now gathered about the cloth. The teasing smell of coffee that bubbled on the fire filled the air. Appetites were enormous except in the two late comers, and they were scarcely noticed once Mary had got Peep's milk from them. He sat serene on her knee, pausing between mouthfuls of bread and milk to gaze in wonder at the expanse of white cloth, at the array of strange food. Once his grandmother popped a bit of ham into his mouth and he beamed at her the long while it lasted him. Nicholas kept the wine circulating, and Malahide, who had seemed enervated and depressed all the afternoon, became animated. "Perfect weather, a lovely scene, good wine, and charming people — what more could one demand?" he exclaimed. Meg murmured, under her breath — "Your removal."

With the coffee they disposed themselves more indolently. Renny carried a large cup of it to Hodge, who was eating his meal near the tethered horses. He sat down beside Hodge and offered him a cigarette. They began to talk of Gallant. The fact that other horses from the Jalna stables were entered in the Show had sunk to unimportance. All hopes were centred on the colt. When Renny and Hodge talked of him they forgot everything else and brooded only on the beauty of lovely horseflesh.

Mary went and stood by herself on the shore watching the dark rose bars of the afterglow. It was growing cool and she held her slender body in her arms while an aching sadness made her eyes fill with tears. She was happy and, because of her happiness and the lovely colour of the sky, she wanted to weep. The voices of the others came to her, sweet and sad, like evening bells.

A small cold hand reached up to touch hers. Her fingers closed over it with tender pressure.

Eden asked — "Why did you come here, Mummie?"

"To watch the colours in the sky."

"And on the lake, too. There are colours deep down in the lake."

"Yes. Do you like them?"

"Do you?"

"Yes. But they make me long for something. You can't understand that."

"I do. They make me sad too."

Philip came across the sand that now lay in shadow. "Time to go! The horses are ready. The girls have the baskets packed and Peep is asleep on Mamma's lap."

Eden put up his arms and tugged at his father's coat. "Oh, I'm so tired! Do you think you could carry me a little way?"

Philip swung him to his shoulder, Mary put her hand in Philip's arm, but she was reluctant to return, even though she too was tired.

XXV

BONEY

HE HAD HAD a lonely day. The dullness of the morning had been unbearable. The sun was so hot that Adeline had kept the curtains of her bedroom drawn, and when he had complained to her, demanded her attention by a harsh coughing sound ceaselessly repeated, she had laid a square of dark cloth over his cage, cutting him off from all sight of her, from all movement of air. In her excitement over the picnic she had forgotten to remove the cloth and he had languished the rest of the day in a silent house, his only pastime the tearing of cloth to shreds and the spitting out of his seed shells on to the floor.

Adeline was contrite when she saw him humped there in his cage, an expression of abysmal gloom on his beak. She uncovered him and spoke to him in comforting Hindoo all the while she changed the black cashmere dress she had worn to the picnic for her second-best black silk. What a relief it was to take off her bonnet and put on a fresh lace cap! She fastened the collar of her bodice with a diamond brooch set in twists of dull gold.

She took Boney from his cage and attached to his leg the slender chain of his perch. She took the perch in her hand and, carrying it in front of her, appeared, as though in procession, at the door of the drawing room, where the rest of the family were gathered.

"Poor old Boney!" she said. "What a day he's had! I left him with his cage covered, a thing I never remember doing before. Now he's coming into the heart of the company." She planted his perch in the middle of the room and sat herself in the chair Malahide placed for her.

Philip said — "Hadn't we better have something to eat? It seems a long while since the picnic tea."

His mother looked at him sharply. "What's the matter with supper? We're accustomed to supper, aren't we?"

"But, Mamma," objected Mary, "when do we eat such a tea as that? For my part I could not touch another mouthful, but of course we can easily have supper for any who want it."

"Nothing but a whiskey and soda and some biscuits for me," said Nicholas. "What about you, Malahide?"

Malahide's preoccupation of the afternoon had returned. He was sunk in a deep chair in a dark corner of the room. He held his chin in his hand and his heavy eyes regarded the family with languid indifference behind which a spark of anger burned. He had disliked the day he had spent almost as much as Boney had disliked his, and he was too tired, for once, to conceal his feelings. He answered, in a low voice: —

"I'll have a whiskey, but no biscuits, thank you."

Adeline said — "What, losing your appetite, Mally? Now I want a pot of tea and some buttered toast and anchovy paste. You children will sup with your Granny, won't you?"

Meg and Renny agreed that they would. Philip went for the whiskey and soda, and in a short time Eliza appeared with a silver pot of tea, a pile of toast, so well buttered that golden globules oozed from slice to slice, collecting in a pool on the plate beneath. Adeline's eyes gleamed as she dipped into the anchovy paste.

"I like things off a tray," said Meg. "I enjoy them more than my regular meals."

"It's a bad habit," said Renny, thickly spreading a slice for himself.

"Nothing that you enjoy is a bad habit," observed their grandmother. "It's the food you eat without enjoyment that plays hob with your stomach." With satisfaction she placed her lips to her brimming cup of tea.

The hiss of the syphon sounded and Nicholas filled his pipe. A steady glow from the ceiling lamp cast a charmed light about the circle, with the exception of the corner where Malahide drooped. He tossed off his whiskey with a desperate air.

If Boney had expected some rare titbit in compensation for the dullness of his day he was disappointed. No one paid any attention to him. He walked the length of his perch, claw over claw, regarding the company with angry glances. He opened his beak wide and brought it together with a snap. He dropped his wings and, thrusting forward, exclaimed: —

"To hell with Cousin Malahide!"

Ripples of pleasure stirred his plumage as he uttered this sentence, for it was the first time he had said it except in solitude.

"What's that? What does he say?" demanded Nicholas.

Boney turned to him with an undulation of his supple neck. He repeated ferociously: —

"To hell with Cousin Malahide! To hell with Malahide! Hell — hell — hell — with Malahide!"

Was there something in the inflection, in the metallic enunciation of these words, that made all eyes turn to Renny? Malahide set down his glass and went green rather than white.

Renny burst into loud laughter. He doubled himself over his folded arms. It was more than Nicholas and Philip could bear. They joined their mirth to his. Their laughter was more than Mary and Meg could withstand. All their dislike of Malahide was loosed in shrill feminine merriment.

Boney rocked in his perch, ribald, relentless, screaming to make himself heard above the confusion he had created. He leered from one face to the other and repeated: —

"Hell — hell — hell with Cousin Malahide — *Paji* — *Haramzada* — *Iflatoon* — *Kuza Pusth* — *Sug prast* — hell — hell — hell — with Malahide!"

Malahide Court rose slowly to his feet and took a long, menacing step in the direction of the parrot. He said, with his lip lifted in a snarl: —

"To hell with you, I say! And to hell with the one who taught you these insulting words! You swear at me? Listen then: *Soor — Soor — Kunjus — Kutni! Churail! Afimche!*"

Bent on his perch, with cocked head, drinking in every oath that Malahide had uttered, as though listening to the ravings of another parrot, Boney could now restrain himself no longer. More furiously than before he screamed:

"Hell with Malahide! Hell with Malahide! Hell — hell — hell! *Iflatoon! Chore!*"

"Filthy bird," sneered Malahide, drawing a step closer. *"Nimak Haram! Nimak Halol! Sakth Dil!"*

"Byman! Sala! Dagal! To hell with Malahide!"

"Piakur! Subakhis! Jab kute!"

In a paroxysm of rage Boney rocked and cursed. It seemed that he would choke with the hate that was in him. And the louder he screamed his imprecations the more his listeners abandoned themselves to laughter — all but Adeline and Malahide.

Renny exclaimed, in Meg's ear — "This is all too much! I shall die of joy."

Her lips formed the words — "Me too!"

Adeline sat, with one heavily ringed hand shading her face, of which it could be seen that the colour was steadily deepening.

Squatting on his perch, with drooped wings, while waves of fury shook his brilliant plumage, Boney confronted Malahide. Their two mouths upcurving beneath their drooping beaks gave them a curious resemblance.

As Malahide delivered himself of a litter of black curses and shook a long forefinger in the parrot's face, Boney thrust out his head and caught the finger in his beak. Malahide doubled up in pain.

Before he could retaliate Boney leaped the length of his chain and settled on Adeline's shoulder. He began to peck wickedly at the ribbons on her cap.

"Too bad, too bad, Malahide," said Philip, ordering his face to calmness.

Malahide turned on him. "Don't you sympathize with me! You have insulted me."

"No, no — but the bird was so damn funny."

Mary said — "I hope you're not hurt."

Malahide almost screamed — "No, you don't! You hope very much that I *am* hurt. And I am! Look at that!" He shook his finger at her, from which the crimson drops sprang.

"Have another whiskey and soda," advised Nicholas.

"I want nothing from this house! I leave tonight."

"Come," said Philip. "We've not treated you badly."

"Badly! Your young ruffian has made life here a hell for me."

At the word Boney swayed on Adeline's shoulder and rasped "Hell — hell — hell with Malahide!"

Adeline snatched the antimacassar from the back of her chair and threw it over his head.

Malahide continued — "Yes, it was he who taught the parrot that insult."

Adeline said — "He shall apologize."

Philip turned to his son. "I agree. You must apologize to Malahide."

"I'm damned if I will."

"What — what —" said Philip, glaring at him, but with laughter in his eyes. "You refuse?"

"I apologize," said Renny, grinning. "I apologize for teaching Boney to say 'To hell with Cousin Malahide!'"

Boney raved under the antimacassar: —

"Hell — hell — hell!"

Malahide bowed elaborately to Renny. He said, in concentrated passion: —

"We will have this out — when the night of the Show comes. Then you — and your bucking bronco — shall bite the dust."

"Well said, Malahide!" declared Adeline. "Now come and let me bind your poor finger."

With something of childlike docility he went to her, while keeping a watchful eye on the parrot. She took her own handkerchief and deftly tied up the wound.

Philip, with a long look into Nicholas's eyes, pushed the decanter toward him. Molly began softly strumming on the piano, while Renny and Meg disappeared behind the long window curtains in a pretended search for the new moon.

XXVI

Tenting Tonight

It was with difficulty that Adeline had restrained her amusement at the duet between her parrot and her kinsman. It had been a scene after her own heart, and when she and Boney were in the seclusion of her room, she gave him not a little praise for the manner in which he had performed his part in it. Yet she was troubled about Malahide. If, as it seemed, he was to nurse his anger too fiercely, it might have an ill effect on his nerves. He and Harpie must win at the Show. Robert Vaughan had set his heart on it. Her championing of Malahide must be justified, her desire to triumph over Philip and Renny gratified. In the days intervening between now and the event, Malahide must be protected, humoured, praised.

But when he appeared next morning at her door he brought with him a gloom that her archest smile could not disperse. He seemed already sick with the taste of defeat. An impersonal blackness seemed engendered at his very core. Her smile wavered as she looked into his face.

"This is the end," he said. "I shall go."

"Go!" she repeated, frowning. "But where?"

"God knows! Anywhere away from here!"

She took the lapel of his coat and drew him into the room. "You're flurried," she said, "and no wonder. But let me tell you how much I admired the challenge you flung at that young rascal."

"That," he said, "was in the heat of the moment. This morning I have no more bowels than a jellyfish."

"Now, I'll tell you what," she said, "you shall spend the time between now and the Show at Vaughanlands. The change will do you good. The congenial company — everyone on your side — will put new life into you."

If it were possible to look blacker, he now did.

"Well," she said, impatiently, "what have you against the Vaughans?"

He dropped into a chair and took his head in his hands. "It is no use, Cousin Adeline," he said. "I could not endure the atmosphere of that house. Robert Vaughan and his wife bore me, crush me, take away what energy I have left. I shall send a cable to my mother and tell her that she must receive me. I must go home." And he added, bitterly — "If one can call it a home."

Adeline's shaggy red brows went up to her cap. She pulled her bell cord and asked Eliza to bring Mr. Court a glass of gin and bitters. He was far from well. Eliza had a great contempt for Malahide. She obeyed grimly.

As he sipped the drink he sank still lower in his chair, but his eyes brightened.

"How is your finger?" Adeline asked with solicitude.

"It kept me awake most of the night. Parrot bites have been known to be fatal." He examined his finger, still dressed in her handkerchief, with an expression as gloomy as though it were already carrion.

"My goodness, Mally!" exclaimed Adeline, "I've never seen anyone so down as you are! What am I to do with you?" There was genuine exasperation in her tone.

"Nothing," he said. "Even you. I'll have to go home to my mother."

"You can't, and that's flat," she returned. "Listen now, I have an idea. There's a very good tent about somewhere which is used for hunting trips. I'll have it put up for you in a quiet spot at the river's edge. You shall camp out for a bit. It will do you a world of good. I only wish I were young enough for it. I've tented in my day."

Malahide reluctantly allowed himself to be led under the harebell-blue arch of the October sky. But when he saw the pretty spot, on a secluded curve of the stream, his gloom lightened. The gin and bitters had also had an effect. He agreed that it would be pleasant to camp here and, under Adeline's fostering, his determination to ride Harpie to triumph was again roused.

Philip and Renny were busied with the schooling of polo ponies. Nicholas was spending the day with friends in town. Meg and Molly had gone on an excursion with the Laceys. It was not till evening that Adeline disclosed to them the erection of the tent by the river and Malahide's migration there. He had taken only one or two travelling bags with him. The rest of his luggage was piled in his room as though for departure. In truth, Adeline felt that the time was not distant when she would be willing to see him set sail for Ireland. The long winter was drawing near and she looked forward to a comfortable and secluded period with her family.

The news was received with amusement and relief. The family could scarcely believe that Malahide was actually out of the house. One after another they went to the door of his room and looked at the mound of luggage which rose with something of the mysterious appearance of the earth thrown up by a burrowing animal. And how he had burrowed into their life at Jalna! Nicholas expressed skepticism as to his leaving. When Malahide found it too cold in the tent, he said, he would come back to the house. Nothing could keep him out.

As, singly, they had inspected his room, they went in a body to overlook his new retreat. It was on the opposite side of the stream, the riverbank there being much lower. So, from the shelter of a group of sumacs and alders they looked down on the white tent set among pines and half hidden by bushes. Before it the stream moved swift and darkling and the setting sun left it in cool remote shadow. There was not a sign of life about.

"I'd give a good deal to see inside that tent," said Mary.

Meg said — "You would discover Malahide stretched at full length on his cot, a bottle of poison in one hand and a picture of Gran in the other."

"Let's hope he'll take the poison," said Renny.

Mary laughed. "He would thrive on it."

"How vindictive you all are," said Philip. "For my part, I feel sorry for poor old Malahide."

"There he is!" exclaimed Nicholas. "Don't let him see us."

They drew back and, from the shelter of the reddening leaves, watched him appear from his tent carrying a kettle. He came to the water's edge, knelt, and allowed it to fill. Every movement he made was regarded with curiosity by the watchers. He collected some brushwood and lighted a small fire in front of the tent, and hung the kettle there on a support evidently made by more experienced hands than his. A blue spiral of smoke rose above the pines and dissolved into the tender azure of the sky. He then disappeared into his tent.

As they returned along the river's edge they had a feeling of unease as though Malahide, leading his singular existence, were capable of exercising a charm, enervating and evil, against them and against their horses.

This feeling was perhaps fostered by an intense glow, of a colour approaching saffron, which now pervaded the atmosphere. The very grass and leaves took on this tone, and their own faces were transformed by its radiance. An extraordinary hush prevailed. Even the murmur of the river was muted as though a finger had been laid upon its lips. Bright-coloured tendrils of poison ivy stretched toward their path. Two old farm horses, now past work but kept as pensioners by Philip, were allowed to roam here. They had grown wild in their ways and at sight of the approaching group were suddenly affrighted. They stood staring a space from under their forelocks, which were clotted with burrs, then neighed loudly and galloped up and down, squealing and kicking. Renny, who had gathered a handful of acorns, began to pepper the beasts with these.

Philip laid a restraining hand on his arm. He asked: —

"How did the colt behave this morning?"

The boy gave him a tragic look. "Like the devil. Scotchmere is in the depths. Says we had better not show him."

"Don't be worried by Scotchmere. Perhaps you've worked Gallant too hard. Give him a rest. Feed him up a bit. What about the ponies?"

"They were splendid."

"If that fellow," said Nicholas, "gets the best of us, I'll never hold up my head again. You must not let him, Renny."

Renny threw up his last acorn and caught it. "Its easy to talk," he said. "I wish you had seen Gallant this morning — rocking about like a drunken sailor."

"I think you excite him," declared Meg. "Why don't you try to be calm like I am?"

"Yes," agreed Mary. "I think we should all try to be calmer about this affair, not let it take such a hold on us. For my part, I can think of little else."

Philip hooked his arm into hers. "Think of me, Molly," he whispered, "for a change."

They did indeed try to regard the approaching contest with more detachment in the days that followed. Gallant was kept quiet for several days, and when his schooling began again, the family disposed themselves about the paddock in attitudes of exaggerated nonchalance. Molly even brought her knitting and affected to count stitches at moments of tension.

The absence of Malahide from the house was indeed a source of tranquility, though Adeline did not allow it to be forgotten how he had been driven out, and it became the habit of Boney, in the most peaceful moments, to ejaculate the mischievous words taught him by Renny.

The weather continued to be perfect, and each morning Adeline called at the tent for Malahide and they proceeded together to Vaughanlands. Each morning she carried some special dainty to him. By her direction his more substantial wants were supplied from the kitchen. Mary was so thankful to have him out of the house that she herself saw that his needs were plentifully provided for.

Malahide's moods were a problem to Adeline in these days. They varied between deep dejection and a boastful hilarity that was unusual in him. She suspected that he was drinking too much. The strain of her guardianship began to tell on her and she did not sleep as she was accustomed to. Her temper was short.

The event in which Gallant and Harpie were entered was the most important high jumping contest of the Show and was set for the third night. Renny was riding on both earlier nights and the family attended in force, with the exception of Adeline, who was storing her strength for the great event.

On the first night Malahide bore her company. But by his alternate fidgeting and gloom he tired her. With his long wrists dangling he sat talking to her, now of his variable past, now of his lacklustre future. He hinted boldly for money to raise his spirits, and at last Adeline went to her room, unlocked the drawer of her small bureau, and brought him no mean sum. She dared not let Boney see his face, and Malahide still wore a stall on his finger.

The next morning Adeline suggested to Admiral Lacey by a three-cornered note that he should invite her and her kinsman to dinner that night. By this means she would know where Malahide was and yet not have the responsibility of his entertainment.

The invitation was warmly extended.

Philip, his brother, and his family were at a dinner in town. In good time Malahide appeared at Jalna and got his evening things from his trunk and in his old room dressed for dinner. Hodge had driven the family to town and Malahide himself was to drive the bays to the Laceys'. Adeline, sitting at his side, declared that he handled them beautifully. There was just light enough to make the drive without the aid of carriage lamps. There was a nip of frost in the air.

The dinner was a great success. The jolly Admiral, his portly wife and vivacious daughters, were always charmed to have Adeline in their midst. The daughters hung on all Malahide had to say of Paris. He posed, he swaggered. He praised the good wine and, to Adeline's chagrin, she perceived at the moment of leaving that he had taken too much of it.

At the door she hesitated, wondering if she should not ask for someone else to drive them home, but it was late. With misgiving in her heart and a bold front she bade her friends goodnight and, taking Malahide's arm, guided him down the steps, managing to conceal his condition. Indeed he looked more alive than usual, helped her in, and mounted lightly to the seat beside her. He took the reins from the Laceys' old coachman.

"I hope you haven't drunk too much, Mally," said Adeline as they spun down the drive.

"Not a drop," he laughed. "Never felt better in my life. How nice the Laceys are! I have a mind to visit them for a little when the Show is over. I suppose those girls have not much money?"

"Poor as church mice. Mind what you're doing! You all but grazed the gateposts."

"Don't worry!" laughed Malahide, cracking the whip. "I'll jump the gate if necessary — carriage and all!"

They flew along the road, Adeline's lace scarf streaming out behind, the moonlight shining on her set features.

"Look there!" said Malahide. "What lovely clouds! To me the moon looks like a race horse leaping over them." He waved his whip skyward and the carriage swerved dangerously near the edge of the road.

"My God!" cried Adeline. "You'll have us in the ditch!"

"What! Do you say I can't drive?" He turned and looked in her face. The bays shied at a piece of paper fluttering in the moonlight.

"Give me those reins," said Adeline.

She took them in her hands and drew the horses to a standstill. She spoke soothingly to them.

Malahide swayed and seemed likely to fall off the seat.

Adeline would have given a great deal to be back at the Laceys' or home at Jalna. But this must be faced. She put one arm firmly about Malahide's waist. His head dropped to her shoulder. His hat fell off, but fortunately not into the road.

What would her children say if they could see her, she thought grimly, as she drove homeward. Never must they know of this. Yet the situation was not without its element of pleasure. It was many a year since she had handled the reins. Her hands felt strong and capable. If only she had not this incubus of Malahide leaning against her!

And what a night! The unseasonable warmth had gone. In a few hours it had turned to this brilliant air, pregnant with frost, filled with sharp warning of the approaching winter. She was reminded of night drives with her Philip. Different indeed they had been, with him sitting straight and stalwart beside her, driving his horses at a spanking rate along the lonely road.

With a challenging air she drew up the bays in front of her own door. Malahide seemed half asleep, but she helped him to alight and made him sit on a garden seat in the shadow of the porch. The bays stood quietly, nuzzling each other.

When the man had driven the horses to the stables she turned to Malahide. What should she do with him? She decided, after a moment's reflection, that he must go back to his tent.

"Come," she said sternly, "get up and take my arm."

He rose obediently and they moved slowly across the lawn in the direction of the ravine. She added: —

"Are you able to walk to your tent?"

"To the world's end with you," he declared, leaning heavily on her.

"You talk like a fool, Mally…. Now, help yourself a little! Don't imagine I can carry you."

She gave him a thump between the shoulders that made him stagger. It did him good. He braced himself. Slowly and heedfully they descended the variable path.

In the ravine a clear and poignant chill stung their nostrils. "Sharp frost tonight," commented Adeline.

"And me in a tent!"

"Have you plenty of blankets?

"Tons of them."

"Good. Ha, here is the bridge!" She would have liked a breathing space here, but she was afraid to stop, for fear he might be difficult to start again.

She found the path on the other side and along it they groped, for it was dark down here, till they saw the whiteness of the tent. Malahide was reviving in the cold air. He bent and, unfastening the flap, ushered her into the tent as though it were a mansion. He found and lighted a candle. The interior was discovered, chill and neat. On a chair, by the bed, stood a half-empty bottle of brandy. He beamed at Adeline. He said: —

"Let me give you something to sustain you on the walk back. But, no, you shall not go! You shall sleep on my pallet and I will lie on the ground outside your door."

Adeline stood firmly on her feet, regarding him with a strange mixture of amusement and despair.

"What account you will give of yourself tomorrow night, I can't imagine," she said. "I'm afraid it's all up with us. For Robert Vaughan's sake, pull yourself together, Mally!"

He stood swaying, the bottle in one hand. "For your sake, and yours only!" he said, fervently. He poured a little of the brandy into a glass and she sipped it gratefully.

She helped him to divest himself of his evening clothes, which she hung on a line that was suspended across the tent. He sat in his woollen dressing gown, his confused mind not quite convinced of her substance, or of the unreality of her grotesque shadow that loomed above them. As she raised her arms the lines of her sides and breast showed something of her early grace. Her face was to him the emblem of fortitude and the arrogance of their tradition.

She had tucked him up like a child and now she retraced her steps through the ravine. Freed of Malahide, she no longer felt tired. She walked strongly, and when she came to the bridge she stood there for a space, looking down into the sliding darkness of the stream. It threw silvery glances up at her. It talked to her — the familiar, long-continued converse of more than fifty years. She stood so motionless that she might have been one of the watchful trees at its brink. An owl flitted by her, its soft wings carrying the moonlight, a mouse drooping in its beak.

"Ha!" she exclaimed, under her breath. "You about your business … I about mine! Funny old birds … both of us!"

XXVII

The Horse Show

In the strong electric light every detail of the spirited scene was garishly visible. The bright uniforms of the bandsmen; their polished instruments, from the throats of which a barbarous march was throbbing; the gently swaying flags and bunting that hung from the ceiling; the varied colour and staring faces of the audience that filled the tier upon tier of seats; the muscular and shining bodies of the horses, and the rich hue of the tanbark. From the boxes, with their array of white shirt fronts and evening cloaks, to the occupants of the back seats, all eyes were directed toward the next event, which was the most important of the Show, the prize being a coveted silver cup and a purse of a thousand dollars.

The Vaughans shared their box with the Laceys, all but Vera, who sat with Meg Whiteoak. Robert Vaughan's ascetic face wore an eager, almost a tremulous, smile. It was his first outing since his illness and he found the excitement of the occasion almost overwhelming. Admiral Lacey sat, solid, red-faced, and benign, his eyes sometimes wandering from the horses to the handsome women who strolled by with their escorts.

The Whiteoak family occupied the next box, Nicholas nervously tugging at his dark moustache, Philip with an expression of exaggerated calm, Mary, outshining both young girls that night, in a gown of silver and blue. Adeline, wearing a white lace mantilla and a grey satin dress and ermine cape, was the most notable figure in the audience. Since her husband had been one of the founders of the Show, she had sat in that box year after year, her appraising gaze on the horses, her challenging smile flashing for the men who ever and again came to lean over her shoulder or raise their hats to her from below. This year, conscious of her new teeth, there was an added self-satisfaction in her greetings. She threw back her cape and sat erect as she saw a society reporter making a note of her appearance. There was nothing of the restrained and luke-warm fine lady about her. She arched her neck and showed herself off, as the vital and eager thoroughbreds in the Show.

Now they were coming! Lifting their dainty hoofs high, distending their full nostrils, holding their sleek, barrel-like bodies in readiness, their riders immaculate, their faces masks of imperturbability. Renny was the youngest rider and Gallant the youngest horse. Yet they excelled the eighteen other entrants in severity of line and scorn of bearing. Gallant was transported to a new world of artificial light and strange sounds. The only link with his old life was the thighs that bound him, the hands that guided him. For sheer grace, give the crowd Harpie and her dark-faced rider, whose languid length seemed to melt into her very flesh.

One after another the riders essayed the jumps. One after another they cleared the easier ones, balked or failed to clear without ticking or knocking a bar from the highest — all but Renny and Malahide, who, with scarcely a fault, circled the tanbark. One after another the sound of a bugle dismissed them till only five were left.

Amid loud applause these five returned to another trial. The three tall barriers together at the end of the course were the stumblingblock. The tension of the audience became pronounced, as three of the riders were defeated and withdrew. Now only Gallant and Harpie were left. Through all their sensitive nerves they were conscious of the atmosphere of enmity. As they passed each other, Gallant made a hideous grimace and bit Harpie on the shoulder.

"Keep that hell's spawn out of my way!" snarled Malahide, and struck at Gallant with his crop.

Three times Gallant and Harpie were pitted against each other. Three times the Whiteoaks and Vaughans were strung up to meet victory or defeat. But the judges could not decide. They bent their heads together in close conclave.

Philip consulted the paper on which he had kept tab of the jumps. He struck it on his knee.

"I tell you," he said to his mother, "Gallant has won!"

"No doubt about it," said Nicholas.

"Nothing of the sort," declared their mother. "Gallant was at fault — *there* and *there* and *there!*" She tapped the paper with a hand upon the forefinger of which flashed a handsome ruby ring.

Mary exclaimed — "Harpie ticked the bar in that last jump! I saw it. She jumped all wrong."

"What do *you* know of jumping?"

"I have my two eyes to see."

"Ha, here they come again!"

At each successful leap there was an outburst of applause. At each failure a sharp outgoing of breath. The excitement was almost too much for Robert Vaughan. He closed his eyes that he might not see Harpie's final leaps.

Throughout the contest the mare's irritation had increased. She disliked Malahide and feared him. In crabbed fashion she jumped the hurdles and sped toward the three highest gates. She felt his hands like iron on her reins. His spur sought her side. In grand swoops she leaped the barriers and galloped from the course, tossing her head and sheering. The vibrant air was shattered by applause.

Adeline smiled triumphantly into Philip's face.

"Renny will be put to it to beat that," she said.

But the world must not know that she was against Jalna. Her face was noncommittal as colt and boy trotted into the arena. She felt a pang as she watched them to think that her heart was set against their victory. Ah, but they were clean-cut and fierce and beautiful! Her nostrils dilated with pride.

As the confidence between Harpie and Malahide had diminished during the contest, so the love between Gallant and Renny had flowered. With an almost jocular air the colt made his final appearance. He arched the granite grey of his neck and leaned sideways a little. He leaped the first barriers with disdain, the music of his hoofs thudding gaily between each. Like a phrase of music he approached the high climax of the three gates.

The audience leaned forward in their seats. Those standing by the palings pressed closer. A woman with coarse yellow hair gave an excited laugh and thrust her breast forward between two men. The colt, almost near enough for touching, rolled his great eyes, saw her and swerved. Strange memories came to him.

His gay arrogance fell from him. His speed rushed back on itself as a torrent in sudden meeting with a rock. He swerved from the jump and balked, showing his great teeth, picking up his hoofs as though they were missiles to be hurled.

Renny too had heard the laugh, seen the face. "Careful, boy — good boy — now for it!" Wheeling, he headed Gallant for the gates. But again he sheered, curveted, rolled his eyes. Now, for the last time — let him try it! All his blood is in a fever — the very hairs of his mane are electrified. "Up! Up! Up you go, my darling!" Renny says to him softly, and with hands and knees and spirit lifts him over the gate. The next looms. Over it the grey body describes a swift arc. At the third his spleen rises, he jumps as though he would fly to pieces, and kicks the top bar from its place. The bugle sounds. The air is shaken by handclaps and cheers and laughter. Like the embodiment of perversity the colt refuses to leave the arena. He gives a massive buck, then kicks at an official standing near. Renny's face is white. His hat has fallen off and his hair shows dark red in the strong light.

Severely Malahide rides out on Harpie amid a tumult of noise. The brazen music of the band, the sharp explosion of applause. But Renny and the colt are the favourites. The air is full of praise for them and wonder at their defeat. Malahide circles the course with the silver cup on his saddle, his sallow face impassive.

As Renny made his way through the crowd he passed deliberately where Lulu stood hanging on the palings. Already she was in close conversation with one of the men, but she turned, her face all alight, to Renny. He said, his mouth beside her ear: —

"I wish you'd been in hell before you came here tonight!"

She exclaimed — "You said you'd send me a ticket, and you didn't! I came all this way to see you ride. Paid for it out of my own money!"

"And made me pay for what I had of you!" he returned, and passed on.

He came to Philip's box and sat down beside him. Philip put a hand on his knee and gave it an affectionate squeeze.

"Well done, old man!"

Renny gave a grunt of bitter dissent.

"What happened?" asked Philip.

"I don't know. Well — I can't explain. But the colt saw someone who upset him. Oh, don't ask me, Father!"

"Never mind. We must just swallow our disappointment. But Gallant's too temperamental. No good for showing."

"I know." He stared blackly at the throng of horses, their riders in uniform, who were entering for the Musical Ride. He could see Lulu, leaning on the palings, talking to the man, who now turned his back on the arena and was looking with heavy curiosity into her face. The knuckles on her hand that gripped the palings stood out. Renny felt that her wanton lips were pouring forth his secret.

Adeline gave him a poke with her fan. She asked: —

"Why did you lose your stirrup? It was bad enough to let Malahide beat you."

"I hope you're happy, Gran," he returned bitterly.

"I didn't like to see my grandson beaten," she answered. "It went against the grain."

Malahide sat simpering in the Vaughan's box, where Robert Vaughan, with a ghastly smile on his face, received congratulations with him.

XXVIII

Designs of Youth

THE NEXT DAY Renny told Philip that he had wrenched his ankle, he scarcely knew how. Certainly it was swollen and slightly discoloured, but he made more of the mishap than was usual with him. He had dark shadows beneath his eyes and looked as though he had not slept. The family doctor came and bound up the ankle. Renny was below par, he said, and must rest for a fortnight. Philip looked at his wilding with some concern. What sort of man was he going to be, he wondered. He wished he knew what was in his heart.

"Beaten! Beaten! Beaten!" mourned Renny to himself, as, with the aid of a stick, he hobbled along the path at the river's edge. "And by that spineless cur! How could I let him do it! Oh, damn that woman — damn her! I never want to see her face again!" Her face mocked at him from among the leaves. Her eyes slanted up at him from the glancing river.

Irresistibly he was drawn to the spot opposite Malahide's tent. He lay down in the long grass and waited for a sight of Malahide. The tent looked remote, unapproachable, serenely virgin, hidden among the trees. Yet, beneath its white dome, it harboured that black viper! "He beat me!" Renny reiterated, clenching his hands on the grass. "He did me in! He licked me! He's defeated me! He got the best of me! And all Lulu's fault!"

The flap of the tent was drawn back and Malahide came out carrying a teakettle. He wore a black jersey and white trousers, and his hair, which Renny had always seen in ebony sleekness, rose in two pointed locks like horns. With the effortless yet cautious movements of a cat he approached the stream, knelt there, and plunged his arms into the icy water. He splashed his face and head with it as though to cool a fever, then, still kneeling, rubbed them with a towel that lay crumpled on the brink.

Unseen by him the family of swans appeared round the bend of the stream. Of the four cygnets one only now survived. How the others had met their end no one knew. But the successive calamities had left the parent birds in a state of unease. They moved in watchful protective strength on either side of the cygnet, who arched his fluffy grey neck and uttered wistful cooing sounds. The female suddenly dived, turning up her snow-white stern, while her mate, throwing her a glance of haughty interest, sailed smoothly round the bend, his cygnet at his side. At that moment Malahide shook out his towel and the swan, fearing some danger to his young, raised his great wings and sped toward Malahide in fury.

Stepping backward, like a matador before an enraged bull, Malahide flicked the towel in the bird's face. He had not anticipated the rage he excited, for the swan, beating his wings upon the water, came close to him, even on to the land. Malahide darted back and disappeared into his tent, while the swan returned to his cygnet, raising his breast feathers in triumph, one dark leg curved above the water ready, if necessary, to strike in its defence. The three then moved together down the stream.

Renny had watched this scene with the most intense interest. He still brooded on it while Malahide returned and filled his kettle. While the graceful smoke rose from his fire and the smell of his frying bacon came across the stream, Renny lay, his head pillowed on his arm, watching as though half asleep, but in truth the most vivid thoughts and pictures were illuminating his mind.

He remained there for more than an hour until he had seen Malahide, dressed in dark tweeds, fasten the flap of his tent and disappear in the direction of Vaughanlands.

Renny then rose and, not without pain, retraced the path to the bridge and crossed to the other side of the river. He went to the spot where Malahide had thrown down his towel and crouched there beside it, half hidden in the bushes. All about was the deep quiet of autumn. The frost of the night before had given way to warm yellow sunlight. The soft tongue of the stream licked at the stones, making them ever smoother.

He had not long to wait. The two swans and the cygnet were returning to the sequestered nook where they spent the heat of the day.

As they were abreast of him Renny appeared abruptly before them and shook the towel savagely almost in the male's face. For a second the bird was overcome by astonishment, holding himself rigid like a piece of sculpture. Then, the very personification of fury, he beat the water with his wings, churning it into a sheet above his head, and rushed to the attack.

But Renny was prepared for this, He darted backward, again and again flicking the swan with the towel while, in clumsy grandeur, it laboured after him.

He was breathless and hot pains stabbed his ankle as he escaped up the path and out of the ravine. He stood motionless for a time, holding his chin in his hand, then slowly limped through a small oak wood and across a field to the road. One of his father's men was passing in an empty wagon with which he had been delivering a load of apples at the railway station. Renny called out to him: —

"Look here, I want you to take me to the Moorings. I've hurt my ankle."

He climbed to the seat and the man, avoiding the painful subject of Gallant, observed: —

"I hear you did something wonderful with the polo ponies at the Show last night, sir."

"Oh, well enough."

"But we heard that you won all before you — rode something grand, Scotchmere says."

"Well, that's decent of Scotchmere. But I didn't win on Gallant and it wasn't his fault."

"Those things will happen, sir, and better luck next time, perhaps." He looked sympathetically into the youth's tired face. "That colt, they say, is the devil born again."

Renny did not answer. He sat, with folded arms and chin sunken on breast, bumping along the rough country road, moved now by only one idea, the necessity for seeing Vera. She alone could soothe his bad mood, drive away his devils.

She was cutting dahlias in the garden when he descended painfully from the wagon seat. She came to the gate to meet him.

He stood silent, till the wagon rattled away and the man's inquisitive eyes were off him. Then he limped eagerly to the gate and held out his hand.

"Oh," said Vera, "you have hurt yourself!"

"Yes," he answered, with a rueful smile, "inside, as well as out."

"Do you mean your disappointment last night?"

"Partly. Only partly. I'm in a beastly mood." He cut at the dahlia stocks with his stick. "Could you help me out of it?"

"Don't!" she exclaimed. "You're hurting the flowers."

"They've been frosted," he answered sulkily.

"But I'm cutting the best ones. Look!" And she held up the gayly coloured bunch.

He stared at them. "The way their petals curl up is like your hair — all those little close curls."

She looked at him suddenly in the eyes, her own suffused by tears. "Do you know what?"

"No. Something bad?"

"Rather. I've had a letter from home. I'm to go back at once. Aunt Violet is going and I must go with her. In a fortnight!"

"Good Lord!" He stared at her blankly. "But why?"

"My daddy isn't well. He wants me with him. I think they worry about my being so far away."

"Vera, you don't want to go, do you?"

"How could I — when you and I are just — getting to be such friends?"

"Let's go into the summerhouse and talk."

They sat down in the little vine-covered shelter and beneath the cold leaves of the dahlias their hands met.

"It's strange," he said, "how one thing after another happens to a fellow. First — I am suspended from college. Second — well, I'll not tell you what that was. Third — I've had a man I loathe in the house with me for months. Fourth — he beat me at the Show. And now — the first girl I've really cared for is being snatched away from me." His mouth went down at the corners. His fingers tightened tremulously on hers.

She felt weak under their pressure. She said, in a small voice: —

"It's been wonderful to me — having you for a friend, Renny."

"And now we must part! What *rotten* luck! Why, I've been planning already what we'd do in the Christmas holidays!"

"I know — I know — isn't it heartbreaking?"

"Awful!"

"But we'll write!"

"I'm no good at letter writing."

"Oh, but you *must* write to me! I couldn't *live* if you didn't!"

"I'll write. But it's small consolation. What I want is you, yourself, to talk to, to have for a — friend…. Vera, you have no idea what you are to me."

"And you can't imagine what you are to me. You're so strong — so courageous — so splendid. My heart nearly jumped out of my mouth — I was so excited last night…. I was afraid you might get hurt…. Is your ankle strained?"

"It's nothing. Look here, Vera …" He hesitated, poking at a rotten board in the floor of the summerhouse. His mouth grew hard. "Look here, if you discovered something about me — like Meg did about Maurice — what would you feel about it?"

She went a deep pink, but she answered steadily: —

"It wouldn't make any difference — if that was all over — and — I knew you loved me…. But, of course, it's quite different. We're not engaged."

A warm tide of desire for her rose in him. He raised his head proudly and looked deep into her eyes.

"But we shall be!" he exclaimed. "We must be! It's the only way. We'll be engaged and marry, too — before they can take you away from me!"

"Oh, do you think we could?"

"Of course, we can — if you want me as much as I want you!"

"Oh, Renny, I can't pretend that I don't. I'm simply dying for you!"

"Somehow," he said, "I must get you an engagement ring."

XXIX

SWAN SONG

A FEW DAYS later Philip was standing in front of his house filling his deep chest with draughts of pure morning air. There was a southerly wind and it carried with it a distinct smell of the lake, which, to a keen ear, could be heard rolling in long waves on to the beach. He said: —

"It looks to me as if that fellow is going to stay till the crack of doom. In any case he must give up the tent, because Nick and I want it for our duck shooting trip."

"The nights are getting so cold," said Mary hopefully, "that he will not be able to bear it much longer. But then, I suppose, he will come back to the house. Your mother insinuated as much last night."

"Did she? Oh, I dare say we shall have him for the winter. Poor devil, I expect he has nowhere else to go! But certainly Nick and I must have the tent. I want my tent, and that's flat." He set his round full jaw and looked stubborn.

"Well, Philip, you must remember that when you come back from your shooting you have promised to take me to New York."

"If I take my horses to the New York Show I shall certainly take my wife too."

"And I want at least three new dresses and some American shoes. They fit so perfectly. It's a misfortune to have such slender feet as I have." She turned one foot on its side and looked down at it with pretended disparagement.

"Don't pretend you're not proud of them, Molly. I know I am."

Adeline had come into the porch and overheard some of the conversation. She demanded: —

"What's this about new clothes?"

"I'm going to New York with Philip," answered her daughter-in-law with a somewhat challenging air, "and I may as well buy a few clothes there."

"Nonsense! I've never heard such nonsense. You buy far too many clothes for a quiet place like this, Mary. Why don't you make your dresses last as I do mine?"

"There is a good deal of difference in our ages, Mamma."

"H'm — well, when you are as old as I am you'll think less of falderals and more of keeping your family in order. Eden is getting thoroughly spoiled."

The little boy came running out of the house. He put his arms about his father's legs. "Are you going away, Daddy? May I go too? Do take me to New York!"

Philip looked down at him with the good-humoured air of a mastiff at a puppy. "You are a little beggar," he said. "You're always wanting something."

Eden saw Renny passing through the little gate toward the ravine, followed by Keno. "Please, may I go with Renny?" He danced up and down in his excitement.

"What a flibbertigibbet scamp it is!" exclaimed Adeline. "Just like you, Molly."

"Run along after Renny and tell him not to walk about too much on that lame ankle," said Philip.

Renny was not well pleased when Eden overtook him. He said, when he had heard the child's message — "You'd better not come with me. I'm in a dangerous mood. I'm quite likely to chuck you into the stream."

"I don't mind," answered Eden, and pressed his small hand into Renny's. "Where are we going?"

"To have a look at Cousin Malahide."

He wanted to be alone, but he could not bear to send the child away. He liked the feel of his clinging hands and dependence on him.

They went along the path till they came to the bank overlooking Malahide's tent. It was the hour when he usually made his first appearance. A brilliant change had come over the landscape in the past few days. The quiet tones of autumn had been transformed to scarlet and gold. Against these splendid hues of the maples and birches, the green of pine and spruce was richly intensified, the wild creepers that draped themselves along the very fence being like a vivid tapestry. The river appeared to move more quickly, and there on its surface was spread the proud reflection of a crimson branch. The swan, his mate, and the cygnet were floating in a tiny cove at the end of Malahide's path. Now and again the male arched his neck and looked expectantly toward the tent. It was from this point that he had for days been harried.

Renny, Eden, and the spaniel settled themselves on the short grass that clothed the sandy soil. Eden amused himself by attacking a densely populated ant hill with the heel of his sturdy brown shoe. Keno buried his nose in a small burrow, snuffling in complete absorption. Renny took from his pocket a snapshot of Vera Lacey and gazed at it intently. Yet, while so occupied, each was alert for the most delicate sounds in the world about him.

They all turned at the faint clink of Malahide's kettle, as it struck against a stone of the improvised stove. Three pairs of eyes bent their clear gaze full on him as he came languidly down the path: Eden's blue, wondering; Renny's brown and lighted by a malicious hope; Keno's, above his earth-covered muzzle, showing a feckless curiosity in their hazel depths.

Malahide was not aware of the presence of the swans till he had sunk his kettle to the brim. Then he saw the male, with upraised wings and gaping beak, poised for attack. As Malahide scrambled to his feet on the slippery stone, he flung his kettle at the swan, which rushed at him, churning the water with powerful strokes of his wings and uttering a trumpet call to battle. His sudden change from pale immobility to dread commotion was comparable to the breaking of a spell.

Possibly because of the slime on the stones, Malahide lost his foothold and was plunged into the stream. In a second the swan was on top of him, and such a confusion of beating wings, contorted neck, and threshing legs and arms ensued that, for a space, nothing could be distinguished through the sheet of upthrown water.

The immobility of the swan's mate was in striking contrast to his convulsive energy. She sat the water at a little distance, watching the struggle with a sidelong, haughty glance, while the cygnet, with tilted head, regarded the scene in roguish detachment.

Gathering all his force, Malahide was able to free himself for a moment and scrambled frantically to the shore. The swan, however, with the air of being master of all the elements, rocked ferociously in his wake. Malahide leaped to gain the trunk of a tree, but the swan, with a grand spread of his wings, leaped too and bore him to earth.

At the beginning of their struggle Eden had given a scream of fright and almost fallen from the bank. Renny caught him by the arm and held him fast while, with his other hand, he gripped Keno's muzzle, and stayed his barking. He sat between the captives, his features fixed in a grin as elemental as that of some playful satyr.

But as he saw Malahide getting the worst of the struggle the grin changed to an expression of human concern.

He released the spaniel, who tumbled down the bank in a frenzy of excitement. Now his great ears lay on the water, his feet trod it, and his wide mouth gaped in eagerness. He was on the opposite shore barking into the snowy depths of the swan's stern. Malahide, half fainting, had dragged himself on to the branch of a tree.

"Let me go! Let me go!" screamed Eden. "I want to go home!" Released, he flew toward the house.

Renny then scrambled down the bank and waded across the stream. He caught up a stick and threatened the swan, which, finding the forces against him trebled, retreated heavily into the water and swam, a great bundle of ruffled plumage, toward his mate and the cygnet. The former showed evident pride in his prowess, the latter tranquil pleasure in his return.

Renny, dragging Keno by the collar, went to where Malahide crouched in the tree.

"Are you hurt?" he asked.

Malahide snarled — "Hurt! Hurt! You ask if I am hurt! I tell you I am killed!"

"You must have angered the swan."

"Can one breathe the air of Jalna without enraging someone or something! You or your family or your damned pets! Your ugly-tempered horses — your biting curs — your vile-tongued parrot — your horrible swan! *Who* are you? *What* are you? You think you own the earth — it's not safe for civilized people to live with you! You tire them out. You assault them — body and soul! Help me out of this tree — if you have the decency."

He held down his hands. Renny took them and stiffened his body under Malahide's weight. He slid to his feet and stood, battered, drenched, and shaking with mingled outrage and relief.

"I have died in this shambles," he said, "and been born again. I'm a different man. If I could live with this visit over again you'd sing a different song." He turned staggering toward his tent.

"Will you take my arm?" asked Renny.

With a surly air Malahide took his arm, but leant on him heavily. They went into the tent with its grassy smell and its flickers of sun on the canvas. Malahide dropped to his couch and said: —

"Get that bottle of brandy from the cupboard. That cursed bird! His wings were like flails! I haven't a whole bone in me!"

Renny brought the brandy and poured a glass. Malahide's teeth knocked on its brim as he drank. Puddles formed about him on the floor and the bed. He tossed off the entire glass, except what escaped down his chin. He wiped this on his fingers, and held them to his nostrils and sniffed.

"Thank God," he said, "that you arrived when you did! That monster would certainly have had my life."

"He has lost three young ones," said Renny "You can't blame him for being fussy."

"Was I to blame if he hadn't the sense to rear his young? Was I to blame if I rode better than you at the Show? Or because you were justly expelled from your school? Or because young Maurice begot a hedgerow child? Or Robert Vaughan had a stroke? Or that you went to bed with a gypsy? No! Yet all these calamities — if they were such — have been heaped up and cast on my innocent shoulders. I have been the scapegoat for both your houses. I have been insulted in yours, and the Vaughans will scarcely speak to me."

Keno had been investigating every corner of the tent. He had discovered a jar of *pâté de foie gras* and now began to devour it in plebeian gulps. A little bird, perched on the ridgepole of the tent, chanted its farewell to this cold country and its plans for flight to the South. Eden's clear voice could be heard chattering in the distance.

Holding tightly to his father's hand, he appeared in the doorway. Philip demanded: —

"What's this I hear about the swan attacking Malahide?" He looked with concern on Malahide, who had sunk into a posture of apathy and made no reply.

"It's lucky I was about," said Renny. "He got a bit of a mauling."

Malahide raised his head. "Your son has saved my life," he answered. "The first act of kindness I have had from one of you. And that only common humanity. Yet I have done everything to make myself agreeable. Even to accompanying your mother sixteen times to the dentist, which you were all cowardly or too lazy to do."

"You got a diamond pin out of it," observed Renny.

"I'm sorry," said Philip, "that you think so badly of us." He looked uneasily at a yellow envelope in his hand, and then added — "I have a cablegram here for you, Malahide. It had just arrived when Eden came. Do you feel up to reading it?"

Malahide held out his hand and took the paper. One of his eyes was closed by a swelling. With the other he read: —

YOUR MOTHER PASSED AWAY PEACEFULLY THIS MOR-
NING AFTER SHORT ILLNESS AWAIT YOUR INSTRUCTIONS
BATES — SOLICITOR

After taking in the meaning of this message, during which moments the only sound was the rasping of Keno's tongue in the *pâté de foie gras* jar, Malahide read it aloud in a grandiloquent tone.

Philip, although he had never heard any good of Malahide's mother and only bad of the relations between them, was filled with concern. He said sympathetically: —

"It's sad news for you, Malahide. I'm very sorry, for your sake. It will comfort you to know that she passed away peacefully."

"It is the first peaceful thing she ever did," said Malahide. "My life has been given over to keeping the peace. You can judge, from my stay in your house, what an adept I am at it. But I shall miss her."

"I am sure you will," said Philip. "What was she like? Would you care to talk about her?"

Malahide sighed. "It would be impossible to describe her. She lived like a queen in a house of which the roof is falling in, the stables are empty, and the garden overgrown by weeds. But she had money in the bank. It will be necessary for me to go home at once."

"In the meantime," said Philip, "you must let bygones be bygones and return to Jalna. As a matter of fact Nicholas and I shall require the tent for our hunting trip. We leave in a day or two."

"You are welcome to it. I shall return, at your invitation, to Jalna."

"You had better come with us now, if you feel able to walk."

"I think I shall stay here today."

Eden came to him and laid his hand on his knee. "The swan may come back," he said.

"True," said Malahide, putting his arm about him. "This is the flower of your flock, Philip, and I hope you will live to appreciate him. Give him to me and I will take him back to Ireland and make a civilized gentleman out of him."

Philip laughed. "What about it, Eden? Would you go to Ireland?"

"Would Renny come too?"

Malahide answered — "There are limits to my civilizing influence."

"What does he say?" asked Eden.

"He says," answered Renny, his hand on the little boy's neck, "that you are safer here, with your big brother."

"Whatever you do," said Malahide, "you'll not make him into a Whiteoak. Mark my words."

"We'll do our best," returned Philip. "Take your hand off his neck, Renny. How often must you be told that?"

XXX

THE ENGAGEMENT RING

THE NEWS OF Malahide's altered circumstances, of his imminent departure, created a pleasurable stir at Jalna. There was a general desire, after the long-continued rift in the family's solidarity, to draw together again. As the evenings now closed in early, Adeline liked her family gathered about her in warm, if sometimes bickering, converse, the dark red curtains drawn, a bright fire blazing, and herself as the centre of their life's pattern.

She acknowledged openly that she felt no regret at Malahide's going. The passing of his mother, Bridget Court, could be regarded only as a blessing, since it rid the world of a tyrannical, two-faced old woman and left her son in a position to govern his own life. Adeline was ready to discuss these subjects by the hour, and, after Malahide was put to bed in his old room, liniment applied to his bruises and a hot-water bottle to his feet, she settled down to the most tranquil hours she had contemplated for a long while.

With a glass of barley water, flavoured with lemon juice, at her side, she sat herself at the writing bureau in the library to compose a voluminous letter to Ernest. She wished very much that he was here, because no one was more satisfactory than he in a prolonged dissection of family affairs.

Seeing her so established, Keno plumped down from the pyramid of cushions Meg had arranged for him and came to her feet. Across her long black kid slippers he laid his long liver-and-white muzzle and gave himself up to somnolent intercourse with her.

On and on her pen, held parallel with her breast, moved across the mauve-tinted pages bearing her initials, from a box given her on her birthday by Sir Edwin. Sometimes her mobile lips were thrust forward or her shaggy rust-coloured brows were raised as she wrote. Occasionally she scratched her head with her pen handle and pushed her cap to a rakish angle. But, in all her movements, satisfaction with her situation was evident, and this being subtly conveyed to the spaniel by gentle movements of her foot, he roused himself sufficiently to thud his plumed rail on the rug.

When she had finished the letter she pressed it to the blotter, the edge of which was decorated with the heads of horses drawn by Philip during his reluctant letter writing. She finished her glass of barley water and called to Mary, who was potting geraniums outside the window, to come and hear the letter.

"Find Philip and Nicholas too," she said. "And Renny and Meg. They'd like to hear what I've writ."

Mary looked at her hands. "I shall have to wash them first."

"Wipe them on the grass. It's clean dirt."

"No — really, I must wash them."

"You're always washing. You'll wash yourself away."

"I'll only be a moment. Then I'll find the others."

The time of waiting seemed long to Adeline. She arranged herself in front of the bureau and fixed her eyes on the door. Meg appeared first, then the two men, who had been already overhauling the tent which had been carried on to the lawn. Last Mary came with Philip's heavy hunting socks to darn.

He brought his gun and settled down to clean it while he listened. His mother regarded this proceeding doubtfully.

"D'ye think you can give proper heed to me, if you do that?" she asked.

"Of course I can, Mamma. I'm all ears." He laid his cleaning cloths beside him and peered along the shining barrel of the gun. Keno sprang up with a glad bark and circled about Philip in delighted agitation.

"Where is Renny?"

"At the Laceys'," answered Mary. "I think it's a case, there."

"The sooner he goes back to college the better," said Nicholas.

Philip turned to Meg. "Do you think he is very fond of Vera?"

Meg looked inscrutable. "I think he admires her."

"Since the Show he spends most of his time with her," said Mary. "If she isn't here, he is there."

Adeline interrupted — "Are we here to discuss the whelp's conduct or to listen to my letter?"

"Fire away, Mamma," said Philip.

"*Will* you stop that dog's barking?"

"Down, Keno, down!"

"Now, then, are you all listening?"

"All on the *qui vive*, old lady," said Nicholas.

Impressively, with strong emphasis on her underlined adjectives, Adeline delivered herself of the letter. Once, at what he considered a false statement of the jumping event, Nicholas would have interrupted, but Philip gave him a kick on the ankle and it was allowed to pass. At the finish Mary exclaimed: —

"What a perfectly wonderful letter!"

Adeline looked at her over her spectacles. "It's nothing of the sort. It's a good plain account of our doings. Nothing exaggerated. Nothing, as Saint Paul says, set down in malice."

"Shakespeare, Mamma," corrected Nicholas.

"Shakespeare, then. Clever men, both of them, but not to be taken too seriously. So you think the letter will do?"

"Ernest will be delighted," said Philip. "He'll read it to everyone of his acquaintance."

She removed her spectacles, gave a benign look at those about, then noisily drew in the last drops of the barley water. "Ha," she said, "that's good! D'ye think it is binding, Philip?"

"It might be — a little. Now — the gun is in good shape, I can tell you. What about it, Keno? Shall we a-hunting go, old boy?"

It was four o'clock before Renny returned. Meg met him in the hall and took him by the lapels of his coat.

"Do you know what they are wondering?" she whispered. "They are wondering if you are in love with Vera. Mother came right out and declared you are."

"Why are you always moping about the house?" he said. "You have no more colour than chalk."

She laughed and shook him gently. "*Are* you in love with Vera?"

"You used to have three funny little freckles on your nose," he said. "But they've disappeared. The sun never touches you."

"If you think you can get out of it with an answer like that, you're mistaken. I want an answer."

"Why don't you cut off that pompadour?" he said. "And make your hair into little curls like Vera's. Then I might like you."

"You *are* in love with her! You *are*! But they'll never let you be engaged! Never! She has told me that the Laceys don't like your being there so much. And, of course, she's going home."

"I'll tell you all about it," he said, "and you can help me."

She threw her arms about his neck and kissed him. Then she said: —

"But first you must come and see Peep at his birthday tea! I promised you would." She led him to the dining room, where the baby sat in state at one end of the large table, on which was an array of small cakes, jellies, and buttered bread. Before him was an iced cake on which two candles burned, their flames reflected in the clear blue of his eyes. From the golden Thames tunnel on the top of his head to the blue silk bows on his shoulders and his blue slippered feet which thudded against the rungs of his high chair, his small being exhaled prideful possession.

"My cake," he said to Renny and Meg. "My cake. My 'obby-'orse!" He pointed with his spoon to the rocking horse which his grandmother had given him.

She sat on his right, and the sight of her, so massive, so grand, at the table with him, made him forget to eat. Mary and Eden sat on his left. Eden, with the slightly subdued air of the child whose birthday is a long way off and who feels his unimportance of the moment.

"By Jove!" exclaimed Renny. "What a fine horse! You must let me see you ride it, Peep."

"Now! Now!" cried Peep, struggling to get down.

"Oh, why did you say that, Renny?" said Mary. "We have had a time to get him off it for his tea."

Renny came and glared at the cake. "Me want cake! Me want cake, now!" he declared.

The baby looked at him severely. "My cake," he said, but his attention returned to his food.

Eden said to Renny — "That's a funny way to talk. You don't talk that way to me."

"You're a big boy."

Mary cut the cake and, as Meg and Renny stood devouring theirs, Adeline asked of him: —

"Where have you been all day?"

"In the stables," he returned, and smiled at her disarmingly.

As soon as brother and sister could they escaped to her room. There, walking up and down, he poured out the story of his love for Vera and his desire to be married to her before she left for England. If Meg had had doubts on the subject they were swept away by his eagerness, his boyish animation. She planned with him how the secret arrangements could be carried out. She and Vera would go to town together, he would meet them there, and in some remote church, or even in a registry office, the ceremony would be performed.

"What a darling you are, Meggie!" he said. "Vera and I will never forget how you have helped us in this, you may be sure. I wish to goodness that I had an engagement ring for her. It is beastly hard luck that I haven't enough money for that! If *only* I had won the prize — I could have bought her a beauty!"

"How tragic!" she said, mimicking Malahide's mincing tone.

"You know, Gran showed me a ring one day that she told me I was to have for my fiancée. The pearl set in diamonds. It would look lovely on Vera's hand."

"If I hadn't given Maurice back his," said Meg, "you might have had that."

He did not take to this idea. "It would be unlucky," he said.

Meg heaved a deep sigh. Her lip trembled, then, after a moment's thought, she brightened and said: —

"Why don't you try to get possession of the ring Gran promised you? She said it was to be yours when you became engaged. You *are* engaged, so it is yours to all intents and purposes."

He looked startled at the suggestion. Such a proceeding would have never entered his head, but it seemed reasonable and just. He said: —

"If only I could lay hands on it!"

"That is the easiest thing in the world," said Meg. "It's only her money she locks up. Never her jewels. After supper, when she is settled in the drawing room, we'll go to her room and, if I don't find that ring, I'll eat my hat!"

"That new Merry Widow one?" he demanded, his eyes shining with excitement.

"Yes. We must take a banana with us so that, if we're discovered, we'll pretend to be feeding Boney — teaching him something naughty. That will take Gran's mind off any suspicion."

Renny regarded her admiringly. There she stood, solid and complete, a world in herself, moving in her own orbit, knowing just what to do. Yet qualms assailed him.

"I wonder if I had better take the ring," he said. "It seems a queer thing to do."

She turned on him scornfully.

"*Are* you engaged to Vera?"

"Certainly."

"*Did* Granny tell you that this ring was for your fiancée?"

"She did."

"Then why do you think it strange to take it?"

"It seems like stealing."

"Is it stealing to take your own? Besides, just as soon as you are married you will confess all."

"What if Gran made me return the ring?"

"She couldn't. Vera would have it and that would be final."

"What if she should miss the ring at once?"

"Never! It's in a box she seldom opens."

He was convinced. He put his scruples behind him.

It seemed a long while till the lights were on in the drawing room and Meg, reconnoitring, declared the way open. She stood at the foot of the stairs, her round, pretty face alight with mischief, a banana in her hand. As he came softly down the steps to join her he had the hilarious feeling of their days of childish plotting. She took his hand and led him to the door of their grandmother's room.

There he hesitated, and said — "Look here, why need I go in? You know just where the ring is. I had better wait here and keep watch."

"Coward!" hissed Meg. "And idiot, too! You may be seen hanging about here. Inside we are safe." Softly she opened the door and led him in.

"Light a match," she commanded.

He struck one and she turned up the wick of the low brass lamp. Now its warm light brought the room to life. The painted fruit and flowers of the bedstead showed their rich colours. The ornate wallpaper, the vivid Chinese rug, the mulberry window curtains and polished mahogany, all revealed the sumptuous taste of the occupant. On the mantel stood a delicate statue of the goddess Kuan Yen, her fine porcelain hands like the petals of flowers. The parrot was asleep on his perch.

Meg put the banana into Renny's hand. "Now," she said, and she was in her element, "let us waste no time. If you hear anyone coming, give Boney a prod and begin to feed him. Let me see, where does Gran keep this box? Yes, in the bottom drawer of the wardrobe." She drew out the drawer and disclosed the orderly arrangement of Adeline's treasures, expensive materials hoarded for many years, ivory fans, a cashmere shawl, lace fichus, and a number of small boxes. The faint scent of bygone gayety rose from them.

Meg pounced on a wine-coloured velvet box.

"Here," she exclaimed and opened it eagerly. Her soft fingers explored its contents, which, characteristic of Adeline, were a mixture of the valuable and worthless. In triumph Meg held up the ring, a pure pearl surrounded by diamonds.

"*Aren't* I a good sister?"

"You're a duck, Meggie! Let me see it." He took it in his hand, a look of proud determination hardening his features. "It will look well on Vera. Have you noticed her hands?"

"Yes, they're quite nice. She sleeps in gloves lined with almond paste."

Renny was silent. He was looking at the cluster of jewels on his palm and thinking what they signified to him and Vera, of their future together, how he would care for and protect her.

Although they had been so quiet they had disturbed Boney. He raised his head, gaped, and spread one wing. His bright eye roved over the room seeking Adeline. It was not right that other people should be there without her. Something in the very attitude of the intruders irritated him. He made noises which were preliminary to an outburst of anger.

"Pretty Poll," soothed Meg. "Give him a bit of banana, Renny."

Renny drew back the skin from the fruit and proffered it, but Boney turned his beak away. He gave a furious peck at the jewel in Renny's hand and ejaculated loudly: —

"*Chore! Chore!*"

"Good heavens!" said Meg, struggling with the clasp of the box. "He'll have the family in here! Offer him the banana.

"He won't take it."

Boney still glared at the ring, screaming — "*Chore! Chore!*"

"It means thief," said Renny, hoarsely. "Isn't that appalling?"

Meg, terribly flustered thrust the box into its place and closed the drawer.

"*Chore! Chore!*" Boney rocked on his perch. Nothing could induce him to touch the banana. Now, between the open curtains, he saw through the window a pale face peering between the branches of the lilac tree. It was Malahide, risen from his bed, and prowling about the garden in a disturbed, yet exalted state of mind. Seeing a light in Adeline's room, he had thought, if he found her there, to enter and have a private talk with her. Seeing instead her grandchildren, wearing the air of conspirators, he stood immovable, watching them.

Boney now burst out with — "Hell! Hell! Hell with Malahide! Malahide! Malahide! Malahide!" He sidled up and down his perch in sinuous spleen.

Renny blew out the light and they fled into the hall. Like shadows they crept up the stairs and did not stop till they reached Meg's room. There she sank into a chair, laughing and holding her side.

"Oh!" she exclaimed, "I've such a stitch! Oh, what a bird!"

"Well," said Renny, "it was just a little too uncanny. We didn't escape a moment too soon."

He put the ring on his little finger and began to eat the banana.

XXXI

THE LAST OF MALAHIDE

NICHOLAS AND PHILIP left for their shooting trip two mornings later. The combined assistance of servants and family was required to get them off. The tent, the great canvas bag of rugs and blankets, had been taken to the station earlier; also the box of tinned goods, bacon, eggs, and jam. Their small bags, their guns and ammunition, they took with them in the trap. Keno sat between Philip's knees, beaming content on his forehead, his muzzle reaching now and again to the case which held Philip's gun. A young pointer, just being trained, was held on a lead by Nicholas.

A severe frost had crisped the grass the night before. The dahlias hung black and sodden on their stalks. Nasturtiums and asters were quite dead, but here and there a marigold raised its bright face in the border. The air was so clear, so nipping, that it was all Hodge could do to keep the horses in order. Mary, in her thin blue dress, hugged herself to keep warm, as she laughed up at Philip.

"Don't fail to send partridges! *And* quail. I like them both better than duck. And *don't* come home with a dreadful yellow beard as you did last year! Be careful of your rheumatism, Nick. Oh, I do wonder if you have everything!"

"Good Lord!" said Nicholas. "I have forgotten my liniment!"

"Molly will fetch it," said Philip. "Run and get it, like a dear, Molly."

"I'll fetch it! I'll fetch it!" cried Eden, who had carried his toast from the breakfast table and was feeding bits of it to the pointer.

"What's forgotten, men?" asked Adeline, who, wrapped in a Scotch plaid, stood in the porch.

"My Minard's Liniment," growled Nicholas. "In the under part of my washing stand."

"Eden will fetch it."

"No. He'll get the bottle buttery."

"Let Meg bring it," said Philip. "Meggie, run and get Uncle Nick's liniment."

Meg had just come out, carrying the baby in her arms. She pouted a little. "And carry Peep? He'll not let me put him down. Will you, sister's little angel?" She buried her face against his soft body and he buried his hands in the depths of her pompadour.

"I'll go!" cried Mary.

"No, no," said Philip. "Let Eden go."

"No!" shouted Nicholas. "Look at his hands!"

Adeline thumped her stick on the porch. "Will no one get my son's liniment? *Where are* the maids?"

Eliza appeared with Philip's pipe in her hand. She said severely, as she handed it to him: —

"I found this, sir, full of hot ash, on the piano."

Philip took it from her meekly. "Well, now, that's pretty bad, Eliza. But, never mind, you'll have the house very tidy while I'm away."

Renny, hands deep in pockets, lounged round the corner of the house. His father and uncle ordered him simultaneously to bring the liniment. He dashed into the house and up the stairs.

"Look at him," said Nicholas. "Did you ever see a strained ankle get well so fast?"

"It was swollen. I saw it," said Philip. He looked affectionately at Renny as he approached, followed by Eden, begging to be allowed to carry the bottle of liniment. Philip had felt that he should have a serious talk with the boy before leaving. He would not see him again before he returned to college. But he could not bring himself to do it. He had simply said: —

"Better luck next time, old man. And — hang on to your temper. Don't go knocking the masters about."

With jocular adjurations from Adeline, cries of goodbye from the children, thrown kisses from Molly and Meg, the bays dashed away, sending up a shower of gravel. The dogs lifted up their voices in glad barks.

But Renny made a trumpet of his hands and shouted — "Dad! Dad! Did you get the whiskey?"

Philip shouted to Hodge. Hodge shouted "Whoa" to the horses and drew them in sharply. The young pointer, strangling himself in his lead, was cuffed by Nicholas.

"Bring it! Bring it!" ordered Philip. "My God, Nick, we might have gone without it!"

Again Renny dashed into the house with Eden after him. Adeline was so excited that she turned around in bewildered fashion in the porch. "When will they be gone!" she muttered. "This is too much!"

Renny, bearing the heavy box of assorted spirits, hastened down the drive. It was difficult to find a place for it. Philip patted him on the shoulder, saying — "Good man!" and they were off again.

It was several hours before Malahide appeared. A breakfast tray had been brought to him and, when the tumult of departure had subsided, he had turned again on his side and slept.

It was nearly noon when he strolled along the road toward Admiral Lacey's house. He found the old man basking in the sun, which was now warm, on a south verandah overlooking his frost-blighted garden. The Admiral was not particularly pleased to see Malahide, for he never quite knew what to say to him, but any company was agreeable, as his family were entirely occupied by preparations for the departure of Violet and Vera.

After a little desultory talk Malahide said, stroking his bluish chin: —

"It is a great pleasure to me to be able to travel with your daughter and Vera. I hope I shall find the opportunity of being of service to them."

"Well, well, I'm very glad they are to have a man with them. I don't think much of ladies travelling alone, even in these days."

"Vera is a charming girl," said Malahide.

"She's a nice child," agreed the Admiral. "But I shan't be sorry to see her go. She's been a responsibility. My son spoils her. It's not the way I brought up my daughters. The child resents being chaperoned, let me tell you. She's determined, and very artful in getting her own way."

Malahide turned a melancholy face on him. He said: —

"Admiral, I can't pretend to think Vera's engagement to young Renny anything other than lamentable."

Admiral Lacey stared at him in astonishment. "Engagement! What d'ye mean engagement? There's no engagement that I know of."

"Is it without your consent, then?"

"Consent? I've never been asked. You are quite mistaken. There is no engagement."

Malahide moved forward and whispered — "They *are* engaged, sir. She has his ring."

Admiral Lacey turned a deep red. "I'll send for her," he said, "and see what she has to say for herself. As though I should allow an engagement! When she was sent over here to avoid one." Then he added, more coolly — "Not that I have anything against the boy. He is a fine lad. But he's not twenty yet. When he is a little older we may consider it."

"A marriage between them," said Malahide, "would be nothing short of lamentable. I repeat the word, *lamentable*. He is not fit to touch an innocent girl — let alone *marry* her!"

Admiral Lacy eyed him with distrust. "I wish you would explain yourself," he said stiffly.

There was a conscious lubricity in Malahide's tone as he returned — "It is easy to explain. Renny has been intimate with a woman — old enough to be his mother — a relative of the girl young Vaughan got into trouble."

"Does Philip know of this?"

"Yes, he knows of it."

"Then, by the Lord Harry, he did wrong to let his young wastrel come over here to visit my granddaughter. I don't thank him for that. As for an engagement — do you say she wears his ring?"

"Doubtless — in secret. The very way he got the ring was perfidious. *He stole it from his grandmother!*"

The Admiral's slow moving blood gathered yet more strongly in his head. He turned purple. "Let me — let me —" he began incoherently.

Malahide laid a quieting hand on his arm. "If you speak to Vera, excited as you are now, it may do more harm than good."

"My dear man," answered Admiral Lacey, "I do not have to wait the opportune moment for addressing my granddaughter!"

"Of course not. But if you wish to be impressive, choose the opportune moment. Choose the moment when they are in the room together. He comes here every day, doesn't he?"

Although delay was against Admiral Lacey's inclination, he did wait till afternoon before descending on Vera and Renny. Renny came, as Malahide said he would, but not alone. Meg was with him, wearing one of the new enormous hats perched high on her head. Admiral Lacey hung about the hall, feeling strangely like the culprit himself, till the three young people were in the drawing room. He wished Meg were not with them. To tackle them alone would have been easier, he thought.

Presently the strains of the "Merry Widow Waltz" came to him through the closed door. The three had been to see the opera only the week before. Sleeping or waking, it was difficult for them to get the melody of this waltz out of their heads. The Admiral softly opened the door and peeped in.

The long, narrow room with its slanting floor and small-paned windows, its water colours and Dresden china, its banner fire screen and crocheted antimacassars, was filled with the golden sunshine of late afternoon. At the draped square piano Meg sat, her face like a round enraptured flower under the enormous hat. She played the waltz as though she had, in that moment, composed it. She raised her hands high above the keyboard, letting the sweet seductive notes fall from them. If they were inaccurate, no one guessed it, for the two who danced were lost in a world of supple movement and youthful love.

As well as they could they were imitating the dancing of the two stars they had seen the week before. Renny, in long agile steps, glided down the room, turning, turning, with Vera in his arms. She, resting in his embrace, bent backward as far as she could endure, gazing up into his face. On the white hand against his shoulder gleamed the pearl and diamond ring.

The Admiral stood gazing open-mouthed for a space. In spite of himself he liked the looks of the waltz. And they way they performed it!

"Bless my soul!" he exclaimed. "You might be professionals."

The dancers stopped short, though the piano strayed on through another dreamy bar. Vera hid the hand that wore the ring.

"Now, Renny," said Admiral Lacey. "I should like an explanation."

"Of what?" asked Renny boldly.

His tone had a hardening effect on the Admiral.

"Of your manner of dancing with my granddaughter. It's not seemly."

"It's the newest thing," said Vera.

"All the worse for it — and for you! Why, you looked like foreigners!"

"It is foreign," said Meg, from the piano stool. "It's a beautiful thing. The scene is in a country rather like Ruritania."

"It is lovely to do," said Vera.

"It is improper," replied her grandfather. "And what about the ring you are wearing? Show it to me."

Vera was frightened. She looked at Renny for help, but he gave her none.

"Show me that ring," repeated Admiral Lacey.

Vera approached him, holding out her hand.

"Hmph! It is not the first time I have seen it. I have seen it on Mrs. Whiteoak. You must explain to me how you came by it."

"Oh, Granddaddy, I can't! I — oh, please, don't insist!"

"I do insist."

Vera began to cry.

Meg spoke from the piano stool. "I lent it to Vera. It once belonged to my grandmother."

The Admiral raised his voice. "You dare tell me that, young woman! No — I say it is an engagement ring, and I say that your brother *stole* it from his grandmother!"

"That's a lie!" shouted Renny. "Gran gave me the ring for my fiancée. And I gave it to Vera. We are going to be married."

The old man and the youth faced each other. The one short, thick-set, redoubtable. The other tall, wiry, passionately alive. They were like a battleship and a seaplane.

"You dare!" thundered the Admiral. "You dare tell me I lie!"

"No — I don't say *you* lie. I don't know who told you, but I do say it is a lie. My grandmother did give me that ring."

"You were seen to take it!"

Renny and Meg looked at each other. She said: —

"We *did* take it. But we didn't *steal* it."

Admiral Lacey turned to her. "Why did you tell me, miss, that you lent the ring to Vera?"

"I was just trying to conceal their engagement. But since Renny has told you that Vera and he are to be married —"

"Married!" interrupted the Admiral. "It's ridiculous! They are foolish children."

"I am twenty," said Vera.

"And I soon shall be," said Renny.

"What have you to marry on, I'd like to know?"

"My father must help me."

"*Must* help you! *Must*, eh? I like that! I do like that, indeed! There's the young man of today speaking. His father *must* help him! Oh, you couldn't have said a worse thing to me! Now, I tell you what we'll do! We'll go find your father and tell him that he *must* help you!"

Renny answered — "We can't. He's off on a hunting trip."

"So he is! I forgot. Very well, we will go to your grandmother. She shall hear all about it."

"Oh, no, no, don't do that!" said Meg. She burst into tears. It was natural for Meg to weep on a man's shoulder. So she came and laid her face on the Admiral's.

His florid face softened. He put an arm about her. Vera, seeing this, came at once to his other shoulder and wept there. Between their two heads his face glared out at Renny like a fine old bulldog's between two dew-drenched flowers.

"I must see Mrs. Whiteoak about this affair," he declared. "You two must come with me, but Vera shall stay here with her aunts. She shall not go out of this house again until she sails for home."

"If you think you can prevent our marriage," said Renny hotly, "you are mistaken. We love each other and we are going to get married."

"Oh, Grandfather," said Vera, "if you only knew how we love each other!"

"If you knew all, my child," said the Admiral, "you would not be so fond of this young man."

"Who says anything against my brother?" cried Meg.

"I do! I say he is not a fit husband for my granddaughter."

Renny said bitterly — "Malahide Court has been here, poisoning your mind against me."

"Is truth poison?" said Admiral Lacey.

"Oh, yes, often," said Meg. "But I don't see what Malahide could have told you that would turn you against Renny, Admiral! You have always been so fond of him."

The Admiral returned stiffly — "I cannot talk about this in front of young girls."

"Listen, Granddaddy," said Vera. "Renny asked me once what I should feel if I found out anything about him like Meg and Maurice, and I said if it was all past and he still loved me it would make no difference. So surely that settles it!"

"Nothing of the sort! You don't know what you're talking about! Now, my dear, you go straight to your grandmother. Your friends and I will go to Jalna."

He took Vera with him to Mrs. Lacey, and ordered the old man who acted as gardener and groom to bring round the carriage. Soon he and Meg and Renny were on their way to Jalna, while Vera poured out the whole story into the not unsympathetic ears of her aunts and grandmother.

They found Adeline, Mary, and Malahide having tea together in the dining room. Adeline was pleased to see her old friend and made room for him beside her. But Malahide, after a swift glance into his face and another and more furtive glance into the faces of Renny and Meg, sank deep into his chair.

"You are just in time," said Adeline, "to share a section of new honey and a nice bit of news about our rector. He's engaged to be married. He brought me the news himself, this morning." She deposited a golden square of honey on the Admiral's plate and beamed into his face.

"That is good," said Admiral Lacey, forcing himself to smile. "He needs a wife. Where is she from?"

"New Brunswick. A long way to go for a bride. But she suits him, he says, and he thinks she will suit of all us." She talked on, but soon noticed that there was something wrong. She looked searchingly into his face. "Are you ailing?" she asked.

"No," he answered gruffly, "but I must have a talk with you, in the presence of the young man here. Just we three. Will you arrange it?"

There was nothing she liked better than a talk on some important subject, preferably controversial. After her third cup of tea, she said: —

"I want you, Admiral, and you, Renny, to come to the drawing room with me. There are things to be discussed." She rose from the table a little stiffly, resting her hands on it. The Admiral offered her his arm.

"Mayn't I come, Granny?" asked Meg. "I am in this affair, too. With my last drop of blood!"

"No, no," said Admiral Lacey. "Just your grandmother and Renny and me."

"Well," exclaimed Meg, passionately, "I know what it's all about, so why shouldn't I be there?"

"And Malahide," said Renny, "Don't keep him out of it!"

Adeline gave a grunt and reseated herself. "Very well. We'll discuss whatever it is — together, as a family should."

Malahide took out a cigarette and lighted it. "After what Renny has said I think I certainly should be present."

"Very well," said Admiral Lacey. "Since you are agreed."

"Will you have another cup of tea?" asked Mary.

"No, thank you." He looked straight into Adeline's eyes. "Mrs. Whiteoak, did you give your grandson a pearl and diamond ring as a betrothal ring for my granddaughter?"

Renny's eyelashes flickered. He clenched his hands beneath the table. Malahide's heavy lids were lowered and his fingers played with his diamond cravat pin. Meg fixed her full blue gaze on her grandmother's face. It was a study, this fine old face, as strongly marked as a weathered cliff. She thrust out her muscular underlip and her eyes moved from Renny's face to Meg's, from Meg's to Malahide's — compelling from each a quiver of defence or acknowledgement. She picked up her spoon and saw her own distorted reflection in its bowl. She laid it down and said curtly: —

"I did."

The Admiral blew. Renny gave a short laugh and his face lighted with vivacity. Meg preened herself.

"But," exclaimed Admiral Lacey, "I was told —"

"Malahide told you," interrupted Renny.

"I saw the theft myself," said Malahide.

Adeline turned on him. "What theft?"

"The theft of the ring."

"And where were *you?*" cried Meg. "Spying! Peering in at the window! Now I understand why Boney screamed — 'To hell with Malahide!'"

Adeline sat, pursed, wary, trying to absorb all, determined not to give her grandson away.

Admiral Lacey looked in her eyes. "Did you *want* this engagement, then?"

"The girl could do worse. He's a fine boy. A perfect Court. Not like Biddy Court's son, there. A real Court — like myself."

"I should not have minded — a few days ago. But — since then — I have heard something very bad about this young man."

"Out with it!" said Adeline.

The Admiral looked at Mary and Meg. "I can't — not in front of the young ladies."

Mary rose. "Come, Meg. It is much better for us to go."

"Yes," agreed Adeline, "run along. The Admiral is squeamish."

When she and the three men were alone together, Admiral Lacey said — "Neither I nor my son can consent to this engagement. You can't expect it, Mrs. Whiteoak. Renny has been intimate with a loose woman. Apparently you know of it."

Adeline fixed him with her fierce eyes. "Did you go spotless to your bride? How many men do? Tell me that!"

The Admiral coloured. "This is different."

"You mean it is found out!"

Renny exclaimed — "Everything I do is found out! I have a shadow who dogs my footsteps. I wish he would come outside with me and he would not be even a shadow when I had finished with him. Come along, Malahide! Come along! Don't be a coward!"

Malahide turned to him with a sneer. "I should be delighted — if you could fight with anything but your fists."

"I can! I'll fight with anything you name. Pistols — swords — riding crops — axes — anything you like!"

Adeline struck the table with the flat of her hand. "Silence! There'll be no fighting between you two. As for you, Malahide — I'm done with you. My family was right and I was wrong. You've tried to diddle all of us. You've tried to turn us against each other. It's a nice visit you've given us. And I'm the one that will not be sorry to see the last of you." Her brown eyes suddenly blazed and she struck the table again. "Be off with you — out of my sight — forever!"

Malahide's mouth was an ugly gash. "Do you imagine," he snarled, "that I have enjoyed myself? Only the extremity of my misfortune brought me here in the first place. Only extremity made me endure the boredom. What are you Whiteoaks? Who are you? What do you know? Where have you been? Nobody — nobody — nothing — nowhere — these are the answers!"

Adeline could scarcely breathe for the fury that was in her. She clutched her throat.

Renny thought — "Let her have it! Let her have it! Let her know what he is!" But he trembled with the urge to spring on Malahide.

Adeline got out the words — "You dare — you miserable — oh, let me have the strength to — and — my sons not here!"

"I'm here, Gran!" shouted Renny. He sprang toward Malahide, dragging the table cover as he passed, and crashing the tea things to the floor.

Admiral Lacey interposed his florid bulk between the two. "Go," he said to Malahide. "You'd better go at once."

Malahide took three long steps to the door. There he turned and raised a dark hand.

"It's time," he said, "that you were told what you are, Cousin Adeline. But I can't tell you. It would have taken my mother to do that."

Before she could retort he was gone.

Now the sound of Boney's screams came from the bedroom. He had heard Malahide's voice raised in anger and he rent the air in raucous reply.

"Hell — hell — hell with Malahide! To hell with Cousin Malahide! *Shaitan — shaitan ka batka!*" His wings could be heard flapping frantically at the end of his chain.

"Go to him Renny," said Adeline in an unexpected small voice. "Go to him and free him. Oh, the poor bird! The poor, poor bird!" She rose, leaning heavily on her stick. "To think," she said, "to think that Bridget Court is in her grave and I can't write and tell her what I think of her son!"

XXXII

Winter Comes

Renny looked about his room to see whether he might be leaving anything behind. The room looked dishevelled, desolate: the drawers of the dressing table gaped; the cupboard doors stood wide open, disclosing an assembly of soiled white duck trousers, faded jerseys, and assorted tweeds; while on its floor boots, tennis rackets, riding crops, and garments for the laundry lay in confusion. A fox terrier had burrowed himself into the middle of the unmade bed.

In this confusion Renny stood, a trim soldierly figure, in the winter uniform of the Royal Military College, the long, dark blue top coat, faced with red and fastened by brass buttons, the wedge-shaped, grey lamb cap, worn at a lively angle. His expression showed unusual gravity and he looked thinner than he had a month ago. His face appeared older, with a look of somewhat taciturn self-possession.

Miss Lacey, Vera, and Malahide were on the ocean. He had seen Vera only once again. They had said their goodbye in the presence of Ethel Lacey, who, against her father's commands, had slipped from the room and left them a few precious moments alone together. Vera, in a controlled voice, had promised to be faithful, never to forget, to wait for him — no matter for how long. How young and stern and beautiful she had looked! The fine, glossy skin beneath her eyes had been tinged with violet. Her hands had been as cold as ice, but her lips were hot and ardent with love for him. She would write by mail and he would do the same.

Looking about the room he felt himself a different person from the boy who had come back to it last spring. Desire for experience, arrogant strength, had hardened within him. He would face the world without fear; he would go his own way.

He bent over the terrier and patted it. Its warm tongue slid across his hand. It rose on the bed, stretched itself, and jumped to the floor, uttering a troubled whine.

"I'm off now," said Renny. "Coming down?"

They went down the stairs together. Meg appeared at the door of the dining room, table napkin in hand.

"You're going!" she exclaimed, wiping her lips in preparation for kissing. "And I didn't have breakfast with you! I slept so badly I simply couldn't wake this morning. And I might as well have been with you while you finished dressing. I haven't eaten three mouthfuls." She came and stood close to him, her eyes soft with sleep, the long braids of her hair wound round her head. He saw that she wore her nightdress beneath her dressing gown.

He removed his cap and bent to kiss her. She held him tightly, the smell of toast and warm flesh coming from her.

"M'm," she breathed. "Nice old thing! I wish you hadn't to go. It's been fun these days, with you the only man in the house and that beast Malahide gone. But you'll soon be back. It will be no time till the Christmas holidays."

He rocked her gently in his arms. "Where are the kids?"

"With Mother, in the sitting room. Eden has a cold."

He found Mary with her usual basket of darning. Peep was astride of his rocking horse, his golden head, his vivid blue suit, a flash of gay colour against the bleakness of the scene outside the window. Eden, bent over the table, was absorbed in drawing. Renny tried to see what it was, but Eden flattened himself on it.

"No," he said, "you shan't see! It's my own private picture."

"Let Renny see," said Mary. "He's going away."

"No. It's not for anyone but me."

Renny's relentless hand drew him back and a crude drawing of a swan was disclosed, standing on a still cruder drawing of a prostrate man. Renny gave a shout of laughter.

"Good for you, youngster!" he exclaimed. "Malahide and the swan, eh?" He bent to kiss the child, but Eden turned his face away.

"Very well, I'll say goodbye to Peep!"

But the baby, intent on his gallop, turned an indifferent cheek.

Renny said, rather huffily — "Perhaps you'll let me kiss you, Mother?"

Mary drew down his head and they exchanged kisses of more warmth than usual. They had been less antagonistic in these holidays than ever before.

"Well," he said, "you'll have a nice, peaceful time, with Malahide out of the way. Make Dad write to me about his shooting. Have a good time in New York."

"Yes, yes. I hope things will go better this term."

He gave a derisive grunt and went to his grandmother's door.

"It's me, Gran. I'm off!"

Her voice came, full and strong. "I'll see you outside. I'm coming out for a breath of air."

"Damned cold air," he thought, as he opened the front door and a piercing gust met him. It brought with it a flutter of dead leaves that heaped themselves, trembling, on those already in the porch. The bare limbs of the trees thrust up starkly out of the ravine. The grass lay frozen and crisp. By the door his luggage waited, and he gave a grim smile, remembering how Malahide's had lain there on the day of the garden party.

He strode across the lawn and through the little gate to the edge of the ravine. The river that moved so secretly among dense growth in the summer now lay exposed in startled brightness, a skein of ice on either brink. As he looked, the swan and his mate appeared round a bend, soft and snowy on the ruffled water. Their cygnet had disappeared as the others had done, leaving no trace of its short existence. Now the parent birds moved by in proud melancholy, their arched necks like question marks of fate.

He thought of his own life that lay ahead of him. What would it be? He and Vera moving close together like the swans. But they would rear their young, by God! He would always love her, take care of her. Now she, like a swan, was sailing across the ocean from him, but the time would pass, horribly long though it seemed in prospect. He would go to her, bring her back for always.

The face of Lulu flashed into his mind, that strange face with its teasing eyes and sensual mouth. With a frown he turned abruptly from the river and retraced his steps to the house. He heard the sound of horses' hoofs. Grandmother would be waiting.

As he crossed the lawn the bays were drawn up in front of the house and he saw her in the porch. She had put on one of her best caps in his honour and she wore her mink cape which had seen much service. She made a picture, he thought, standing there in the porch, with the reddened leaves of the Virginia creeper festooned above her — a fine, formidable old woman. He was proud of her. He felt a quick throb of pride in the house, too, standing foursquare to the cold wind, brave wreaths of smoke rising from its chimneys. One day it would he his. Not for many years, he hoped, but still — one day it would be his.

She came down the steps toward him.

"My goodness!" she exclaimed. "How cold it has turned. Cold as a stepmother's breath, hey, Renny?"

He smiled a little sheepishly. "She's been very nice to me these holidays."

"Nicer than I have, eh?" she eyed him jealously.

"Oh, that's all over, Gran!" He laughed cheerfully.

She came and tucked her hand in his arm. "We've made it up, haven't we? And I've admitted that I was all wrong about that vagabond Malahide. And I stood by you in your love affair, didn't I?"

He pressed her against his side. "You did indeed, Gran!"

"Too bad they made Vera return the ring! But I have it safe for you. Whenever you want it — you'll know where to find it." She gave him an arch look.

"You were a brick about that, Gran."

"Walk me up and down a little. It's cold standing here. Capes are cold things. I've always said so."

They took a turn up and down the drive, a striking pair, she in her cap and mink cape, he in his cadet's uniform. Hodge had the luggage in the trap. The bays were pawing the gravel.

"Goodbye, Gran." He bent to kiss her.

She laid her hand on his chest. "Don't be in such a hurry. I want to say this…. You must not set your heart too strongly on that girl. You never know how things will end in these first love affairs. I've had 'em. They die a natural death. But when a great love comes you'll know it. Let me tell you that!"

He looked unbelieving, sure of the endurance of his love. She kissed him on each cheek and he got into the trap beside Hodge.

"Goodbye, Gran, goodbye!" He waved his hand to her and to Mary and Eden, whose faces were at the window. He heard Eden's shrill voice calling to him. He saw Peep's bright form flashing to and fro. The trap bowled along the drive, its wheels and the well-groomed flanks of the bays glimmering behind the evergreens.

Adeline stood looking after them, leaning on her stick. A fine boy, bone of her bone, a perfect Court! Strange it would be now, women alone in the house together, no man about. Strange to think winter was coming on … no man about … strange how quickly the summer had passed … like a dream … now the cold weather was coming on … a long, long spell of it.

A chill sunlight flickered out between the indigo clouds and fell on her, on the frozen grass and bare trees. "Those clouds mean snow," she said aloud, looking up at them. A poem of Moore's she had used to like, but had not thought of for years, came into her mind. She stood, leaning on her stick, looking straight ahead of her, and began to repeat it: —

> "I saw from the beach, when the morning was shining,
> A bark o'er the waters move gloriously on;
> I came when the sun o'er that beach was declining,
> The bark was still there, but the waters were gone."

She trudged along the drive to the small wooden gate and laid her hand on it almost caressingly. She had always liked this gate. Her husband and she had often stood at it together. But how cold the wood was to her hand! Still, it was more sheltered here. With an almost rapt look in her eyes she repeated the next verse: —

"And such is the fate of our life's early promise,
So passing the spring-tide of joy we have known;
Each wave, that we dance on at morning, ebbs from us,
And leaves us, at eve, on the bleak shore alone."

"A good poem," she thought. "My Philip used to like to hear me say it. Queer how I can remember every word of it this morning. I feel very clear-headed and strong this morning." She turned, facing the wind, and marched back toward the porch.

The cloud had indeed held snow. Now it came, hard and white, dancing on the wind, stinging her cheeks. The air was full of it. Its falling did not ease the bite of the wind as it sometimes does, but made it all the more bitter. She had to put her head down and struggle against it. It filled her cape, so that her body looked huge, and smote her sides. She was out of breath when she gained the porch. But she was proud of herself. She said, aloud: —

"Not many women care to be out on a morning like this — let alone a woman of my age!"

She stood in the shelter of the porch gazing out at the snowstorm. Some flakes hung in her shaggy eyebrows, her shoulders were white with them. She smiled a little, a smile in which there was poignant regret, but no bitterness. Still out of breath, and in a much lower tone, she continued the poem: —

"Ne'er tell me of glories serenely adorning
The close of our day, the calm eve of our night: —"

Her memory failed her. She groped in her mind for the next words, while the wind, veering vindictively as though in quest of her, rushed in on her where she stood, scattering the dead leaves and carrying its weight of whiteness. She faced it, as though at bay, and the next lines returned to her. But she said them haltingly: —

"Give me back, give me back the wild freshness of Morning,
Her clouds and her tears are worth Evening's best light."

A gleam of sunlight flickered into the porch. She gave a triumphant nod of her head, but she realized that she was bitterly cold. She put her hand on the door knob and turned it. The wind, as though coming to her aid, pressed its savage weight upon the door and threw it open, pressed her into the hall.

Try as she would she could not shut the door behind her. The terrier came snuffling from the hot stove and stood beside her. She rapped peremptorily with her stick.

"Eliza! Eliza!" she called. "Come and shut the door!"

Eliza hastened to her aid, crisp in her clean print dress. Her strong bony arms mastered the wind. The door shut with a bang.

The warmth in the hall felt delicious. Adeline gave a proud grin at Eliza.

"I've had a walk, Eliza," she said. "A walk in that wind. Not many women — of my age — would do that, eh?"

"No, indeed, ma'am! It hardly seems safe."

Adeline took off her lace cap and shook the snow from it. "Don't worry, Eliza," she said. "I'm not going to do it again. I'm stuck here in the warmth — for the winter — ha!"

THE END

THE JALNA NOVELS
BY MAZO DE LA ROCHE

In Order of Year of Publication

Jalna, 1927
Whiteoaks of Jalna, 1929
Finch's Fortune, 1931
The Master of Jalna, 1933
Young Renny, 1935
Whiteoak Harvest, 1936
Whiteoak Heritage, 1940
Wakefield's Course, 1941
The Building of Jalna, 1944
Return to Jalna, 1946
Mary Wakefield, 1949
Renny's Daughter, 1951
The Whiteoak Brothers, 1953
Variable Winds at Jalna, 1954
Centenary at Jalna, 1958
Morning at Jalna, 1960

In Order of Year Story Begins

The Building of Jalna, 1853
Morning at Jalna, 1863
Mary Wakefield, 1894
Young Renny, 1906
Whiteoak Heritage, 1918
The Whiteoak Brothers, 1923
Jalna, 1924
Whiteoaks of Jalna, 1926
Finch's Fortune, 1929
The Master of Jalna, 1931
Whiteoak Harvest, 1934
Wakefield's Course, 1939
Return to Jalna, 1943
Renny's Daughter, 1948
Variable Winds at Jalna, 1950
Centenary at Jalna, 1953

From *Mazo de la Roche: Rich and Famous Writer* by Heather Kirk

INTERNATIONAL BESTSELLERS
BY MAZO DE LA ROCHE
BACK IN PRINT!

Jalna
978-1-894852-23-4
$24.95

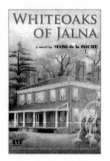

Whiteoaks of Jalna
978-1-894852-24-1
$24.95

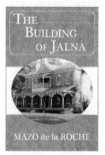

The Building of Jalna
978-1-55002-878-2
$24.99

Whiteoak Heritage
978-1-55488-411-7
$24.99

Mary Wakefield
978-1-55002-877-5
$24.99

MAZO DE LA ROCHE was once Canada's best-known writer, loved by millions of readers around the world. She created unforgettable characters who come to life for her readers, but she was secretive about her own life. When she died in 1961, her cousin and life-long companion, Caroline Clement, burned her diaries, adding to the aura of mystery that already surrounded Mazo.

Available at your favourite bookseller.

🏠 DUNDURN PRESS
www.dundurn.com

CPSIA information can be obtained at www.ICGtesting.com
Printed in the USA
LVOW11s0510041214

416997LV00002B/7/P